Kissing Bandit

LOVE AT THE LAKE BOOK ONE

MARGARET ROSE

KISSING BANDIT

MARGARET ROSE

HODSON
Press

For the risk-takers and list-makers. And for those struggling to be brave, remember, you can't win if you don't play the game.

Prologue

A flowerpot that hasn't seen a flower in years is still doing its job and hiding my old key. But the front door to my childhood home flies open before I can use it.

"Oh, *cheese and rice*." My hand clutches at my heart to make sure it doesn't jump out of my chest. "Mom!"

She's standing before me as if she had a vision and saw me coming, a concerned look working across her face.

"Frannie?" Dad races into the entryway, pulling up short behind her and whipping readers off his nose as if he's ready to take on an intruder with his bifocals.

"Hi, Dad." I shift on the welcome mat in my sneakers, hoping my eyes aren't so red they give me away.

It'll be hard to fool him, though. I am his youngest, sensitive-to-a-fault daughter, after all. "Where are all my boxes?" I sniff, taking in their worried faces.

"Boxes?" they answer in unison. At least they see me. I'm not actually invisible or an insignificant detail. Unfortunately, my boyfriend doesn't share the same regard—scratch that, ex-boyfriend.

"Garage. Why?" Mom pads into the hall in a short seventies

house dress—a true product of the time she probably picked up for a dollar at a Flea, not a fast fashion knockoff. It's cute enough to wear out with flats.

"What's wrong, honey? Rough night?" Dad wraps me up in a hug as I step into the entry. He's wearing the same stripped terry robe he's had since I was a kid. I lean into his shoulder and it's soft and warm. Solid.

"We had a fight," I sniff again, desperately trying and failing to hide the wobble in my voice.

"You and the girls?" His fatherly bemusement is downright charming.

Sure, my best friend, my sister, and I sometimes get on each other's nerves, but it's never serious enough to warrant tears. And that says a lot coming from me. I cry when I get a flat tire or when I smash a spider and feel bad, but smash him anyway because I live three flights up in the Marina District, and I'm too lazy to walk him out.

"God, no." I rub at my eyes.

They exchange a meaningful glance, realizing it must be my relationship with the man I'm supposed to marry. He's been hinting at proposing. Any day now, we thought.

"You know how sensitive she is, Mike," Mom whispers, high and light, but it hits like an accusation all the same.

That's exactly what he said. I've spent the last hour of my life sifting through years of a relationship with a surprisingly stoic man I *thought* I knew. After he unceremoniously tossed me out of bed, he said I was too *sensitive*, and he didn't want to be with someone he had to tiptoe around for the rest of his life.

"She's like her dad." His strong hand squeezes my shoulder.

"No, she's tough like me, but she doesn't know how to bubble wrap that fragile heart of hers."

"She doesn't need to change herself for anyone. She doesn't need bubble wrap," he insists under the glow of an antique chandelier I know he hates.

Good god, they are the Bickersons. "Not helping, guys," I say, toeing off my shoes. Some things never change.

I march through the living room, still paneled with warm walnut and littered with Dad's vintage collectibles, and barrel through a door off the kitchen leading to the garage. My family is organized. We have to be in our business, and sure enough, stacked against one spiderwebbed wall are a handful of cardboard boxes labeled *Fran* in black sharpie—a thick slash under my name, as if the person packing was entirely certain about stuffing all their memories away. That person was me. I boxed up everything I used to be without blinking an eye, slapped on some duct tape, and threw away the boxcutter.

That was when I thought I was getting married, well, not married, but at least proposed to. At the very, very least, he was days from asking me to live with him. *I thought.*

Instead, I've been dumped. Literally. And, I know how to use that word, I mean, literally *dumped onto my ass.*

I rub my right hip, still smarting from landing on a giant dog bone, and dig into the first box.

"Frannie, what's this about?" Mom's hovering behind me, hating that I'm so breakable and terrified for me nonetheless. "It's late."

Dad's probably gone back to whatever book he's reading now that he knows the only threat in his house is the argument Mom and I are about to have.

"Nothing. I need something." I need a lot of things. And maybe my mom is right, I need to toughen up. Clearly, I'm not cutout to be a doctor's wife. He was right when he said I'm sensitive, emotionally messy, and a chronic oversharer. Hearing him list off my offending qualities has made me feel like a child who's just made a big mistake.

Mom hums, knowing if she stays silent, I'll end up spilling my guts.

3

She's not wrong. "We broke up," I say with another big sniff, but my voice holds firm this time. *Tough!*

The tears I shed on the drive over here have all dried up, leaving my cheeks salty and scratchy. Now, roughly thirty minutes post-breakup, standing in a garage that smells faintly of mold and memories, I'm numb and looking for answers. Numb is good. I'll take numb over pain any day.

"What happened?" she sighs.

I snort, laughing through my nose. "He forgot I existed."

Or rather, I kinda forgot myself. This might be one of those moments I look back on one day, realizing it was a turning point. Did I ever really love him? Did he even know the real me? Or did I hide it all away? Fake it to be what he needed?

And in the moment he rolled over to cuddle his dog instead of me, all the clarity came crashing down like a sheet of rain.

"Oh honey, you've always taken things so personally. You're almost thirty. Don't you want to make something stick?"

"Mom, he pushed me out of bed!" I sure hope she's ready to hear this. *I'm twenty-eight*, as she likes to point out, Cat is thirty. "After we had sex!"

"Francesca," she chides.

"Wait for it"—I continue—"*to cuddle his dog.*"

That's a punch to the gut and pride, full of clarity. You'd have to be comatose to ignore it, and maybe I have been.

She purses her lips. My mom isn't a prude, per se. She gave Cat and me some really good talks about sex growing up. But she doesn't like to hear negativity of any kind. And she doesn't like to have these conversations without a pen and paper, sitting at the kitchen table as if conducting a business meeting. Listing out a plan of attack.

"That can't be what happened."

"Got it!" The third box I've torn through contains my treasure.

"*Not the keepsake box,*" she groans, following me back into the kitchen.

"It wasn't only that, Mom. It was a lot of things," I say quietly and mostly to myself. "Things that I've been shoving in a drawer because I wanted it to work so badly."

The box inside the box is covered with Mod-Podge, slightly tacky—pun intended—and screams *young-angsty-teen.* I dump it on the kitchen table unceremoniously. I'm so desperate to remember who I was and becoming more shocked by the second at how much I've forgotten.

"This is how I deal with my feelings, *Mom*," I blurt, sifting through handwritten notes, faded photos, and trinkets of all shapes and sizes. All these little things hold such *meaning.* Everything I used to be.

"She was after the keepsake box?" Dad appears in the living room doorway, a cup of sleepy-time tea in a Winnie the Pooh mug that I guarantee Mom found at an estate sale.

I remember tediously cutting clippings to make this box up in my room with all the familiar smells of childhood and the built-in comfort that came with it.

"I keep telling her she's too sensitive—"

Ugh, that *word*. I know she means well, but I'm holding back tears with a weak dam of determination right now.

"One day, that'll be someone's favorite thing about her." Dad winks. "Night, Frannie-Bananie," he adds before Mom can protest.

"Night, Dad."

"Is this from the lake?" Mom, now invested in my journey against her better judgment, holds up a fish keychain. She taught me how to dig for the good stuff in a heap of junk, after all.

"Yeah, I loved those trips. Why did we stop going every summer?" I take it from her and put it in the pocket of my cutoffs.

"It's hard to build a business and a family at the same time. I guess we stopped going once Cotton Candy Carnie began to grow. We did have fun, though." Her blue eyes turn wistful, and I wonder if she regrets forfeiting family time for the vintage games business she built with my dad. But my parents have worked hard for their livelihood and their relationship, over twenty years and going strong.

"Those summers are my best memories," I say, picking up a photo of me and my sister on Spirit Lake, paddles in hand, fighting to stay upright on boards in bikinis. We are complete opposites in so many ways—Cat with her short brown hair and me wearing mine long and blonde, her brown eyes taken from my dad, my hazel, a muddy product of the mix with Mom's clear blue.

I scoop everything up and drop it back in the box. I'm never letting my treasures go again. I'm never letting myself go again. From now on, it's self-preservation all the way. No men. Maybe I'll date when I'm fifty. A nice, stable silver fox would do me just fine.

"Why don't you go talk to him? You two never talk to each other." She follows me through the entryway, out onto the front lawn, where a full moon hangs high. "You can fix things if you communicate with him, honey." She wants stability for me, she wants me to be taken care of and I wonder if it's because she doesn't believe I'm capable of taking care of myself.

"Like you and dad?"

It's a low blow, but we've never held back in this family. I both love and hate that about us. My parents have stayed together and made their marriage work, even when there were times we all wondered if it would.

"We're not perfect, and we never hid that fact from you girls. But we try, Fran, we work on it every day."

Why did I stay with him? I worked on it every day while he barely showed up. But I let everyone think we were perfect. I told myself I was happy.

It was a lie.

And now, I'm determined to figure out why I did it. And the

only thing I can think to do is go to the source, look back on my past, and figure out when I was most myself.

"I want to feel like I did when we spent summers at the lake," I say, plucking another picture from the box to prove it, this one of me on the back of a boat while Dad played captain. I was sixteen.

"Honey, everyone wants to return to their childhood—especially after they've been burned—but I'm sorry to say, it's not possible. Life doesn't work like that."

"I think you're wrong," I breathe, looking up at the moon, and yeah, I make a wish.

My mom's not the only one who likes to make lists. That part of her—along with turning trash into treasure—is nestled inside me. And I think I can do something with that.

Mentally, I begin to number my to-do's, starting with finding a rental on Spirit Lake. Starting, with finding my happy place.

CHAPTER 1

Fran

I t's a rush of adrenaline, that feeling you get when you're about to kiss someone.

The club is stifling on the first warm night of summer, packed with bodies bouncing to vintage rap. Throwbacks is known for eclectic sets, wild theatrics, and glittery lights, pulling a mix of San Francisco's finest. Every age group, ethnicity, gender, and personality are here on full display. And you never know what the DJ will play next.

"Uh oh, she's got that look." Willow, my bookish best friend since fifth grade, shifts in borrowed heels from my sister's closet. Her Marilyn Monroe curves are all the kids talked about in school, motivating her to constantly hide them in outfits like the sack dress she's wearing.

"I don't have a look."

I'm out late tonight to chase that feeling of rushing adrenaline, fuzzy thoughts, and skipping heart beats. I'll pay for it tomorrow on my first official day of Frannie's Finds, a fledgling estate sale business I hatched a few months ago after my breakup with a man I thought was *the one* began to curdle.

"Who's it gonna be, Frannie?" My sister Cat laughs, pulling her short, dark hair into a tiny pony. After meeting us here straight from work, she removed her suit jacket to reveal a black tube top with skinny black trousers and heels.

Why do I think keeping a list of safe, one-time-only kisses is going to protect my heart from getting smashed all over again?

Mentally, I run through *Fran's Post Breakup Kiss List*, meant to numb myself and put all my too-quick emotions and feelings in a box. The goal is to get all those delicious vibes from a hot kiss without sinking into an immediate you're-the-man-I'm-going-to-marry mindset. My whole life, I've naturally been a serious-boyfriend-girl—not anymore.

Fran's Kissing List

1. Reverse Happy Hour sushi kiss— raw fish after midnight, paired with kissing, is a bad idea.
2. Dude from dog park... Okay, fine, I was there scoping out my ex, and a tiny part of me hoped he'd randomly be there and witness me getting over him in real-time.
3. Brunette from Cat's work party, she was so hot and I was so tipsy.
4. Guy from Cat's work party. First time I've ever kissed two people in one night. They went home together. I went home alone.
5. (Tonight) TBD....

My senses are on alert, my heart pounding with anticipation. Sure, the first four kisses were failed attempts at finding that fizzy, gut-happy feeling minus the emotional vulnerability, but I'm going to give it one more try.

Someone *has* caught my eye. I can't believe I'm doing this, *again*.

"That one," I finally answer with a slight nod toward a group of men at some sort of bachelor party.

"The one in the suit with the big hair? Or the one with the Super Bowl ring?" Cat asks.

"Show-offs are more your brand." She makes a sour face, and I counter with a raised brow. She's a know-it-all who doesn't know her own type. "Backward hat, white T-shirt, *tight* jeans." I bite my straw between my teeth. "Biceps for *days.*"

"The wallflower?" Simultaneously, Willow and Cat look over their shoulders.

"Guys!"

"He doesn't look like he's got any moves." Willow's disappointed with my choice. She's also not on board with the kissing list.

Cat's eyes go wide. "He doesn't need moves. She's making the moves!" My sister, forever the feminist cheerleader, ladies and gentlemen.

"She doesn't want to make the moves!" *Aaand*, the best friend, the hopelessly hopeless romantic.

"Anything akin to Superman is her type. Have we learned nothing over the past few months of watching her play Kissing Bandit?" Cat asks.

Willow plops a round of shots on our tall table as if procured from a puff of DJ smoke. Seriously, I look around—no idea where she got them.

"Frannie," she lays a gentle hand on my arm, "is this really how you want to handle it?"

Willow's lack of enthusiasm might have something to do with finding me in our kitchen clutching a box of childhood memorabilia like a life raft six months ago. She made me a cup of cinnamon tea, and a list of to-dos was born that night.

Fran's Happy Plan

11

1. Resign from my position in the family business
2. Rent a place at the lake for the summer.
3. NO dating, only fun kisses.
4. Build website.
5. Post new business for hire on Spirit Lake social media.

Finding a cheap room and blowing my savings was easy enough, but first kisses with no strings, no feelings, or fire hasn't been working. They've been sloppy, sticky, or just...*fine*.

But there's something about the guy across the room. His big gray eyes that shine in the low light and the way he keeps fiddling with the baseball cap on his head as if he's trying to hide from the crowd captivates me in a way I can't explain. He looks like a challenge, and I don't shy away from a challenge. Number five might turn things around and deliver what I've been looking for: a toe-curling make-out that leads to absolutely nothing. No dating. No relationship. No broken heart. Nada.

Just *vibes*.

"Let her do what feels right," Cat says. "She needs to get that idiot out of her system."

She *does* support the kissing list, as well as my sworn declaration not to get serious with a man until I'm fifty. So, I've got, what, twenty-two years of kissing to go? That seems exhausting, which is why tomorrow, I turn into a work-only pumpkin.

Cat faces me. "I'd go with the one in the suit with the hair. The other one looks...emotional." She scrunches her face as if it's a bad thing. "He's all broody."

"I do love broody." Willow smiles into her drink, her thoughts clearly elsewhere. She leans in, pulling our circle tighter around the high-top table that's barely big enough for the three of us. "I've got books that will erase"—Cat gives her a withering look, and I realize they must have an agreement not to say his name—"*him* from your brain for hours on end. A kiss is a moment, a flash." She snaps her fingers, and her pretty blue eyes ignite. "A *book* is—"

"I know exactly what kind of books you have, Wills."

I have quite a few copies on my own shelf because Willow won't loan her books to anyone. Instead, she reads them without cracking the spines, and then they sit color-coded on her shelves like trophies.

"He's here by the way," Cat says.

My chest tightens. "What? Where?"

"I saw him about half an hour ago slamming martinis at the bar." She hands me a plastic shot glass, a metaphoric bow on a box of bad news. "Starting tomorrow, you'll be miles away from him. At the lake all summer because you've banished yourself."

"I did not—"

Cat holds a hand up, effectively silencing me. I snap my mouth shut. "We all loved our childhood trips there." Willow nods. She came with our family to the lake every summer because her parents died young, and her aunt was in no shape to travel. "But I also know you used your savings to escape for the summer so you could be as far away from him as possible—don't deny it."

I hate it when she's right and I make a face.

"Doesn't matter." Cat shakes her head. "Go out there and dance your ass off, exude all the pent-up sexual energy you've been holding inside since he didn't know how to find *anything*—"

"Hey—"

Why am I about to defend him? I no longer need to feel embarrassed by his shortcomings—or mine, which he seemed to enjoy focusing on so often. Maybe I am too sensitive.

"Show him what he's missing." Cat's mouth quirks in a challenge. Her eyes hold mine and a lifetime of sisterly banter is exchanged in a matter of seconds.

I'm far enough away from the breakup now, from the comfort

and the delusion of a relationship that was about half as good as I thought it was, to think about how he might miss me. *Might*. But I'm not sure because he did have a lot going for him: fancy job, family money, a Great Dane that made him look pretty damn hot at the dog park. I supported him through med school, and told myself he wasn't *not* paying attention to me, he was busy. I'm starting to think he had no intention of sticking around. I was merely an item on *his to-do list*. Graduate, *check*. Finally get around to breaking up with Frannie, *check!*

"Oh, he's missing plenty!" The feeling of being thrown away is a hard one to shake, but I try on some of Cat's empowerment and borrow a bit of Willow's self-discipline—if only for tonight.

"You look hot in that vintage Calvin Klein."

If this dress could talk, I bet it'd have some serious stories to tell. Picking up ten-dollar dresses has been a side hobby of mine since I started sifting through estate sale closets with Mom.

I *do* look hot. "One more kiss, just for fun, then tomorrow I'm married to my new job."

Cat gently presses a hand to the small of my back, giving me a push.

I tug on the slender straps of my dress, turn toward the crowd, and lock eyes with my prize. He's still holding up the wall with shoulders as wide as goalposts, long lean muscles stretching out over the rest of him. And he's at least a foot over my five foot eleven height, maybe more. His boys whoop and holler as I approach.

Superman pulls the brim of his cap forward, discreetly watching me weave through bodies on the dance floor. It hovers low over his eyes, and my attention is immediately pulled to that strong jaw. That pleasant pout. The bachelor party whistles and claps as my pointer finger hooks the collar of his T-shirt.

See, I'll do all the work. You just have to come along for the ride.

Dating a guy I thought I'd marry but have come to realize

never loved me has given me blind courage. At least when it comes to a stranger I'll never see again. I can't get hurt when there's only one tiny kiss involved. No one can claim I'm too sensitive when I walk away, head held high.

But my feet freeze mid-step.

I know absolutely nothing about seduction. My ex was typically bored with me in the bedroom—embarrassing but true.

I can do this and I've got a list to prove it. This guy is going to be lucky number five.

His friends go wild, smacking him on the back and exchanging high-fives when I resume my pace. Have I picked the groom? Another woman's man is not my style.

A built man with closely cropped hair wearing a *Bride* sash jumping to the beat near the DJ booth two-finger whistles in encouragement, and I realize I'm safe.

"Hi, I'm Frannie," I holler over the volume in the room, tipping my head back because I have to.

He leans in, the bill of his hat pulled so low I can only assume his eyes are on my neck. "What?"

"FRAN!"

I catch a whiff of minty breath as he dips even closer and shouts directly in my ear, "WHAT?"

Forget it. I grab his hand, overly large and engulfing mine, and pull him into the heart of the dance floor. He leans in close to hear what I say next, "LET'S DANCE!"

Dropping all pretense of reluctance, he grips my hips. The DJ flips to a new song, and I hold my breath, praying for something we can actually dance to instead of the mosh-grind I was about to attempt.

Marvin Gay, "Let's Get It On," pours through speakers, and somewhere red lights turn on while a disco ball drops into the center of the sweaty room. The crowd roars, people coupling up and launching seamlessly into a scene from *Dirty Dancing*.

We quickly find a rhythm. I can't believe my luck, but one glance at my dance partner's friends reveals Cat and Willow have made their way into their group, one of the guys currently fist-bumping the DJ.

They've set this up. My best friends laugh along as if they'd ridden here on the bachelor bus we passed on our way in.

The newly acquainted crew flashes thumbs-up and kissy faces as Marvin croons. The *Bride* clutches his heart and makes a puppy face— obviously, my girls didn't let him in on the plan. This is not a lovey-dovey moment.

"I think our friends bonded." Marvin is much easier to talk through. He nudges the brim of his hat with the tip of his thumb and we lock eyes.

"I see that." His grip on my hips tightens.

"The brunette in black is my sister, Cat. The redhead in the pink dress is our best friend, Willow... So, come here often?" *Oh, hi. It's me Frannie, a walking blonde cliché.*

"Not normally."

I shake my head and look away. I need a break from his intense gaze, taking in every inch of my face as if committing it to memory on the spot. The room was already hot, and still everywhere his eyes land is a slow burn.

"Don't like dancing?" I ask, speaking into a firm, T-shirt-covered chest.

"Isn't this dancing?"

His words cause me to take stock of my body. Up to this moment, I've been lost somewhere in his earnest, handsome face, sharp white incisors, the slight cleft in his chin, and that baseball cap pulled so low, making him look mysterious and delicious and—

"Hey, you still with me?"

"My ex didn't like to dance," I say, glancing up.

"Ah." He pulls me closer, lightly nudging my chin between his knuckle and his thumb so our eyes meet again. "What an idiot."

Then he trips over his own long legs, just a little, catching himself quickly and giving me a lopsided smile that makes me giggle.

I can't believe I giggled.

This guy is just...yummy. *But not too yummy,* I remind myself. This is not going to lead to anything. It's one delicious kiss—if I'm lucky. Lucky number five. Five is my new favorite number.

He spins me out and pulls me back to face him. It's endearing. He doesn't really know what he's doing, but the old-fashioned slow song is helping him improvise. There's a way about him, a willingness to try, and a confidence that automatically makes me trust his every move.

I glance at my sister, and sure enough, her face is a tangle of worry. *Don't gush all over the random make out, you dummy!*

Focus, Fran

"Is something wrong?"

"Sorry," I say, looking back up at him. "It's been a long..." Week? Month? Life? "Long time since I've danced with someone."

"It was a serious relationship?" That's a surprisingly sincere question for the dance floor.

"Since college, off and on here and there, but yes, pretty serious in the end." I look up at him, pressing even closer so I can see his whole face under the brim of his hat. "I thought he was the one. We were talking about getting married." His eyes are clear and thoughtful, listening to every word. "I'm sorry." I shake my head. It's gotta be the heat that's making my mouth run away with me, about my personal life, to a stranger. This is exactly what I'm *not* supposed to do. "I didn't mean to bring any of that up. That's not what I came for."

Full lips twist into a confused half-smile—*what did you come for? they ask.* "Don't apologize. I may not know how to dance, but I won't let you fall."

He wraps a hand around the back of my neck, his thumb grazing my collarbone. The movement is startling and my body responds even more to him despite my brain warning me not to. My ex never touched me with so much intention. I don't think anyone has.

"You haven't told me your name," I say, feeling more unexplainably drawn to him by the minute. I want to savor this moment because it's almost over. After tonight, I'll never see him again.

"John." His solid thigh wedges between my legs, causing my dress to hike, and I slot right into place. His eyes ask, *is this okay?* And my returning gaze gives him the answer.

A glance at the bachelor party tells me they love it. Willow has one hopeful hand resting over her heart—*I thought you weren't on board, Wills!* One of his buddie's, clad head to toe in denim, glares at her while clutching a small water glass that looks one hundred percent out of place in his bear paw.

"And you are?"

"Francesca," I rasp with a dry throat. "I'm Francesca." Our chests press together, and his arms circle around me in what can only be described as a much-needed *hug*. "Everyone calls me Frannie." Without meaning to, I speak into the crook of his warm neck, and goosebumps pop on his skin.

I let my cheek rest for a second on his chest. Who cares if he's a complete stranger or that I'm quickly veering off the path of *get-in-and-get-out*?

He holds me tight, then in a whirl, drops me low, my back almost resting against his strong thigh. My hair skims the floor, but I'm locked in solid arms as if I'm light as a feather. And yes, my heart throbs.

"I've never been dipped." My words come out rushed and surprised.

His eyes dig into mine, searching—for what I'm not sure.

I blink, and he whips me upright. "Francesca." My full name rumbles in his throat, creating a trickle of *want* that rolls down my spine. "That is a tragedy."

Marvin is about to wrap it up, which is fine because I can't take any more of whatever this is, anyway.

His face softens as he leans in, his full lips showing the beginnings of a shy smile. "Let's go outside."

"Can't," I squeak. "I'm good here." Nothing about this moment feels like a kiss and run. He's being too careful, too serious, too real.

The first four kisses on my list had zero butterflies or buzzy feelings attached to them, effectively safe in their mediocrity. This guy has *swoon* written all over him, and for me, that spells danger.

"Okay." He nods, grasping my hips again even though the song is hanging on to the last note.

And then it's over.

The bachelor party, Cat and Willow part and parcel, whistle and clap. Every inch of me turns cold when he lets me go and steps back, the entire bar cheering and staring at us. The DJ has gone so far as to play an applause track to rouse the crowd even further. We've put on quite the show.

"Why is everyone applauding?" I ask, confused, sweaty, and a little dizzy.

"I used to play some ball." John reaches out a hand with a sheepish shrug, slightly tilting his head toward a patio door that flows into a chic beer garden. "I won't bite."

He *is* Superman, asking me out onto the veranda for a private chat. To get to know me. To talk to me. More adrenaline and a hint of fear licks down my neck, settling heavy in my chest.

A new song starts, one about throwing a wish in a well. One glance at Willow, and I know she requested it, and I remember my plan.

This is just a kiss, and then I'm gone, simple. Easy. That's all I want.

I step back up to him, and he leans in instantly, his body possibly affected by the same odd gravitational pull I've felt since I laid eyes on him. This is the moment where I brush his lips with

19

mine. Where I kiss him once and walk away. No commitments. No emotions.

Instead, I *run.*

CHAPTER 2

John

It's damn near impossible not to chase her, but I don't know this woman. She danced one song with me, so close and knit together until my balls hurt, then *poof*. Gone. My eyes track the room, following the curve of a fat hallway leading toward the front doors. She didn't go that way. She's still here, I think.

No way I should go after her. This night was supposed to be me getting out, post-athletic career. I'm not twenty. I'm getting close to doubling it, actually. One-night stands, the slapdash emotion, and the eventual awkward parting of ways aren't... appealing, anymore.

I should get back on the bus. Get back to town and pour my friends who've overindulged into sleeping bags and let them snooze it off at my cabin by the lake while I stoke a fire with a stick. Deliver the bride safely back to his worrying groom, red-eyed but alive in the morning.

"That was something." My buddy, Winter, saunters up to me as the crowd peels from the dance floor. The lights are turned up now, bright and jarring, everyone squinting as they scatter.

It sure was...something. But I have no idea what, so I dodge his comment. "Is it closing time?"

We only danced for a song, but I've lost my grip a bit, on time, on my senses... All I can think of are strawberries and sunscreen. Her hair smelled like summer, even though tonight is the first real night of the season.

"Coming from you, that's a shocking question. You and Logan were counting the minutes until that girl nabbed you. Plucked you straight from a candy dish. My ego would be bruised but—" Winter's got an actual royal title, dusty and buried under a crest somewhere overseas; his ego is fine.

"I just..." I pull my hat from my head because my blood is still boiling from her touch, unsure how to answer him. I can still feel her cheek pressing into my neck, her hands gripping my arms and holding on.

I put the hat back on and pull at the bill until it's covering most of my face the way I like it. "I lost track of time."

How the hell has no one ever dipped that woman on a dance floor? *And my clumsy-ass attempt was her first?*

"You lost yourself in that girl, Fran."

That has my attention. "How'd you know her name?"

"Let me give you the highlights. The second you two collided, her friends hit the DJ to make a request. Logan 'bout scared them off in all his unkempt lumberjack glory, but Jack and I bought them drinks. I think her sister's name is Cat?"

"How's Jack doing?"

"The bride is face down on the bus, gave me his Super Bowl ring, and told me none of it mattered now that he's in love. Wagner's gonna kill us. We're all ready to head. I came to get you, the drive back is going to be long and vomit-inducing, I fear."

Our hometowns, ridiculous places that share a state line and a long-standing feud, Clover, California and Novel, Nevada, are roughly two hours from San Francisco and take up a good chunk of Spirit Lake waterfront.

"You're not wrong."

It's a gut reaction to look for her. People are heading toward the door, a few of them hanging on at the bar nursing dredges in drinks. That's when I spot long blonde hair that's soft as new leather—I know, I've run my hands through it—connected to a lean body in a little white dress.

She's not alone. "Hold on, don't leave without me—"

"Or, I could leave you, and you might have the best night of your life," he says, following my gaze.

"I've got to open the bar early tomorrow to let the construction crew in—"

Dad's voice when he asked me for my last check to save the bar he'd mortgaged up to its eyeballs rings in my head. And then when he, on a drunken rampage, announced in the middle of Main Street on a Tuesday night that his good-for-nothing son refused to bail him out, that family was bullshit, and that he was moving to the mountains and didn't want a damn soul to follow him. I was dead to him.

Well, back at you, old man. Now, the bar is my problem, and I'll be damned if it doesn't succeed to spite him.

"I'll buy you ten, but they're getting rowdy. There's only so much Logan and I can do to hold it down before our driver chucks us for the drunken assholes we are."

"I'll be there in five."

"Best of luck."

"I'm not... I mean, she's not..." I let my words drop because I don't know what I'm doing or saying. Other than my sister, Meg, the guys are all I've got, and they've all assured me it's time to remedy that.

"Remember what we talked about? You've raised your sister, you've retired, you're ready, right?"

"I remember." Why the hell did I confide in my best friend? I've been a sniveling, jacked-up mess since Dad left. Like losing him made losing mom come back tenfold. I'm not afraid to cry, but I am afraid of getting hurt like that again.

Winter puts a firm hand on my shoulder. "Tonight is the first step. Go get her and give her your number. You need backup?" We both watch as she attempts to walk away when a dude in a sports coat and tie pulls her back.

It's pathetic that he thinks I need help getting a woman to go on a date with me. But that is the goal. Meg said if my dad and I can't fix our admittedly toxic relationship, maybe I should work on another one and start dating, and my baby sister has never steered me wrong. Winter said meeting a girl in a club would be easy, but he's steered me wrong plenty of times.

"Nah. I'll make sure she's okay."

"And give her your number."

"And give her my card if she wants it."

He rolls his eyes at me. "Buddy, I got hard watching you two on that dance floor," he scoffs, "and I'm not too proud to admit it. She wants it, and even though passing out business cards is such an old-man thing to do," he quirks his head and pats me on the shoulder, "On you, it's almost cute."

The guy she's talking to right now appears to know her pretty intimately by the way they're speaking, arguing while he puts his hands on her, and she bats him away.

She didn't bat me away.

"Wait for me," I say, pointing at him to make him know I mean it. It's going to take some real determination for Winter not to leave me here in hopes I end up in her bed. But that's not the plan. I've had enough of that.

"Don't throw down. Remember, your shoulder isn't what it used to be, man. It's not worth it."

We bump elbows, and I watch Winter for only a second as he leaves. His warning was a joke. He knows I'd never throw a punch in a bar on principle, even though I was known for being hot-tempered on the baseball field back in the day. But damn if my hands don't start to curl into fists when my attention is back on Francesca. Things are escalating with Mr. Bulldog Print Tie and I don't waste another second crossing the room.

"Everything okay here?" I ask, inserting myself between them. Men putting their hands where women don't want them is a big *no-no* in my book.

"Oh, hey," she says. There's surprise in her tone but not the bad kind, I don't think. She moves behind me and slightly to the side, subtly welcoming me as a shield.

"*Oh, hey*?" Bulldog Tie repeats. He spits a little, and we all notice.

"Let's call it a night, okay?" she says around my shoulder.

"Who's this guy?" He drops his wallet and stoops to pick it up. "You've moved on already, Frannie?"

Instantly, I hate him and the way he slurs her name.

"It's been months, and you ignored me half the time we dated, anyway. *You don't care*," she assures him. "You'll remember that in the morning."

"This guy is the one now? You've fallen for uh, uh," he stutters looking for words he can't find through the haze of alcohol," an *old jock*?"

Goddamn, I'm thirty-nine, not one hundred. Still, I'm surprised when she doesn't correct him. She doesn't tell him we just met, minutes ago.

"He might be," she fires back, standing straighter and moving closer.

I think she's having one of those fantasy moments where you actually get the revenge you've been wishing for. Honestly, I'm rooting for her.

If this is the game, I find myself more than happy to play. "You ready?" I ask, dropping an arm around her shoulders. She's tall, but I'm much taller, and she curves into me. Her honey-blonde hair brushes the back of my arm.

He slams an empty glass on the bar.

"You got a ride home, buddy?" Hating him for no real reason aside, someone needs to make sure the kid isn't driving.

"I've got friends," he spits again, hands on hips and swaying a tad. "And believe me, she's not that much fun."

Heat courses through my arms and my chest flexes unbidden. "Clearly, she's just been in the wrong hands," I say, low and clear so he gets my point and she misses it entirely.

I look down into her wide hazel eyes and smile as I ask again, "You ready?"

"Yeah." She returns my smile with an even bigger grin, we're in cahoots. "See ya," she tosses over her shoulder.

"Hey, wait a minute..." But his words quickly fade as we walk away, my arm around her, all the way to the parking lot.

The bachelor bus has pulled up to the curb, and her friends are standing outside with my friends, presumably waiting for a car.

"Frannie! Did you tell that moron where he could shove his video game controller?"

Francesca pulls from me easily. I want to reach for her, but she's not mine. I don't even know where she lives, what she does for a living, or if she has any pets.

"Come on, lover boy!" That's Jack's voice bellowing from inside the bus, apparently not face down anymore. The man is a formidable athlete, a two-time super bowl champ, and the biggest sweetheart I've ever met.

"Time to burn, Boss." Logan slaps me on the shoulder as he boards the party bus, looking even more stricken with his current situation. He's itching to get back home.

"You too, Frannie," her redheaded friend says as an SUV pulls up. She slides in, adding over her shoulder, "Wrap it up."

Her sister, the dark-haired one, wiggles her eyebrows before climbing into the car. The two women couldn't look less alike, one bright sunshine and one sleek shadow. The door stands open like a gaping mouth waiting to swallow Francesca up next.

With the guys loaded on the bus and her friends in the car, she pauses on the curb. "Thanks. For in there."

"I-I want to talk to you." *What does that even mean, Boggs?*

I pull out a business card, shiny and brand new, for the new-to-me bar I'm about to re-open on the lake.

"Here." I shove it at her, half crumbling it in her hand.

"What's this?" she asks, but she doesn't even glance at it.

Damn, Winter was right. I am an old man with a business card.

"My card, if you want to call and…."

"Oh, uh, yeah. I'm not." She's shaking her head at my chest and looks over her shoulder at the waiting car. "I'm not really dating or meeting people right now. I just started a small business…" she trails off.

Exhaust from the bus spews into the night, lifting and dissipating in the air. Breaks whine as the driver shifts into gear. Of course, she's not looking for anything serious. *Just my luck.*

"I'm opening a business, too," I offer in comradery, still a glutton for punishment. I can't let her go so easy. "Just call. Even if it's to scare off another guy." This is why I don't talk to women, pursue women, or date women. I'm bad at the talking part because I never had to be good at it. But she felt so right in my arms on that dancefloor, and instant chemistry like that doesn't happen all that often. Or ever. Despite how many times you try, I should know.

"I could have handled him—"

"Of course you could," I answer honestly.

"But I'm glad I didn't have to. That was sort of a win in there." She nods her head toward the club and laughs lightly.

She's not looking for anything serious, and I'm done with one-night stands. I have to shove my hands in my pockets so I don't reach out.

Walk away, Boggs. Step around her and get on the bus.

"Night. And good luck with all that." She motions to the bus just as Jack drops a window and yells, "Kiss her, you Neanderthal!"

The entire bachelor party starts chanting, "*Kiss her, kiss her, kiss her.*" Even the driver, who must be looking to relive some glory days, chimes in.

My gaze meets hers, and I wonder if our eye color might match exactly. It's the only cloudy thing about her, those hazel eyes.

Screw it.

My hands grip either side of her face, trying my best to be gentle because all I want to do is throw her over my shoulder and run. Jack, that ass-hat, knows me well.

"I get that you're not looking for anything serious..." God, I sound like an idiot, but if my sister has taught me anything, it's to be straightforward with women. I always have been, and it's served me well.

She takes a step back and bumps into the bus as if pulling away, but then I watch as her eyes fire up, talking herself out of whatever hesitation she had, reaching out to dip a finger in the pocket of my jeans and pulling me close.

"Francesca, can I—"

She's bouncing on her toes as if she's drawing all her energy together. "Lucky number five," she whispers, as she closes her eyes.

Her face is eager, honest, excited, and scared. "What?" I laugh, cupping her cheeks with my hands again, my eyes roaming her features, trying to take them all in at once.

Wait, what was I going to say? Can I kiss you? That's exactly what I should say, but my mind is all jumbled. I blame the chanting, which is still going strong but has faded into a buzz around us.

"What did you say?" I ask again, slowly drawing her lips up to mine. Brushing a stray strand of hair from her cheek.

Her eyes crack open, and I pause. Can I kiss you? *Say it.* My mouth is seconds from taking hers.

"It's silly. I like making lists," she says, but I don't understand. My pause deepens into an actual stop.

"I'm not following." I nudge her chin with my knuckle, enjoying the moment and just sharing breath.

It's a shock to both of us, I think, that I'm not dropping the whole thing and kissing the shit out of her. But I'm curious. There's something in her eyes: nervousness mixed with courage, an intoxicating combination.

She chews on her bottom lip. "He said I'm too emotional," she nods toward the door and presumably the drunken ex, "so I'm keeping it light. I started a list because they make me feel more in control." She laughs at herself even though I know she's not saying anything funny.

This isn't settling well in my gut. I want to ignore the feeling that this woman is a red flag walking, but I can't. "And you want me to be number five?"

"Frannie, we gotta go!" The shout comes from the SUV, her sister poking her head out and giving me a glare.

"Can't hold my foot down forever, son," the bus driver, sitting feet from us with his door open and a make-believe bag of popcorn in his lap, taps a watch on his wrist.

"Do you want to be number five, John?"

Before I can answer either of them, Winter shoves his head out one of the windows and yells at the SUV, "Keep your shirt on! Can't you see they're making a connection here?" He gestures between us as best he can through the small window.

"You want me to make a connection with my palm to your face, pretty man?" her sister, Cat, hollers back.

Wow. I've never heard anyone talk to him like that—other than the dudes, of course, but we're grandfathered in. We knew him in high school when he was a shit stain concealing his identity so he could experience American life.

"Baby, maybe don't keep your shirt on. And—YES." Winter's attention is fully on Cat now. Francesca and I watch them shout at each other like a tennis match.

"You better be the lead singer of a boy band. Otherwise, nobody calls me baby," Cat tosses back.

Our heads swing to Winter. "How about my queen? Kitten?" he croons, "Whatever gets me in your—"

Back to Cat. "Don't finish that sentence. I'm warning you, pretty man!"

"Sorry," Francesca says, pulling slowly from me. "Raincheck?"

Funny, our town hands out rainchecks all the time when a boating event, the school's ice cream social, or the annual Flea gets rained out. They're purple, handmade tags with glitter and string that people actually cash in at a later date.

I tap my pockets. "I'm fresh out of rainchecks."

It's for the best. I don't want to be anyone's *number five*, no matter how delicious she is in this slinky dress.

"Too bad." She exhales long and slow, a pout on her lips that's downright adorable.

She dips into the SUV and slams the door.

CHAPTER 3

Fran

A man-boy wearing a green *Get Lucky At Maureen's Estate Sales* T-shirt hefts a cement swan to his shoulder and winks at me. The shamrock on the back of his shirt must be giving him confidence, considering he's got to be on summer break from high school. No way he's going to be number five on my list. I'm not even sure there will be a number five on the list. Last night...

It might be time for a new approach. I've been kissing and running for months now. But last night, I couldn't risk it. I was dangerously close to wanting more. And more will inevitably lead to heartache—I'm done with heartache. I couldn't kiss him because I already felt a connection after a chat and a dip on the dance floor. Ridiculous, and way, way too sensitive.

When John pressed me up against the warm metal of that bus, I almost ripped down the walls I've carefully built to welcome him into the massive hole that seems to be my heart. He was mature, rugged features cut and chiseled with a little more time than me— nowhere near a silver fox, but definitely hinting at older— asking me to go talk, watching out for his friends, and opening a business with actual business cards. I don't have any business cards. In short, Superman has his shit together, and I clearly do not.

My eyes continue to assess the items around me in our third grimy house of the morning. There's always a good sale to hit around the eclectic neighborhoods of the Bay Area, and I dragged my roommates out this morning to take full advantage. The room is filled with kitchen appliances and accessories, also with stacks of newspapers and magazines from the eighties selling for fifty cents each. One man's trash...

Is this the right choice for me? Did I blow my savings on a summer vacation and a bad idea? Can I make a profit on junk and half-baked dreams? My thoughts spiral, and the urge to jot down a list of to-dos comes over me. I pull my phone from the waistband of my shorts to get it down.

Fran's Marketing Plan

1. Yard Signs
2. Business Cards
3. Ask Cat for ideas to post on socials

Now, back to perusing.

"Do we have one of these?" I hold a skillet up to a crack of light sliding through country kitchen curtains.

Other people's stuff has a certain life to it. This cast-iron skillet, for example, has been through some tough times. I feel a kinship with this skillet. We've been burned. We've been tossed aside and mistreated. We've been neglected and taken for granted.

"Put that down," Willow says. "You don't cook, and I think you have to season it or something."

The room is tepid, the feeling of vacancy permeating the air. I blow a piece of hair out of my face and pull a scrunchie from my arm, wrapping it into a nest of blonde on top of my head.

"Like a steak?" I ask, picking it up again for further inspection.

Willow lets her fingers glide over a collection of cut crystal figurines that have no business being in the kitchen, her ropes of curly strawberry hair glowing golden in the bits of sun seeping into the old house. "Like, that's how you clean it. Or, cook in it?" She rubs at her temples, her nose scrunching. "You don't need it."

She slips heart-shaped sunglasses from the neckline of an over-sized sweatshirt and puts them on, the large frames perched on her thin nose. She's the only person I know who celebrates Valentine's Day year-round.

"Maybe I do," I hedge, though my bicep is already burning from holding the thing up.

"Cat will tell you how you can't cook up Dorito's in a skillet and that you should make yourself something healthy. It'll sit on a shelf in the kitchen—and you're leaving, anyway!"

"Fine," I say, putting it down in a pile of burnt baking sheets. "You're right."

"Where did Cat go?" Willow likes to keep us close.

I turned in my resignation weeks ago to Cotton Candy Carnie. My bosses weren't pleased, but starting my own business was something to focus on, something to fill up my future besides a relationship. If I can't have love, at least I can have work, like Cat. I'll make my business my passion. And one of my passions is repurposing junk. You can't kiss a yard sign declaring twenty-five percent off, but you can pay your bills with the profit—I hope.

"She's probably hiding in a closet taking a work call. Cat," I shout.

Fellow estate vultures give us the side-eye as if there are rules for poking through other's people's things. Like you've got to be respectful, quiet as if you're at the actual funeral instead of the aftermath of a life. Estate sales aren't always about death, though. Some people are downsizing, some are moving into retirement, and some have bought school buses they plan to renovate and live in on a whim. Either way, they're ready to unload things that were once prized but now hold little to no value for them.

"Present and accounted for." My sister pops up next to me, head to toe in signature black on a sunny San Francisco Saturday. "Learn anything?"

"Err," I look around the ranch-style floorplan for inspiration, "better lighting?"

"Fran," she chides, sliding right into protection mode. "If you're serious about this, you should be taking notes. Taking pictures. That is going to be you—tomorrow. What's your brand? What sets you apart from the others?"

Discretely, she points at an elderly woman sitting at a card table near the front door with a Big Gulp that makes my mouth water and a yellow adding machine. Maureen's been running *Maureen's Estate Sales* for twenty years. I've already interviewed her and asked about a newsletter swap once I get my own venture off the ground. Shocker, Maureen doesn't have a newsletter, so I promised to set one up for her and send her the details in exchange for ten minutes of her wisdom. I took copious notes and made a list of her rules, of course.

Frannie's Finds is going to be the biggest estate sale business to hit the lake this summer, but when I get back to the Bay Area, I'll need some friends in the business.

"I have taken notes." I hold my phone up open to the Note's app with my multiple lists to prove it. "This is purely a research trip. I'm not buying," I huff while we follow Willow to an old study with peacock print wallpaper.

"You bought that vase."

"Doesn't count. It's for Mom and Dad. My '*I'm sorry I'm leaving the family business*' gift-vase."

"Ah!" Willow screams into a stack of dingy spines perched on top of an ancient microwave on the living room floor.

I jump and bump into a grandpa shuffling through the study.

"Sorry, sir." He takes one look at me in my off-duty biker shorts and no-makeup-aviators-indoors ensemble, grumbles, and continues pushing through the burgundy shag under our feet. "What is it, Wills?"

"First edition, signed! The Flame and the Flower! Kathleen Woodiwiss. Holy shit, this thing is mint. And they have no idea what they've got. It's two dollars, Frannie!"

My sister and I exchange a glance. Willow needed a win. The girl is always fighting a flu bug, temporarily injured with a superficial sprang or scrape, or buried under fourth-grade book reports and week-old salads. We follow her as she skips up to Maureen's card table to get in line.

Once we're outside on the sunny sidewalk, we decide to call it a day and hit the road in my convertible with the top down. Willow's hair blows wild, and she does nothing to stop it in the backseat, smiling up at the sun. Cat's next to me in the passenger seat, black Prada shades in place, frantically texting on her phone. Her blunt-cut dark hair is pulled back into a nubby pony. Wisps escape, but she doesn't bother tucking them behind her ears. She's in business mode. Nothing stops Cat when she's in business mode. Something I aspire to.

"I can't believe the band's breaking up," Willow says as we all push through the door to our cozy little home for three. Bacon and three different brands of perfume cling to the air.

"You two are on breakfast. I'm on margs. Showering first." Cat strides to her room, nose still in her cell, and closes the door.

It takes no time for Willow to whip up breakfast for dinner, our weekend go-to.

"You can't put that much syrup on your pancakes. Your plate looks like one of my students got hold of it," she says, watching me with a scrunched-up nose as I let globs of golden sugar pool.

Her concern makes me smile, but I ignore her, peeking out the window of our pink, three-story walk-up. This is my last night with my sister and my best friend, the last night in the adorable dollhouse we've gotten to live in for the past five years—the brutal twenties phase of our lives. We're all within a few years of hitting thirty, and things feel stagnant but comfortable. Is it possible to feel both?

"No one's ever died from living on sugar." Breakfast for dinner, with tequila, of course, is our tradition.

"That is one hundred percent false." She takes her plate of pancakes, pads her way into the living room in socked feet, and slides into the crook of the sofa nearest her bookshelves.

"Oh my gosh, Wills, stop staring at that book." The book she bought today is placed face out on the middle shelf.

She groans, "I just love it."

"Tomorrow's the big day," Cat says, striding through the kitchen and passing out mismatched glasses before she gets to work on the margaritas. The smell of lime and salt is an instant comfort while we all sit our butts on the floor around the coffee table, pitcher in the middle.

"To our last night as roommates—for a while," Willow says.

I give her a look. "I'm only breaking up the band for the summer!"

She raises a pink champagne coup filled with spicy margarita. "And to all Fran's recent make outs." I can't get a handle on how she feels about my kissing list. Willow is a lover of romance, but she doesn't date—like, ever.

Almost number five flashes across my mind—that soft cleft in his chin, tan skin, and strong hands gripping my hips.

"Yeah." Cat narrows her eyes. "Why didn't you go for it with that guy last night? I thought that was the whole point?"

I'm about to get grilled for the rest of the night, or at least until the tequila runs out.

"You were about to start a brawl with his buddies," I say, using it as an excuse not to answer her question.

His eyes were so, so intentional, like he was really looking at me. It was amazing to be seen, and maybe I am reading too much into one nightclub dance, but he was being careful with me. He was taking things slow.

Exactly what you don't need, I remind myself.

"To Frannie's Finds," Cat says with a supportive wink, releasing me from the spell of memory.

We clink our glasses in unison, sloshing our tequila and licking our fingertips.

Fran's To-Do List

1.Order business cards (check!)
2.Pack
3.Drop off flowers
4.Drive
5.Stop for treats and scratchers

"You're up early."

I startle with a freshly toasted waffle in my mouth, coffee in one hand and my phone in the other. Willow stares back at me from across the kitchen island. She's sleepy-eyed, rubbing the palm of her hand into her forehead as if she might be getting a migraine.

Busted. "Sorry for waking you."

"I know my codependence is showing right now, but I really don't want you to go."

"Take a book to the beach and have yourself a nice start to your summer break. I'll be back in two weeks."

The second I signed a contract for my first sale with Frannie's Finds, my mom announced she and my dad were throwing a second wedding, and she needed me back in town for a whole weekend right smack in the middle of my sale dates. The family was understanding and magnanimously agreed to me coming down to organize, prep, and work on selling the collector's items, then coming back home for the wedding weekend before going back to wrap up the job.

The toaster pops, and two more waffles shoot up. I toss one to her, but it knocks her elbow and goes spinning like a disc into the living room.

Her expression doesn't lift much, my efforts at comedy in vain. "Oh yeah, for your parent's thing?"

"Vow renewal. I feel like it's a bad sign."

"I hope it's not," she grumbles, still groggy and heading in the general direction of the coffee pot. "I love your parents."

"They love you, Wills." Her smile quirks and her eyes soften as she pours. Steam lifts from her favorite pink coffee mug that says, *Howdy*.

I hustle Willow through her morning and into a responsible long-sleeved scuba-style swimsuit—girl burns like a match stick in the sun—all but pushing her out the door with her massive straw hat.

The first thing I do after Willow heads to Crissy Field beach with two books stuffed in her favorite book sleeve is pack. Half my wardrobe is tossed haphazardly into one bag while I load another bag with two weeks' worth of sustenance: corn chips, salsa, cereal, popcorn, and granola bars—the ones with the chocolate chips and caramel drizzle.

On the way to the Cotton Candy Carnie warehouse, I stop by

a local farmers market and buy a load of rocket-red tulips for the vase I scored yesterday.

The warehouse is teaming with activity, exhaust from an early morning delivery truck hanging in the air as employees move pinball machines and pop-a-shots into a corner to make room. The concrete under my feet is cracked and gray, instantly making me think of being here as a kid on rollerblades.

Zenni, an employee and friend who's been with us since I can remember, is directing the organized chaos like an air traffic controller and yells, "Watch the Toy Story Pinball—that's twelve grand you're tossing around like a dollar store Koosh ball!" Spoken like only a director of operations at a gaming vendor could.

"Enjoying being me, are you?" I ask her, baiting and waiting for her to banter back.

She directs the truck back toward the dock. "Stop!" she yells, holding a fist in the air to signal the driver. Employees open the back door and begin unloading. Vintage carnie games pour out of the truck: whack-a-mole, crates full of bottles and glass rings, down-a-clown. This is a good haul.

She finally responds only with narrowed eyes, tucking salt and pepper-streaked hair into a bandana that's holding short waves back. "I'm keeping your title warm for you in case you don't win millions. But if you do, I expect to be cut in."

The lottery is my thing. I could be doing drugs! And while I'm no longer taking chances on men, I am always going to throw my hat in the ring for a jackpot.

"Dream on, woman. You've given me a hard time about my lotto obsession for years. If I ever win—I actually don't know what I'll do—but giving you a penny won't be on the list."

The vase is starting to weigh heavy in my arms; it took two dozen stems from the market to fill it. "I'm dropping off a thank you before I head out."

"Where's your first sale gonna be?"

"In Clover."

"Clover?"

"California. On Spirit Lake, just past Tahoe. Sits on the state line with Nevada."

"Really, offsite already—oh wait— you don't have a site. You don't have a warehouse or an office."

"You don't think I can pull it off?" My voice wobbles more than I mean to allow.

She drops the tough love act and wraps an arm around my neck, pulling me in by the crook of her elbow as if she's seconds away from giving me a noogie. "I'm worried about you, kid."

"I'm almost thirty years old, Zen."

"You're thirteen. That's how old you were when I met you, and you'll always be French-braided and brace-faced in my eyes. A terror on rollerblades in one of your dance costumes, red lipstick-stained teeth. You really were something, kid. Your sister's got fire, but you have the heart. Don't lose that, okay?"

Misty-eyed—damn it, Zen—I make my way to the office where I know I'll find Mom and Dad and knock on the door.

"Come in," Dad calls.

It's a broom closet with no windows and faded drawings signed *Frannie-Bananie* and *Kitty-Cat* taped to the walls behind him. You'd have no idea they're running the largest vintage games business on the West Coast in this hovel they call an office.

"I wanted to say thanks again for giving me your blessing to go out on my own."

"I don't like it," Mom says, elbow deep in a filing cabinet.

"But we support you," Dad adds, stretching at his desk. "What are you doing here, kiddo? Day one out from under our thumbs?"

I drop the vase of tulips unceremoniously on the desk. "Nothing. One last goodbye."

"Where did you find that vase?" Mom asks, and I'm proud that I've pleased her with a good hunting eye. "Sweet of you, honey."

"A sale I went to yesterday with Cat and Wills." I knew she'd appreciate the antique Blue Willow vase. It was a big score when I found it hidden under a Christmas tree in a basement.

Dad leans back and folds his hands behind his head. "Frannie, are you nervous to leave?"

"No." But my hands graze his desk as I go to stand near the wall of childhood art with my name scribbled all over it. "Maybe."

"We've been over this. No way but through, right?"

"Right. When posed with an obstacle," I recite words that have been lovingly drilled into me since I first started working in his office, "there's no way around, only through."

"Can't go under it—" he says, reciting one of my favorite childhood books.

"Can't go around it—"

"You gotta go through it. Atta girl," Mom chimes in. She may not love my choice, but she's on board.

"Your business plan is solid. You're ready." Dad pushes up to stand and rounds his desk to grasp my elbows. "Listen, kiddo. We're going to be just fine without our baby girl here in the warehouse, much as we'd love to keep you and Cat tucked between our wings. Truth is, we might actually sell. Now that we know you and your sister aren't interested in the business."

"But this was your dream."

"And we've enjoyed it," Mom chimes in, still at the filing cabinet, still on task. "But maybe it's time for a new dream... You've inspired us, Fran, even though I'll be up all night worried for you."

Inspiring my parents, anyone for that matter, is a shock. So is the warmth and pride that blooms in my chest.

I hug Dad hard and mouth *Love you* over his shoulder to Mom.

"I can't believe all it took was a handmade website, and someone booked me for my first estate sale just like that." I snap my fingers.

"It happened fast, for a former sports guy? Ricky Boggs? I didn't realize he'd died."

"I've been communicating with a member of the family, Meg Martinez. She didn't give a lot of details, but I'll have a load of memorabilia. And a thirteen thousand square foot lakefront in Clover to clear out."

"*Fancy!*" Dad claps me on the back. "You've been around this sort of thing your whole life. You've worked with stock from liquidations we've done here, and you've sifted through more estate sales than normal for a girl your age with your mom. I'm telling you, you're ready. Where's Clover?"

Taking a deep breath, I launch into it all again. "It's past Tahoe, on Spirit Lake." Hasn't anyone ever heard of this town? "Shares a state line and the lake with another town, Novel. In Nevada."

"Must be tiny. I've made that drive for our trips to Tahoe a hundred times at least, and I don't recognize it. But I had two young daughters shouting in the backseat and your mom navigating down to a nat's ass, so."

"Excuse me?" Mom jumps in, quick as lighting. "Before your car told you where to turn, *I did*."

"Anyway, that's my girl, leaping right into the deep end. Do you need a rec for the sports stuff?" He moves back around his desk and starts rifling through a drawer.

"You got one?" The family business is games, all makes and models of anything game-related. We sell new but also old, refurbished, desirable, and collectible. He's scrappy, my dad. "That would save me a ton of legwork, yeah, thanks."

He fishes out a card and hands it to me. "This guy owns a B&B out that way in Genoa, sells on the side. Tell him you're my former protégé, and he'll treat you well."

"Thanks, Dad. You're a peach." We look at each other for a moment, and I know he's sizing up what he sees in me, a little of himself, a little of my mom. Both our eyes turn watery.

"Remember, sell the goods in a big lot, nickel and dime for the crap," Mom says.

I make a checkmark on an invisible list. "Got it."

I'm really going to miss seeing them every day. We're not perfect, but what family is?

CHAPTER 4

Fran

I-80 East has a few tolls, but I'm prepared. Road trips are one of my favorite things to do. Our family used to drive this exact route for summer getaways to the lake when Cat and I had sticky raisin fingers and coloring books in the backseat. I don't remember my parents being together much. Even on those trips, they both peeled off for separate business calls often. But I do remember I was happy. A floating in the water without a care in the world, blue sky, endless, weightless kind of happy.

After an hour of driving, I pull off the highway, desperate to pee. I also need more snacks. The shock of air conditioning hits me hard, so I move quickly, do my business, gather my spoils, and dump them on the counter with a smile. My heart is jumpy as I eye the man dragging my items through a scanner and dropping them into a flimsy bag.

"And I'll take two Mega Millions and some scratchers, please." After all, you can't win if you don't play the game.

I don't know if it's being rid of my ex, starting something new, driving out on the open road, or the pull of the unknown I feel tugging at my chest that's making my pulse suddenly race. It's possible my subconscious has been begging for this change, this escape, but the rest of me wasn't ready to take the plunge. Maybe I'm still not ready, and that's what the pounding heartbeat in my ears is all about...

Too late now.

The time for second-guessing has passed, Frannie. You already booked the motel and a job.

"You know, young lady, it's risky to gamble," the man at the counter says. He's got a large hoop earring in one ear and a tattoo homage to music notes scrolling down both arms.

"Just some fun." I shrug and sip my soda while waiting for my tickets. The bubbles tickle the back of my throat while sweet syrup settles my antsy stomach.

"If you consider toying with your destiny fun."

Prickles rise on the back of my neck.

I turn and look over my shoulder. For a second, it felt like someone was in line behind me, watching this awkward little chat go down in this bizarre little gas station.

For his benefit or mine, I'm not sure, I let out an awkward laugh. "This is my only vice, okay?" I hold up the book of ten scratchers he's slid across the counter, unsure why I feel the need to justify myself to a stranger. All this change is making me itch.

"You're searching for something?" He eyes me as he pushes additional printed big pot tickets across the counter with two fingers.

"Err, I was. The bathroom, found it. Yours are very clean, by the way."

Again, I scan the store. The windows are mostly covered with decades-old signage. And still, there's that sensation we're not alone, and it's not the nineteen eighties Marlboro Man staring at me from behind a dingy stand of mass market paperbacks.

My gaze drags back to his. Deep brown eyes bore into me with a kind but clear challenge. "You can't run from your destiny." He hands me the bag he's finished ringing. As if I'm supposed to understand this conversation, he tags on, "What do you hope to win?"

For an absolute stranger, he's being awfully forward, but I get the feeling he's a curious person. It's a loaded question. A different life, contentment, safety? Isn't that what everyone dreams of when they go to bed at night and wish for a winner?

But I settle on, "Happiness."

When I'm buckled safely back in my bug, I take stock of all the essentials I've gathered: a jar full of coins, cinnamon bears, peppered beef jerky, and the biggest travel tumbler full of gas station Dr. Pepper I could fit into my cup holder.

Music pumps through my speakers, early *aughts* rap blasting as I bob my head and let my messy bun get messier in the wind. My favorite aviators sit lightly on my nose, and my best vintage jean shorts are soft enough to sit in for three hours. A white tank top that I probably should have swapped for something long-sleeved so I don't get too much sun whips in the wind.

Unable to check my phone, I mentally run through my to-do list: check into motel. It's called *something* and Burr. I remember the Burr because it made me think of how cold it must be in the winter up in the mountains that surround the lake. Hit a grocery store for things I forgot—like a razor. If there's time, check out a highly recommended antique shop in Novel, but I'm not sure how far it is from my business in Clover. Shower, change, and meet my client, Meg Martinez, at six for a run-through of their estate needs. It's going to be a lot to juggle, and I'm terrified I'll drop a ball.

I press on the brake and slow, the smell of asphalt and the shock of stillness a welcome change from the battering wind. After dropping coins in a toll bucket that sucks them down, I drive on, and before I know it, I pull up to my motel in Clover. Hot and sweaty.

Thistle and Burr. It's charming and slightly rusty with flecks of hunter-green paint chipping around the latticework in the windows, just off the main road in a strip of ice cream shops, clear kayak rentals, and T-shirt stores. If I did my research right, I can walk to the restaurant where I'm meeting my client, called simply, Boggs. Must be a play on rain boots? This area is all about outdoorsing. You can't throw a stick without hitting a gear rental shop.

"Welcome. Checking in?" I nod to a cheery pixie girl around my age. She watches me closely, eyes fixed, head quirked, hair poking in different directions from a claw clip. She's wearing a shirt that says, *Holiday Boat Rental, Novel, Nevada*, with the sleeves cut off and a string bikini underneath.

"Bloomfield, Fran," I answer, trying and failing to keep groceries from tumbling to the checkered tile floor. I should have gotten my room key before lugging everything I packed in with me.

"Got you right here." She taps on an ancient computer screen. "Room eight. Two months?"

"Yup."

"I'm Heidi," she says, tucking wisps of hair behind her ears. "What brings you to Clover?"

"Work, work, work." I mean it to sound cheery, but it comes out stressed instead. The place smells like fresh lemons and pine needles, so I take a deep breath and try to chill. "I've got friends coming to stay later this summer too. Work hard, play hard, I guess."

"You're in the prime summer months here. So much to do. Hiking, concerts, bar specials, bike rides, and boat rides. Let me know. I'd be happy to help you book."

"Thanks. I had planned to book another room for my friends—"

"But waited to make sure the motel wasn't filled with cockroaches first?" She laughs as she punches at a keyboard and pulls a key from a wall of hooks behind her.

"Err, something like that." I can feel my own cheeks heat and hope she doesn't notice she's onto me. "Do you have any openings?" I swipe the diamond-shaped key fob off the counter.

"I'll scrounge something up for my best customer. We'd be happy to have you. I haven't had anyone stay a full two months before. We'll be besties before you know it!" She fidgets while I digest her comment. "No pressure." She laughs, her eyes tired but bright. "I'm really bad at making new friends. Small town and all. Can't imagine what I'd be like in a big city. Wish I could find out, but can't imagine I'll ever get the chance while chained to this place."

Careful what you wish for. The night my ex and I broke up, I looked up at a full moon, standing in my childhood yard where I'd skinned my knees and dug in dirt, and with tear-stained cheeks, I wished I could start over, fall madly in love with the right person instead of wasting time and faking it with the wrong man. And here I am. Starting a business in a lake town. Maybe not exactly what I'd had in mind at that moment, but I've gotten myself this far, and I'll take it.

"I bet we'll be exchanging friendship bracelets by the time it's all over." I give her my best smile.

Heidi continues watching me, holding my gaze expectantly until her stare finally resonates, "Oh," *A tip, of course!* "Thanks again!" There's zero cash in my pocket, so I hand her a few scratchers. "Sorry, no cash, but I'll get you next time. And maybe, this'll pay off in the meantime."

I shouldn't have spent all my money on the tickets and snacks —but I've never been able to hold back when it comes to *tickets and snacks.*

She looks at the scratchers, then back at me. "Thank you?" Her voice ticks up into a question. "You really don't have to," she sputters. Maybe she wasn't waiting for a tip, maybe she really wants to make a new friend.

"Good luck!" I laugh, not quite sure if she's pleased. "Hope you win more than fifty cents. I'll see ya around."

"Yeah, same to you. And thanks. I could use a little luck." She holds the tickets up and shakes them as a wave goodbye.

My room is four doors down from the main office, and it's perfect. The kitchenette I'll hardly use and mini fridge are clean. A plush bed with white linens beckons after my drive, but the open bathroom painted a deep forest green with bright white tile is even more enticing—I stink.

My skin is still warm to the touch from all the sun I got on the drive, and despite the sunscreen, I've added to my year-round tan. I push on my shoulder with the pad of my finger and watch a white spot form and then disappear into golden brown.

A cold shower cools me off, and I wrap wet hair into a tight bun and pop gold earrings in. A few dresses hang in my motel closet after unpacking, and I pick the sunny yellow one. I want to make a good first impression on my new client. Meg Martinez doesn't know she's my first client—*ever*.

With a crossbody over my shoulder and a party bag of Doritos in hand, I head out the door to check out the antique shop that should be on my route to the restaurant. The second I pulled into Clover, I knew checking things out in Novel wasn't going to be a problem. The towns are pushed up against each other like bookends with no books.

Sure enough, it's down the sidewalk, but I stop short.

There's a street sign proudly stating that I am now entering Novel, Nevada.

I look behind me and see I missed a similar sign, stating Clover, California. *Birthplace and Home of Ricky Boggs.*

Between the two signs on the street, up a grassy green lawn, is a mint green Victorian-style house with an ornate wooden yard sign proudly proclaiming in script: *Town Hall, Clover.* And below that in the exact same script, *Town Hall, Novel.* If you were looking down at a map, the two towns seem to be split in two. Like a cake cut in half, the Town Hall divided down the center, continuing across the street and through the lake. But maybe lake waters are like international waters? Who knows?

Before I can read the fine print, two men burst through the double front doors.

"I wasn't finished speaking, Harry!" A man in an out-of-season sweater vest says.

"You can't have that date for the Clover Fire Festival because we've got that date earmarked—in red pen— for the Novel Flea Market," Harry replies, a shorter man in swim trunks and loafers.

"What's an earmark? You book the date, or you don't. It's ours. And it's a fall tradition!" Hollers sweater vest.

"You, sir, are out of order. I'm taking this to the lake committee." Harry stomps his loafer-ed foot.

"Ruth is not going to see things your way. She's by the book! You, you, you snake oil salesman sneak!"

"Virgil Troutwine, what did you just call me? You, sir, aren't fit for the lake committee. When I take my case to Ruth, I'll tell her just that!"

"There's no such thing as an earmark, Harry!"

"And when was the last time anyone used the term *snake oil salesman,* Virgil?"

I look around, trying to figure out what sort of Dorothy/Oz situation I've stumbled into.

The two men continue to barrel down the sidewalk. "Excuse me, miss," the snake oil salesman says.

"Fine. At the next committee meeting, we'll settle this," the other bellows. "Until then, you stay on your side of town, and I'll stay on mine!"

The two of them march away from each other, and that's when I notice a painted red line extending from curb to curb across the street. White letters sprayed into the asphalt, *State Line.*

The two men speed walk in opposite directions while I stand on the street, gapping at them. *What on earth was that?*

Traffic is picking up. The one light I've seen for at least a mile turns green as a slew of rusted trucks, fancy Land Rovers, and topless Jeeps drive on. I step back onto the sidewalk and continue past a specialty dog treat café called Dazzel Paws, finally coming to the sign I've been looking for, Revival!

Inside, a mishmash of antiques and eighties furniture accost the eye. There's taxidermy in stark contrast across the back wall, and I literally shield my eyes.

"Welcome," a gruff male voice greets me from somewhere in the store, but I can't see anyone.

It's not quite warm, that welcome.

Another—cheerier—voice chimes in, and a man pops up from behind the counter in the center of the store. "Welcome! Looking for anything specific?" This welcome is honest and true and full of a high school stage production's worth of enthusiasm.

I put on my best smile. "Just looking."

"I told you we shouldn't put that Art Deco settee up front," the grumpy voice mumbles. A fit White man steps out from behind a bedframe with a toolbelt around his waist and a screwdriver in hand.

The man behind the counter who's the size of a linebacker with stubble and a dimple in his cheek puts up his hands— he's weaponless. "Okay, okay, honey. You win. Move it wherever you want." He looks faintly familiar, black skin, dark eyes, dark hair, but I can't quite place him. He adds out the side of his mouth like a ventriloquist, "It's the taxidermy, isn't it? I kept telling him."

"Are you the owner," I ask.

"Yeah, I'm Jack, and this is my fiancé, Wagner." He motions to his partner. The grumpy blonde with freckles on his nose nods in my direction. "He's got a cinnamon roll center, I promise."

"Opposites attract," Wagner says, winking at Jack.

"I run an estate sale business, Frannie's Finds," I say to Jack. He's so familiar, his face ringing a bell in my mind, but I can't quite place him. "I'm in town for the next two months for a client sale. Are you guys currently buying?"

"Who's kicked the bucket?" Wagner asks.

"I'm not at liberty to say." Maureen made me take an estate sale oath to never share personal details.

"It's a small town. Let me fish the gazette out of the recycle bin." He eyes me with an arched eyebrow and digs through a box behind the counter.

"Sorry, I can't release personal information, but I wanted to introduce myself and let you know I may have some items you'd be interested in seeing."

"We might be interested," Wagner says, stopping his search when he clearly doesn't find what he's looking for. "But we're about to elope, then honeymoon." He saunters through a back door without another word.

"Ignore him. He's on his period," Jack says, his bright, wide smile stretching enough for the both of them.

I blurt out a laugh. "You're so familiar. Is it possible I've seen you around the estate sale circuit? Do you ever visit the bay area?"

"Possibly. Listen, you come in anytime and let us know what you've got. We're always buying."

"Thanks." I smile at him and the warm welcome. "I will."

Pushing out the door, I backtrack down the street, stepping over the state line from Novel, back into Clover. Dazzel Paws has a client currently being brushed and groomed in the window, a poodle who's gotten her hair dyed every color of the rainbow.

Boggs is an unassumingly chic place, about a five-minute stroll from Revival. A chalkboard sign outside says, *closed for renovation, reopening ASAP.*

With some effort, I push on the heavy door, and when I finally squeeze through, I'm met with an expansive birds-eye view of the sunken restaurant. The walls are bare. Painters on scaffolding are spraying them a fresh white, and the bar is completely taped off under plastic—except it looks quite ruffled, exposing deep mahogany, as if recently disturbed.

A large trashcan is full of solo cups, everything smells like primer and sweat, and there's a hammer pounding away as if it's got something to prove to all the power tools lying around. Dark wood beams overhead look to be safe from the paint, and I instantly adore the aesthetic. It's modern but old and warm at the same time. Rustic, but with a fresh eye. The owner is letting this place say what it wants to be, just giving it a polish so it can shine.

But none of it can hold a candle to the view. The back of the restaurant is all windows—an entire wall pulled back accordion style to open the place up to the outside. And outside is water. The bluest, greenest, clearest water dotted with rocks and boulders. I caught glimpses on the drive, and I faintly remember it being really cold as a child, but seeing it close is like a visual shock. One long dock that must be for Boggs customers who boat here instead of drive juts off the restaurant's pristine white beach.

As I approach for a better look, tempted to tiptoe downstairs onto the sparkling sand with large Adirondack chairs sporting fluffy nautical pillows, I trip over a beer bottle. Someone definitely took this bar for a test drive, and recently. I pick it up and place it gently on a table.

"Francesca?" A warm voice startles me, and I freeze.

No. It can't be...

CHAPTER 5

John

Bang, *bang, bang.* A hammer is pounding away somewhere, doing unspeakable things to my nerves. But no matter how much my two-day hangover and red eyes plague me, I know what I see. It's her.

"Francesca?" She jumps, and I sputter, "Wha-what are you doing here?"

She spins around, and I read the confusion that washes over her face. "What are *you* doing here?"

My heartbeat sprints on a treadmill. "This is my bar." I take a deep breath, trying to figure out whether I should laugh at the comedy act we've got going or pinch myself because I must be dreaming. "*What are you doing here?*" I ask again.

I stand very still in jeans and a worn-out T-shirt full of holes in the armpits that I wish I would have thrown out months ago so I wouldn't be greeting her in it now.

"I'm supposed to meet Meg Martinez about selling a relative's estate. I think he used to own this bar? John Boggs?"

Now, it's a nail gun firing in the background, making her look around for the source. The guys are in Chef Alec's kitchen right now, making it the Martha Stewart wet dream he demanded in order to relocate here permanently and transform Boggs Chicken Tender menu to Fresh Catch cuisine.

"Meg Martinez is my sister. *I'm John Boggs.*"

"*Noooooo.*" She covers her face with her hands.

It would be funny, the way her eyes go cartoon wide. Would be, except now she's hiding behind her hands, and her voice is filled with pure dread.

"What do you mean, *no*?" My hands are on my hips, and I think I'm puffing out my chest. I'm not accustomed to this reaction from women. I'm excited to see her, but this is clearly the worst-case scenario in her mind.

I should have put it together sooner—Frannie's Finds. But the professional email I'd been copied on between Meg and *Fran* never clicked with the girl in the bar from two nights ago, telling me about her shitty ex-boyfriend, some sort of kissing list, and a startup business.

She holds her phone up like a beacon, fingers shaking. "This is who I'm meeting."

I adjust the brim of my hat before taking a few steps closer to read her screen, and I hate that my stomach drops to the floor with the proximity.

"Yeah, that's me." The signature on the bottom of the email correspondence she's holding up like a shield has my name all over it. Blah, blah, blah, then *Best, Meg Martinez.* Then underneath that, the logo I spent way too much money on and—"Jonathan Boggs, Owner. Boggs Bar and Grill, Clover, California. My sister booked you to sell my dad's things. Did you even look at my business card before trashing it?"

She shakes her head, giving me a sheepish look and going slightly green around the gills. "I'm sorry for your loss," she breathes. "This is a beautiful space."

She looks up, looks down, then focuses again on me. As much as I want to launch into something that resembles the other night, I do my best to keep it professional. This isn't Throwbacks in the dark on a dance floor with a disco ball. This is broad daylight, and she's here on business.

Shit, that's going to complicate things.

With nothing better to say and in no rush to explain the situation with my father, I utter, "Thank you," and shove my hands into my pockets.

A saw begins an eternal, never-ending buzz cut, and I cringe. I'm acutely aware of the bottles littering the floor along with paper plates stuck together with cheese sticks. All remnants of the after-party I should have picked up yesterday. I used the oven in our brand-new state-of-the-art kitchen, and Chef Alec has already made it clear if it happens again, he'll have *my* head on a platter instead of his house specialty coconut shrimp.

With a fake smile glued to her pretty face, she strains to speak over the racket, "I guess we should go look at the stuff—what I'm here to sell."

If she can work through the palpable awkwardness, then so can I. Apparently, we're going to pretend we didn't almost make out against a bus. Shit, I might be old news. For all I know, she's already filled slot number five. Maybe even six. *Damn, five used to be my lucky number.*

"Right. Meg couldn't make it today, so you're stuck with me." I scrub the back of my neck and adjust my hat.

My mind has been circling her like a hawk since the moment she pulled away from me. I've given up women I was interested in before. The game doesn't really lend itself to being in a long-term relationship. Giving up on a spark is nothing new. It's old hat, comfortable territory. Even though I'm ready to date, it seems this is just another thing I can't have.

"Oh. Okay," she says, cringing a little.

The hammers and noise of renovation are too much to take while I try to wrap my brain around why she's here. For my dad's stuff, that's right. *Pull it together, Boggs.* "Hey, Gus!" I shout, wincing when I see her jump. I try to tone it down a bit but still get through to him. "Can you guys take five?"

"Sure, boss!"

The noise stops, thank God. It's been months of this, and my head is still pounding from the bachelor party. "Most of it's upstairs in an office we're using as storage. Once it's cleaned out, my sister is going to use it for school, and she helps out with the books around here, too."

"Lead the way," she says. At the same time I say, "Follow me."

I gesture toward stairs near the front door that lead to the loft. Her lips work into a tight smile, and she smooths her dress down with the palms of her hands as she moves past me in an arc so wide it's comical.

I take a stab at small talk. "So, did you find a number five?"

"What?" Her head snaps to look at me over her shoulder.

Shit, Boggs. Well, I never was good with the small talk.

"Sorry. Didn't mean to pry."

"It's okay," she finally answers, trying to laugh it off. "And, uh, no."

Why does that small admission make my chest feel all light and jittery like it used to when I dropped a bag of gear in a locker room before suiting up for a game?

"How was the drive?" I try again, doing my best to put her at ease.

All I can think about right now is the way my hand dragged down her body, neck to hip, on that sticky dance floor. Shit.

"Easy enough. The weather was nice, and the view was great." She climbs the stairs, and I keep my distance casual. "So, your sister is Meg, the one I emailed with, right?" She seems to be working hard to keep her voice light.

We reach a spacious landing that looks down over the restaurant. Cylinders of protein powder are stacked in a corner, and I feel my own cheeks heat.

"Meg, yeah," I finally get out. "She needs a place to study and helps out bartending during the busy season, which basically starts this week, but we missed that deadline as far as the re-opening. You'll be working with her. I'll be around overseeing the renovation and prepping to open, but I don't want anything to do with the sale."

"Okay, sure. We may need some signatures from you from time to time."

"Fine." I nod.

"Hey, boss?" Gus calls from somewhere down in the kitchen.

I lean over the railing to answer him, "Yeah?"

"You want this baby done in time for fireworks on the water. I gotta make some noise..."

The racket around us resumes. If it's possible, I think they even turned up the volume to spite my hangover.

"The Fourth is a real big deal around here. All the boaters drop anchor in the water for the show."

"I remember."

"You do?"

"Yeah, as a kid, my family came to the lake a few summers in a row. I loved the fireworks show. Kinda a finale to summer, it always made me sad because I never wanted it to end. They went above and beyond with, like, five finales, right?"

"Yeah. That was my dad. He'd spend what most people make in a year on a five-minute show. People boated in from all over. This place used to belong to a buddy of his before he bought him out. It was beautiful."

I fish through my jeans for my keys, tapping each pocket, forgetting where I stashed them.

"I'm sure you miss him," she offers politely. This is probably tricky territory in her business. With this job in particular, she has no idea how tricky, and I'd like to keep it that way so she doesn't realize I've got enough emotional baggage to fill this office.

"Um, yeah," I hedge. I don't want to lie to her. "In a way. So, you run estate sales?" Have we established this? My brain goes to mush every time I remember the smell of strawberries on her tan skin and the feel of her honey-blond hair.

"I'm brand new in the business. I guess we didn't really get into the details the other night, did we?"

"No, we didn't." I find the ring of keys in my back pocket and open the door to the office.

"My mom used to drag me to sales before and after school when I was little. I'd hold her place in line while she ran to get doughnuts." She smiles at the memory, and I want to soak up the way her glossy lips move, the one freckle under her eye. I can't look away from that freckle. "My sister was usually in some overachiever club or another, so it was just us. I liked searching for treasure, a natural magpie attracted to anything shiny."

She breezes into the stuffy room. I follow and almost smash into her when she turns abruptly.

I take her elbow to steady her, my hands turning to fire where we touch. "What brings you here?" I ask, wishing my voice hadn't dropped so low. "Why Spirit Lake?" Her eyes widen. I step back.

She licks her lips. "That's a great question. My relationship ended, you remember the guy?"

"Oh, I remember."

"It all feels a little clandestine." She laughs at our shared experience with her drunk ex. "Anyway, I wanted a change. My whole life, I've loved painting furniture found on the side of the road, being creative, and I don't know why I ever stopped. Estate sales popped into my head. I built a website, put up a job post, and your sister booked me. Then I met you," she finishes, her eyes fluttering here and there, everywhere but mine, as if she's telling the story to the room full of stuff instead of me.

"Are you from there? The Bay Area? What does your family do?"

"Born and raised. We sell new and vintage games. You?"

"I've traveled with a few teams over the years, but this is the only place I've ever called home."

"John, can I be honest with you?" She stops in the center of the room, clocks me with a direct gaze, and takes a deep breath. "We sort of connected the other night, right?"

"I felt that way," I say, "yeah." Where is she going with this, and why is my body all tingly?

"I feel like I can be honest with you..." She hesitates, but I'm glad she feels comfortable enough to speak with me freely.

"Shoot. Whatever's on your mind." I stuff my hands in my pockets and wait.

"I've spent my entire savings getting my business off the ground and on a room here for the summer. I'd appreciate it if we could start over, forget what happened the other night."

It's deflating, and the ego smarts a tad, I can't lie. But I understand where she's coming from. "We'll move forward like nothing...happened." *Idiot.* Nothing happened. "Just so you know, the office door is always locked. Meg will have a key for you tomorrow."

She nods with a stiff upper lip. I tug the brim of my hat lower.

The makeshift office smells slightly moldy from the leaky roof we recently repaired, stacked floor-to-drop ceiling with storage tubs. Framed Jerseys lean against walls, and baseball bats pop out of boxes like toothpicks in a cup.

"This is the entire collection?" she asks, more relaxed, which helps me do the same.

"Of sports memorabilia. A couple of buddies of mine took what they wanted, but this is the bulk of it. Ricky's house is about ten minutes from here on the other side of the state line, in Novel. I'll need you to handle that, too, but it's mostly personal belongings and furniture. He decorated the restaurant with this stuff—obsessed with the game."

"Baseball?" she asks. It's a fair question, though I'd figured anyone in the surrounding states knew who my father was. There's a lot of crap in here spanning multiple sports. She won't make it long in Clover or Novel without hearing about the great Ricky Boggs.

"Yup. He played ten years in the majors."

"Really? Exciting. What about you."

"Me?" How can I still be shocked at this question? The son who was supposed to *eclipse* Ricky Boggs, if anyone could do it, they said, it'd be me. The next generation. *Bigger, badder, stronger,* they said. "I played almost as long and almost as well."

"It makes sense, the other night, the applause." She twists her hands, and I wonder if she's thinking about the same moments I am. "You said you played some ball... So, baseball, then, like your dad."

She smiles, and it's sweet—no idea the shit sandwich she's just stepped in. She thinks I followed in the family business, so to speak. Too bad it isn't nearly that storybook.

"Yep." It's difficult for me to force a smile, but I try—it's stiff, like my shoulder. "Blew out both shoulders before I could beat any of his records. He was the oldest major league player in history and finished up his career as a coach for a few years. Bought this bar off his buddy as his retirement plan. It's kinda a big deal around here." I let my words trail off because I'm unsure how to finish. "We were both born and raised here, he and I. Now, I'm back. And I'm retired, too."

"Well." She claps her hands and looks around some more, anywhere but my face. "I'll work on finding a collector connection for most of this—someone who will buy the lot. Or, we can try to stage it inside the house for the main sale."

"If it was you, what option would you take?"

"Collector. If we can move the lot, you'll take a small hit, but it's highly unlikely I can sell it all for the price it's worth in a two-week estate sale. Better to take a small loss on a decent profit than have this stuff sitting around on your personal eBay account for years." She shrugs and then catches herself, stills, and stands taller.

"That's what I'd recommend, but I apologize. I'm not trying to downplay the difficulties of letting go of your father's things."

All I manage is a grunt in her direction, which she takes in stride.

"The little antiques store in town, Revival, do you know it? I spoke to the owner. He might be interested in things that don't move. After that, it's a donation drop, and I cut you a check."

"Jack would not like to hear anyone call his shop a *little antique store*—"

"You know him?"

"Everybody knows everybody in this town. Also, he's won a few Super Bowls. This time of year, though, we get the tourist rush, so it doesn't feel quite so suffocating."

"Sounds nice to me, having people around who know you. My friends, the ones you met the other night, are coming to visit at the end of the summer. Sort of like a celebratory thing." It's clear she regrets bringing up the night we met the second the words leave her soft pink lips. Her cheeks turn an even brighter shade of magenta.

So, I press her a bit because I want to see that blush deepen. "I remember your sister, Cat. And the one with the freckles?"

"Willow." She looks away and continues wandering around the room as if she hasn't already seen it all. "We'll do a nice dinner out or something," she rambles, her yellow dress swishing around her thighs. "Anyway, they're going to like it here. It feels..." She turns quickly toward something that catches her eyes: a trophy from my Triple-A days.

The hem of her skirt lifts an inch, fluttering around tan skin. "It feels kinda magical. You know, on my walk here, after I shopped around to get my bearings, I stood for a solid minute in two places. One foot in Nevada, one foot in California. Magical."

There's something lodged in my throat, but I manage to grind some words out. "That's a pretty way to look at it."

All sugary sweet and thoughtful. Pie in the sky. Where the hell did this woman come from? Why is she suddenly here and not in San Francisco? I understand the logistics she's explained. The mix-up is understandable enough, but it all feels too good to be true. Because I was dying to see her again the second those bus doors closed. Pathetically praying she'd use my number.

"Should we go see the house?"

"Meg will help you with that," I say, pulling at my neck and readjusting my cap. Francesca is off-limits for so many reasons. She's selling Ricky's stuff, for one, and that's a story I really don't want to tell. And she's told me straight up she's not dating. She lives almost three hours away. "She was supposed to be here today but had to take a meeting with her advisor at the last minute. I think she failed economics."

"Ouch."

"Yup." We let an awkward moment stretch long between us. The more this charade goes on, the more I feel like I'm not going to be able to work with her at all while she's here. Pretending like I haven't already had my hands all over her, like I don't know how silky soft her pretty blonde hair is, is taking a toll. And she's acting as if none of it happened.

"I'll see myself out and let you get back to it." She turns and hits the door jam. "Ow!"

Maybe she's a little affected. "Magical, huh?" I can't help laughing. "You alright?"

She laughs it off. "Sure, sure." There's something in the way she's dancing around on her toes, nervous energy rolling off her as she tries desperately to control it, all pink-cheeked and deep breaths. It could give a guy hope. "Nice meeting, or um, seeing you again Mr.... John."

"Oh, and Francesca—"

"Yes?" She turns her head while trotting down my stairs and beelining toward the new front door I had installed, the Boggs name branded into the wood. The woman sure has a knack for running from me.

"Find a collector, sell the lot, and get it gone." It's a miracle I manage to get the words out without including an expletive.

She stops short, and we hover in the doorway. All too desperately, I soak in the extra time with her, knowing there's not much left. Her smile is just... Magnetic. That's the word I'm looking for. That damn freckle under her eye is magnetic. *Everything* about her seems to draw me in.

What am I going to do with her in my office, in my bar, day in and day out for the next two months? I already don't want her to leave. It's like dancing with her all over again. The song ends way too soon.

But I haven't forgotten her asking me to be number five. I couldn't explain it if I tried, but I had a visceral reaction to being a notch on her list. It's even more powerful now.

Out of all the moments to give up casual sex, why did I have to choose now?

"I'll let you know when I've secured a deal." She nods, pulling at the heavy brass handle as I reach over her head to support the weight.

We say our goodbyes on the sidewalk in the sun, me adjusting my cap and her avoiding eye contact, still not mentioning the details of what happened the other night and how insane it is that we've connected again.

Magical, indeed.

She peeks over her shoulder and waves as I walk down the sidewalk, following her until I realize it and stop.

Meg will contact her tomorrow. She'll take her to the house and show her around. She'll answer any questions she has and make all the decisions. There won't be a reason for Francesca and I to see each other. Maybe a glimpse from time to time when we're coming and going at Boggs.

She turns back again, and I'm still watching as she crosses the street. I check my feet. I'm halfway down the sidewalk, so I didn't stop following her after all.

The sign for Thistle and Burr Motel hangs over her head. She gives me one more smile despite what looks like her trying not to, her shoulders raising in question and a look of delighted confusion on her face as if saying, *What the hell are you doing?* Then she simply shakes her head and disappears through her door.

Patty pops out of her pastry shop across the street from Boggs and gives me a bewildered wave before clearing one of her bistro tables. I'm standing like a dope on the sidewalk as cars and the first trickle of tourists move around me. In this moment, I'm sure of one thing: I'd refuse to be a name on Francesca Bloomfield's list again, because one kiss with her wouldn't be enough.

CHAPTER 6

Fran

I've got a new email from Meg Martinez apologizing for missing the meeting yesterday. She gives me directions to meet her and tells me to dress for a picnic and bring a bathing suit. They're having a Sunday soiree on Boggs' beach at four, and she won't take no for an answer.

All night, I tossed and turned in my motel bed after the epic shock of running into John. At the lake. Hours from the nightclub where I danced with him less than three days ago. The odds have to be minuscule.

My pulse kicks up as I drive my bug with the top down, a canopy of towering trees overhead, to the address in Novel.

I shut down completely during our meeting. Did I even speak? Did I come off professional or like a two-by-four with no personality? Did he see right through me, down to my jittery nerves and desperate confusion? I tried so hard to mask my racing heartbeat every time he took a step toward me. I put those feelings in a box and used industrial duct tape.

He made it clear I'll be working with Meg for the estate sale, but I'll probably see him from time to time at Boggs. That thought is equally terrifying and enticing. Maybe he'll be too busy doing "bar owner" things—signing paychecks and shining shot glasses, one of his signature baseball hats pulled low and highlighting beautiful cheekbones. Maybe he'll be around but hanging with his buddies, and we'll barely have time for a hello.

Maybe I'll add him to my list of kisses, finally filling slot number five. Just one kiss to get him out of my system.

Frannie, no. I shake my head in my bug and check the rearview, but no one's behind me on this winding road dappled with sunlight. I let out a long breath.

Kisses with no connection haven't been working. It's been mediocre vibes and lackluster thrills at best, and while I haven't felt a connection or uber-sensitive about any of it, which was the goal, I also haven't felt...anything. *John would be different*, a tiny voice in my brain says, and I know it's true. I knew it when he dipped me at Throwbacks as plainly as when my stomach dropped when I saw him yesterday.

But now he's a paying client, and while I know people wrangle working together and sleeping together often—my parents' case in point but also, *ick*—I'm not looking for anything serious. Serious leads to pain. I've been through all that. So just—*No.*

Clover and Novel, fancy as they are with their high prices and stunning views, are unexpectedly casual. It felt like the right move to wear my yellow one-piece suit with cutoff denim, so I don't have to change. An indulgence via raffia wedges on my feet. Generally, feeling like a blonde amazon is a *no* for me, but if I do see John again and I happen to stand next to him, he'll still be a foot taller than me. And that's damn exciting for a tall girl.

Ricky Boggs's home is bookended by mountains, surrounded by slim but towering Jeffrey Pine trees that are a staple around town, and backs right up to a large lawn leading to pristine water dotted with smooth gray boulders accustomed to the area. I did some research, and Mr. Boggs was a freaking great athlete, which explains the rustic mansion with acreage and a tiny cabin in the distance.

If I'm going to front to a former baseball player that I know how to handle his collectibles, I need to know my stuff. I've soaked up everything I can. One detail I noted is that there's no information about Ricky's passing online. Odd, since most celebrity signatures increase in value after death, and besides the fact I never came across an obituary, there's not one article about the athlete passing. But I get the feeling John just wants everything gone and couldn't care less what price I get for it. The family has obviously kept things private. I certainly don't want to ask him for details about the funeral or lack thereof. Maureen's world-weary words ring in my ears: *you will find skeletons in closets, but keep it professional!*

He seems to be a very private person, anyway. It's no surprise he wants to deal with his father's estate quickly and quietly.

The truth that I've been dutifully avoiding while setting up my website and buying scallop-edged price tags with grosgrain ribbon ties is I haven't the slightest clue and couldn't care less about sports. Antiques, hand-carved and dovetailed, birds-eye maple, and pass-downable heirlooms are what I'm into. But I took this job because the Boggs family was the first to book me. I've already got an email into Dad's guy, two towns over, in Genoa. One way or another, I'll sell this estate, enjoy the rest of my summer chasing that elusive bit of childhood happy, and return to San Francisco ready for anything.

As I'm pulling up a winding drive that allows quite a bit of privacy, a woman pops out the front door.

"Hi!" she yells. "Cute car. I'm Meg." She's petite. I dwarf her when I get out of the car by about a foot, and she sports curves for days with wavy black hair with an assortment of chestnut highlights. We're shaking hands in a flash.

"Francesca."

"Frannie's Finds, right? Follow me, Miss Frannie." She smiles at me wide and warm before leading me up the pebbled drive.

"I'm sorry I couldn't meet you yesterday as planned. My guidance counselor roped me into a summer class to make up for a boo-boo on my report card, so I'm juggling that as well as helping out at Boggs."

She has no idea I had the surprise of my life when I heard her brother's voice behind me, a voice I thought I'd never hear again. "Thank you for booking me for the job. I'm excited to be here."

"Sure. I like supporting women-owned businesses." She leads me across a rustic threshold stacked with speckled stones. "I could tell you're new and trying to build something—no offense, your website screams start-up." She says it with a smile and unabashed honesty. It's impossible to take the comment for anything other than what it is: truth.

"You got me," I admit while maintaining a confident smile like my mom taught me, but my palms start to sweat. Am I in completely over my head? Can she tell? "This is my first job aside from my family's business. I've worked for them since college. Close to ten years as director of operations for Cotton Candy Carnie, new and vintage games in San Francisco."

"I saw that in your bio." She laughs. "I bet you have a really fun house."

I nod, taking in the warm terra cotta walls of the foyer lit by a chandelier made of antlers. "Let's just say I spent a lot more time playing pop-a-shot than building websites."

"Not a bad childhood."

"We were the envy of the neighborhood for sure. Every kid should have Pinball. And their own cotton candy machine. My dad used to pull it out on Sundays. Drove my mom crazy; she was so worried about our teeth."

"Not gonna lie, I've got a sweet tooth the size of the lake." She drops a key in a dish with a golden mirror hanging above it. Our reflections continue to work through small talk.

"Me too," I say, happy to have met a fellow sugar head.

"I would eat cotton candy for breakfast if my brother would let me. John and I are over ten years apart, and he's mothered me since ours passed young."

"I'm so sorry," I say, and I mean it. My heart breaks for them both, so much loss at such young ages, the likes of which I've never experienced. I know how lucky I am. Sure, my parents argue, but they refuse to give up on each other.

"Thanks." She waves me off because what else is there to say?

"My friends are a lot like your brother," I add in solidarity and to shift the somber mood.

"I think the man is addicted to healthy eating podcasts. It's weird, but whatever floats your boat, right? Our mom was very into healthy lifestyle. John says she hid pureed carrots in everything she made me."

"He does seem pretty straight-laced. Can't say I'm surprised to hear that."

"I'm not surprised that's what you got from your meeting yesterday. Did he ask you to color-code everything? Because that's the first thing he asked me to do when I took over the office." She makes a pained face, as if we're in cahoots now working for her stickler brother.

This is not the moment to admit I've met him before, right? How do I explain to a new client I did a slow grind on a dancefloor with her brother? So, I skip it and reply, "That wasn't the first thing I noticed about him, but no, he didn't mention color coding."

There. That was honest enough.

"But he did explain what he wants from the sale? Or do you need me to go over that? Basically, it's a clear out."

"He told me as much, and I won't let you and your brother down. I'll be as respectful as possible while dealing with your father's things."

I hold in all the questions I want to ask about the late Ricky Boggs and follow her into a bright kitchen with high ceilings, light pouring through massive windows highlighting walls with slatted-wood that go all the way up the two stories.

"John and I share the same mother, but Ricky Boggs isn't my father." She gives me a wry look. It's true, she and John don't look anything alike. Where he's all strong Roman nose, plump lips, and lightly tanned from summer with wide hazel eyes like whirlpools, Meg has piercing eyes, brown skin that suggests Latin roots, and heart-shaped lips. "My dad lives in LA. We're half-siblings." Her eyes squint as she looks me over. "What did he tell you about this job?"

"He wants it all gone ASAP, but I'm in no rush if that's what you're worried about. I'm here for the summer. You can both take all the time you need if you're still sifting through items to keep."

"Oh, I don't think you need to worry about that." Maureen warned me about this. When people are in mourning and dealing with the realities of clearing out a life, they're understandably going to be upset.

She walks me around the house, pointing to various items that will be difficult to move or especially valuable. When we make it to the primary bedroom, I ask the question that's been poking around my mind for the last twenty-four hours.

"He says he doesn't want anything of his dad's, or seemingly from his own career, but most likely, that'll change when strangers start manhandling precious memories and the moving truck pulls up." She doesn't respond or react, and I wonder if I've offended her, gotten too personal, but I can't help myself and plow on. "Do you think, maybe, you should convince him to keep a few things? He may regret getting rid of everything one day."

She fluffs a pillow on the king bed and takes her time responding. "I'm not exactly sure how to answer that."

Have I forced her to put a guard up? That's the opposite of what I should be doing. I should make both of them feel as comfortable as possible as they live through this change.

Now my palms and my armpits are sweating. I'm handling this all wrong, and I wave her struggling response off. "I'm sorry. I shouldn't have pried."

"Listen, I'm an open book, but he's gone through a lot the past few years. Lost his career. Lost his dad. I'm not saying I agree with how he's going about it, but I am glad he's finally moving forward." She stops in the hallway and looks straight into my eyes. "He's getting serious about his life. Have you seen enough here?"

Meg Martinez sure doesn't hold back.

She switches off the lights, unconcerned with my lack of response, and moves through the hall, trotting down a winding staircase that delivers us back in the entry. Quickly, but holding on to the railing because of the wedges, I follow her all the way out the door. She locks it behind me.

"Whelp," I say, standing by my bug and searching for some way to wrap this meeting up professionally. "I'll get started first thing tomorrow morning: organize, catalog, tag. It seems your brother wants everything out of the office first. He mentioned you could use the space"—her face softens—"so I'll start there. Then, I'll get to work on the house. We'll have the big sale in about three weeks."

Her lips tip up into a smile. "He puts everyone else first, that man. He deserves to have this done for his own piece of mind. That sounds great, Fran. Thanks."

"You can reach me anytime by phone or email. Whatever you need, but I'll be gone one weekend before the house sale for my parent's vow renewal in San Francisco."

"Works for me. And Frannie?" She takes a deep breath. "Come to me with any and all questions, okay?"

"Of course."

"Great," she says again, nodding but not looking completely convinced. "Work, over. Let's go catch a buzz."

Meg rode her bike to the house, so I drive us around snake-like roads through Novel toward Boggs with a shiny red bike in my rearview. She loves my little bug and props her elbow on the window, letting her hand roll through the breeze as we wind around curves.

"You need one of these if you're enjoying the ride this much," I say, turning the volume up.

"You know what? I think you're right. Finals nearly killed me, and the summer program I'm in is intense. This car feels like a vacation."

"What are you in school for?"

"English, philosophy, not sure. I'm already in my fifth year... I might go for my master's to become a librarian. But I've got rowdy roommates and love to hike, so it's taking a minute. John gave me the job at Boggs to help cover expenses while I figure it out."

"My friend Willow would love you. She's an avid reader."

"What does she do for a living?"

"Fourth grade English teacher. She's addicted to romance novels."

"Nice," Meg says as her cheeks begin to flush. From the sun or the subject, I'm not sure. "That's my genre of choice, too."

"Too bad," I say as I park my car on the street a block from Boggs. The parking lot is roped off, having new concrete poured tomorrow if a spray-painted sign is to be believed.

"What's too bad?"

People mingle outside sherbet-colored shops in bikini tops, kids run with Frisbees printed with local logos, and a line for a shaved ice truck with a penguin painted on the door wraps around a corner. "I gave it up."

The view alone is giving me happy vibes. Despite being worried about pulling off the sale, I made the right choice being here for the summer. It feels right.

"Books?"

"No," I laugh. "Just romance. I'm recovering—" Why do I overshare? If I was smart, I'd keep my big mouth shut. But while I haven't gotten an exact read on Meg, I think I like her.

It looks as if she's trying to zip her lips too, but breaks and asks, "Got burned?"

"Real bad."

She makes an *ouch* face as we push through Boggs's front doors.

Once inside John's bar, we sidestep tools and overturned chairs on tabletops. Construction is over for the day, the large windows creating a perfect picture frame for the clambake going on outside. The accordion wall is wide open.

On the beach, shallow pits are filled with shellfish, corralled by simmering coals and ears of sweet corn. Memories of evenings like this with my family flood my mind when Cat and I were still pre-teens and feigning disinterest while secretly loving every minute of wet hair, setting sun, and mouths full of salty, fried food.

"I'm sorry, sis. I knew I liked you the moment you cruised up in that teeny, tiny, topless car. But anyone who knows romance knows if a fan has given up the genre, they're most likely in a deep, dark pit of despair. Are you in a pit, Frannie?"

"I am not in a pit!" I respond too quickly, trying hard to say it with a winning, toothpaste commercial smile, but her question caught me off guard and hit surprisingly close to home.

"Day one of a brand-new job, essentially moved to a small town to start over, gave up on her favorite books, misses her friends back home..."

We step onto the deck of Boggs. Like magnets pulling to metal, my eyes snag on John in the sand, wearing a pair of red trunks. He's manning the grill, shrugging on a Patty's Pastries T-shirt, pulling it down over golden tan pecs and knotted abdominals. I stop short, my feet suddenly wooden. *Good god.* I knew his body was honed, but I didn't quite realize *that's* what was wrapped around me at Throwbacks.

"You got all that from me giving up romance novels and mentioning Willow?" I breathe, warring with myself to dislodge my eyes, currently glued to his white smile and the divot in his chin.

Flags flap in the wind on the dock where a few boaters are tying off. Savory smells coming off the beach make my stomach grumble while I hopelessly drool over a man I had the chance to kiss but foolishly ran from instead. Because he was just too much. I'm entirely unsure of how I'm going to live and work around him for the summer. He's got *off limits for Frannie if she's trying not to fall head over heels and get hurt all over again,* written all over him as if the paragraph were a warning on his T-shirt instead of a dancing cherry pie.

"Girl, you are the epitome of the pit of despair. It's written all over your face. And..."

She stops before we start down the stairs to the beach.

"What?" Reluctantly, I pull my gaze from her brother and realize I am going to have to get some really dark sunglasses and avoid him at every turn this summer.

"It's you..." she says, eyes narrowing.

Oh shit. "What's me?" But somehow, I think I know. Even though it's impossible she knows. *There's nothing to know!*

Meg calls my bluff as her curls blow softly in a breeze. "You didn't meet him yesterday, did you?" Her eyes hold mine relentlessly.

The burning in my cheeks is strong. "Meg." I turn fully toward her, putting John and the scene on the beach behind me, trying my best to block out the Norman Rockwell vibes and focus.

"The way you're looking at him... He told me he met a girl, *Francesca*." She goes on without waiting for my response. "It's you, isn't it? You're from San Francisco. They were at that club because Jack loves it, for his bachelor party."

"It was nothing. We met, yes, but very briefly."

"It wasn't nothing to him. He told me everything," she says slowly. "Would kill me if he knew I was saying this." We both watch him now, slapping members of the construction crew on the back as he pulls food off the grill and plates it for his guests. "He wasn't himself the day after that bachelor party. He literally woke up a different man. And then, *bam!* You appear in his bar, and—"

I laugh off her words, instruct my head to stay clear and not let what she's saying affect me. "We hardly know each other, and we've already agreed to start fresh." I can feel her gaze land back on me, incredulous and still putting everything together.

My traitorous gaze stuck on him again as he walks a full plate of food over to an older man and woman at a table on the beach. He carries on a conversation with them, his big smile on full display with his hat turned backward.

Meg takes a step closer and we both lean on the rail watching him. "He was more awake that morning—the morning after he met you. Hungover as hell, but his eyes were wide open. Like he'd been walking around in the dark this last year, and you turned on a light. I can't believe he danced, like, in front of people."

"That's... I can't believe he told you about me. It was only a moment," I repeat, more for my benefit than for Meg's because this means he thought about me long after the dance. The almost kiss.

I affected him? *Turned on a light?*

"But you're only here for the summer, right?" Her words are an arcade game powering down, *whomp, whomp.* Game over before it's even begun. "And you've just been burned, given up on romance, right?"

"Well, yeah. I..."

"Frannie, you can't get involved with him." She's a sister in full-protection mode wasting zero time getting to the point, and I know exactly what she's going to say next—because she's not wrong.

I try to beat her to it. "I'm here to work, that's all."

"I'll say it plainly, so there's no confusion." She stands up straight and looks me in the eyes. "Please, don't break my brother's heart. You're beautiful, fun, smart, and motivated like he is. I can see why he was attracted, but don't string him along for the summer only to leave. His home has always been here. He's attached to the trees and the water, and now he's starting a new life with Boggs and..."

"I won't." It's an easy promise to make. "The last thing on earth I'm looking for is a serious relationship." This is no big deal. I can promise to stay away from John Boggs with a clear conscience. It's for the best—for both of us.

And I really don't want to be on this woman's bad side. She is clearly strong, determined, but in this moment, she's being vulnerable. She's asking me not to hurt her brother, and she's truly worried. It's written all over her striking face.

Meg nods once and smiles. "Alright, I'll trust you to make good on that promise. Let's go see if we can find something edible down there. Knowing John, he's gonna tell us the sweet corn is dessert."

"That didn't work on me as a kid. No way it's working on me now."

"Same. I've got three cherry cheesecakes hidden in Chef Alec's fridge. You'll help me carry them out later?" I'm not exactly sure if we're friends at this point or if Meg is keeping her enemies close. I don't want to be her enemy, and I certainly don't want to hurt her brother.

"Absolutely," I say, replacing what wants to be a frown with a winning smile.

We head down a short stack of weathered wood steps. John's eyes snag mine immediately, but I look away, squinting behind my aviators. My brain works overtime trying to dissect the conversation I just had. I made a promise, and I'll have to keep it. I *want* to keep it. That's all there is to it.

The party's already flowing on the sandy beach, and Meg peels off to greet guests. People tend pits filled with coals and shellfish with sticks, and some kids are flying a kite down the beach. The day is sunny and full of that super breathable lake air, crisp but warm. The savory smells of brats on a grill make my stomach rumble. I'm ready to eat my foot, I'm so hungry, or eat my feelings until I no longer feel the sting of a protective sister warning me off her brother.

Slipping out of my shoes, I stow my things on one of the folding tables set with butcher paper and mallets and make my way to the food line. John stands at the end, still working the grill, his forearms flexing in the sun. His green baseball cap is turned forward now, shielding his face from the rays and reflection off the water, and his bare feet sink into the sand. Short red trunks hang on his hips, a bit frayed at the edges.

Butterflies flutter in my stomach, but I dig my heels into the sand and squash them. *Even if he was up for it, there's no way I can add this man to the kissing list now.*

The buffet is littered with fresh seafood. Piles of clams swimming in butter and garlic, stacks of shrimp with potatoes still steaming from the coals, so much food on display that I bolt toward the table with an empty tummy. I think the entire construction crew for Boggs is here, already eating at a low-slung table near the water, sitting in the sand on tufts and mats.

My heart warms for this clearly close-knit brother and sister team. This is a thank you to their workers, to the town it seems, as the beach is filled to the brim with people, and it's such a statement of respect and gratitude I swear, I almost tear up. It's my goal to help them, to do a good job not only for my business but because this family deserves it.

Down the food line I go, icy grapefruit-infused beer in hand, putting nothing on my plate but chips. *Damn, shellfish allergy.* I'm newly energized, building a wall up with each step I take. This can't get personal. Maureen was right; this is a job. I'm here to help these people move on after a loved one's death, clear out their spaces so they can live again. I'm not here for anything romantic. That was never part of the plan. Work was the plan, and it's going to stay that way.

When I make it to the end of the line, I look up at him. I knew this was coming, and yes, it's hard to look at him knowing how attracted my body is to his. That was established the second he touched me on that dance floor, again in his office yesterday, when his mere presence made me walk into walls, but I can do this. I can keep things friendly.

I squint up at him, shielding my face from the sun with my can of beer. "Hi."

John looks at me horrified, flipping brats by memory on the grill. "Francesca?"

I startle. Did he not know Meg invited me? I bump my aviators up my nose with my knuckle. "Um, yeah?"

"Why is your plate full of chips?" His forearms flex as he transfers a few brats to a mounting pile on a silver platter.

I'm thrown. "I like chips?"

His eyes narrow, and heat blooms in my chest. Am I in trouble? The line behind me chatters away. No one seems to care that I'm causing a halt in traffic.

He exhales a string of almost frantic comments. "You need veggies. Why no clams? I made the hummus fresh."

I take a long pull from my beer, sizing him up. Is this man about to tell me what to eat? Slowly, I lick the sweet grapefruit hops from my lips and give him a quizzical look. How am I supposed to respond to that?

His eyes snag on my mouth for a moment. "What about the shrimp salad?" he pleads with big, hazel puppy eyes. "There's a whole bowl of fruit..." He is a kid trying to find words while perplexed by my plate.

"Bleh. Salad."

"Oh my god, Francesca." The pleasure of unexpectedly winding him up washes over me. "Please don't tell me you eat like a toddler." His lips form a slim, firm line.

I kinda do, and my entire family is on me about it all the time. But in this exact moment, my plate is not my fault. If I eat the fish, I will puff up, turn red, and keel over.

Why does this man care what I eat, anyway? Meg did warn me he was passionate about food, but I'm a stranger to him. Well, a stranger who was in his arms three nights ago, but we're past that!

Right?

Instead of explaining, I change the subject. "Please don't tell me you're going to call me Francesca for the rest of my life. Most people call me *Fran*."

Oh, no.

I was aiming for casual, but he takes a very deliberate step toward me and drops a banana on my plate. My head tilts up further as he eyes me down.

"For the rest of your life?" He clears his throat.

Of course, he's going to zone in on that innocent turn of phrase.

"I misspoke," I say, my cheeks burning. "For the rest of our relationship."

The words *our relationship* hit the sand between us like a bomb—*boom!*

I didn't mean *relationship,* relationship. Emphasis on *working!* *Did I forget to add that word?* And why are both our chests heaving as if there's not enough oxygen on this beach?

"Hmm," is all he says.

What? What does *hmm,* mean?

He eyes me from head to toe. "I guess I'm not most people."

"But, and hear me out here," I add playfully because I can't stop myself, "is that a good idea? I think it might be best if you *were* most people." *Instead of so surprisingly special.*

And there it is, that feeling of attraction turning into emotion which will inevitably turn into attachment. It's clear any inside jokes or nicknames are a bad idea for me. *I'm weak* for the implied intimacy.

"Brat, please," I stammer, feeling anything but pulled together, under control, or professional. I need more coaching from Maureen. I need to be tough!

He plops a brat on my plate next to the banana and flips his hat around backward to accost me with a full-blown, boyish grin.

"Come back when you want dessert, Francesca," he says.

And then he licks his lips.

CHAPTER 7

Fran

The party rolls into the evening. The sun right at the edge of the water, about to fall fully splattering the mountains in the distance with hot pink and blood orange. My belly is full of meat and chips, and just as I'm thinking I might head back to my room for a solid eight hours of sleep before a grueling work schedule begins, my phone rings.

"Hey!" I dig my toes into sand. The small screen gives me a view of Willow and Cat sitting in the kitchen of our apartment. "What's up?" Cat looks to be in tears, which would be totally out of character for her, but it's hard to tell with the glare on my screen.

"Man, the beach looks good on you," Willow says. "Swimsuit and sunnies on like you do it every day." I grin goofily at her through the screen because for this summer at least, I think I will do it every day. "Everything's okay. I got it covered, but we needed to call you before we opened the second bottle."

Ugh, oh.

Cat holds up her favorite wine glass as if she were toasting through the phone, the one with the kitten rolling around with a sprig of mistletoe. "I'm fine!" Her voice is uncharacteristically light and forced.

"What happened, Kitty-Cat?"

She doesn't answer and brings the glass to her lips, sipping slowly.

Willow's face pushes into view. "She lost the client."

"The punk who needed a new image?" I say, wishing more than anything I could reach through and hug her. "You'll sign another big fish. You always do."

"And you don't have to travel as much," Willow rubs her back in big circles, "which means you get to stay with me for the summer!"

"We were depending on the billing for this one client to fund an entire year. We're not going to make it with mid-listers only. We needed this guy. No." She shakes her head, raking a hand through her hair. "This is going to ruin us. Alan might close our doors."

I've met the owner of Cat's women-owned PR agency, Alan, a spitfire blonde in her seventies, I can't imagine she'd let one client take the agency down.

Willow looks at me without breaking the circles she's got going and mouths, *OMG?*

I know! I mouth back.

Cat's head pops up from her wine glass, and we both school our features back to normal.

"I'll be back in two weeks for the wedding. We'll work it out," I finish, making sure to catch my sister's eyes as she sips sullenly.

"Go have fun," Willow says to me, her face filling the screen again. "We'll be okay. How's the job so far?"

"Odd, actually. That guy that I met in the club the other night at Throwbacks? It's for his father."

"Whoa," Willow's face is incredulous. "That's a coincidence." She peers at me through the screen trying to read my reaction so I do my best to keep my features neutral. I do not need to be grilled about John—again.

"People suck." Cat shoves her hair into a tiny pony then picks her wine glass back up and gulps. "*Loyalty is dead*," she declares as if she's lived many more years than thirty. Zenni was right. I might be the sensitive heart in our family, but my sister is full of passionate fire.

"Do me a favor." Cat's face fills the screen, pieces of dark hair falling haphazard around her face. "Do something fun while you're there. Do something just for you. You never know when it'll all be ripped right out from under you. Might as well live it up while you can. I mean, damn, I should have at least gotten a selfie with him before *his people*," she makes air quotes with one hand, the other clutching a now empty glass, "fired me."

My chest tightens. I'm trying to be a good businesswoman like my sister, and she's crumbling right before my eyes. "Right. Will do."

"They're going to regret this day!" Cat oaths to the wine bottle, holding her tears back like she always does. "Just wait, I'm gonna do something so big, so major, the industry will take notice, and they'll be begging to have me back." She holds her glass up like Liberty's torch.

"Okay, time for us to go," Willow says.

"Love you guys. Cat, you'll fix it. You always do. You'll see." For a moment, I let my eyes drift out to the lake. My sister has always been the strong one, she can do anything she sets her mind to. It's scary to watch her waiver but also, a little comforting, if I'm honest. Her imperfections make mine a little less painful, knowing I'm not alone.

"Fix it, like I always do," she murmurs, her eyes fall and she's suddenly still. Then she wails, "I'm the laughing stock of the PR world!" And lets her head fall to the counter, her empty glass now a dead fish in her hand.

Thank goodness Cat has Wills right now. "You're not. Okay, love you guys."

Willow mouths the words, *I've got this,* over Cat's head.

There's no good way to end this call. I wave once at the screen and hit the red button after Willow gives me a thumbs-up my sister can't see.

Guilt pools inside me, I hate that I'm not there to comfort her. My eyes focus again on the beach ahead, a Boggs flag flying high on a mast with a colorful fish embroidered on it. I'm going to do exactly what she told me to do—something for me. A few people are dangling their feet in the water off the dock, and I shimmy out of my shorts so I can have a swim.

"Hey," Meg says, running up to my side. She's shrugged a sweatshirt on that says *bookish girls do it better* that looks two sizes too big. "You jumping in?"

"Yeah, gotta swim off the carbs your brother can't believe I survive on."

"I warned you he's a health nut. Ignore him. You know it's cold, right? People don't really swim yet, dangle your feet, maybe jump in a kayak. But no swimming, especially after the sun's gone down."

She's right, but I'm tough, I remind myself.

"The thing is," I chuck my earrings into a pocket in my bag, "I just got off the phone with my sister, who's super emotional, and she's never super emotional, which has made me super emotional. You were right. I am kinda in a pit of despair, and I'm going to change that. Right now."

"Girl, do we need to sit down with a cozy blanket and a box of tissues?"

"Nope." I shake my head. Meg looks genuinely concerned despite *her hands off my brother* chat from earlier.

"You need an audiobook with a sexy narrator?"

That does make me laugh, and I pause on my way up steps that lead down the long pier.

"Nope. I'm going to jump off that." I point to a spot at the end of the dock. "Right now."

Meg takes my declaration in stride, "Okay, Miss Thing. You go on and go for it, but don't say I didn't warn you."

A couple of guests clap as I make my way down the warm wood planks of the dock, their faces bewildered, but I don't pay much attention. Maybe it is slightly chilly out, but the sun makes up for it. Maybe people don't usually swim at parties. But I couldn't care less and continue down the long stretch of weathered boards that run about two hundred feet out, bookended here and there with pretty sails and wooden speedboats. There aren't any people toward the end of the dock, so I won't be making a total spectacle.

Coming here is a fresh start; starting my business is a fresh start. Something in my sister's so rarely watery eyes has made me acutely aware of my freedom in this moment as if fingers have snapped inches from my face.

Wind rushes past my ears and a bubble of laughter pops from me unbidden. How much did I ignore to end up here? How unhappy was I that I literally removed myself completely from my old life the second I had the chance?

The water is slightly choppy but not too bad. I can see straight to the bottom, it's so clear, definitely deep enough to dive. But as I line up my toes at the edge, I feel a slight thunder rolling through the weathered boards and turn.

John is running, bare feet pounding one after the other in a sprint. He's still wearing his cook's apron smeared with ketchup and coal from the grill and pulls his baseball cap off his head. I'm rewarded with a glimpse of wavy brown hair streaked by the sun.

Still holding the cap, he cups his hands with the bill to shout, "Francesca, wait!" He starts tugging at the strings of the apron.

But it's too late. I've got my arms overhead at a perfect point.

I'm going to get his goat again, like I did with my plate full of meat and GMO carbs. I don't know why this thought is thrilling —just as thrilling as a jump in the lake that's going to be the personification of my fresh start.

Pushing up onto the balls of my feet, I spring off the dock. In some corner of my mind, I hope the dive looks pretty, and I think to point my toes as I hit the water.

The frigid cold smacks my chest. I lose all my breath, and my eyes squeeze shut. I think I lose consciousness until I finally jar my frozen legs into action and kick up.

It's suffocating—the cold.

When my head pushes through the surface as thick and heavy as a sheet of ice, I have just enough time to hear him yell, "It's too cold to swim!" before I sink again.

The heavy pull to let go is there, to let my muscles succumb to numbness. My body is wrapped in cold, like weights around each ankle, each knee, cinching at my chest, my waist, my elbows. The urge to give up is strong, but my urge to kick up is stronger.

My head breaks the surface of the water again, just in time to see strong, bare, broad shoulders dive.

CHAPTER 8

John

Frantically, I swim toward Francesca while she tries to tread water. Really, it's more like thrashing. She pushes herself up to spit out water, only to sink again. Kick up, cough, choke, sink again. It's as if she's fighting a monster. She is. His name is hypothermia.

The water is choppy today from start-of-summer activity. Boats are shedding their winterization and going for inaugural spins around the cove. Already, she's being pulled away from the dock, not out further, thankfully, but farther and farther from the dock that's raised high above the water on six-foot beams.

Fiery pain rockets through my shoulder as I visualize myself cutting through the water. It's all-consuming and encompassing, the weight of the cold and the wet combined with a paralyzing burn from my old injury.

I bite down, trying to ignore it, to focus all my attention on Francesca. She tries to swim, hands cupping to scoop while strong arms attempt to rake through the water to pull her to me, to something that can hold her up and keep her safe.

"Stop swimming!" I manage to get out. The cold expands in

my chest, making it impossible to draw a full breath, but I've got to get to her. She's got to stop struggling. I'm coming for her.

"Tread! Kick hard!" I spit icy water from my mouth and launch into a freestyle stroke, damn my shoulder. All those physical therapy hours spent swimming laps to stretch and strengthen ligaments blown out from throwing ball are grateful for at least a modicum of muscle memory.

"I'm... I'm..." she sputters as I get close, then sinks right before my eyes. I stretch my arm as far as I can, grasping for her, but she's just out of reach. She pops up again, coughing, and I almost get my hand around her wrist, but she sinks again, literally slipping through my fingers.

I dive down.

My eyes are open, and the water is clear, affording me an unobstructed view of her struggle. Her legs have gone still, but she continues trying to pull up, scooping at fistfuls of water and nothing.

Hard as I can, I kick down toward her, closing the last stretch between us, and reach out through the water. I catch hold of the straps of her swimsuit and yank her to me.

Despite my force, the motion is slowed by the mass of water between us. Rays of sunlight poking down from above illuminate the gold in her hair, surrounded by the greens and blues of the lake. Finally, she's flush to my chest, and for a wild moment, I drop into a fantasy where I'm pulling her toward me to kiss her.

I press my warm lips to her cold ones and push my heat into her. I want to wrap my body around hers, make her warm, and keep her safe. Cupping her neck, I take her with my mouth like I've been longing to do while she brushes her fingers against my jaw and kisses me back deeply.

Shaking my head, I push and kick up. Gripping her around the waist when we break the surface of the water. It's hard to get anything close to words out with the weight of the cold squeezing

89

her lungs like a vice, I know, but she tries, gasping and choking on her attempts. I wish she'd stop.

"Hold onto me," I demand, gruffer than I intended, but she's scaring the shit out of me. Her teeth chatter, lips already blue. She stops thrashing and lets me take all her weight. "Good girl."

Strong and swiftly as I can manage, I pull us both through the water, the muscles of my back taking more of the brunt of the work because my shoulders are spent. I'm completely working off adrenaline now. The cold doesn't exist anymore, only Francesca. Her back is flush to my chest, slippery and small as I drag her through the water.

In a short amount of time, the waves and wake coming off the main channel have moved us at least a hundred feet from the dock. I could tow her there, but pulling her up without a ladder would be impossible. There are large rocks scattered throughout the shores of Spirit Lake, and Boggs's private beach is no different. I thrust her onto one the size of her car and quickly cradle her head so it doesn't smack against the stone.

"Can you breathe?" I ask, hovering above her. She's laid out like a cold, dead trout. A drip of water rolls down my chin and hits her chest right in the center where her breasts slightly swell.

"I'm a strong swimmer," she stammers, defending herself. A small laugh gets stuck in my chest.

She's a fighter, but her strained breath might beg to differ. Her body is strong. She's laced with lean muscle and long limbs. I absolutely believe her, but I know even the strongest swimmers struggle in water this cold, especially when it takes you by surprise.

Instinct takes over as I press two fingers to her neck to check her pulse, surveying the situation, looking to the cloudless sky, and welcoming the last few streaks of the setting sun beating down on her skin. I'll take all the warmth she can get right now.

Her breathing calms. She rubs her arms and then presses her fingers into the warmth of the stone before looking up at me. Sucking in breath after breath, I stare back at her, laid out under me. Before I can stop myself, I push hair that's stuck to her forehead back and out of her eyes, letting my fingertips trail the curve of her chin. That freckle under her eye mesmerizing me.

She's safe. She's going to be fine. So why can't I settle my racing heart?

"Lake has a low of thirty degrees in the first week of June," I say as a way of answering the shocked look on her face. "It's the snow from the mountaintops. Feeds the lake, keeps temps chilly even through the height of summer."

Shivers roll through her, so I pull her into my lap, her back to my front again, and form a cross over her chest with my arms for body heat. My hands grip each of her shoulders, and we shiver together, goosebumps along our forearms. Our chests draw breath in tandem.

"I don't remember it being quite so cold," she stutters. "How will we—"

"Here comes Meg," I say over the top of her head, resting my chin there, but only because any form of warmth right now is necessary.

A small speedboat that I recognize as one of Ben's from Holiday Rentals coasts up to the rock. Meg's driving, looking like a badass lady captain.

She tosses an ugly orange life vest at us, and it lands in Francesca's lap with a *plop*. "If it's any consolation, it was a real pretty swan dive, Frannie."

I secure the ancient orange vest around Francesca's neck and snap the belt around her waist. If she falls back in, she won't have to work so hard to keep her head above water. It's a precaution I'm fine with taking, even though I won't let her out of my grasp until we're on solid land.

I stand, hoisting Francesca to her feet by her armpits. She slips, but I've got her and tuck her into my side. "That was some damn good driving. Keep it idle while we climb on but don't hit the rock. Ben will pop a hernia if we damage the hull."

Meg expertly shifts the motor to idle, letting the boat hover close to the rock. "Benny tossed me the keys himself. I was off the dock before anyone could pull their gaping jaws closed. I warned her."

"Not enough," I say.

"Hey, we're big girls. We make our own choices, and I thought she knew what she was getting into. The woman said she needed a fresh start."

"Is that so?" I eye the top of Francesca's head, but she appears to be pouting and doesn't look up.

"Sorry, Frannie." Meg shrugs, then extends a hand to help her aboard.

"It's not her fault," Francesca says, finding her voice. "I don't know what got into me."

She stretches her legs so she can step into the boat while I spot her and make sure she doesn't slip. Her swimsuit has become a thong in the back, her full, round ass on display. I'm a sucker for a tan line, and it's all I can do to reel in my thoughts and adjust my trunks.

Once she's in, I follow and settle myself on the bench seat in the back of the boat beside her. The motor rumbles to life as Meg floors it back to shore, kicking up an enormous amount of wake in a no-wake zone.

We get a round of applause back at the dock. I sneak a peek at Francesca, wondering if she's thinking of the first crowd that cheered us on at Throwbacks.

"Thanks for fishing me out," she says, climbing the steps to the deck of my restaurant.

The response I'm looking for is you're welcome, but instead, I say, "You're trouble." I'm not upset with *her*, but I'm still shaking off the nerves of what just happened—of what could have happened. "Follow me, I'll find us something dry."

"The normal me is actually the opposite of trouble." She blinks as if surprised by her own comment. "I'm fine. I promise," she adds a bit softer.

The party is breaking up on the beach, but I don't have time to stop for goodbyes. I need to get this girl into something dry and fast.

"What you is this?" I motion toward her as she follows me through the restaurant, around the bar, and toward the office stairs.

"The new me?"

It concerns me that she thinks she needs to reinvent herself. From what I can tell, she's damn fine the way she is. I should leave it. I should let it lie.

Even so, I hesitate on the first step and turn toward her.

Half the party is spilling through the back doors we came through, milling and chatting on their way out for the evening. I wave goodbye to a few guys on the crew over her head.

"Are we talking about bulldog tie?" I ask, leaning in close, trying to keep my tone soft and easy. When she doesn't answer, I press again. "Do you want to talk about it?" Sure, it's odd that I know this intimate detail about her and not much more, but we bonded on that dance floor. I'm invested.

"I'm over it." She gulps. "It wasn't love. I know that now. But unlearning some of the lies I told myself, *about myself*, to please him are harder to shake than I thought."

Even though I've come in direct contact with the guy, I will myself to drop it. It's not my place. "Good, because you don't need to change to please anyone. *You do* need something dry and more than a pair of teeny, tiny shorts to wear."

She sputters but has no comeback ready. She knows I'm right.

I move past her on the stairs, careful not to brush her arms with mine, both of us still dripping wet and leaving our puddles behind. I shiver all the way into the office and rummage through a few tubs I keep in the closet. She's shivering too, her tan skin has turned gray as a stormy beach day. I grab a towel first.

"Here," I say, wrapping it around her and rubbing her arms.

"Oh god, that's heaven," she says, and I chuckle at how easy it is to please her. "Water's damn cold, huh?"

"It hurt!" she exclaims, looking up into my eyes. "Like an elephant sitting on my chest and poking me with tiny needles at the same time."

I'm not sure if she means to, but she nuzzles into the towel and my chest while making a happy little hum, then pulls back quickly. "Sorry."

The spot on my chest where her cheek was keeping me warm goes cold.

"No problem," I say, patting her arms as if that instantly makes things feel friendly instead of intimately familiar. I dig through the closet again and hand her the thickest shirt I've got.

She disappears into the bathroom, and I drag a hand over my face when I hear her wet suit hit the tile with a *smack!* My breath catches, and I gulp, working hard not to cough. When she pulls the door back open, I'm treated to the view of a lifetime. My jersey comes halfway down her thighs. I can't stop staring as she gingerly leans down to pick up her suit.

"I hope this isn't one that's worth a ton," she says. "I'll have it cleaned before the sale, I promise. A few leads are getting back to me on how to manage the sports collection."

94

I clear my throat, but my tone is dry and raspy. "Don't bother. That one's yours to keep."

"Really? Is it an important player?" She twists as if she could possibly read the name and number on the back.

The universe has a funny sense of humor. "No, it's mine."

"From when you played?"

"Yeah." I run a hand through my hair, hoping it's not sticking up in all sorts of ways.

"Here." She offers me her towel.

"Thanks." I take it and rake it over my head. She holds my gaze and I'm so torn in this moment between slipping right back into the way we were with each other on that dance floor, and keeping my distance in my office.

"I'm so sorry," she says, filling a silence that wasn't awkward but instead full of a magnetic pull I know she feels too. "I shouldn't have jumped in the lake. That probably wasn't the kind of entertainment you wanted for your party. The random estate sale lady raining on your parade." She laughs at herself, but I can tell she's worried I actually give a shit about her affecting the end of the party.

I fish through the small closet for something to wear. "I don't care if you jump in the lake, sunshine. Just let me get you a wetsuit first."

That makes her smile, and I feel like I've lassoed the moon. She is the opposite of rain, with all that golden hair and bright, honest energy.

"You're doing a nice job downstairs. It's beautiful."

"It's a fresh start." We exchange a meaningful look. "My dad and I didn't exactly see eye to eye. He lived on the edge. I lived with a safety net. Had to, after losing Mom and watching out for Meg. I'm sort of turning over a new leaf, too. Seems we met each other at the same moment in time... Fighting through something."

"Jumping into something new before you even understand why...." She muses in agreement.

Exactly. "Something like that, yeah."

"It's hard, isn't it? Growing, taking chances, being brave?" She can't look at me when she says it, letting her gaze zero in on a box of baseball cards on top of an old wooden desk. Even going so far as to leaf through them as if she knows what she's looking at. I knew the night I met her, she's not a fan. She had absolutely no idea who I was.

The truth is, I don't know if I can forget the smell of her strawberry sunscreen skin, the way her hazel eyes mirror mine, or the little wisps that fall from the buns she twists her sunny blonde hair into.

Shit, I do know—I can't.

"Do you still want to start over?" I let out big breath because I just couldn't hold that question in one minute longer. "Can you really do that?" I ask.

"Ah, yeah?" Her answer comes out squeaky, like a mouse. She starts again, squaring her shoulders and intentionally holding my gaze. "Especially after all that out there. Can we add that to the list of things we're forgetting?"

"Sure we can, sunshine. Don't think another second about it." Her cheeks heat. Good, she needs to get her color back.

I haven't had a woman in my life for a while now, was content to deal with my family drama, and after I'd finally made the choice to block it all out for good, I was content to run a bar overlooking a lake and entertain the idea of eventually finding someone to share it with me.

And here's Francesca, who's determined not to get involved. It'll be hard to wrangle what's going on in my chest, the fire that she lit inside me. Just knowing she's standing feet from me with nothing underneath my old jersey—

"Let's shake on it. A friendship pact," she clarifies quickly.

"Excuse me?"

"Friends. Let's shake on it, you know, like a handshake deal."

Her eyes are bright with anticipation, almost as if she's wondering if I'll fight her on it.

"Yeah. Okay." On a knowing laugh, I shrug off all my silly feelings. This is a classic case of potentially the right person, at exactly the wrong time.

We shake, and it's like I've been tossed back into the lake. I shiver while an absolute circus goes on in my belly from a single touch.

My gaze trails from where my fingers wrap around her wrist, up the crook of her elbow, past her delicate collarbone generously on display in my too large shirt, and land square on bright hazel eyes. The urge to kiss her is fierce. I'd do about anything for one taste. This woman is affecting me to the point that I wonder if I'm making it all up in my head.

"Friends," she reiterates.

"Yup." It's going to be hard for me to stick to this deal, but I'm going to try.

Her eyes are still locked on our hands, and when she looks up, I see it. Hidden poorly on her sweet, tell-all face is absolute want and desperate need.

Friends who have extremely hot chemistry. *A friendship pact?* It feels like an inside joke. Staying away from her is going to be impossible.

"Works for me," I agree again, in stark contrast to my own thoughts, my hand grasping hers and not letting go. "I'd refuse to be a number on your list, anyway, Francesca."

That's clear to me now. I knew the night I met her that I didn't want to be nothing, another notch on her list. But now I know it'd be impossible to kiss her just once. For anything between us to be meaningless—at least, for me.

"But be careful in the water, okay? I was really worried about my *friend* today."

She pulls away. Her eyes flash fire, and I do my best to ignore what that look does to me. "Gotcha. Good to know, JB." She punches me on the shoulder, and I can't help my chuckle. It's as if she's thinks our handshake has magically made us good buddies.

In an effort to put distance between us, and the fact she hasn't stopped staring at my chest since her eyes fired up, I pull on a T-shirt, then move into the bathroom to quickly step out of my trunks and into a dry pair of jeans.

"You know," she says, stretching the words as if thinking out loud, "the whole list thing?"

I peek out, and she dutifully looks away, faces the wall. Cute.

Maybe friends talk to each other about their kissing list? I have to say, I like where this is going. Mentally, I'm in the friend zone, but subconsciously, I'm already thinking of how I can break out of it.

"What about it?" I ask, trying to keep my tone even.

"I always thought the first kiss was the best. And the list was so I could prove to myself I didn't have to get all emotionally attached for it to be good..."

"I'm old hat at meaningless, mediocre make outs. That's mostly all I've had in life." I move toward the door, ready to be out of this box full of half-naked tension. There's been too much undressing, too much wet and cold, with only hot emotions running through me. My head is all jumbled. I'm afraid I'm making promises I can't keep.

"Well, none of it felt all that good." She shakes her head. "Why am I saying all this? Is it the near-death experience making me feel like I can unload on you? Or is this what my mom means when she says I'm too sensitive?"

"Friends unload on each other, right? So, this is actually on track for us." I motion between us and lean against the doorway. Maybe I don't want this to end. I could talk to her forever. "But I can agree with you from personal experience. Kissing strangers—no strings—isn't all it's cracked up to be."

She shrugs as if she can no longer hold her guard up. "I don't think so, either. So far, random kisses have been terrible."

98

It would not be terrible with us.

She leans against the opposite side of the doorway and when she meets my eyes she gulps. Both of us seem to know exactly what I'm thinking.

She tugs on the hem of my jersey.

Are her words an invitation? Is she rethinking this ridiculous list she's invented for herself as protection?

We need to get out of here, but I stand taller and can't stop what I say next, "Would you ever, give it up? Maybe try—"

"John…"

"Francesca." I take a deliberate step forward and brace my hands above her head in the doorway, not touching her but trying to wrap her up anyway. Her hair is still dripping creating wet spots on my jersey, her chest heaving and that damn collarbone looking entirely too lick-able.

"When you say my name like that, it makes my head go real fuzzy." She shakes her head as if I've asked her a question directly. "But that doesn't mean I'm changing my mind. You're looking for something serious. And Meg—"

"I've already done the *no strings stuff*," I whisper, watching her throat work through a gulp, "in *my* thirties." I arch an eyebrow for punctuation as dawn flushes over her face. *That's right. I've been in your boat.* "It didn't work," I rasp, trying to lean in close enough to see if her skin still smells like strawberries without being too obvious.

"Hey, you two still up there?" Meg's voice trails upstairs. "Is Frannie okay?" Neither of us moves. "Hey! *Johnathon Boggs*, answer me right now!"

A half-smile plays across my lips, and it's contagious. Francesca smiles back.

"It's all good, *Megan*," I reply without breaking eye contact. She exhales long and slow, her shoulders relax. Safe, for now. "We're coming down." I motion ahead of me, asking her to lead the way.

We hustle downstairs quickly so Meg will stop screaming and I watch Francesca's long blonde hair swing across my name, my number.

"Oh, there you are," Meg says, eyeing my jersey and Francesca's bare legs. "Everything okay?" She hands over a small bag and the ridiculous shoes Francesca walked in here with—the ones that make her legs look two miles long and me wonder how they'd feel wrapped around my neck.

"We're good!" she says, way too bright and cheery

"We're great," I echo in solidarity.

Meg's eyes narrow, and I wonder what she's seeing that she clearly doesn't like.

My bar is covered with plastic, but I pull it aside and begin to rummage through supplies. "Painters are done here, and I need a drink. You two?"

Outside, the party is broken down. Ben's company, Holiday's Boat Rentals, doubles as a catering business, and he must have hauled everything away. The water is calm, and the sun is long gone. A large summer moon demands attention against a backdrop of stars. It's the kind of moon that makes you want a fire, maybe a book, and a bed.

"Drinks two nights in one week? That's rare for you—but I'm in." Meg pulls up a stool, and I give her a lopsided smile, surprised she's hung around this long already. She has school, roommates, and friends she's usually eager to get back to after checking in with her big brother.

"Same." Francesca hops onto the stool next to her. "If you guys don't mind. Near drowning sure does make you want a drink." She's pink cheeked now, panting slightly. Maybe her throat is dry for other reasons. Maybe because I almost kissed her silly in the doorway ten seconds ago. We came so close, despite the little friendship agreement, and despite the damn list.

Meg smiles and shrugs her shoulders as I pour tequila and fizzy soda water with mottled lemon and spiced salt for the rim. There's something odd going on with my sister, but for the life of me, I can't imagine what.

"It'll keep you warm," I say, handing Francesca a drink.

"Thanks, I love tequila," she says, her lips tipping up in a no-holds-barred mega-watt grin. So easy to please.

I smile back at her, then after a clearing of my sister's throat, I remember to hand Meg a drink.

Get your head on straight, Boggs.

Francesca's good mood is contagious. Despite our handshake deal, I'm pretty sure the look I'm reading on her face is *giddy*.

Fuck it. I pull a set of keys from behind the bar, spread them out on a cocktail napkin, and slide it across polished wood in her direction. The bar is the first thing I rehabbed in this place when I took ownership, stained and polished it by hand after watching a shit-ton of tutorials online.

"What's this?"

"To the office." I point to a blue key. "The house." I point to the red. "And to the restaurant, just in case you need access when I'm not around, while we're closed to customers."

Meg quirks a brow in my general direction. "I thought I was supposed to make keys?"

"Gus needed a pack of nails, and the hardware store didn't have a line. I took care of it this morning."

"I'll check that off my list of to-dos, then." She licks salt from the rim of her drink, her eyes flicking back and forth between Francesca and me. "Do we have everything we need for Alec tomorrow? He requested a grocery list a mile long, still perfecting the new menu."

"I'm going to the market first thing in the morning. Grover is territorial about his produce. Gotta get there early to get Chef the best broccoli."

"Bleh, broccoli." Francesca laughs over the rim of her drink. I try to ignore her, but I can't help it. She makes me laugh as I sip my drink too.

"To new friends," Francesca says, raising her glass. She glances at me out of the corner of her eye.

"To new projects," I manage. "Meg finishing school, re-opening Boggs, Francesca's business." It's all I can do right now not to kick my sister out and press Francesca against my bar, lean over her, and drop my lips to that damn tantalizing collarbone. It's a fantasy I'll surely indulge in later—alone. Because that would not be in keeping with the friendship pact, and I did make a promise.

"And to waiting 'til August to swim in the lake! I told you to bring a suit so you could get some sun, not take a polar bear plunge." Meg's finished off her drink already but raises it none-theless, shaking the ice.

We laugh, we clink, and we drink, but not before Francesca's knuckles brush mine.

My heart skips a beat while she inhales sharply and her cheeks turn pink.

My sister looks away.

It's going to be a long two months, constantly reminding myself of one golden rule: Francesca Bloomfield is a magnet, and I'm not allowed to be attracted.

CHAPTER 9

Fran

Knock, *knock.*
I crack one eye open, then the other. Apparently, my brain runs through a to-do list in REM. I'm mentally halfway through:

Frannie's Finds, first day to-do's

1. Add John's keys to my key ring and remember what color goes to what
2. Haul tubs to office to start categorizing
3. Follow up with collectibles contact
4. Don't think about the tall, handsome bar owner

It's still dark. The knocks come again just as I'm drifting back off to sleepy land.

Knock, knock—knock—knock, knock.

The knocks keep time in an annoying musical beat that sounds faintly like Stayin' Alive by the Bee Gees. It's way too early for cleaning. Heidi must be an early bird.

"Francesca, open the door." But a deep voice—John's voice—carries through the thin walls.

I shoot up like a whack-a-mole. Everything is black until I push my face mask up and stare at the back of my motel door.

"Please open the door?" he shouts again.

What does John Boggs want at the crack of dawn?

I turn and dive back into my bed, pulling the covers over me to keep the world out.

The knocks turn to bangs. "Francesca?" He sounds worried.

"Coming!" I shout with a kick of my legs. How am I supposed to stop wanting him when I'm always around him? "I'm coming!" I yell again at the door. I need to go over Frannie's Finds business hours with him.

My eyes aren't fully open when I twist the deadbolt and crack the door. There he is in a baseball cap, khaki shorts that end well above his knees, showing off muscled thighs, and a crisp Throwbacks Discotheque T-shirt that makes me wonder if I'm still dreaming. Hallucinating?

I blink.

He's juggling bags of produce and barely catches a red bell pepper that comes close to the edge with his chin.

"I'm not staying," he blurts, seemingly more to himself than me because it sure looks like he's got a bag of groceries and intentions to come in.

"What are you doing here?"

Last night, we ended my almost drowning incident with a few drinks and a friendly, *see ya later*. His sister giving me the stink eye the entire time. I didn't expect to *see him later* so soon. I figured I'd go about my business the next few weeks, put it out of my mind that I'm desperate to kiss him, and we'd have minimal interaction.

"Feeling okay? After last night?" he asks, ignoring my question while assessing me from head to toe. "There's this thing called silent drowning. You take on water in the lungs after an experience like yours yesterday, only you don't know it. I didn't want to over-

104

react and drag you to the emergency room, but it kept me up all night."

He wasn't the only one who couldn't sleep. I only dreamt about him fishing me out of the water over and over and over. In every watery scenario, he had to warm me with his body from head to toe so I didn't freeze to death, Meg never came for us, and we lived on that tiny rock that morphed into a private island. And then everything got very *Blue Lagoon* but without the cousins part.

"I'm good, but it's early."

I rub the crust from my eyes in time to see his gaze take me in from head to toe. I'm wearing sleep shorts and a slinky white tank that has been washed so many times you can absolutely see a detailed outline of my nipples—now hard under his full attention. Not exactly a friend zone ensemble, but I didn't ask him to knock on my door at the crack of dawn.

A Christmas tree scrunchie Cat gave me bobbles on top of my head and I pull it out to give me something to do. I've got a scrunchie collection that is my pride and joy, a quirk I acquired as the youngest girl in the family, up to one hundred sixty-one and counting.

My hair cascades around my shoulders in chunky waves from drying naturally last night. The eye mask hits the floor.

He clears his throat. "I brought dinner. I'll set it up and be on my way."

"At seven in the morning? Do you do this for all your friends?" I tease him. Also, I hardly know him, and I'm working for him. This is unexpected for a hundred other reasons I can't think of because I'm asleep on my feet.

"Crockpots in the truck. I'm not Chef Alec, but I can do a roast. Thought it might be nice to have something hot and ready at the end of your first day in town—hot food always makes me feel good."

"Listen, I realize nearly drowning yesterday and you fishing me out of the lake means we bonded or something," I start, because whatever he's got planned is already making my heart melt, and he hasn't even unpacked. We need to reestablish the boundaries.

"And I helped you brush off your moron of an ex—"

"And that," I agree, "but we're *just friends*, remember? We shook on it. You don't need to do all this..." I wave my hands toward the groceries and can't find the right word.

"We are friends. This is nothing." He shrugs, avoiding my eyes.

"This feels like more..." I push because Meg's words are ringing in my ears, and I need desperately not to hear them. *You turned a light on in him...*

"I couldn't help myself at the market this morning. All this gorgeous produce on display." The groceries are precariously on the verge of toppling. "My mom had a thing about food and feeding people, and she was way into organics before anyone understood what crop dusting was doing to our gut. It sorta stuck. It's the only thing Chef Alec likes about me."

"I need to meet this Chef Alec. He seems like an important person in your life."

"His French country salad with lemon Dijon vinaigrette is an important person in my life. I can pack it away by the gallon." He motions to his stomach as if he's hiding more than a flat eight-pack I meticulously counted from behind my aviators yesterday on the beach.

That makes me laugh out loud, and I feel my body loosen as my hesitation crumbles into a comfortable lean against the doorjamb to hear him out while he shifts on the sidewalk. "If you're offended I didn't eat everything on the beautiful grill of yours yesterday, it's because I'm allergic to shellfish. It wasn't personal to you or Chef."

"Oh."

"Yeah."

"Well, no shellfish in a pot roast." He winks at me, and my

pulse stutters. "The nutrients in one green bell pepper are so high in iron and vitamin C—"

"So, you're going to cook for me...in my own kitchen at seven in the morning. Do all good friends do this?"

"My friends do. By the way, I stopped by the hardware store, and the crockpot is new. Yours to keep."

"You do realize you're pampering me with food and gifts? You're going to make me love you more than my sister—" Oh geez, there it goes again, my mouth running away with me and making my cheeks heat and my pulse race.

Make me love you? What the hell, Frannie?

He takes it in stride, my rambling giving him the green light to make intense eye contact that makes a shiver dip in my belly. "Is it working? Please, let me in."

"Maybe." Slowly and against my better judgement, I open the door fully, giving him cart blanche to my tiny room.

"I'll take maybe." He huffs at me but that smile of his cracks, showing bright white canines, his strong jaw framed by the brim of his cap. I mentally smack my own hand away from the candy as soon as the image of kissing his full lips races across my mind. *Again.*

While he runs to his truck for another load of supplies, I quickly change into a sky-blue romper, splash water on my face, and apply tinted SPF and strawberry lip gloss. He's back in time to watch me pull my hair into an intentionally messy bun from the corner of his eye while he sets up shop on my kitchenette counter.

"You peel." He hands me a potato and what I'm guessing is a vegetable peeling device. It looks medieval. "I would have prepped at my place, but I came here straight from Grover's market."

Gingerly, I take it from him but hesitate when he hands me a grimy potato.

"You have peeled a potato before, right?"

"I've peeled a piece of string cheese?" My smile waivers, I really do wish I knew how to cook.

"Francesca," he groans.

"What? My parents own a small business, and they worked a lot. My sister and I were basically on our own past the age of seven, and it was frozen pizza and mac n cheese city growing up."

"I understand over-worked parents. Believe me, I do. But..." He's stunned. Stands there looking at me like I'm a talking eggplant. "Has no one ever cooked for you?" My eyes must give him his answer. My ex never cooked a meal. Then again, neither did I. "My God, Francesca, what are we going to do with you?"

Shrugging, I plop onto my hastily made bed and watch as he does all the dirty work. "Cat cooks sometimes, but mostly, Willow makes sure I eat something green every few months."

He chops, de-seeds, and rubs and pats a piece of meat with a baggie full of what he explains is his *secret weapon*. The whole time, his shoulders take up a ridiculous amount of the kitchenette. When he's happy with his assembly, his biceps flex as he washes the wooden cutting board and neatly stacks it against a microwave. I guess it's my cutting board now, in addition to the shiny red crockpot. He puts the lid on and turns it to low.

"Now what?" I yawn.

"Now, I take you to breakfast."

The breakfast place is in Novel and aptly called the Breakfast Place. Inside, the cafe is teaming with life. Servers hustle around an old farmhouse turned cozy diner, complete with mallard print vinyl tablecloths.

"Hi, welcome to the Breakfast Place," a cheery teenager behind the hostess desk says. She's got a buzz cut, a hot pink nose ring, and an explosive smile.

The main floor is bookended by knotty pine staircases on either side that lead to a loft level sporting more tables with skylights overhead. The entire space shines with early morning sun, rings with creaky wood floorboards, and yawns cozily with the promise of a summer season that's just begun.

"Morning, Savannah. We'll find a spot out of the way upstairs," John says, pulling me by the hand. "C'mon buddy."

The way his long fingers weave through mine makes it feel like he's done this a hundred times before, very Deja vu. I have to shake my head to remember this is not my normal.

"Shit." He curses under his breath as we hit the top of the stairs, and I bump face-first into his shoulder blades. It's all I can do not to nuzzle my nose in his soft T-shirt right here in the middle of this restaurant.

He tries to turn quickly and usher me right back down, but I balk. "What's wrong?"

Now that I've smelled all these breakfast smells, I'm not really in the mood to leave without an actual breakfast.

"Boss, over here!" A round table in the back of the loft is filled with an assortment of ridiculously good-looking men, now waving in our direction. Of course, it is. I look around, wondering where the pixie dust and the portal to Neverland are hidden. The table is set with a silver pot of coffee and large cream cups and saucers, all currently in use.

"I didn't think they'd be here. We usually meet on Thursdays."

"Who are they?" I ask, hesitantly backing up from the table currently filled with raucous laughter.

"The dudes, and they already see us. They've been blowing up my phone about fishing you out of the lake yesterday."

"How do they know about that?"

"Well, the fact that most of them were there and that word travels fast between our handful of coffee shops, restaurants, and tourist traps does the job. No secrets around here. I found that out the hard way when I tried to sneak into our high school senior year with a glitter bomb on a dare."

"How does this story end?"

"With my photo, wanted-poster-style, all over town."

"They snitched?"

"Nah, some other kids did. I played varsity ball all four years. They had it out for me." He looks around as if there might still be a way to escape the table of men waving us over with shit-eating grins. "Logan, Ben, and Winter were freshmen at the time, but the little punks came to my defense... Listen, it'll be better if we introduce you, and then we can be on our way. Otherwise, they'll be a pack of dogs after a bone."

I cough a laugh. "The dudes?"

"You met most of them at Throwbacks, and don't ask."

"Oh, but I already did. Do you, like, *actively* call yourself the dudes? Or do other people call you that?"

"Since grade school, actually. I was five years older and stuck up for Logan and Ben when they needed it. Winter was initiated in high school. He went after the glitter bomb snitch and earned his place in the crew that day."

We walk over to the table. "Guys, this is Francesca."

They all stand, and I fidget in response to their respectful hospitality. "So, you're the fish. The jumper—" The man with a wave of hair that any GQ model would kill for and a pony on the pocket of his shirt says. I instantly recognize him from Throwbacks. He's the one who argued back and forth with Cat. I've never seen anyone antagonize her the way he did.

"You remember Winter," John says, a boyish frown pulling at his lips.

"You're Willow's friend," the bearded one pipes up, dragging a hand over his face. I'm surprised he remembers her so immediately.

"And Logan," John adds. "And this is Jack." He points to the formidable man from Revival, and it suddenly hits me. He's the *bride!* Of course.

"She's the *dancer!*" Jack exclaims.

"You're the Super Bowl ring!" I exclaim back. "I knew you looked familiar," I say to all of them, though the bearded one, Logan, isn't paying attention anymore.

"I'm Ben, Holiday boat tours, gear, and party rental, at your service." I remember Meg mentioning he wasn't at the bachelor party. He's got skin clearly tanned by hours on boats in the sun, and his stone-gray T-shirt says everything he's just said in a playful font. Mirrored sunglasses perch in a mess of wavy hair on top of his head.

"Please, sit," Winter motions to a chair and pulls it out for me.

"Vikingstrong!" They chorus around him.

"Excuse me?" Am I being initiated into a fraternity?

Glancing over at John, who's taken the chair on my other side, I ask him *what the hell's going on* with a squint and a shoulder shrug.

"Winter's family founded Clover. There's a castle called Vikingstrong in Paradise Bay that's pretty popular with tourists. His dad's a king. It's a whole thing that I promise isn't nearly as interesting as it sounds, but his manners make up for it," John supplies to bring me up to speed.

"Can't argue with that," Winter says, moving back to a chair opposite me.

"Ah, but what our prince lacks in an actual title, country, people, or funds for that matter—" Jack starts.

"Hey, I do just fine," Winter interjects with ease in his voice that makes me believe him—that and the very expensive watch the size of a saucer on his wrist.

"He makes up for it in sheer determination to ruin the good family name," Logan finishes. "Nice to meet you," he adds to me.

"Damn right." Winter pounds his fist lightly on the table twice as if holding court.

"Boys, you're scaring the new girl," Jack says, delightedly taking in his friends' banter.

Our waitress is speedy, probably because she wants the guys to free up her table. She's wordlessly placed a mountain of family-style eggs over my shoulder, bacon, assorted grilled peppers, and a pile of flapjacks on the table as we've been talking.

"More coffee?" she asks.

When I look up, I'm shocked to see Heidi above me with a fresh silver pot in her hand.

"Yes, please. Heidi? Aren't you..."

"Supposed to be at the motel?" She's wearing a classic diner apron with a pencil perched behind her ear.

"Sure?" It's none of my business, but I am curious.

"I put an out-of-office sign up a few times a week when Shirley and Ned need me to take a shift. They own this place, and they're getting too old to wait tables. And the extra cash is nice."

"You're an angel, Heidi," Ben says, watching her make her rounds filling cups.

"I'm not putting a word in for you with my sister, Ben." She makes her way back around the table to lean over my shoulder. "Now, don't let the dude crew scare you, Frannie. They're all good boys. Been around most of them all my life. But don't let your guard down, either. They're also a gang of troublemakers in men's clothing."

"Hey, now. That's not fair. I fixed your sister's front step last week—"

"That was you?"

"Hell yeah, that was me," Ben says, affronted. "Who'd you think it was? Winter?"

The table laughs together as if Winter is the last you'd suspect to lift a finger.

"Well, thanks, Benny. Thanks a lot." She plops the fresh pot in the center of the table in exchange for our empty. "Anything else boys? Fran?"

A round of no thank you's from full mouths sends her on her way, but she stops short. "Oh, and Frannie, I scratched your tickets—"

"And?"

"Nada. But thanks. It was fun," she says, taking off with a skip in her step, her apron bouncing.

"What tickets?" Ben asks.

To my surprise, it's easy to tell them all about my lotto obsession and my drive into town. They're good listeners, mostly because they're stuffing their faces, but I think they like me too. The food is delicious, and when I stop chatting to devour my own plate, John gives them a recollection of our escapade yesterday in the lake. He puts emphasis on the fact that any *out-of-towner* could have made the same mistake, and I love him for defending me so easily.

"Colt's being born." Suddenly, and just as we'd started in on our third silver carafe of coffee, Winter jumps up from his chair, phone in hand while he pulls an engraved money clip from his pocket.

Everyone grabs the edges of the table to stop it from rocking.

"You need any help?" John asks while he and the rest of the men follow suit, pushing from their chairs and throwing bills on the table. I guess people still like to pay in cash around here.

"I've got a big cedar delivery today, but I'm free after four if you need me," Logan offers. He stands in utility pants, suspenders, and a clearly laundered but very worn T-shirt that suggests he works in the woods and fully embraces the lifestyle.

"Shit, I gotta open Holidays," Ben says. "Keep me updated in the chat."

I watch as the rest of them wait for Winters's reply. He's halfway down the stairs already. "John, I'll take your hands if you've got time. Doc is getting too old for it himself but promised direction."

"I'll be there," John says.

"Thanks to the rest of you. We'll have a soiree for the new baby soon as she's weened."

John gently puts his hand on the small of my back, guiding me to follow the train of men downstairs.

Out on the street, it's full-blown summer vacation. Bikers ding bells, shopkeepers sweep steps, kids play tag with rainbow-colored ice cream cones at nine in the morning. It's freaking picturesque.

Winter jumps in the passenger side of khaki-colored Jeep. Ben hops into the driver's. Jack takes the back. They're gone before I can ask, *What the hell is going on?*

John reads the confusion on my face. "He's got a thing for horses. Rides almost daily."

"Colt? As in, horse? I thought I was watching a proud new papa run out the door."

"Winter? A dad? That's funny. He's been so burned by his family. I don't think that guy will ever procreate."

"Doesn't look much like a cowboy."

"Not that kind of riding. Owns a few hunter-jumpers and a barn with a state-of-the-art arena within walking distance from his place. He added it when he moved here full-time. A mare's been 'bout ready to pop, and I guess she finally did. He'll be a mess of worry 'til it's done."

"I don't want to keep you. I should get going, anyway." I pull my old fish keychain from my purse. John's three colorful keys and the doors they go to that I've memorized by heart jingle together. "Thanks for breakfast...and dinner," I add. "I'll let myself in. Start in the office, then move to the house. Each will only take a few weeks. The sale will really depend on how fast things move, but I'm here for two months, so we can extend if needed."

"I thought you said your friends were coming to stay?"

"Oh, they are but not 'til I'm done with the job."

He looks out at the street full of morning traffic, cars slowly winding down the road that borders the lake.

"I'll be at Winter's if you need me." His jaw ticks as he clamps his mouth shut even though it seems he's got more to say.

"Birthing a horse?" I don't know why I'm dragging this out, only that I'm not ready to say goodbye to my new *buddy*.

The idea of him doing something like that makes me feel a curiosity that needs to be snuffed out like a breath to a match. I cannot get involved with this man. I cannot wonder what's going on in his life that makes him want to erase all memory of his father so badly, cook hot meals for new friends, or help deliver an animal with his bare hands.

He looks back at me. "A colt."

There's a feeling, a vibe that's gluing our feet to the concrete. He doesn't want to walk away any more than I do, even though I know something pressing is waiting for him. His friend is waiting for him. Yet, he's standing here with me as if we've been tethered together with bungee that won't stretch but a few inches.

"Go on." I jingle my keys at him. "I'll be in your office."

That seems to pull him from whatever he was contemplating. "You know, we could use an extra pair of hands..."

"You mean me?" I raise a hand to block the sun.

"That's right." He nods with his chin, then pulls the brim of his cap around so that his hat is backward. Rays of sun highlight the strong cuts and angles of his handsome features. How am I supposed to say no to that?

Still, we silently hesitate, but it's not awkward. The pull to stay together feels totally natural. It should be embarrassing, but it's not.

Families and backpacking couples push around us, making

their way toward beach access with chairs strapped to their backs, inadvertently giving us a reason to close the gap. Step by step, we move closer and closer together as they pass on the sidewalk.

"'Scuse me, sir," a woman in a Yankee's cap says.

"No worries," he answers, grasping my elbows and pulling me in so she can wheel a stroller around us, a man following close behind with a toddler riding piggy-back.

I quickly run a list of pros and cons through my mind. On the one hand, I've sworn not to get close to this man, any man. But John Boggs is a particular kind of temptation, one that feels built specifically for me. On the other hand, I scheduled plenty of time at the lake this summer to do my job and have fun, too.

"You comin', sunshine?"

I nod. *We're friends, right?* I remind my heart. It quickens with every step I take toward his truck as he falls into step wordlessly beside me. I'm pretty sure his hand flexes, wanting to reach for mine. But he doesn't.

Why can't I have a little fun with John Boggs, my new bestie, at the lake?

He opens the passenger door. "You sure? This might get messy, but I promise it'll be worth it in the end."

I can't stop myself from giving him everything I've got, the best smile in my arsenal, as I slip my aviators on for effect. "Absolutely. I'm in."

CHAPTER 10

John

The lake, for me, is the home I never had. The safe place that was there in high school when Ricky didn't show up to my games because he was out traveling for his own doubleheaders. It was something stable in my adult life too, when both my parents were gone and I was raising my baby sister.

Whenever it was too much, or I felt alone, the water was there.

When mom died too young, it rocked me to my core, but the mountains didn't crumble around me as much as I thought they would. It occurred to me when Ricky left that I didn't allow myself to break fully apart because he left me with a business to save. And while I didn't see cleaning up his mess as a gift at first, it has sunk in over the months that he tethered me to this place. Gave me a purpose just as my career ended, when I needed one most.

He made sure I didn't lose the lake, the land, the view at night I'm so obsessed with I started sleeping under the stars as my only comfort. I just couldn't be boxed in by walls after I first got cut from the game. Maybe it was my time, I was old in baseball years and injured beyond repair, but I'd planned stupidly to play forever with mere grit and determination. So, I was furious about it even though I understood it. My anger was too big for walls. I needed open. I needed space.

In his own ugly way, he did give me that.

I've tried to be a rock for Meg, making sure she has a paycheck while she chases her dreams and doing my best to be around for her while staring into my campfire each night instead of whatever it is most men do at the start of their forties. This isn't where I saw my future heading. I never planned to settle down, never thought I'd live in the town where I grew up.

And now here I am, with a schoolboy crush on a girl, and a buddy who needs me to pull a slippery colt from its mother's hindquarters.

And Francesca, said girl, sitting next to me in the cab of my truck ready and willing to help, all pink-cheeked and sun-kissed.

Parking at Winter's *home* means fighting tourists for spots. Vikingstrong is a Scandinavian masterclass in craft, woodwork, and stained glass just off the beach in a copse of trees in the crescent of Paradise Bay. Winter's family home has been standing for over a hundred years, now a national landmark that still belongs to the family even though they donated the land to the state long ago.

"A state park?" Francesca asks as I pull into the lot, grateful to grab a spot before it fills for the afternoon. At least I know the secret way to the shoreline so we don't have to hike the two miles down, which isn't bad and is pretty beautiful, but we don't have time for that today.

It's hard not to grimace for the families unpacking cars and kids, heading down the mountain with heavy coolers and striped towels toward Paradise Beach. That hill is a princess on the way down and a total bitch on the way back up.

"You'll see," I say, enjoying the chance to surprise her, to show her something she's never seen before.

I round the truck and open her door, watching her hop out

and immediately go to the edge of the retaining wall to take in the view. It's there she gets a proper look at Winter's place.

She gasps, "That's a castle," then spins on her heel to face me. "His?"

"Don't swoon too hard." I feel that same frown pull at my face that I felt at the breakfast table this morning. Already, the thought of another man pleasing her makes my stomach turn.

Trouble.

"I'm not swooning," she smirks, easily reading my jealousy which makes my entire body feel hot, "but, wow. A real castle."

"Follow me." But she doesn't. She's too confused about the direction I'm heading, into the trees versus toward the well-beaten path down the mountain.

I grasp her hand, something I've been wanting to do since I lead her through The Breakfast Place with her fingers twined through mine, and while it's not my place to do so, it feels damn natural, anyway. We hop in the back of the automated outdoor elevator that takes a code to operate. It's more of an open-air boxcar, hidden between tall trees and off to the side of the parking lot at the top of the mountain. It's remote enough that tourists never find it. But a handful of years ago, the Hammer boys found it, and a few joyrides and prank doorbell rings later, Winter had it updated with a touch screen code. That's about all he updated, though, preferring to keep as much of his family history intact as possible—despite his own rocky relationships with said family. He's a complicated dude.

"It's a tight fit." It's more than that. She's going to have to sit on my lap.

But she takes it in stride, conspiring right along with me. "Surprise, surprise."

She perches on my knee, but when the thing jolts into motion, I have to grasp her around the waist to steady her. The car precariously jostles as we descend, but she's laughing. It's a tin can on tracks—old, rusty, but quiet enough and does the job.

"What are you getting me into?" she asks, eyeing me over her shoulder, leaning back more than I know she thinks she should.

My arms tighten automatically around her. "Well, I've seen one of Winter's horses give birth before. He had more backup then, and Doc was a younger man. But it's a beautiful thing, Francesca. Both the birth of something new and innocent and the way Winter loves his animals. You'll see."

"I can't imagine bringing something into the world like that."

"Kids in the cards for you?" It's probably too personal to ask, but I need to know. My intentions toward this woman are changing by the second. I'm not sure I'm equipped to be a father —ever.

"I mean, maybe? But it's honestly the last thing on my mind right now."

"Right. Kissing list. No strings."

"Right." And I'm thinking about kids and picket fences. I shake my head at my own foolishness, *idiot.*

Except she said kissing strangers isn't working. No strings isn't working. And there's no denying our bodies react naturally to one another, much as we're both trying to hide it, we're failing with every nonchalant touch and innocent hand-hold. I squash my next thought as best I can because I've promised friendship, but it's there.

Maybe I can change this girl's mind?

The car grinds to a halt and dumps us at Winter's back door. Granite boulders embedded in mortar make up most of the structure. We wrap around a fat turret that I know is the winding staircase that takes you to Winter's living quarters.

"Unbelievable." Francesca takes in the intricate carvings over the doorways. Polished wood glows in the summer sun, scales in the form of serpent-like dragons crossing at the head over the main entrance.

"It's got thirty-six bedrooms to offer. He lives on the top floor like Quasimodo, complete with Scandinavian-style gargoyles."

Her neck arcs back to take in the view. It gives me the chance to do the same, gazing at her. "What a life he must live."

"I wouldn't wish it on my worst enemy."

"Really? That's so sad. Is his family around?"

"Funny how, yes, they are, but they're completely unavailable to him all the same. We sort of raised each other, the guys and me."

It's the closest I can come to explaining we're a family, all of us filling gaps in our coming of age that we couldn't possibly comprehend at the time. I was a protector at first, being five years older, but we've given each other advice along the way. We've pretended not to see the other cry while simultaneously giving staccato pats on the back, catching frogs and baiting fishing poles, passing the whiskey around one of Logan's cedar fires, and rolling out the sleeping bags well into our thirties.

"You weren't close to your dad?" she asks.

That's a tricky subject, so I take the chicken exit and go with, "No. You?"

"Yeah, I'm close to both my parents. And my sister. We're a pretty tight unit."

I nod. "Meg and I are like that."

"That's good, that you have that. And the dudes." She smiles at me, but it's a sad smile, not her normal mega-watt.

"But?"

"Nothing, it's silly. We should get going." She waves me off and starts winding around the castle on a path that, whether she knows it or not, is the right one.

It's tough to stop my own hand from reaching out to hers. "I want to hear what you were going to say," I prod, slowing my own steps to keep in time with hers. The trees here are so wide and tall with age. I let myself look at them, knowing they'll settle me and wondering if they'll do the same for her.

She shakes her head. "They say I'm too sensitive. I need to toughen up. I know they're worried about me—want the best—

but as much as I love them, sometimes it's hard to separate their opinion of who I am from my own."

"And what do you think?"

"I think I'm here, trying to be tough."

Finally, I take her hand in mine and simply place it on the trunk of a tree that's probably two-hundred or so years old.

"What are you doing?"

"Sometimes this helps. Grounding. Logan taught the guys and me this years ago." I had just started my freshman year and the rest of them were still finishing up middle school. He's always been wise beyond his years.

"Oh," she drags her palm over the bark.

"Listen, I'm not saying change is bad, but you can't let anybody or anything make you feel like you're not good enough the way you are."

Neither of us can forget that I met her before this new lake life. I saw her that night on the dancefloor. She walked straight into my arms and wrapped me around her finger in minutes with her nervous determination.

She nods and walks on, I think to hide some water in her eyes. I wish she wouldn't, I'm the last persona she needs to hide her emotions from. We stop half way around the castle, and she takes in the architecture from a new angle.

That douchebag should have kept his mouth shut if her feelings were too intense for him, if he couldn't see what a lighthouse in a storm she is. How strong she is, and simultaneously soft.

Before I can wonder if I'm overstepping, my big mouth goes on. "Never let anyone make you feel small. You're not small, Francesca."

She turns from reading a plaque on a wall, probably a history lesson on Winter's lineage, and pins me with her gaze. "What if I feel it? Small."

It's an effort not to put my hands above her when she leans

against the stone, to cage her in and demand she know how beautiful she is, how bright.

"You weren't small on that dance floor," I rasp, using every bit of my self-control to stay put. "You weren't when you marched into a business meeting the other day, shocked as shit when you ran into me—you held your own."

She glances up at a window, birds taking flight over the lake stained yellow and blue. "I can't decide if it's a good thing. Running into you again, like this, against all odds."

I scratch my neck and adjust my cap, trying to play it cool. Truth is, it feels clandestine as fuck. "Are you open to figuring that out?"

"Maybe."

My lips curve effortlessly and I flip my hat around backward. "I'll take maybe, Francesca." I give into my own need and pull her hand into mine. She lets me. We both pretend it's entirely normal. *Friendly.* "Come on."

The stables are about a hundred yards offshore and somewhat hidden by the forest. Unlike the castle, whose main level is open daily for tours, the stables are private and closed to the public.

Nodding to a few groundskeepers as I pass, we enter through tall barn doors and head down a cobblestone hall toward Winter's sanctuary. Wrought iron chandeliers hang overhead, and the whole place reeks like horse, oats, and hay. If my home is the lake, his home is his horses and this barn.

It's eerily quiet, the heat from morning rays turning the wooden walls into a cedar sauna. "Winter? You back here?" Francesca stays close by my side. "I brought some extra hands," I holler as we make our way down a line of stall doors with iron nameplates. Horses of every breed whinny and nicker as we pass.

"Yeah. You're just in time." His voice is calm, and I follow it to the last stall.

"Dr. Derek, we about ready to pull?" he asks the vet as we

123

stand outside the half door of Daylight's stall. "Thanks for coming, Frannie," he beams, sweat and anxiety covering his face. "John, we could use your muscle as long as you don't mind risking your shoulder. Fran, can you grab that stack of towels behind you and bring in that stool?" He motions to the items behind Francesca. She grabs them quickly as I gently open the gate open.

Of course, I'll risk my shoulder. I'd give any of the crew a kidney, an appendage, my soul, and the shirt off my back if they needed it. I can't stand to see anyone suffer, especially if I know I can help, including the mare in front of me, fat, lying on her side, and panting.

And that's why I'm Winter's go-to right now. He knows I'm good for whatever the situation calls for. The soft spot I've got for the guys I grew up with means I couldn't live with myself if I wasn't.

"Tell me what you need," I say while Francesca hands the items to Winter. He takes a seat on the stool. The labored, panting mama lets out a low groan and rolls as if she's trying to stand but can't, hay sticking to her back and neck.

Dr. Derek, the best veterinarian for miles, steadies the horse with long strokes of his weathered hand. "She's labored a good eighteen minutes. It's time."

Winter is wringing his hands, nervous in the eyes, and chucks the shirt he's wearing over the stall door in one swift move. "It's cashmere," he says when he meets my incredulous look. "If you care about what you're wearing, you'll do the same. And take that glove from Doc. You're pulling. I'm keeping her calm. She trusts me." He kneels by the horse's side, gazing into Daylight's eyes while he gently pets her straining neck. "Don't you, girl? That's right. I've got you."

"I'm good," I say. But still, I roll the short sleeves of my T-shirt high on my shoulders.

"I'm good, too," Francesca pipes up from the corner. "What can I do?"

"Sit here, where I am," Winter says, exchanging places with Francesca so she's cradling the horse's neck. "Long strokes down her flank. It'll help calm her. I'll move around the front so she can see me better. She needs to know I'm here. And I'll be ready to help with the baby when it's time."

Francesca doesn't miss a beat, petting the horse down her long neck, whispering low and sweet under her breath. Ready for anything, the girl is a total ray of sunshine in a stall full of tense men.

Dr. Derek is in his mid-sixties and in no shape to do the pulling. That's why I'm here. He helps me into a long latex glove that goes up to my armpit.

"What's this for?"

"You'll see."

"Got any tips."

"Pull like all hell, son."

I nod, then chuck my hat into a pile of hay in the corner where I hope it stays safe. I really like that hat.

Winter steps out of his bathroom, steam following like a trail of wizard's smoke.

"Why do you get to clean up, and I have to sit here trying not to get after-birth on your fancy chairs?"

Francesca and I were both stunned watching Daylight have her colt. Even with the doctor there, Winter was rattled. Everything went well, but I called a car to take Francesca home to clean up. She understood that I needed to stay here. I still didn't feel great putting her in a car and letting her go. Not after watching her react fast as lightning during the labor, moving confidently at Winter's side, not at all squeamish or put out, aiding him and the doc as if she'd done it a hundred times before—all with a million-dollar, Hollywood smile. Damn, that woman can alter the energy in a room, any room. I can attest to that now.

"Go use the hall bath. There are extra shirts in the armoire. Give me five to blow dry, and I'll make it up to you with lunch." He rakes the towel over his head, causing hair that's normally in a gravity-defying wave to flatten. He almost doesn't look like himself. "And John?"

"Yeah?"

"Thanks for being there."

"Any time, bud."

Five minutes later, as promised, Winter and I are sitting in a large bay window at a round, marble-top table probably brought here on a ship from a royal palace across the globe.

"That should do it," his housekeeper, Annie, says as she turns to leave. "Anything else I can get you, sir?"

"No, thanks, Annie. We're all set."

"Breaking out the crystal and sterling for me?" I lift a glass to my lips and chug some much-needed water. "I'm honored."

"She's on me to clean up my act before my parents get here. Normally, I eat standing over the sink in the main kitchen, hoping a tour doesn't catch me in my royal britches." He takes a bite and wipes his lips with a monogrammed napkin.

I dig into steamed vegetables on a stack of sticky rice, and a piece of seared halibut continues to sizzle on my plate. "I love your life."

Winter tugs at a button-down collar that must be feeling a bit tight. "Yeah, well, it comes with a price. You know my parents are all over me to marry? Like a regency aristocrat, I'm supposed to continue the family line or some shit. They're threatening to set me up."

"Like an arranged marriage, set you up?"

"Like the dark ages."

I look him dead in the eye. "Damn."

"Thanks."

We eat in silence, the adrenaline from the new baby colt—he named her Destiny with zero hesitation—still rolling off us in waves.

"I got a problem," I say. Changing the subject is the least I can do.

"What's that? Other than a ruined shirt."

"Thanks for the loaner." I shift in Winter's shirt since mine is in the garbage in the hall. It's too small and has stripes. He was right. I should have taken mine off from the start. But my hat survived, now happily tucked into my back pocket.

"So?" He motions with his knife and fork for me to go on before he cuts a baby carrot in half and chews with astonishingly straight teeth.

Finished with my meal, I push back in my chair and let my knees go wide. Out the window, the afternoon has taken hold of Paradise Cove. The beach is littered with blankets and towels, lovers and parents. Boats anchor here and there in the emerald bay. Some fancy stretches of sleek white wood, Gar Woods and Shepherds restored from the seventies and eighties that Ben would drool over, some with sails that reach for the sun, and some rented pontoons from Holiday's that have seen better days.

"I made a promise, and I want to break it."

"That's concerning, coming from you. I've never known you to break a promise." He chews and appraises me thoughtfully but with zero judgment.

"Exactly. It's not sitting right, but neither is the promise."

"Might it have something to do with a certain blonde that blew into town? A certain blonde who happens to have hazel eyes that, combined with your stormy gray, would produce unfairly gorgeous offspring?" He folds his hands and rests his chin on his knuckles, giving me a mocking smile. "Hmm?"

"Who says shit like that?" I ask.

Winter never fails to keep you on your toes. The man can be razor sharp, mischievous to a fault, but also polished and even deep.

"Don't sidestep. And my parents are all over me to procreate. It's top of mind how I can get out of it."

I wipe my mouth and drop my napkin on my plate, resigned. "It might have something to do with her, astute, young prince."

Now he's playing with a make-believe beard. "My spies are everywhere. And also, I loved watching you fish her out of the lake. That was some star-crossed shit."

"How much did you see? I never even saw you at the party."

"I stopped by but had to leave before you'd finished playing the hero. Daylight was close, and Doc had another call that night. Ended up sleeping with her in the barn."

"The horse? Not some unassuming damsel you found on the side of the mountain?"

"Correct."

"Of course you did."

"Yeah, well, back to *your* love story. You want her."

"You're not telling me anything I don't already know."

"Seemed like she was into you at breakfast. What's the problem? Location? How long is she here before she heads back to the bay?"

"I haven't even gotten that far because I made a friendship pact—"

"A what, now?" He lays his silverware delicately across his plate and Annie instantly appears to remove our dishes. We both murmur our thanks.

"You heard me."

"But you think she might be open to more? To sharing a meatball, drawing hearts in the sand, filing taxes together, having all your babies?"

"Hold up. I didn't say anything about babies. Not sure I should recreate Ricky's mistakes—"

"You wouldn't. You were made to be a dad, but your clock *is* ticking, grandpa." He removes his napkin from his lap and drops it on the table. "Shit. My mom has really gotten to me. I'll have to ask Annie if she's sneaking in the hypnotist while I sleep *again.*"

I can't even acknowledge that comment. There are a lot of things I can be honest about. I sure as hell should know myself by this stretch of life, but I cannot go there right now. I had a shit dad, and that sets me up to be a shit dad. "She's not looking for anything serious, got burned recently. Her ex was at Throwbacks the night we met, classic idiot who doesn't know how to treat a woman, but I don't know all the details—"

"That's what you do!" He jumps up and points at me for emphasis.

"What?" He wants me to startle, to widen my eyes at his antics. So I keep my features stoic instead. He should have been an actor, he can't help himself.

"You get the details. You find out exactly how he hurt her, and then you kiss the boo-boo all better."

"How am I supposed to do that? She wants to keep it to business. She's going to clean out my office, sell all Ricky's shit, sell all the shit in his old house, and then she's out. She's made that clear."

"You like her, right?"

I look out the window and focus on the water. "Yeah."

"Like not just a one-night thing, right?"

"I haven't done that in a long time."

"Exactly. You've been living outside, a vagabond married to the stars like fucking Romeo. All I'm saying is you're ready. For something serious, for the real thing. All that stuff with Ricky was hard for you, and if you'd had someone to lean on instead of worrying about how you were going to take care of Meg, it would have been good for you."

"I lean on the crew plenty," I say, looking back at him and pinning him with a gaze that says *tread lightly*.

"We drink with you. We sit around your campfires as long as we can stand it and smell like shit the next day for you. But you need more than that."

"Logan likes to camp, too."

"Logan is an actual bear. That's why we all tolerate him. He's nothing but a misunderstood animal in suspenders. It's endearing."

I track him as he moves around the room, suddenly restless and excited. "When did you become a counselor?"

"I'm an only child. You'd be horrified if you knew how much time I spend thinking about feelings and shit."

"I've been flirting." My own cheeks heat at my omission and I push from my chair to stand and shrug off the awkward feeling.

"We need more than flirting, man. You need to woo her."

"Woo her." I drag a hand down my face slowly, taking my last eyeful of the view from the top of the castle. "I did buy her a crockpot."

"Very on brand of you and a good start," he replies, honestly invested in the conversation as if it were his own potential relationship. "There's no turning back, now." He declares it like a king. His face turns somber as he claps me on the back.

"Even though she's told me point blank, she doesn't want to be wooed. I promised the exact opposite. We made a friendship pact. We shook on it."

"Even better, buddy. She'll never see it coming. You're a wolf."

"I'm a wolf?"

"In the grass."

"That's snake. The saying is *'snake in the grass.'* I don't want to be a snake, man."

We walk, shoulder to shoulder, to the door of his apartment.

"Fine, you're a wolf in the hen house. You're sneaky, but only because you're determined to get what you want. You and I both know no one could love harder or treat a woman better."

"Fuck, you're making me blush."

"I'll spoil your kids," he confirms as if I've already proposed or moved her in. "I've seen how you take care of your sister, and I watched you take care of your mom right up until the end. You didn't deserve what Ricky did, but I also know how much that man loves you, even all the years he wasn't around as much as you would've liked."

I pull my hat from my pocket and pull it firmly down over my eyes. "I don't want to talk about Ricky."

"Don't walk away from this, Boggs," he presses, quirking his head to meet my eye. "I'm serious. I'm watching you toss your life in the garbage. It's different for me. My life has already been sorted, but you were born for a wife and a family. Just because your own didn't work out, it'll only make you better—"

"That's enough, Win." My own shit childhood is not going to make me a better husband or potential father. In fact, it makes me wonder if I'm good for anyone at all. Maybe I'm the worst thing for Francesca, and she's right to avoid a relationship with me.

"That was passive-aggressive bullshit, Ricky dropping the bar on you out of spite when you refused to pay his bills. Walking away. But you and I both know deep down he cares. Ricky loves you—"

"Enough," I say again, firmer while I walk to the door. I didn't sign up for this today. And truth be told, I feel guilty about refusing Ricky.

"Not everyone is gonna leave you if you don't give them exactly what they want, man." He's an incessant buzz in my ear that I can't stand. "Your mom didn't choose to leave you. If she could have stayed, she would have. I still believe Ricky's sobering up in the woods as we speak for you. Have you told Frannie what's really going on there? With the sale and cleaning out the house as if he were dead to you?"

"Winter, I love you. But I'm telling you to stop. I-I don't want to do this."

"You can make mistakes. *You don't have to be perfect.* And you deserve something good, just for you."

He's pushed me too far. I turn on him in the doorway and push back on the chest that's way too close, pressing me too hard. "Are you talking to me now? Or to yourself?"

He stumbles back but holds his own. He could throw a mean punch if he wanted, and I wouldn't blame him. I put my hands on him first. But he has the good sense to stop coming at me, to take another step back, and let me push him out of my personal space.

"Let's get one thing straight," he says, his face turning dark. "You and I are nothing alike. Regardless of what's happening here right now." He motions between the two of us. "I'm telling you— you deserve her. Because you need to hear it."

That's the thing about Winter Larsen. He's all fun and games and lavish parties and flippant jokes until he's not. Until he goes somewhere deep and dark, and I promise, you don't want to be his enemy.

"Okay, I hear you." I nod at him once.

My mind is made up to go after Francesca Bloomfield, make her mine, and hopefully convince myself I'm good enough for her while I do it.

CHAPTER 11

Fran

For the next week, I try my darnedest to avoid John Boggs. But he's everywhere. When I'm working in the office, he's below in the bar. When I take a break and stop by the house to drop off a load of necessities for the upcoming sale, he's magically out back, poking at a fire with a stick.

I'm avoiding him because I'm so wildly attracted to him and I can't do anything about it. Yet he surrounds me in his office full of baseball bats and little league trophies with his name on them. The bar he polishes daily stacked with meticulously shiny glasses. It's a problem.

I got an early start this morning, showering while munching on chips and salsa for breakfast. I really want the Breakfast Place, but I can't risk running into John. I wouldn't have the strength to turn him down if he asked me to eat with him. And then my brain would dissolve into fantasies about him fishing me out of the lake and hauling me off to a castle somewhere. And then where would we be?

I threw on athletic shorts and a T-shirt and pulled my hair through the back of a black baseball cap. I did not think about John and his signature broody baseball hats when I contemplated my outfit this morning—you never know what you're going to find when rummaging through people's stuff. It always includes involuntary cleaning, and some sort of foreign substance will eventually fall, crumble, or rain down on your head.

Wear a hat. That's the first rule in organizing an estate sale. It's Maureen's commandment number one, and I will live by it. I'm following all the rules since my nerves will be jittery, and my imposter syndrome will be whispering I can't actually pull this off.

I nudge the brim low and instantly picture John doing the same as I step out my door. The morning air is dewy with that distinct smell of algae that creates a film over the water's edge. If I listen closely, I can hear the lake lapping against the stone behind the old motel.

"Need any fresh towels?"

"Oh! *Cheese and rice.*" I struggle to keep hold of my phone after jumping out of my skin. "Are you trying to kill me dead on your sidewalk?"

Heidi stops pushing a cart full of towels and tiny bottles of shampoo. The shampoo is lavender and mint, smells divine, and I'm glad she's restocking despite clutching my heart in shock.

She's wearing a bikini top, cutoff shorts, and green wellies. Large headphones sit on her head. "Ha, sorry. Getting a crack at it early." She pulls the headphones off and lets them rest around her neck. The volume is so loud we can both listen along now to Fleetwood Mac. "I'm covering at Ben's today. He's been swamped." She offers a stack of towels, but I wave them away.

"No thanks, I'm good. I'll be good with the one towel for the week. Hang it over the door to dry."

"Good for you. You're going to fit in just fine around here. Conserving energy and water is important. Most tourists aren't quite so thoughtful."

"No? Why *wouldn't* someone want to preserve what you've got here?" I take a deep breath of crisp air. "It's so invigorating."

The oxygen clears my head, and I instantly feel like I'm ready for whatever the day throws at me.

"I've been eyeing some energy-saving machines. Can't afford it, though. My sister lost all her money shortly after she bought a place here, and I've been struggling to help while I keep the motel afloat. She doesn't get out much. People make her nervous. I could sell the place, but I'm not sure how much I'd get for it and how long I could live on a lump sum... I mean, what else am I going to do with my life? I'd love to travel and live off beans and toast like kids did in the seventies, but I've got this bikini addiction, you know?" She scratches her head.

Dumfounded, I nod. *Where is this going, Heidi? And how long do I stand here before politely walking away?*

She goes on as if in a world all her own. "I'm kinda torn between 'I need to save money,' and 'you only live once.' Very chicken or the egg. Of course, there's always winning the lottery." She chuckles and punches me good naturedly in the arm.

I shift in my sneakers and commiserate with her. "That's what I always say—but, didn't you lose?"

"Yep. It was fun, though." There's a large ring of keys on her cart that she uses to unlock the door next to mine. "Well," she says, stubbing the toe of her wellie into a crack in the sidewalk that could use a patch, "guess I should get to it."

I nod. "See ya, Heidi."

"See ya, Frannie."

After a sharp right turn, tourists and pots of flowers hanging from lampposts lead me to a quaint coffee shop I've been hitting every day called Patty's Pastries. It's across the street from Boggs.

"Mornin'. What can I get ya?" the proprietor, Patty herself, asks, wearing paint-splattered overalls. She sets down a pen and a pink silk rose she's twisting with green floral tape. There's a tiny pot of coffee beans with similar floral pens in assorted colors near the register.

"Um..." I peek inside her case of pastries, a slight sheen of fog

135

on the glass from the cooler. "A dozen, whatever your favorites are, and a gallon of dark roast to go. I'll need a stack of cups and coffee accouterments, too."

"A dozen? Fran, right? You've been a one coffee, one muffin-top girl for the past week straight."

"Taking treats to work this morning. There's some heavy lifting I foresee needing some help with."

"Ah. Smart."

She pops open a pink box and lines it with parchment before filling it with gooey cinnamon rolls, folded croissants oozing with cheese and chunks of ham, and muffin tops of every flavor. So far, the blueberry is my favorite, and I couldn't care less if that makes me basic.

Her overalls are covered with an explosion of color and I can't look away. "What do you paint?" I ask her to fill the time while she works.

"Ah." She slides the box across the counter. "Get a load of my newest." She reaches under her register and quickly flashes me a canvas.

"*Oh, my!*" is all I can say. The painting is of a very nude, long, wavy-haired—very well endowed if the artist is to be believed —man.

"I know. Drive all the way to the community college in Genoa for this class. Worth it." She waggles her eyebrows, waiting for a reaction.

I lean in and play along, fanning myself for effect. "*Totally.* You are very talented." My dry spell is getting to me, I think I was a little attracted to that painting.

"Thanks." She wiggles her hips and stows the canvas. "Here for a summer holiday?" she asks while I poke around the store filled with logos. Patty likes merch.

"No, well, yes. Here for the summer. I'm at Thistle & Burr for a few months while I sort and run an estate sale. Built in a week of vacation after."

"Profiting off the dead. Good margins, no arguments. I like your style." Her wide smile shows off quite a few teeth filled with silver; cavities in this line of work must come part and parcel. Her hair is silver, too. "I like old stuff. Where is it?"

"A really nice house a few minutes from here in Novel. I can't release the address, yet. But lots of sports memorabilia. The house is gorgeous, too, worth a trip just to walk through."

She stops, hands on hips and harrumphs. "It wouldn't be at Ricky Boggs's place, would it?"

"You know it? Not saying that it is. It's technically against the rules to release the address early."

She shakes her head. "Such mules! The both of them."

"I didn't know Mr., uh, Ricky."

"He and his rock-headed boy are two of the most downright stubborn men I've ever known. Both of them put Clover on the map. Ricky because he's got the longest career in the majors. John because he set some big records his rookie year. Made everyone in Novel want to eat their shoes. 'Course then, they outright coerced Lucy Lark to move back to Novel to get our goat—"

"Lucy Lark. The famous pop-star, Lucy Lark?"

"That's the one. She lives in a little cottage on a few acres, on the tippy-top of a mountain. Heidi, the owner of Thistle and Burr where you're staying, she's her sister."

"Shut up—" I start, but the door to Patty's jingles with a group of hikers walking in.

"I better take them. Gotta make a buck."

"Thanks, Patty."

"See ya, sweetie. Nice meeting you."

They're a rowdy but upbeat crowd, all of them hitting her merch wall and picking up T-shirts, hats, and coffee mugs proclaiming *I love Patty's Goodies, Clover, California.*

I make my way down the street, taking what's become my usual route, and haul my treats into Boggs and lay them across the bar. All the workers, including the general contractor, Gus, thank me profusely. Periodically, they hover around the snacks and serve themselves, which makes me happy.

Up in the office, I get to it, sorting into tubs what I've already pre-categorized 'til my head hurts.

There are baseball cards, signed shoes, signed bats, signed jerseys...basically, anything sports related you could write on with a sharpie. Ricky was obsessed with all sports. A box full of Michael Jordan shoes are what snagged our buyer's interest, along with signed footballs and some hockey pucks that I'll be shocked if I find they're worth anything. I'm glad my dad gave me his contact in Genoa. Dave is buying the lot and expecting my delivery promptly on Monday morning. Of course, everything has to be authenticated first, but Dave said he's got a guy.

The only nook I haven't cleaned out is the closet. Gingerly, I push all of John's clothes to one side so I can squeeze in there and make sure I haven't missed anything. My ass sticks up in the air in black shorts like a cat doing a stretch but I still manage to knock my head on the shelf above me, dislodging a hanging bar. *Ouch!*

T-shirts, a few pairs of worn jeans, and collared shirts that look slightly dated and rarely worn rain down on me. But it's not so bad, because I'm instantly wrapped up in the smell of the outdoors, water, and spice. I know this smell, it's the smell that pulled me into a tight hug on a dance floor, the same that fished me out of a lake. All John Boggs.

Focus, Frannie.

Once I get the bar back in place, I continue crawling on all fours all the way to the back of the closet. A job worth doing is worth doing right, after all, and a fat accordion file shoved in the back catches my eye. I better do my due diligence and check to make sure it's not filled with signed ballplayer undies or something.

Inside the burnt orange file folder, I don't find more signed cards or photos. Instead, it's filled with paperwork on the house in Novel, all transferred to Jonathan Boggs. Along with a stock portfolio that I don't read because I don't want to be a total snoop. When I hit banking statements, I stop altogether, but not before noticing a lot of them have *Final Notice* and *Warning!* stamped across them in red.

I snap the files shut, and dust flies all around me as I do my best to shove them back where I found them. Whatever his father intended his relationship with his son to look like, he clearly transferred all his assets to him a while ago—when he was living. Well before his death.

Maybe he knew he was dying and wanted to save John the trouble. It's all so sad.

By the time lunch rolls around, I've got piles of equipment, collectibles, soft goods, and paperwork all separated and stored in tubs. I've only had to use one Band-Aid from my emergency kit, another Gospel from Maureen, for a bloody finger that got into a fight with a packing tape dispenser. My next step will be renting a small U-Haul and then driving everything to Genoa.

During all the organizing, I've realized John is living in this office or at least, existing in this office. There's a small cot in the corner. It can't come close to fitting him comfortably, which is probably why it looks unused. And the long skinny closet he pulled towels and clothes out of yesterday is filled with more than just a few extras. It's got necessities, including a shower caddy.

My work is mostly done here but I can't help myself, I step back into the closet and pull the caddy from the top shelf to sniff his shampoo. It only adds to my memories of that night in the club, and I'm catapulted into the scene we must have made while he let his hands roam my body, while I grasped his neck and looked into his eyes, trying to memorize him. I wanted to hold onto him that night more than anything and desperately tried to convince myself I was better off running away.

"Meg! You up here?"

I scream into the closet and then slam the doors.

"Oh, it's you," John says, stepping into the doorway.

There's a touch of shampoo on my nose, and I wipe it away with a sniff. "How's Daylight doing? How's Destiny?"

It's the first thing I think to say, though I am wondering how the new mama and baby are. I'm also wondering how he is. Wondering way too hard while delighting in his scent like a teenage girl in a Sephora.

"Fine, sunshine. How are you?"

His words hit me like a rollercoaster drop, the familiarity, the easy friendliness that feels a step away from intimate. "I've scheduled a drop-off to a collectibles dealer, so I'm almost finished here." Work, focus on work—not pet names and those full lips that utter them. "Next week, I'll start on the house. I budgeted more time than I probably needed for the sale, but I wanted to make sure I got it right. Memorabilia can be tricky."

To my horror, he walks right up to me, pushes the closet door open, and pulls the shower caddy that I'd just been fondling out in one swift move. Desperately, I try to hide the fear in my eyes.

Can he tell I was openly fantasizing about him in his closet, memorizing his smell?

"Take your time," he says easily, making my nervous gush stand out to my ears even more. "I hide this in here so people don't get nosy when they come upstairs to use the bathroom when we're crowded."

Does he know I was just nose-deep in his products, absorbing his scent like a sponge?

"I'm intruding in your space." I gesture toward the closet and his sad single cot, covered in rainbow-trout sheets while taking three large steps back toward the door. "I'm wrapping up. I can be out of here well before you re-open."

"No problem. I'd love you to be here for the opening, anyway. Both towns are coming, I think." He stops and leans in the doorway to the tiny bathroom, eyes still groggy as he rubs them. There's a piece of grass in his wavy brown hair.

Finally, he shrugs and grips the neck of his T-shirt, pulling it over broad shoulders. His abs flex.

I gulp. *Time for you to go, Frannie!* But all those rolling muscles span his stomach and disappear in a *V* beneath the band of his sweatpants. I can't *not* look.

"I'll start later, loading all this up next week, so I don't mess up your morning routine," I blubber. But all I can think about is how close he held me the night we met, with all those muscles now on display. He dipped me as if my body weighed nothing.

Probably wondering if I'm going to watch him actually take his shower, he says, "Francesca, you're fine here. Take all the time you need. I don't really use this space for much."

Except for living and showering, though he doesn't seem to want to highlight that fact.

"We haven't caught up, talked, in a while..." *Where are you going with this, Fran?* "I haven't really seen you around?" I add in a rush, my tone rising in question when I'm not sure I mean it to be one. The words shock both of us. So does the fact I'm still standing here, prolonging the moment.

"I camped last night," he answers immediately. "And I've seen you, right? Or was I dreaming?"

It's true, we've technically seen each other—from afar. But after the crockpot cooking, the breakfast with the dudes, and delivering a baby horse with his best friend, I've felt... Something's been missing, these days I've spent in his space, with his things, but without actually talking to him.

I've missed him.

"I camp most nights," he continues. "I checked for you here early this morning. I've wanted to, uh, find you all day." We both lean against the doorways we're standing in as the conversation floats into uncharted territory. Neither of us seems willing to stop it. "So, everything will be gone by next week?"

"Yup, this'll be your last chance to keep anything you want. I'll load a U-Haul first thing Monday. They're delivering the shell—"

"I don't want anything," he says, looking around at mostly tubs stacked against walls now that I've organized and consolidated all his treasures, folding his arms across his tan chest. The flex of his biceps and all that skin on display causes me to lose track of my thoughts again. "That's why you're here. Did you rent a trailer? How are you gonna pull it?"

"Hmm?"

"How are you going to pull the U-Haul?"

"Oh, I have a car."

He huffs a laugh, and his broad shoulders shake. "That tin can?"

"Uh, yeah." When he says it like that, I think of my dad and all the times I've seen him hauling vintage games—in trailers, pulled by large trucks, not a tiny, vintage VW bug.

"Not safe." He shakes his head. "You can take my truck."

"No, no, no." I hold my hands up. "That's not necessary." Hot embarrassment washes over me. I must look like a total hack. "And there's no way you'd want to drive my bug. If we traded for the day, I mean. You wouldn't fit."

"I'll fit." He strides toward me from the closet while I hover in the doorway like a stunned woodland animal you'd find in the forest outside these walls. My body instantly braces for... What? I'm not sure.

"Francesca, what is it about this doorway?" he asks, crowding my space. I smell him, the woods still on him and a spice that's all his.

"No way. Now way you'd fit," I laugh, nervously pulling at the brim of my hat, a move I've seen him do many times. *What are we talking about, again?*

He lightly pushes the brim back up so he can look me closely in the eye. "I can live without my truck for a day. *You can take it*," he says, with deep gravelly insistence.

My brain stutters, slips into salacious thoughts where it absolutely should not be. *You can take it...*

Our proximity is making it hard for me to rein it in. "It's fine. I've got it covered. Pretend I'm not here. That's part of the service. No worries for you."

He's breathing as rapidly as I am. Maybe it'd be hard to tell if he was wearing a shirt but he's not. It's plain to see as his pecs flex as his chest rises and falls in succession with mine. Inches from mine.

"That should be your tagline. Frannie's Finds, *no worries for you.*"

"I haven't seen you all morning because you're busy," I reason, letting my eyes plummet into his. *So what if it hurts when I have to rip them away? It's worth it.* "You have things to do."

Is that my voice? All soft and husky? Why do I keep bringing up how long it's been since we've seen each other? And for god's sake, why do I sound *pouty* about it?

"You're taking my truck." He leans over me just a little more, crowding my space until my spine is flat against the door-jam. "What time Monday?"

I laugh, imagining him twisting into a pretzel to fit in my car. "Eight, sharp," I breathe, absolutely frozen by his command, by the heat coming off his skin. "But it's putting you out, with everything going on downstairs. If I need to, I'll rent a truck—"

His eyes are soft, still holding mine, almost pleading while his body is still in domination mode. "I've got a truck sitting outside. Meg will be here, working in her new office. If I physically can't manage in your car, which I can, I'll grab her bike in an emergency. Have Winter pick me up in his G-Wagon. I probably won't even need to leave before you're back."

It's incredibly thoughtful he's doing this, clearing out a space he could live in, despite the huge empty mansion in his name, for his sister—offering me his car for the day like it's nothing. I dig the toe of my sneakers into the shaggy blue carpet and wish he wasn't right about all this—making so much sense. I'd be a fool to decline.

"Okay, thank you. I'm heading to your dad's today after lunch.

It'll take me about a week to organize and stage. Next weekend, I've got to head back home. That was in the schedule I sent—"

"I remember. Back to San Francisco?" He relaxes a little, leaning away and no longer seconds from possibly touching me. Apparently, satisfied now that he's sorted the truck situation.

"Yeah, my parents are getting married. Re-married. We are the quintessential modern family, but I'll be back for the sale. I've budgeted two weeks for that since our location is kinda remote. Again, anything you might want to keep needs to be out before."

"I don't want anything. Please, Francesca, don't ask me again." He says it with such weight and strained emotion. Those sad eyes are wide and honest.

I regret my words immediately. I want to take them back and kiss it better. But "Okay" is all I can offer him.

He continues to wait, and I think he's working up the nerve to say more. Maybe he finally wants to talk about what all of this stuff means to him. Why he wants it gone. Why it clearly pains him to look at it, even now.

Instead, he takes one step back, then two, three, until he's standing again in the bathroom doorway. There's a palpable shift in the room, the tension that was about to boil over like an abandoned pot turned cold. Can he feel it? Can he tell I hate it?

He pulls at the strings on his sweats and raises an eyebrow in my direction.

Oh! He needs a shower. He's waiting for me. *For me to leave!*

"Right! Bye, then!"

He shakes his head, laughing into his palm. "Bye, then, Francesca." He takes pity on me and closes the door.

For the billionth time I wonder why he's living in this shabby office rather than at his dad's beautiful chalet off the shore. If he notices how I squirm when he gets so close. I can never bring myself to move away because I love the way his smile twists at the corners, and his canines shine like he's always hungry. When he looks at me like that, it makes me want to toss my list and all my fears in the lake. It'd be worth the pain to have him just once, I think, even if my heart got too tangled up.

Francesca! This is the definition of too emotional—getting wrapped up in a man's teeth? Geez.

My mind is circling exactly what those teeth could do, and exactly how he could use them as I make it down the stairs and out the front door of Boggs, my dignity barely intact.

What is wrong with me? I was never this dumb around my ex.

CHAPTER 12

John

Box after box, bin after bin. My calves hurt merely watching her try to load Dad's stuff into the back of a tiny U-Haul trailer. She shouldn't be munching on a candy bar, or randomly texting while she does it. She's gonna pull something.

It's taken me a minute to figure out how to woo Francesca Bloomfield. I've never had to woo a woman. In my former line of work, the uniform did the wooing, and I was content with that. It was enough that women loved my jersey, loved my number, loved that I still had a smudge or two of dirt on me when we tumbled into bed for the night. But I'm desperate for a connection now. Everything that used to be enough just, *isn't*, since I met her. I don't know if it's because of the shit going on between me and my dad or because I miss the hell out of my mom. Suddenly, I'm needy. I need to try with her. I need something real to tie me down so I don't disappear.

The weekend crawled by. I busied myself at Boggs, doing a few chores for the cabin behind Dad's place, and even helped pull kayaks off their mounts for tourists at Holiday's during a Saturday rush. All the while, my brain was turning over ideas. The wooing has to look nonchalant. I can't show all my cards at once, can't let her know I'm interested and pursuing her because we've promised each other to keep it platonic. I can't believe Monday is finally here, and I convinced her to take my truck. Now, for phase two of my plan.

How am I going to convince her to let me drive?

I chewed on this question yesterday while I hung out in Chef Alec's kitchen, pestering him for his pesto recipe, which he self-ishly will not share. He finally kicked me out. I went to Winter's to visit Destiny. I even went to Logan's and sat on his couch and watched *Naked and Afraid* reruns. I drove Jack and Warner to the airport so they could elope to Canton, Texas, get married in cowboy boots, and hit the world's biggest flea market. There was talk about a road trip to Waco to track down Chip and Joanna Gaines, but I'm hoping they forgo stalking their interior design dream couple.

The moments I spent talking to her last week in my office have plagued me. It shocked me when she acted as if I'd hurt her by staying away. To say she hadn't seen me or talked to me as if she wanted me around more. That's when I realized she's *interested*, but because her dickhead ex did some sort of number on her, she's gun-shy. I hope I'm a humble man, but even I can read the room when we're together.

But she's counting kisses, for fuck's sake. All so she doesn't get attached and doesn't get hurt. Well, I know a thing or two about self-preservation.

It's up to me to show her how good I'll treat her, to do what-ever it takes to erase all those bad memories. I can't think of a better way to start than a road trip for two.

She's completely zoned out on her phone screen when I approach. "Good morning," I say, walking up behind her.

"*Cheese and rice!*" she screams and then glares at me.

"Sorry." I hold my hands up and beg for mercy. "Morning," I try again.

"You scared me."

She watches me for a second too long. There's a big portion of her stomach exposed because she's clutching an old baseball mitt, one of mine, against her chest as if it's armor. A honey-tan sliver of skin that's as mesmerizing as staring into a campfire on full display. She looks like a modern mermaid in a tight pair of faded cutoffs, with all that blonde hair cascading down her back.

"Forgive me?"

She notices me noticing her exposed skin, I'm sure I look hungry as a wolf, and her cheeks deepen in color to a rosy pink. She pulls the hem of her shirt down. "Forgiven."

A streak of dirt runs across her forehead. I have to squint to see it, but it's there. I also look like a wreck, I know, and pull my baseball cap lower. I woke up after another night sleeping in the woods. I can't settle on the cot in the office and definitely not at Dad's house—on principal. I slept in yesterday's Henley and jeans, and now I know I look like death warmed up.

"Let me help you with the rest," I offer, keeping my chin level and my eyes easy.

"Thanks. I am in a rush." She checks the time on her phone. I love her drive. She's not going to let anything stop her from getting this job done.

"I'm fast, I promise."

She laughs, and my gut plummets. *Idiot.* Innuendo hangs in the air. The entirely wrong kind of innuendo. There's always this sexy undertone between us, between our words and the looks we try not to give each other. Well, she tries. I've got a different plan. But I sure as shit don't want her to think there's anything fast about what I'd like to do to her.

"You know what I mean. I'll grab the keys," I say, making my way around her to the gaping backend of the U-Haul. I lift with my knees, not with my back—because I have to think about shit like that these days—and push the last heavy box in.

When I grab the keys off the dash of my truck and bring them back, I find her pacing and full of nervous energy.

She squares her shoulders and plasters on a happy face. That enormous smile made for the movies doesn't quite reach her eyes, though. "Any tips on navigating? I've noticed GPS gets confused around here."

"Err," I scratch my head. Is this my opening? *No, too easy.* "I can write down the first couple turns out of town toward the highway you want." How am I going to convince her to let me drive without it looking obvious?

"And, any tips on, um..." she trails off, biting her bottom lip. It's the first time I've seen her do that, and my chest gets all achy and light. My fucking heart flutters. She still can't make eye contact. She's so damn nervous about whatever it is she's going to say next. "Stick?"

"Stick?"

"Your stick. No, damn it," she says, scrubbing her face with her hands. "The stick. You know—stick."

Oh, my ever-loving God, how many times is this woman going to say stick? "You don't know how to drive manual transmission, do you?"

"I do. It's just been a while."

Boom. Perfect opening. It's my lucky day. "Don't worry," I say, keeping my voice level. "I'll drive you. I've been to Genoa a hundred times." This is it. This is my shot.

"Oh, no. I'm fine on my own." She rushes on, clearly uncomfortable accepting help, "You're already being so generous."

I scratch at the three-day stubble I've let grow on my cheeks. It'll be better if she thinks I don't want to go. *Play it cool, Boggs. Don't let her see how much you want this or she'll bolt.*

Before I can speak, Meg rolls up on her shiny bike, laptop strapped into the front basket.

She glides to a stop. "Hi. What's up?" Her eyes focus intently on both of us, standing next to the U-Haul.

"Francesca doesn't know how to handle stick."

"Hey!" Francesca yelps. It's fun watching her hands prop on her hips. All this embarrassment over a manual transmission and dick jokes. I've never talked about sex without saying a word this much in my life.

Meg eyes her sharply, then says, "I can drive you."

"No, really. I can manage, I'm sure. I just need to brush up." She's pleading with both of us, but mostly herself. She tugs lightly on a hair-tie around her wrist.

I hate seeing her worry. "Now, wait. This is my truck. And you're pulling a heavy load."

"That settles it. I'll drive you." Meg dismounts and leans her bike against the shake-shingle wall of my bar.

Shit. What am I going to say now?

"I was going to make a day of it, hit a bunch of sales on the way."

"No problem. I'm game," Meg says. "Oh, wait." She halts mid-step. "I forgot I've got a call with my advisor. But I can take it on the road, I guess. I'm interviewing to be her TA next year—"

"Service is too spotty, you know that," I remind her quickly. A tad too quickly. *Idiot, be cool.*

"You guys, really, I don't want to cause either of you this kind of trouble. I've got it. I'll get it. Give me a few pointers," she turns to me, "and I'll be on my way."

"I'm sure she can pick it up." Meg shrugs.

"Nope, I'm driving, and that's that. My car," I go on when I see Francesca is ready to launch into an argument. "My call."

"I'll make you sing along to all the songs," she threatens, shifting her feet nervously. "You'll hate it."

"I'm fine with that if I know the words." My shoulders shrug on their own, and I feel every bit the big dummy I am.

"I'm stopping at every sale I see along the way. And the flea markets." She points right at my chest, and I laugh at her. "You'll complain about how long it takes me to browse."

"He always rushes me when I'm shopping," Meg chimes in, popping the kickstand on her bike.

Francesca's face twists into a frown. She's genuinely concerned I'll complain.

"I will not complain." I hold up three fingers. "Scout's honor."

"Of course, you're a Scout." She lets out a groan but then suddenly straightens. She's got one more trick up her sleeve. What could it be..."You have to eat the junk food and drink the soda I stop for."

This one gives me pause, and I bite down hard on my molars. She thinks she's got me.

"Fine," I grit out through clenched teeth.

Meg's got a look of absolute horror on her face as Francesca squirms, clearly uncomfortable. I don't want to agree to this, but I'm afraid I'll blow the whole operation if I don't.

"But," I say, rolling around an idea. "I want you to eat some of my food too."

Am I pushing it? Yes. But am I selling it? I think I am. Both women think I'm hesitating when, in reality, I'd probably wash down a bag of M&M's with a Mountain Dew right now. My body shivers at the thought. But Francesca can't know that, not yet.

"Fine," she relents. She's exasperated and tosses her hands in the air. "I already ate all your roast!" she adds, completely flabbergasted by my agreeing to her terms.

And the fact she ate my food, well, it makes me weak in the knees. Is it crazy that I fantasize about future dinners with her? That feeding her makes me feel all caveman and protective? Am I reading too much into this? I don't even care.

"I can be ready in five minutes." There's a breath lodged in my chest. I release it quickly and try to act natural and not like I haven't spent time one-on-one with a woman in over a year.

"I hope you like vintage Brittany," she mutters.

"She's okay, but I'm really more of a Christina."

She tries and fails to hide a laugh.

Shower! I'm about to be in a car alone with this woman, and I need to be smelling right.

"Here, take my keys." Handing my keys over to a woman is something I've frankly never done. My truck is my baby. The first thing I purchased with my last big paycheck when I blew back into town. But with Francesca, I don't think twice.

"Ahem," Meg mock coughs, still standing in the doorway of Boggs and watching us like a streaming drama in the driveway, but now with concern washing over her face. "I guess I'll see you guys when you get back tonight. If it's after ten and I haven't heard from you, I'm calling the cops. So—keep me updated." She's a pissed-off parent who got talked into a co-ed school trip against her better judgment.

What I don't understand is why?

She lets the door close swiftly behind her. *What is she all in a huff about?*

"Thanks for doing this," Francesca says, closer to me now, more relaxed and apparently resolved to our situation.

She plucks a twig from my hair.

I lean into her touch. "Don't worry. I got you."

So why does it feel like *she's got me?*

CHAPTER 13

Fran

He's fresh as a daisy. The guy must have scrubbed with that bottle of body wash to get the woods off him so quickly. It's unfortunate that I know he doesn't use a loofa or a bar of soap, just his hands. Just the bottle. He looks well-rested, clean-shaven, and showing off the cleft in his chin—way too delicious. It's too bad he refuses to be number five on my list and that his sister has warned me off like bad voodoo. Now it's too late, and I really, really would have liked to know how the man's mouth would feel on mine. I bet damn good.

Maybe I don't care that I'm emotional, and all I need is the right person who won't care either. *John seems like that kind of person...*

"You ready?" he asks, opening the car door and motioning for me to get in.

"As I'll ever be." My palms start to sweat as I situate myself in his passenger seat.

He reaches across me wordlessly with the buckle of my seat-belt, clicking it into place, and I swear on all my karma, he drops his lips gently to the top of my head and inhales.

My whole body is a goose bump when he finally closes my door.

How am I expected to sit here now? A whole day with John Boggs. I mean, the man is beautiful—rugged in fresh dark denim and a moss green henley, well-defined muscles pulling taut through the fabric. He's mature, and full of unshakable, easy charisma. All he has to do is breathe in my direction, and it's sexy as hell.

Outside, the sky is a powder blue, with a few birds swooping toward the lake for a late breakfast. The truck rocks as John slides in, slamming the door, lips tipping up in a sweet smile, encapsulating me in his scent as if he knows it's driving me wild. It's everywhere, all over this truck, and I drink it in, breathing deep down into my lungs. I savor the notes of fresh outdoor air, the spicy wood from his body wash, and a touch of campfire that lingers on his skin.

"So, your guy's in Genoa?" His fist grips the stick between us, and my thoughts begin to wander. "Francesca?"

"Hmm?"

"The guy we're meeting?"

"*Dave.*" Right! Stop fantasizing about his hands. "He's my dad's guy and offered a more than fair deal."

"You've taken care of everything so efficiently. You've got no idea what a weight it is off my shoulders." A muscle in his jaw ticks as a strong arm lands behind my head and he turns in his seat to back the truck out.

My brain simply can't track the conversation. I keep wondering, can human beings really feel the tension in a room? Or the cab of a truck? Is that phrase about it being cut with a knife a real thing?

"I haven't eaten anything today. You mind if we make a quick stop?" he asks.

I manage to comprehend his words and reply like a regular human. "Sure, but it's not getting you out of stopping at the Flea and sales I've planned. I've budgeted time. We don't need to meet Dave 'til six at his warehouse."

"I don't mind shopping as much as you might guess, sunshine." He gives me a lopsided, playful smile, and I rip my eyes away to stare out the window as if it's the most riveting season of a TV show my sister might make me watch.

Knowing what's on the side of the road as we drive is my new full-time job.

We cruise for a bit around the lake, out of Clover and through Novel, in the general direction of Genoa based on the GPS on his dash.

Basic Kneads bread company has arching letters above its front door. All sorts of colorful boughies still sporting moss from their time in the lake hang from a shake shingle roofline.

"Carbs?" I gasp.

"Hey, it's not like that. I prefer to eat real food. Food without chemicals found in fertilizer. Do you have any idea what the FDA allows in the US? It's all banned in Europe. Don't get me started on—"

"Okay, easy, big guy. I get it. Food is fuel."

"Exactly."

We seat ourselves, ordering bagels with smear and drinks.

John nods toward the front of the restaurant, where a grandpa is sitting with his morning coffee and pastry. "Number five?"

All I can do is scoff at him.

"Why not? Looks like a decent guy," he presses. There's a smirk painted across his face. "Number five on your list is still open, right?" His smile falters and the tendons in his neck strain where his Henley gapes open, the top button undone.

"Who wants to know?"

"Not me," he amends, dropping his forearms to the table and looking at me through inquisitive eyes. He absolutely wants to know.

The waitress deposits our food and drinks on the table. She

smiles wide at John and lingers, though he doesn't seem to notice her noticing him.

I see it, and it makes me question what the hell I want from him. And what he wants from me. And if maybe it's not friendship at all?

When I've polished off everything on my plate and ordered a refill of lemonade, I break the silence. "Did you and Meg grow up together?"

"Yeah, my mom had me young and then Meg years later when she met her father."

"What happened between your mom and your dad?"

"The game. Ricky swore up and down that he'd make time for her—that he'd put her first, ball second. Didn't come close to holding up his end of the bargain. She left while six months pregnant. He let her."

"That had to be so hard for her."

His face is pained as he speaks. "She thought he was going to be her knight in shining armor, you know? She pursued him because of who he was at first, always admitted that was her first mistake, but she believed him when he said he'd settle down for her and had this whole story made up in her head about how their fairytale would go... He crushed it. Crushed her."

The pain in his voice shoots straight to my heart and takes up camp. "And Meg's dad?"

"Her dad's never been in the picture. Mom got sick shortly after she was born."

Their relationship sharpens in my mind's eye, John acting as a father figure to Meg. Their dynamic makes sense.

"You two have always stuck together." It's not a question, and I smile around my straw, the lemonade is hand-squeezed for sure with fat chunks of raw sugar around the rim.

"We're two peas in a pod," he confirms.

We're still fully engrossed in our conversation when John insists on paying the bill.

"You sure you don't want to take a shot?" he asks, nodding again to the cute grandpa as he pulls the door open for me to walk through. The man is still sipping his coffee, cutting tiny slivers of his bagel, bite by bite.

That thing inside me that wants to get John's goat, that wants to surprise him, gets the best of me. I march over to the grandpa and start to chat him up, beginning with complimenting his Air Force cap and thanking him for his service.

His eyes are bright when I wrap it up with, "I hope you have a wonderful day, sir," then run back to John and out the door.

I barely catch his reply, "Will do, darlin'. You two have fun now." And peek over my shoulder to see both men give each other a two-fingered salute.

"Nice try," John muses when he catches up to me in the parking lot. "I thought number five was a goner for a second. Still, you probably made his day."

"I know you want to know what the list is all about, but the truth is, I'm figuring it out myself. Lists make me feel more in control, less confused, and spiny when there's too much to do or to think about. Getting over a relationship that ended so badly was harder than I thought, and when I did, I realized I still wanted all the adrenaline-fueled, thrilling parts of love but without the threat of getting my heart pummeled all over again. It's a safety net."

"Okay, sunshine. I hear you. I get it," he responds quickly, not at all ruffled by my emotional outburst. Whether he knows it or not, it's a weight off my shoulders to overshare and have him take in stride as if it's totally normal to spill your guts to a new friend.

We wrap around to the back of the lot where we parked, tall grass popping up through the gravel and tickling my ankles. We're far from the lake's edge now, more inland, but the towering trees make up for the loss of view. They are skyscrapers, totally awe-inspiring and a little mystical. Calming when you measure yourself up against their stature, their history.

I know he's pestering me about the list in good nature, but it's holding a mirror up at the same time. It is silly, what I've been doing but it was a coping mechanism.

Maybe it is time to move on.

"You know all about me now. What about your parents?" he asks, dutifully changing the subject. "Vow renewal. That's big."

"Yeah. I hope this does the trick for them. They're meant to be, but they bicker constantly, too. I think they're both terrified of retirement." I laugh, as if the thought of my parents without Cotton Candy Carnie, or Cat and I, to hold them together doesn't terrify me.

"They're not looking forward to a break? Palm trees? Tiny umbrella drinks?"

"Like the umbrellas in the drinks at Boggs?" I'd noticed him practicing at the bar, always popping them on top of hand-pressed concoctions with a flourish.

"I'm working on something special, something for you, actually." He follows me all the way to the passenger side of the truck and steps so close that I have to press my back into the door so we don't touch. "You'll get a taste at the party when we open. And the umbrellas are inspired by you."

His hand grazes my cheek as he pushes tendrils that have fallen from my bun back from my face. "Something sweet, just like you."

"Why for me?" I breathe, letting myself take this moment to memorize his eyes as they lightly roam over every inch of my face. Yes, they're stormy gray but ringed around the edges with golden flecks. And his lashes, they're so long. When he blinks, they dust his cheeks and make him look as vulnerable as he's openly been with me since we first met.

"Because they're happy, and they make me think of you, especially the yellow ones."

"Oh," I say, drinking him in, happy to get lost in the moment. "That's adorable, actually. Stop being adorable." I push against his chest playfully, it's firm and so warm.

He holds my hand there, my fingertips barely reaching the bare skin of his neck. "Tiny umbrellas, I'm convinced, could solve the world's problems... Along with the effects of tequila, of course."

"I love tequila," I agree in a rush.

"I know."

"Stop being adorable and thoughtfully observant!" I pull my hands away because if I don't, I'm going to push up on the tips of my toes and make him number five right here, right now.

He opens my door. "Sorry, no can do."

Shaking my head at him, I get into the car and let him buckle me in as if we do it every day.

He wraps around the car, and when he's back in his seat, he reverts easily back into the conversation, as if he didn't just hold my hands against his heart with a reverence I've never known.

"What are your parents like?"

"Both of them love to work," I continue, easily falling back into our chatter.

"I get that. Feels good to accomplish something."

"Exactly. Mom fell in love with spray paint at a young age, rehabbing old things. Dad fell in love with *Donkey Kong* as a kid and has been chasing that high ever since. They like working on things together, finding the common thread. I think they're scared they've got nothing else, and that's what the vow renewal is all about."

"That's one of my biggest fears, actually," he says as he pulls out onto the road.

"What is?"

"Breaking up, like in your old age."

I raise an eyebrow at him.

"I'm barely ten years older than you, Francesca. I'm talking about retirement age, like your parents. I'd rather live alone my whole life than go through losing someone when I should be settling down to enjoy them."

"Do you think you want something serious now, to do better? Be better than your dad was for your mom?"

Luckily, he takes it in stride. He's been open with me from the start. "When you grow up the way I did... Shit. I don't know how to say this without sounding like a dick."

"You wouldn't even kiss me in a club... I'm pretty sure you're firmly in the nice guy category." My heart jumps at the mention of our meeting, all those adrenaline-soaked seconds spent pressed up against each other coming back full force. More so now because it's *him*.

"You have to know, it's not because I didn't want to."

I gulp. He lets me off the hook and continues, a cocky but cute grin on his face. "I was good at baseball from the jump. A natural, everyone said. Had a pretty full career until I retired—lost my arm. Lost a lot of those meaningless flings, and the crazy thing is...."

"Yes?"

"I've never said this out loud." He chuckles slightly cryptically. "The crazy thing is, a part of me is happier without it. Without all the fake bullshit that comes along with fame and money. It took some time, but I'm finally honest enough with myself to want more."

"It's ironic that you and I had the opposite for most of our lives. I was never a serial dater, just a few relationships. Until I thought I met the one...."

"Mmm," he hums. "You with your serious relationship, me with my flings... I don't think it's funny. I worry every day that I'll never have something like you had... I mean, I know it didn't end well, but—"

"I did have something special for a while. But the way it ended made it all feel like a lie. He told me I was everything, and in the end, I was less than nothing to him. Hardly worth a conversation to break up with me." I look at him. "All that aside, it would be an absolute tragedy to never have felt love, even once."

He gazes at the road ahead, clearly unsure what to do with my comment. But he started it. He started picking open both our old wounds.

"Ever since, I've had this fear I'll kick it alone anyway, in a tent somewhere, with a pet fish. That's how the guys convinced me to try to meet someone that night at Throwbacks. They told me it was time to get serious. Meet someone and date. It's as if I'd been waiting for permission, and moving home and getting off the road, the guys challenging me, was all I needed. And then you," he glances at me meaningfully, "pulled me by the neck onto the dance floor." He raises an eyebrow.

"Oh, so now, if I don't date you, it'll be my fault you end up alone with a pet fish?"

He pushes out his bottom lip and bats his eyes, looking truly pathetic. It's easy to punch him in the arm to give us both the out we need in this moment.

Is that what he really wants? To date me? To be something more than friends, something more than a kiss, even? *Could I trust him? Count on him?*

"That won't happen to you, JB."

"No?" He eyes me quizzically as if he can read my face and features to get the answer he's looking for.

"Not possible." I shake my head. "You're a keeper."

"Is that right?" His face softens, and his shoulders relax. I'm ecstatic, knowing I did that—it's just as good as getting him all riled up—making him happy, if only for a moment with a passing comment.

He flips his hat backward and glances at me, meets my eyes, and exhales long and slow as if he's exasperated.

Looking for something to do with my hands and my face, I drop the vanity mirror and apply lip gloss.

He watches from the corner of his eyes. Back and forth. Me, the road, me, the road, me...

Slowly, I line my lips with sticky, opaque gloss. Taking my time to get the tips of my Cupid's bow. Anything to get a reprieve from the look he's giving me. My cheeks are red as the sangria they serve at Boggs.

161

He adjusts in his seat and I pretend I don't notice him pulling gently around the crotch region of his jeans.

"Need to stop for anything?" He breaks the silence as I flip the visor back up.

My gaze rockets back to his. "No, I'm good. There's a sale coming up, but we've got a little further to go. I'll let you know when we get close."

We cruise while alternating between personal playlists, his full of old country and mine full of emotional ballads. I will my racing heart to settle, but every time I steal a glance in his direction, all I can see are flexing forearms as he grasps the wheel.

He fiddles with his hat, taking it off and tossing it on the dash.

Focus on something else, Francesca.

I try to count how many highway signs we pass, but it becomes painfully clear after sucking down three lemonades and a latte at Basic Kneads in record time, I have to pee.

Longingly, I watch three stops and counting go by, but I don't ask him to exit. It's the principle! I think I can make it to the first flea market we've planned on stopping at. Surely, it'll have some sort of grubby restroom I can use.

I let out a small squeak as we pass an exit with a really nice Shell station. I bet that one had state-of-the-art bathrooms. "Err, can we stop soon?"

"Knew it," he says with a gloating grin and pulls off at the next exit.

CHAPTER 14

Fran

"Be right back." I'm halfway out the door before he shifts into park.

Instead of waiting like I expected, he follows me inside. I head directly to the bathrooms, do my thing, and when I come out, the soda fountain is my first stop. If I could mainline Dr. Pepper, I would.

He's standing near the entrance taking up nearly an entire doorway with his shoulders, clearly waiting for me and fussing with his phone, twisting his cap backward, then forward again.

"Just a couple snacks," I say innocently as I begin to peruse the offerings.

He barks a laugh as if he already knows a couple will be a bagful and heads in the opposite direction toward a sad basket of bananas.

A woman with a nametag that reads *Dixie* rings us up after I've piled my choices high on the counter. I don't say anything when John pulls out his wallet and buys my soda, a package of sour gummi worms, watermelon Bublelicious, a bag of spicy corn chips, and a Snickers bar. I can tell it's difficult for him to hand over cold, hard cash for a pile of sugar, but I feel it's my duty to help him get over this unnatural aversion to junk food.

When we're back in his truck, which resembles a happy nest with treats, he says, "Can I ask you a personal question? Since we're friends and all?"

"I'm an open book." Between my sister, Willow, and me, it's true. I'm absolutely the one who wears her details on her sleeve. And John's easy to talk to because he's pretty open, too.

"What happened in your last relationship that was so bad it forced you to stop...trying? To make a list to desensitize yourself from, well, feeling? Can I ask that?"

Except for that. But for John, I'll try because we're *literally* barreling down a road together, which makes me laugh to myself but also I'm desperately trying to put on the brakes. Truth is, I don't want to.

"It was a bad breakup," I whisper. "Nothing no one else hasn't dealt with for the last billion years."

"Don't negate your feelings like that. Pain is pain. You don't have to measure it on someone else's scale," he presses, glancing at me and then back at the road. Little white dashes get eaten up by his car like a *Pac-Man*.

"It'd been falling apart for a while. I just hadn't noticed. Or didn't want to notice... Wouldn't let myself notice. He said so many things that made me feel really bad about myself..."

"Like, how bad?" His hands grip the steering wheel.

"Gaslighting. Guilt trips," I say softly, adjusting my arm between us, grazing his. "To name a few. He became more and more critical. In the end, we felt like strangers. Our interests were so different. I wanted so badly, no, I *craved* affection, and I think he knew it and used it to punish me after a fight." I shrug my shoulders. "I was too needy for him."

"Sounds like he didn't know his head from his asshole, Francesca. If he didn't want to be in the relationship, he should have been a man and said so." He takes a breath. "Why do I get the sense it ended dramatically?"

I'm making this much bigger in his head than it needs to be. John cares. I'm not sure why or when this started, but I think I might be on the list of people he cares about. He's scooped me up, a stranger in a new town, and has decided I'm worth looking after. And that makes me want to put him out of his misery.

"You really want to know? It was like the cherry on a bad relationship sundae. It was already over for him, I realize that now, and he made it very clear the last night we were together."

His jaw flexes as he bites down, a tendon popping in his cheek. "What did he do to you?"

"He pushed me out of bed."

He waits a beat. Then two. I add, "Like accidentally, like he forgot I was there."

"No, he didn't."

A teeny, tiny smile plays on my lips. "It's okay. You can laugh. I can laugh at it now. I really should have seen it coming. He ignored me in every other aspect of our life by that point, and I let him. I took it because I felt like I'd be wrong to ask for him to do better. To ask for more. Too needy. Too emotional."

"Wait, wait, wait. I need context... What do you mean, *pushed you out*?" He twists his cap around and drops a heavy arm across the back of my seat. His eyes are dancing between exasperation and amusement.

"I mean we, *you know*." He growls a little and my heart flutters. "Then we were finished. Well, he finished. And then he sort of kept scooting over. Did I mention I'm the big spoon in this situation? So, he scoots again and again until I was at the very edge, and he was all spread out like a starfish. Then his dog, a Great Dane named Paul Rudd—he thought that was so funny—it was always, 'I need to feed Paul Rudd dinner,' or 'Paul Rudd piddled on my rug.' Anyway, the dog jumps up and gets in bed, and he just pushed me off the mattress to make room. *For the dog.* I bruised my hip."

He twists the bill of his cap back around, visibly trying to hold back an angry smile. He's mad, but he's also trying not to laugh. Honestly, I get it. Those are the exact emotions I've been working through for the past few months.

"It's not funny," he says, straining to keep his lips turned down in an even line.

"It's not," I agree, straining just as much. "But it was the light-bulb moment I needed to wake up and realize I wasn't happy there anyway."

It feels good, the fact I'm ready to laugh about it. Am I angry? Yes. Did it strike a chord within me, making me realize perhaps I pick guys who don't care as much as I do? Yeah. But I've been working to bandage my wounded pride, and I think I might have managed it.

And I think Johnathon Boggs has a lot to do with it.

"What a dickhead!" he finally cracks, laughing into his hand and looking relieved when I join in. "What did you do?"

It's funny how animated he gets, kinda like I'm talking to Cat and Willow, but instead, he's a dude with a beautiful mouth and laughter dancing in his eyes.

"I mean, not what I should have done." I list the options I obsessed over after falling out of bed on my ass. "Hurl a bunch of *tiny, you know what,* jokes at him—which actually apply! Instead, I cried. A lot. I finally said all the things I'd been feeling, the things I'd been holding inside. That he ignored me, that I didn't feel like a part of his life, that I thought we were headed toward marriage, but I couldn't marry someone who clearly forgot I was even present in the bed, let alone someone I was afraid to share my feelings with. Someone who was incapable of returning those feelings."

"Did he apologize? Did he beg your forgiveness on his knees?"

"He told me what my mom always tells me, that I was reading too much into everything. I was being too sensitive. He'd been in medical school and was a month from graduating. He said I was too much drama for a doctor's wife anyway and that he'd been thinking that for the past year. I went to my parent's house that night, then back to my own house. The next morning, he sent me a text telling me he'd left a box of my things on his counter and that I should pick them up and leave my key. That was the last I ever saw him."

"Until the club? At Throwbacks, the night we met?"

"Yup."

"What a punk. Who doesn't have the balls to man up and just say—"

"I don't want to be in a relationship? This isn't working? I'm no longer interested. Maybe we should stop seeing each other?"

"Right?" he responds, mirroring my exasperation.

"Exactly, right! It's everything I should have said. I was too worried about pleasing him, not upsetting him, convincing myself of everything. Even so, I'm a big girl, he could have told me—"

He's nodding playfully. "I know you are!"

"I can take it!"

"Of course, you can!" he chants, animated and waving his hand toward me as if I'm clearly not someone to tamper with.

We laugh together as I pop Skittles in my mouth. I hand him one of each color across the console, a pile of red, green, yellow, and purple, and he takes them down in one go, shaking his head, eyes still laughing.

He just pounded a handful of Skittles in solidarity. My heart swells.

"What really ticks me off," I say, making my tone turn sober, "is that I believed I was powerless." I notice him straighten in his seat, raptly listening to me. "I let him take all my power," I say, looking out the window. The sun is suddenly not so bright. "I can't shake that feeling sometimes."

"What do you mean you can't shake that feeling? All I've seen from the moment I met you was a woman who knows what she wants, goes after it, and gets it." He reaches across the car and wraps his hand around the back of my neck.

Rapidly, my chest moves up and down, and I can't seem to catch my breath. Can he see how much his touch affects me? Especially now, after I've poured my heart out to him?

Finally, as if he knows we can't continue like this, there's nowhere for us to go with this moment. He squeezes once and pulls his hand back.

"This is me taking my power back, I guess. The list, this trip, the business. I'm trying to erase the feeling of being thrown away. I supported him all those years when he needed it, and then he tossed me like a half-eaten burrito. If I don't give someone that power, it can't happen again." I can't look at him. Instead, I watch the world on fast forward through my window as we fly down the highway.

"Sunshine, he didn't throw you away."

"That's exactly what he did."

"No." He shakes his head, determined. "You can't throw something away if you don't know what you've got. His loss, baby. You hear me?" His eyes crash into mine so briefly before snapping back to the road that I wonder if it even happened.

Abruptly, he pulls the truck off an exit ramp. We wind down a small side street until he takes another sharp turn on a dirt road.

"What are you doing?"

"You'll see."

"Where are we going? This isn't the direction of the sale! What about Dave?"

He pulls into a pasture of sorts, some bumpy, worn-out land with a weathered for sale sign boasting acreage, and exits the car, quickly moving around the front.

He taps on my window.

I give him a *what the hell* face through the glass.

He opens the door. "You said the meeting is at six. We have

plenty of time to hit the sale and meet Dave. Scoot over," he says when he opens the door.

I scramble over the console, and he hops in the passenger seat.

"What are we doing?"

"We're teaching you how to handle a diesel engine." There's a look of determination on his face—a smile too.

"But that's why I have you!" I argue.

"Happy as I am that you *have me*, and you do, you know. It'd still be good for you to learn. So, we're learning. Right here, right now."

"Ugh. No, we're not!"

"Yes, we are." The smile dissolves into a fierce look, one with longing attached.

"John, no. I can't drive this beast." We're in a wide clearing, but there are tall trees on three sides of his big truck.

With the exception of startling easily like one of Winter's ponies, I'm not a scaredy-cat. That's Willow's territory, and Cat? She makes us both look like wimps. But right now, I want to crawl into the ditch on the side of this road littered with oddly pretty, prickly purple flowers standing tall against the rushing wind. I am not strong like those flowers.

"You can," he says, pulling me out of my spiral. "You mentioned earlier you've driven stick before—"

"Yeah, like in high school," I stutter, rubbing my palms together, sticky with traces from colors of the rainbow. "My first boyfriend taught me, but I think it was really his idea of foreplay."

John groans as if I've caused him pain with the mention of foreplay, starts the engine, and it roars to life. My feet find the clutch, the gas, out of sheer necessity.

"Not a bad idea," he adds with a wolfish smile. "You can do this."

"Maybe," I say, letting my cheek graze the soft fabric of his sleeve as he reaches across my lap to press a button, bringing my chair closer to the wheel.

Can I do this? I really don't want to put a scratch on this man's truck after he's been so generous with me.

"Here are the gears." He takes my right hand and places it gently on the stick shift. "We're not actually going to shift. Feel the motions and repeat after me."

My hand is shaking, his palm covering the top so that I can no longer see. "Okay," I whisper.

With every command, he increases pressure on my hand, gently squeezing as he pushes to the right, then forward, then down. I don't know if it's the adrenaline of fight or flight rising up in me, but something about him getting me through these gears, strong and steady, warm and supportive... It makes me believe I can do it.

As he continues to move my hand through the motions, shifting together, the car feels too small. It's too hot.

My high school boyfriend *was* onto something, but he wasn't a man. He wasn't in control, easing me through the motions like John does now with rough hands that I'd love to feel drag down my body like they did at Throwbacks. But this time, my naked body. I want to feel his fingertips burn into my spine and dip between my thighs.

My chest pumps for air as I try to focus on his instructions. I might pass out if my heart rate gets any higher.

He reaches across me again, this man is trying to kill me, and pulls the seatbelt until it clicks at my hip. "Ready?"

I gulp and look deep into gray eyes, swimming with—what? Excitement? Anticipation? Appreciation?

"I feel a lot of pressure—" I say, honestly.

"What kind of pressure," he asks, letting his hand float to my temple. He lightly pushes a wisp of hair back into my bun. I don't have an answer for him.

"Listen to me," he says slow and sweet. "If I didn't think you could do this, I wouldn't be asking you to drive my truck. You're so strong, Francesca. You're unstoppable."

It's everything I've craved hearing for a long time, I think, but... "Why are we doing this again?" I whine, still not quite ready to accept my fate.

"I can't stand the idea of that bastard making you feel powerless. You're not. You're a skyscraper, you're an ocean, you're a—well, right now, I want you to be a turbo diesel engine."

He takes my hands that I hadn't realized I'd been ringing in my lap, and gently places one on the wheel, the other back on the stick shift between us.

"You know that line in *Dirty Dancing*—" he presses, slow and soothing, as if we've got all the time in the world.

"How do you know about lines from *Dirty Dancing*?" My mirror is high. I adjust it so I can see. Before he can answer, my mouth runs on, nerves getting the better of my patience. "Which line? There are many."

He settles back in his seat. His knees push out wide as he answers me calmly, "Basically raised a teenage girl while I was still a kid myself, probably let her watch a bunch of movies way too young." He laughs lightly. "*Dirty Dancing* was a favorite."

I shift into gear and begin to ease off the clutch. "Wait, how old was she? How old were you?"

"When mom died, Meg's dad wasn't interested in raising a toddler. It was important to my mom that we stay together. It was important to me, too. Luckily, I'd just turned eighteen. She was three."

"Oh my god, John." I keep my foot on the brake while my heart cracks down the center. "How did you manage?"

"You know Patty?"

I nod. "The quirky woman from the pastry shop?"

"She was there every step of the way. When I started to travel, Meg stayed with her. We made it work."

"John." I turn in my seat and, without thinking, reach out to squeeze his shoulder. He shivers as my hand glides up to his cheek. He leans into my touch, closes his eyes for a moment, then says, "You need to focus, sunshine. Or I won't be able to either."

I remove my hand, my palm still warm from his skin.

Right, I guess I'm doing this.

"Anyway," he says, eyes back open and on the field ahead of us. "Right now, this is reminding me of that line, 'Don't put baby in the corner.'"

Looking over my shoulder, I gauge my distance from the tree-lined perimeter of the clearing. "That is a good one."

"Exactly. Don't let your moron of an ex make you feel powerless."

And then I'm flying. I'm doing it based on tiny bits of sensory memory, but mostly guided by John's steady voice as he coaches me step by step.

We circle the clearing, coming closer to a few trees than I'd like, but I keep us from hitting anything solid. The more I get used to the feel of the truck, the stick shifting smoothly in my hand, the more I'm able to pick up speed. I even roll my window down, and then John does the same.

"Hell, yeah," he hollers as his tires kick up a wide circle of dust.

Wind fills the cab of the truck. My hair blows wild in my messy bun, tendrils tickling my face. He flips his hat backward, still yelling out at the sky and cheering me on.

When I glance at him, I notice his huge smile matches mine.

And then, we smash into a tree.

CHAPTER 15

John

She's finally stopped crying, I think. God, I hope so because the ache in my chest over watching her go to pieces made it hard to breathe. When Meg cried when she was young, I usually sat down and cried with her.

We made a quick pit-stop at a Walmart for some duct tape for my bumper, and then I dragged her to the flea market she'd been looking forward to, hoping it'd turn her frown upside down. I even nabbed a few things for Boggs while she shopped— some old sails and a large, bleached-out piece of beach wood I'll use for something but have no idea what. But the two estate sales after that were a bust. One house was empty; one closed early, which Francesca said was a big no-no according to some friend of hers named Maureen. So, I googled around a bit and found another sale that hadn't been on her list.

Two stragglers let the screen door slam, happily hauling a cedar chest off the porch.

"Seventy-five percent off," the woman with a bandana around her head says.

"Tools aren't worth a booger in a bear's nose," the man holding the other side of the cedar chest offers.

Francesca runs to them, her face mostly free of the redness from crying now. "You're about to lose a treasure!" she says, scooping fabric that was dragging behind them up and stuffing it in the chest.

"Thanks, dear, those are all hand embroidered tablecloths from the twenties."

"Nice find."

"Good luck in there," she nods a bit sympathetically.

Francesca and I step in unison up wooden treads onto a sun porch. I eye a few garden gnomes because Meg loves them, but they're all chipped. "She didn't seem too hopeful for you."

"Last day of a sale is always hit or miss. This is when you really gotta look close. Hunt for the sparkle in the dirt."

I shake my head, but she's smiling again. She really loves this, and if it's taken her mind off our fender-bender, I'm all for it. She profusely apologized while crying a river and I'm glad she seems to be getting over it. I have.

"So, what are we looking for?" I clap and rub the palms of my hands together. Trying to be a good sport as promised, I'd hang out with her at the dentist if it meant we got to spend more time together.

"Anything." She bats her eyelashes at me—just a little. I don't care if it's because she's feeling guilty. I'll take what I can get.

"I'll need you to narrow it down a bit. You've got to have some sort of plan, right? Or system?" We step inside a spindled screen door with peeling paint. It slams behind us with a *smack!*

The Flea was like an adult carnival. People pull carts with all their found treasures while sipping on spiked Arnold Palmers and munching on kettle corn. This house, on the other hand, looks haunted and vaguely Western. There's fringe hanging in the windows.

"Seventy-five off," a woman in a navy mechanics jumpsuit says. She taps a pixie stick into her mouth, one of the old paper kinds. I tell myself she's not my grandma, and it's not my place to worry about her health.

We both nod our hellos, but she doesn't look up from her crossword.

Maroon walls are warped with age, and industrial shelves that I assume were installed specifically for the sale are packed with crap.

"Okay, so here's how I work when I'm shopping in a house and not an open-air market: I scan for certain colors I like first. What's your favorite color?"

I follow her down a row of knick-knacks, my eyes glued to her tan thighs and tiny shorts. I couldn't care less about the crap on the tables, but I'm really trying. "Green."

"Wow, most people are torn between two, or at least have to think about it for a minute." She turns to me and almost bumps into my chest. I'm tailing her too close.

"I know what I like, always have."

"Okay, Mr. Confidence," she chokes on her words. Good. She should be prepared for what's coming. I'm just getting started. "Keep your eyes peeled for green. What sorts of *things* do you like? Art on walls? Unique furniture? Do you need dishes? I love the old sails you got at the Flea."

The sails have splashes of red, yellow, and navy, and while I've got no idea how to decorate, I thought they'd look nice hung on a few of the larger white walls in the bar area. I'll think of her every time I look at them—bright, unique.

"I don't need anything. I live pretty trim."

"No? You can't say no to everything—"

There's no point in holding back. She'll figure this out sooner or later if she hasn't already. "Currently, I live in a tent."

"Yeah, why is that?" Her tone is soft, but she quirks a brow, treading lightly.

I shrug. Doling out the details is harder than I thought it'd be.

"Can I ask," she uses the same words I used to ask her difficult questions, hazel eyes darting around my face with curiosity, "why you've got a mansion in your name that rock stars would covet, but you don't live in it? Is it too soon? Too painful?"

It's about time I come clean with her about what really happened between Ricky and me. It's a shock she hasn't found out from one of the busy-bodies around town. But I can't. Because I'm still burning mad at the man, and even if Winter was right, I'm stupid mad at *him* for making me work over it all in my head again, second-guessing, questioning. I'd put it to bed. Made my choice and moved on...

"The last time I saw him, spoke to him, was a fight. It was pretty intense." That's the truth, at least.

"I'm sorry," she says. "Do you want to talk about it?"

No, is the answer, but before I can stop myself, I hear my own voice saying, "It was stupid. Money."

"Oh." I can tell she's confused, and for some reason, even though I'm not quite telling her the whole truth, I still want her to understand. "He asked me for money for the bar. It was going under. The house, too. I said no."

"But the bar is—"

"The bar is mine now because he signed it over to me. He was going bankrupt—was going to lose everything. When I said no, he pitched a fit in the middle of Main Street. Said I was dead to him. Then he gave them both to me, out of spite, I think. Wanted to prove to the town he was the good guy, and I was in the wrong for not backing up a family member."

"Did he say all that, exactly?" She's put her hand on my shoulder, and I hear her words, softened by her touch and the fact she actually seems to care.

"No, not in so many words, but I know Ricky, and he doesn't do anything for anyone other than himself. After that, I poured everything I've got into Boggs."

"And the remodel was a fresh start?" She gets points for not pressing. I feel my heart crack open, and it shocks the hell out of me.

"The remodel..." I trail off, unable to get the words out. To tell her how pissed I was that my absentee father decided he needed me in his life just in time to ask for a bailout. All he wanted was the money. He didn't want me.

I can't say all that, so I change the subject. "I drink coffee, and I only have one mug. Guess I could use two?" I offer, hoping we can get back to the shopping.

"Only one mug!" she repeats, giving me the space I need. "We can do better than that. I happen to be a connoisseur of glassware."

"Then I've got the right girl," I say. She turns toward me, holding a mug featuring a kitten in a basket licking its paw that says, *I need coffee right meow.*

I shake my head.

"I'm getting it for Cat, then. She'll love it," she says, delighted —over a cat mug.

"You're so cute, and thoughtful. If your sister seriously likes cheesy mugs." I let my hand glide over her hair and wrap my arm around her shoulders.

She pulls away after a moment, but her cheeks flush. Heat builds between us in this tiny, rundown house that smells like cheese.

"You're cute too, JB," she says playfully.

"I'm trying to charm you," I press, deciding to lead blindly with the truth.

"I've picked up on that." Light sparks in her gray eyes.

"Is it working?"

"Maybe," she answers, letting her hand drag across items on the table. "This is fun. I like doing this with you."

"I'm glad you let me come along."

The slow, brick-by-brick, intentional deconstruction of the friendship pact I'm attempting seems to be working, as unpracticed as I am. Sneaky, maybe. But necessary. I want to win this girl over.

Then what?

We scan the shelves for mugs but come up shockingly empty-handed.

"You know, there's a big flea market in Clover in the fall. Actually, there's one in Novel, too. They have them at the same time. It's a competition, but I think both sides realize it draws a bigger crowd having two. So really, everybody wins. Maybe there'll be some good mugs there."

"Oh, ye of little faith," she says as we head down a creaky hallway covered in horse-print wallpaper and taupe trim. "But fall is a great season to Flea."

"So, you'll come back?" My question hangs in the air with much more weight than a mere answer can settle.

"What's up with the town rivalry anyways?" she asks, effectively changing the subject of distance between us and what we're going to do about it when I inevitably miss her after she leaves.

For now, I let it drop. "Long story—" Abruptly, we halt in front of old-fashioned saloon-style louvered doors. "No way," I say when I get an eyeful of honey wood hanging on hinges. It seriously looks like a cowboy might blow through them at any minute, spurs jingling, looking for a whiskey or a brawl. "There is nothing in there I want. I guarantee it."

"I'll admit, this is my first saloon door experience. See, if this was my sale, I'd remove these doors. Easy, here and here." She points to rusty hinges. "They can be replaced after the sale if the owner wants, and it would make customers less likely to judge. Make lowball offers, that sort of thing."

"Like thinking it's full of seventies crap."

"Exactly."

"But so far, all we've seen is seventies crap."

"We don't know that yet. The perfect coffee mug could be waiting for you in there. This is the fun part." She playfully hits me on the bicep, finding ways to touch me. "Lots of times, people will try to hide good stuff in unexpected places so they can come back for it on markdown day."

"Get outta town. They have to come back for a mug on markdown day?" The meow mug was only fifty cents.

"The thrill is unbeatable."

"I'd beg to differ."

She scoffs at me, but those cheeks turn pinker. My eyes meet hers in a gilded mirror in the cramped hall, and suddenly, I'm desperate to kiss her.

"Francesca," I hear myself murmur before I can stop it. Stepping close and leaning over her.

Is she still determined we stay friends? I was drawn to her the night we met, but this feeling is different. It's escalated quickly because of all the details I've compiled about her, like her sugar addiction that makes me want to cook her warm meals, her love of junk sales, and her pension for taking leaps of faith into frigid lakes. Her truly horrible driving. All my new favorite things...

She pushes through the doors before I can talk myself into making a move, and I jump half out of my skin when she whoops, "You're not going to believe this!"

"What?" I ready myself for anything and push through the doors. I come up short behind her. "Oh, I can't wait to tell the guys."

The room is encased with floor-to-ceiling mirrors. The walls, doors, and even half the ceiling over the bed are mirrored. She's reflected everywhere.

"I've seen mirrored rooms like this, but only in Vegas."

"My thoughts, exactly."

"This is supposed to be a historic town founded by the Amish. Seems like this couple liked things a little spicier." I plop onto the bed and look up at her.

"Seriously?" She laughs at the intentional bedroom eyes I'm giving her.

I raise a brow. "Come on, play the part?"

"No way I'm sitting on that bed with you!" I track her movement in all the mirrors until she disappears into a small bathroom.

"Found it!" she yells.

"What?" I ask, staring at fat tassels hanging off the corners of the canopy bed.

She pops out of the doorway and says, "Catch!" before disappearing again.

Barely, I catch a coffee mug before it smashes into the wall. "Francesca!"

She laughs from the other room. "You're a baseball man, I figured you could take it."

Looking down, I turn the mug over and read, *save a cowboy, ride a trucker.*

"Absolutely not," I yell to her, chuckling but placing it gently on the nightstand. "But I'll probably give it to Jack for Christmas!"

"Perfect!" she hollers back. "The bathrooms are hands down the scariest place in any estate sale, by the way. I'm really taking one for the team right now."

"Why go in there at all?" I laugh. "Let's get out of here and go someplace nice. I'll take you anywhere. A mall? A designer furniture store? There's probably a whittler on a corner in this town—"

"A whittler?" She pops her head out to squint at me, then disappears again.

"Someone who whittles wood," I clarify. "We could commission a table or something."

"And miss the thrill of the hunt? No way, JB! No guts, no glory."

"Why are you enjoying this so much?" I ask, still laughing at her antics and kicking back on the bed, trying not to think about germs. Outdoors, dirt, sticks, worms, no problem. But other people's funk kind of gives me the creeps.

"Because it's fun," she yells, running back into the room and shocking the shit out of me as she leaps onto the bed.

"What's on your head?" I demand.

Pushing up on her knees, she leans over me, delighted with herself. She's wearing a jet-black wig, long and stick straight, with fringy bangs hanging in her eyes.

"I bet they called this one Wanda. I found stacks and stacks of cowboy romance in the closet. Where's your phone?"

"Take it off! I like your normal hair!" I grab her hips, and she squeals when I dig my thumbs in to test if it's a ticklish spot. It is.

"No way. I'm Wanda now!"

A growl escapes me, and she gasps.

"On second thought, I like you, Wanda. Why don't you keep your sights set right here? Also, why do you want my phone?"

"I left mine in the truck."

She wiggles her hands in a gimmie sign, and I sigh, pulling my phone from my back pocket. I'd be lying if I said I didn't want a photo of her, any photo, even one of her as Wanda. "Okay, one photo, Wanda. Then I want my sunshine back."

"But why, sugar lips? When you haven't given Wanda a chance." She bats her lashes at me, this time exaggerated, and I don't think she realizes it looks more like she's got something stuck in their eye.

Extending my arm long and leaning in, I make sure we're both in frame and snap a pic. Both of us look into the screen with silly expressions and ridiculous smiles.

Time stills. Her chest rapidly rises and falls as we stare at the picture.

"We look really happy," she says but contradicts her words by rolling to the edge of the bed, putting space between us.

I shove my phone back in my pocket. *Shit.*

I can't let her tense up now, can't let her run. "Stay in the moment, Wanda." Lunging across the bed, I grab her and pull her under me, pinning her arms with determination. "Stay with me.... Please don't pull away..." When she squirms I add, "I'm serious. My heart can't take it."

Her eyes go wide. "John—"

181

I can't believe what I've said, and while I meant it, it's hard to sit in it. Does she have any idea what she's doing to me?

My forearms brace against the mattress. "I hope whoever owned that thing doesn't miss it too much." She takes pity on me. "Oh, I bet Rita and Rick are living it up with new wigs in new digs."

"Nice," I say as she lets me move in closer, her thighs widening underneath me and making room. I'll play along with anything if it means I can get this close. "They still dress up to go to dinner every night, though," I breathe. Letting my nose and then the faintest touch of my lips trace the edge of her jaw, then her ear. She smells delicious, like strawberries and sugar, totally edible. "Don't you think she misses this one?" I ask, twirling a piece of black hair between my fingers.

The shocking black only helps to frame those big gray eyes. They remind me of the sky reflected in the lake at dusk—bright but mixed with a muted tone from the mountains.

"You think they're still in love?" she breathes, her arms wrapping around me.

Her heart is beating rapidly. I watch her pulse jumping in her neck.

"That's a big question for a fictional, elderly couple who had a kinky sex life."

"Let's pretend they are, though. I'm just... It's hard to believe these days that people make it. All the way to the end..."

I stare into her eyes, trying to come up with something she'll want to hear. Torn about what I'm doing and if I should be doing it. She wants friendship from me, and though I've decided to secretly woo her, is that the right move? The right thing for her?

Something about Rita and Rick being soulmates makes my blood run cold. Surely, she deserves someone better than me. I'm not sure I'm soulmate material.

She shifts her hips and makes me forget my trail of thought entirely. "They met in a local bar. Rita asked Rick to dance. Rick had never seen something so beautiful. It was love at first sight. When Rita kissed Rick—"

Does she want this? She's telling our story, only this version seems to have a much different outcome.

"You got it all wrong. Rita didn't kiss Rick. It wasn't their time, not how the story was meant to be. It happened right here when they decided to take a chance on each other, with each other. Rick kissed Rita on this very bed." I lean in, still settling my weight between her thighs where I ache to be. Our stomachs and chests press together. "And Rita let him because she was ready. Because she knew in her heart that Rick would never, ever hurt her."

My breath dusts her lips. They part, waiting for me—

"It's five o'clock. We're closing." The woman running the sale appears in the doorway in all her jumpsuit glory, hands on her hips.

We startle like teenagers, scrambling off the bed in a tangle of limbs and shooting to our feet.

I bump my knee on the nightstand and almost crumble from the jolt of pain. Damn body beat to hell from the game. Jack's Christmas present rolls off and hits the ground but thankfully doesn't break. Thank God. He's gonna hate it.

"You break it, you buy it," the woman grumbles. She's exchanged the candy that was in her hand when we walked in with a motorized fan, whirling and blowing on her face.

Francesca grabs the cup off the floor and clutches it tight to her chest. "We're buying it!"

The *thump, thump, thump* of my heart racing pounds in my ears. "Sorry, ma'am," I finally manage. Why am I so nervous? Like her mother walked in and caught me trying to make a move.

"You gonna buy *that*, too?" She asks, pointing at Francesca's head. There's a thousand *hers* surrounding us in the mirrors, poking a finger at us.

Francesca blows plastic bangs from her eyes. "Oh, yes. Just making sure it fits."

I drop both my hands on her shoulders in a show of solidarity and let my heartbeat pound into her back. She's shaking with laughter but holding it in. The tone of her voice is so strained. I wonder how she's keeping a straight face.

It's tough, but I paint a crooked, fake smile on my face, too. "It fits. I like it."

"All right then, you two finish up. I've got a Lean Cuisine and a Bud with my name on it."

"Will do. Thanks for your time," I offer.

We fall into a puddle of fits and laughter on the floor after she leaves.

Francesca pulls another mug from under a pillow. She must have covertly hidden it when she accosted me in the wig. "Found you a good one after all. See, JB, it was all worth it."

I look at the mug in my hands, white and chip-less. Hunter-green letters in scrolling script proclaim *happily ever after is a choice*.

CHAPTER 16

Fran

The sign for Dave's B&B appears, and I make a quick turn onto a winding gravel drive.

"Do you realize how well you're doing?" Despite me crashing his truck into a tree, he's still cheering me on. "It's like you were born to drive this truck."

I punctuate the overstatement of the century by grinding his gears. He grimaces but, to his credit, says nothing. I know this truck means the world to him, and the fact he's let me torture it one down-shift at a time is telling—he's a damn nice guy.

That blind faith, and the fact that he didn't act for a second like I was too emotional when I cried a waterpark's worth of tears over almost knocking his front bumper clean off, is making me want to master this damn thing just as much.

He's got a small cardboard box in his lap with our breakables from the sale we were almost kicked out of: his new *Happily Ever After* mug an apology gift from me, Jack's Christmas present, the mug I plan to add to Cat's "cat cup" collection, my new wig, and a pristine garden gnome for Meg we found under the bed in that terrifying room of mirrors. An estate sale bounty, if I do say so myself.

And we almost kissed.

I glance at him, responding to an email from Gus on his phone, his pouty lips calling my name. As much as I'd like to give in to what I think he wants, find out for myself how soft those pillow lips are, I'm not sure. His history is love 'em and leave 'em. My goal for this entire summer is self-preservation, refresh, start over. These two things do not go hand in hand. Getting involved with him when he's turning over a new leaf and looking for serious is not a guarantee while working for him nonetheless. And even if I've seen nothing from him but kindness and stability, I'm not looking for serious. Serious equals pain in the end.

It's a bad idea, I think again, shaking my head as he chews on his bottom lip in thought. I try focusing on shifting his truck down this summer-sun-streaked, deserted road. *Third, no fourth,* I pull down on the stick.

It's a welcome distraction—from his mouth. Those lips that almost devoured mine. I could tell he was about to—*stop, Frannie*! What's the cliché in this scenario? Think about baseball, *but not John playing baseball*, because I'm human. I've stared at photos of him in his uniform, and John in uniform takes *yummy* to the next level.

Okay, I can do this. Boring old baseball, old man baseball. I've certainly had my fill of humdrum stats and collectibles research this week. Boatloads of Ricky Boggs stuff. John's gloves the size of my face taking up bin after bin. His long, hard, wooden bats... *Shit! Focus, Fran!*

"So, the plan is to meet Dave around the back of the B&B near a warehouse he keeps." I swallow hard, speaking out loud for my own distraction while watching the road like a hawk—as if we're not the only car on it. "We'll unload the collection. He's got an agent that will verify the most valuable signatures, and then we'll be off with a check."

My last turn pings on GPS. I'm headed for a rather worn-looking B&B with half-dead flowers on the porch and a smattering of cars parked off to the side. A nondescript, pre-fab barn painted green is a few yards from the property with a large hand-painted sign.

I throw the car into park.

"Are you absolutely, positively certain you don't want to keep anything?" I hold up a hand to stop him from speaking. "I know you said 'don't ask again,' but I wouldn't be doing my job if I didn't confirm one last time. This is it. After we sign, all this stuff is gone."

John turns to me and puts a hand on my forearm. "Francesca. I appreciate what you're trying to do, really, I do, but I need to tell you something about Ricky."

"Shit, I'm sorry. You've been very clear about your intentions. My family always says I get too attached to stuff and feel too hard in general—"

"It's not that—"

"I shouldn't have brought it up. I'll drop it for good this time, okay?"

His eyes detonate and blur from their normal tinge of sad hazel to full-on stormy gray.

"Okay. But just so you know, you don't feel too hard. I am," he seems to push himself through what he says next, "extremely torn up about all this. I feel hard, too. Maybe your ex didn't understand that about you but, I do."

I gulp. He sees me, and I see him. He does feel as hard as I do, and it's a relief to know I'm not alone. "Thank you," is all I manage before hopping out of the car to escape the weight and meaning of our combined emotions. Something I'm not ready to face.

A bearded old man steps onto the sagging porch. Dave is very, very old and matches his inn's decor down to the worn eighties loafers he's wearing. Not what you'd expect an eBay mogul to look like, but that's e-commerce for you. I'm lucky I've got Mr. Muscles in tow because I don't want to unload this trailer by myself, and Dave couldn't lift a baby bird.

We're directed to unload onto wide wooden tables in the warehouse. Collectibles line shelves around the room, neat and orderly, and a packing station with all sorts of postal necessities is situated beside industrial barn doors. Box fans whirl overhead, and a few desks are scattered about, leading me to believe Dave does have employees, and he's not a supernatural grandpa entrepreneur.

"Alright, kids," he says with twinkling eyes. "This looks good. I'll have the signatures authorized in the morning and cut ya the check."

Wait... "In the morning?"

"Indeedy. My man Carlos had a family emergency, or rather, I think he forgot his daughter's piano recital was this evening and caught all hell from his wife. He won't be able to come and validate the collection until bright and early. But I'll give ya a good breakfast and a discount on my last room to make up for it."

"We need to be getting back tonight." I gesture between John and myself.

An overnight with a beautiful man is the last thing I need if I'm trying not to fall for him. I'm already at the edge of the cliff as it is. He's kind, thoughtful, cooks, looks great in gray sweatpants covered in woods, and seems to be trying to flirt with me at every opportunity he gets. I mean, it's a miracle I've held out this long.

"Can you put it in the mail? Or, use a money transfer app?"

"And get stuck with all this crap if it doesn't verify? No, siree."

I gesture incredulously to John. "This is Ricky Boggs's son. It'll verify."

Dave eyes John. "Why ya selling, son? Did you come by this stuff legally?"

That's an odd question. He's his son. His dad passed, and it makes sense his things would go to John legally. I would've thought that was obvious.

"It's fine," John says, more to me than Dave. He's actively avoiding Dave's eyes. "We can stay. It's fine."

"Your sister specifically said to be home before ten!"

"My sister said to call so she wouldn't worry. I'll call."

That's going to be an interesting call. Something tells me Meg has only voiced her opinions about the two of us not getting involved to me.

"Don't forget now," Dave does a turn in the warehouse like the ringmaster of a traveling show, "I'm buying quite a load off ya. Won't find another dealer willing to take all the pieces you got here. Yes, you got some biggies, and that's why I made an offer on the lot. But it'll take you a while to find another in a drivable distance. You'll have to ship, and that'll cost. I run a niche business, ya know."

Spoken like a true geriatric hustler. No wonder this guy came recommended by my dad—you'd think he was running a mafia ring the way he takes favors in exchange for vintage pinball parts.

I eye John sideways, trying to read how he's taking this, then shrug because he's clearly fine with it. "You drive a hard bargain, Dave." I shake his hand because I know when I'm beaten, give him my sweetest smile, and say as brightly as I can, "Slumber party it is!"

Wait, am I excited about this?

"There's a hot spring around back of the B&B called Spell-bound. It's a short hike that's easy enough. Nice spot to relax and enjoy the evening." He nods with light in his eyes, deal done, and motions for us to follow him up to the main house on foot, completely oblivious that he's thrust John and me into a precarious situation.

Sharing a room.

On our way up a slight hill with a mountain view of the setting sun, John drops an arm around my shoulders and whispers in my ear, "Dave's place looks kinda weird, right? I like the idea of a swim in a hot spring tonight, though."

John and me...in a hot spring. *How exactly is that a good idea?*

I change tack and answer his first question. "It does look kinda weird, but you're the one who lives in two town—towns. Clover and Novel, the way they operate, is seriously weird. What is up with sharing a town hall?"

He starts to rapidly gesture as if he's also telling the story via mime. "Happened a hundred years ago, so the story goes."

He leans in closer, and it makes me shiver. I'm onto him, the little touches and close proximity. Smelling my hair! He's trying to wear me down. It's working. And tonight, I'll have nowhere to hide.

"Winter's people built the castle in the bay, and two guys got the same idea to build towns around the royal home—"

"Who are the guys?" I interject.

"Not important. Just some guys that were settling, or hunting, or around at the time, I guess. They both figured tourists would want to visit the royal summer house, and that if blue bloods wanted to live there half the year, then it was good enough for them, too."

"Still doesn't explain how two towns ended up on top of each other and sharing a town hall."

"It started as a barn raising—that's how the structure was originally built one winter, during an old-time festival our towns still celebrate every fall. It's the kickoff to the holiday season, the Fire Festival. They say all the men pitched in to frame the city hall in a day because the season was turning. It was freezing for the settlers, especially up in the mountains. They used wood purchased by Clover but encroached and built the damn thing right on the state line without knowing it. And instead of figuring out who owned the building, in the end, they split it—the two towns cropping up around it over the next hundred years."

"That's nuts! Who would actually think that was a good resolution?"

"I'm telling everyone you said that. You're gonna get blackballed by Patty, who swears she's related to the settlers, which means no more coffee and pastry for you."

"You wouldn't," I say, trying not to inhale his scent as we follow Dave slowly up the drive to the Inn. "Why don't the towns combine and call it a day?"

"You have no idea the can of worms you're digging into."

"Jar of worms. It's *jar* of worms you're opening—"

"No, it's can—"

"No, it's—"

"You see," he covers my mouth completely with his hand and pulls me in close, his eyes full of laughter. We're nose to nose. "You see how quickly a little misunderstanding can escalate."

"Let me go!" I shriek, laughter spilling from between his fingers. My voice is muffled by his hand, but he does. I punch him in the bicep while he pulls me back into him by my shoulders.

He's manhandling me now, and I'm letting him. Not only that, I like it.

He leans in close again with laughter in his eyes, this time letting his mouth linger over the shell of my ear as he speaks, "Behave. You wanted to know the story."

My gasp is audible, and so is his chuckle as he pulls back again to a respectable distance.

"Anyway," he continues, grinning because he knows exactly what he's doing to me with all the innocent touching, "the rivalry roots run deep. For years, they've competed over everything."

"Mm-hm," is all I manage, trying to regulate my breathing so he doesn't notice my chest heaving from his attention. "So, about tonight..." Words fail me. I have absolutely no idea what to say about tonight. I'm staying in a room with him. Dave made it clear there was only one free.

Francesca, you are so doomed! You can hardly walk a straight line with him next to you.

"Let's tell Dave we have dinner plans, so we're not stuck here with strangers," he says, tugging lightly on chunks of hair that have fallen from the back of my messy bun.

When my gaze meets his, it's clear I adore his hands on me, his words, and his breath on my ear. I can feel the heat in my own cheeks.

"It's like, six-thirty. You don't want to mingle and see what sort of people hang out at Dave's?"

"Do you?"

There's no more ignoring the way he makes me feel. I want him to keep touching me, want him to keep brushing my hair and playfully putting his hands all over me. Suddenly, I'm desperate for it, and the intensity shocks me.

I stop to take in the mountain view, gravel crunching under my sneakers, trying to settle my racing heart. The stairs to Dave's are moments away. We're really doing this.

"Pretty, isn't it?" he says, jolting me from my thoughts. And when I turn to agree, he's staring right at me.

"How about we grab some snacks and take them up to the hot spring with us?"

My jaw drops. "You're offering me a snack dinner?"

"If it means missing whatever social gathering Dave plans for his guests and spending time alone with you, yes, Francesca. I'll have a snack dinner with you."

"We hand out baskets with some meats, some cheeses, a bottle of house wine," Dave says without turning, halfway up steps to his front door. "Packed up in a pretty little basket, perfect for toting up to Spellbound springs. Take a dip. Make a wish. Of course, I'd love to have you at happy hour if that suits better."

Both of us tense and look at each other. *Does he have the hearing of a hawk? Has he been listening this whole time?*

"I like the old man's idea," he whispers, leaning in again— presumably so Dave can't hear—but it makes me shiver all the same. "You up for it?"

"Okay."

"Yeah?" His stubble scrapes lightly against my cheek as we quietly conspire against an old man.

Dave leads us through the main house, babbling about stocking some toiletries in all his rooms so we'll have a way to brush our teeth and grab a shower.

John's all smiling eyes and head nods as he follows Dave up a tight set of stairs, pulling me along with him.

CHAPTER 17

Fran

"Here's the rub, kids—" Dave says as he stands outside our room for the night. "The only room I hadn't booked by the time Carlos told me he'd be a day late and a dollar short was the kid's room."

"You have a dedicated kid's room here?" I ask.

"For the families that come through in Airstreams and need a night away from the kiddos, if ya know what I mean." White eyebrows dance. "But the thing is, all my adult rooms are taken. I got the Tulip room, the Valentine room, the Camelot room— that's the ladies' favorite," he says very seriously to me.

"Of course," I reply. "I had no idea that this was such a romantic destination."

"Yep." He takes a deep breath, clearly ready to reminisce. "My wife Wendy—rest her soul—and I came up with the whole thing 'bout fifty years ago. We loved runnin' this place together, working with interesting people passing through, hearing stories about what brought them to our little slice of heaven. It was her idea to have a kid's room so that parents with kids old enough to bunk on their own could get the time they need. Any-who, that's all I got tonight."

The front of the door is adorned with a large, shiny red apple. I can't fathom what's inside. An orchard theme? Seven beds made for dwarves?

But it's not an orchard or a boatload of off-brand mouse propaganda that meets our eyes when the door falls open.

John busts out laughing and pulls his hat off before willingly walking in. He's a good sport because I'm still processing and balk in the doorway. I don't believe it. I have to turn away for a minute, rub my eyes, then turn back—trying to keep it respectful for our man Dave here.

Finally, I blurt, "It's a school-themed room?"

There is nothing remotely romantic about this room. Bubbles of laughter release in my throat. We are totally safe in this room. The most un-romantic, un-sexual, non-canoodling-inducing room I've ever seen.

Dave's got a mischievous look in his eye as he hands me the key. "Sleep tight. Don't forget, hot breakfast when the birds start chirping, and Carlos will be here at seven a.m. sharp."

He shuffles away, whistling a tune.

I take one step inside—one. "We can't stay here."

"It's almost 7." John roams around, touching the chalkboard, gazing at the three vintage desks lined up in a row. Toward the back of the room is one large bed that at least looks cozy with a fluffy patchwork quilt and tiny cots stacked neatly next to it. "No time to find another place, and I'm starving."

"I'm sure I can find something else," I try again. "Something with *two normal* rooms."

"This is high season. Summer months are booked solid way in advance." He's fiddling with props on a teacher's desk, sitting catty-corner next to the chalkboard. It's like the set of a 90s TV show with an on-suite bed, a mini fridge, and a nightlight.

"Why do you look so happy about this?"

"I'm not," he protests, his ears turning red against the sides of his white hat.

"You are," I say, the smile on my face growing. I've caught him in something. I just don't understand what. But then it hits me. "Ohmigod—"

"Okay, before you get too worked up, my teacher in eighth grade was really, really, really attractive. Everyone thought so—"

"John!" I protest, belly laughing, my hand over my heart because I don't know what to do with this information. "That's... That's—"

"Totally normal for a kid going through puberty. Now drop it." He tries to use his commanding voice. He's figured out I like it, I think. But he cracks a smile and looks away sheepishly, too, knowing full well he's busted. "Let's go get some snacks that we can toss in the basket for the hot spring in case Dave's sausage isn't appetizing."

The word *snacks* has my attention, and the mention of Dave's sausage does kinda make me want to hurl. Also, any reason to get out of this room, especially if I'm destined to sleep here, is one I'm going to take.

Like two burglars in rewind, we tiptoe down creaky stairs, careful we don't bump into anyone, but the main foyer is still empty. We pick up a basket of welcome goodies near the unmanned front desk, make our way down the porch stairs, and head back to the truck.

"Anything good in the basket?" he asks as we both slam our doors.

"Um..." I hold up a bag of homemade jerky, no label, no indication as to what sort of meat has been used to make said jerky.

"No way." He chuckles darkly, taking the steering wheel in one hand and driving us down the road. His other arm drapes naturally over the console, his fingertips dust my thigh. "Snacks have never been so appealing."

My eyebrows wiggle because I've finally gotten my way with him, even though it was his suggestion. "You're going to love gas station pizza. It gets a bad rap, but—"

"I said I'd get *you* a snack dinner. But I'm not eating junk foo—"

I reach over and drop my hand clumsily over his mouth to hush him. "That's the deal, JB," I say, trying but failing to hold in my excitement while way too close to his face. He can't do anything about it because now both his hands are dutifully at ten and two, his eyes on the road. "If you want me to sleep like a kid, I get to eat like a kid with no complaining out of you. *And* I want you to partake in the bounty I provide for us."

After a good, long look, I drop my hand, now warm from his skin, and allow him to speak. "You drive a hard bargain, sunshine."

"Anything I want?"

"Anything you want, except Dave's mystery meat."

"It might be good..." I toss the basket in the back. "Anything else you'll do?"

He eyes me sharply as he throws his truck into park in front of a brightly lit gas station.

"Have you not realized that you're the one holding the reins in this *friendship*?" he says, his voice husky and low as he maintains my gaze. "Anything. Name it."

I believe him. "Deal," I breathe.

The sun has dropped. His truck, our little cocoon, is surrounded by twilight, which only makes the soda fountain and rows of candy inside the convenience store stand out more.

"But let me remind you, you promised me a swim in the hot springs." There's determination in his voice, and again, there's a strong tug in my chest. All the butterflies and sparks we had the first time we met feel amplified now because I know him. I know how he works, how kind he is, how much he loves his friends, how he takes care of his sister...

"Have you called Meg?"

"I will right now."

I don't want to hang around for that conversation. "Okay, I'm going in."

He reaches across me, letting his forearm graze my chest, and pops the door open. "If you're not back in twenty, I'll come after you."

Inside the store, I box up my feelings so that my hands stop shaking from his touch and beeline for the slushy machine so I can properly drown them. I get one cherry and one blue coconut. The least I can do is let him choose his flavor. Then it's row after row of candy and assorted crunchy, crackery, crispy, chippy sort of snacks. Eighty-three dollars and change later, I'm back in the car and slam the door.

His face is green. *Oh no, Meg must be pissed.*

"Watching you in there, I kept thinking, that's it. She's done. That has to be the last thing she's getting. No way she can find more junk food... And then you did. Every time. How much did you spend? Wait, no, I don't want to know."

I hold up the two slushies, letting them teeter-totter in my hand as if on weighted scales. "What's it gonna be? Anything blue or red in the junk food category is a classic choice. You can't go wrong."

He grimaces. "Blue. No, wait, red." I hand him the slush, and he takes a long pull, eyeing me the entire time. "You know red number nine will literally kill you," he says, mouth full of slush but keeps drinking. The way he sucks on the straw...

There's no hiding it. I'm sure my face, my hot cheeks, and my heavy breathing are betraying me because my resolution is absolutely crumbling like a cookie.

Sheer, unabashed, carnal want pools inside me and rockets through my bloodstream fast as a sugar rush.

"Good?" I choke out my words, lightheaded and tingly all over. Blue coconut ice burns the back of my throat.

"Fucking delicious, Francesca." His eyes detonate and hold mine. When I think I'll combust, he turns and fires up the truck, the grumble of the engine a welcome distraction from the pounding of my heart in my ears.

He drives us back to Dave's, and like kids, we sneak through the foyer where we hear the faint chatter of a crowd forming in the living room. John picks up a bag of Twizzlers that falls out of the basket I've piled high with junk. But we make it all the way to our kindergarten room and slam the door behind us, panting.

"I don't know what would be worse," he says. "Having to make small talk with Dave and a room full of strangers or eating all the junk you're about to force on me."

"Dave. Dave would definitely be worse." He clocks each step I take to the bathroom door.

"Hey, can I wear your shirt?" I gesture down at my shorts and T-shirt. I'd rather wear his shirt like a dress into the hot spring and rinse it out afterward instead of my entire outfit. I am not getting down to my underwear with this man. Friendship rule or not, there'd be no coming back from that.

"Oh, uh, yeah, sure." He blinks.

"You're gonna have to give it to me then. And there's only one robe." I peek into the bathroom and see the single white terry robe on a hook. It's big enough for John, but I'm claiming that puppy. "That's mine too. You can grab one on our way out, okay?"

"Sure, sure." He gazes at me, possibly realizing we'll be coming back to this room at some point. Sleeping here together in the dark.

"John," I prompt, unable to hide my delight. Usually, I'm the one getting all dazed and confused when we're alone together.

"Right." He tugs at the back of his T-shirt with one hand, swiftly pulling it off, and before I can catch my jaw, my mouth drops open at the sight of him. "Hurry up," is all he says, chuckling the shirt at me.

It hits me square in my gob-smacked face.

"Stop looking at me like that, sunshine, or I'm going to beg you to let me do something about it."

I accidentally slam the door to the bathroom with a loud

smack, listening to his chuckle as I collapse against it, sliding all the way to the penny-tile floor.

He's beautiful. There's no other way to describe it. The muscles that cover his body look hard-earned, real, bought, and paid for with an athlete's training schedule. He has no right to be as handsome as he is, and as good, honest, thoughtful, patient....

I'm in so much trouble.

Pulling myself up purely because I want another eyeful of him, I do my thing, lying to myself all the way and pretending that I don't relish the feeling of slipping his shirt over my skin. As if my pulling the neckline up to my nose and huffing it isn't a giant warning sign that I'm in too deep. I've caught feelings for the man. That's clear in the way I'm physically reacting to the sight of him —the smell of him.

Francesca, why? Why do my emotions turn on like a faucet when I'm trying so hard not to let them? Except, in this case, I know exactly why. It's because John is, well, John. He's special. I can't un-see who he is.

"Ready," I say, all too cheerily for the tumultuous waves rocking around in my chest.

We head down the hall, me in my Dave's Motel robe, him in jeans and showing off an insane amount of bronze skin.

Sure enough, Dave's hosting cocktail hour with an odd assortment of guests as we sneak toward the front door. The odds are against us with every step we take. There's probably no way we're going to get away with sneaking out a second time.

"Are you going to ask him for a robe?" I whisper after an absurdly loud creek in the ancient wood floor.

"Not worth it. Keep moving," John says, rushing and hustling me toward the door, his pecs jumping with every step.

"What about towels?"

"We'll use *your* robe."

"Then what am I going to have to get back here in?" I forcefully whisper, looking back at him.

"Francesca, you'll be fine. Keep moving. I'm not—"

A woman spots us from an arched doorway leading to the living room and moves with commendable speed in very tight jeans and a blouse covered in a nautical print. "Well, frost my cookies! What on God's green earth do we have here?" She's inches from John already, her cheeks turning the color of bright red apples. I mean, you don't see a half-naked man, cut the way John is from years of sports and clearly keeping up on his health, in the entry of a B&B every day, so I can't fault her.

A man in a Dave's motel hoodie, cargo shorts, and hiking boots that look like they've never seen a dirt road comes up short next to her. "Son, you're missing a shirt."

"Oh, Gerald, leave him be." She bats the man away before popping a piece of jerky in her mouth. "This is the highlight of my trip!"

Gerald harrumphs and moves back to the living room, where the rest of the company has filled the archway to stare and sip from Dave's B&B plastic cups.

"Sorry, no more robes," Dave says. "We're at capacity. But here." He moves to a front desk near the door and pulls two towels from behind. "These'll help you get back without having the cops called for indecent exposure. You two be good now."

As we make our way out the front door on whiny hinges, I can't help but realize we've got everything we need—but I'm afraid I conveniently forgot to pack the friendship pact in our basket of goodies.

CHAPTER 18

John

The hike around the back of the property into the tall trees and surrounding mountainside is surprisingly short. A gravel trail turns to dirt as it winds up a hill through dense evergreens. Every hundred feet or so, weathered signs cheer us on to our destination: *Spellbound Hot Springs.*

"Doing alright up there?" I ask. I love watching her truck up this hill in a robe that splits up to her hip with every step she takes. The longest legs I've ever seen disappear under *my T-shirt.*

"I'm great. I love it out here!" she says, throwing her hands up to the sky. She is sugar with a touch of spice, and it's a miracle I didn't devour her in the room when she looked at me as if I were just as edible.

I tote our basket filled with both the mystery jerky and Francesca's haul from the gas station. "I'm considering Dave's jerky. You have no idea how many chemicals are in the stuff you bought. At least with Dave's, I could be eating rabbit, but I won't be eating phosphates I can't pronounce and chemically engineered colors that'll kill me."

It's fun to tease her, and it gives me something to think about other than how much I want her under me, in my arms, in my mouth. Everywhere. I want her everywhere.

"We're getting a workout right now," she pants. "This is the healthy part *for you*. The treats are for me. You get something you want; I get something I want. It's called compromise, JB." She trips on a branch, and I reach out, grabbing her around the waist easily with one arm to steady her. Her back comes flush to my front, and we both freeze.

If I kiss her now, it'll crush me if it means nothing. *Shit, when did that happen?* I've always been averse to being a number on her list, but these feelings are new and damn powerful, so I release her.

She's too much to look at as we make the final push up the mountain. When I hike, I'm normally shirtless and in the same boots I'm wearing now, on my own or with the guys. But Francesca is struggling to stay on her feet in her B&B robe and sneakers. Hair is wrapped into a knot on the top of her head with smiley faces staring at me from her hair tie.

I gulp and hope it's not audible. "We're here."

"What?" She turns back around and reads a sign she must have missed, giving a short history about the springs. "*Ohmygosh*," she gushes as we wrap around some brush and rocks and find the clearing for the spring. "This is—"

"Gorgeous."

She turns and looks at me. From the pink in her cheeks, she knows damn well I'm only speaking about one view in front of me.

"Spellbound hot springs," she turns back, reading another plaque near a small bench. "'Known for mystical healing properties. Total emersion in Spellbound Springs has been said to change the destinies of those willing to ask for what they truly want. Legend has it, to alter your destiny, simply submerge your body completely and count to ten under the water. Think only of what you most truly want, and it shall be so.'"

Of course, my eyes are still trained on her. She looks back and reads my expression, her gaze firing up and going stormy.

What I truly want, I think she knows. "Do you believe in destiny?"

Her cheeks turn downright crimson, and I know it's not just from our hike. Good. I'm about done playing games. If there was a perfect place to rip off the label of our ridiculous friendship pact, it would be in a mystical hot spring promising a fated destiny.

"Honestly, I've never thought about it."

"Never? What about soulmates? Do you believe in soul-mates?" I watch her chest rapidly rise and fall. Maybe she's afraid of her answer. Maybe she's afraid of mine. "Well, do you, Francesca Bloomfield?"

"Not anymore." Her voice trails off, and before my heart totally plummets for ridiculous reasons, she adds, "But I might be warming back up to the idea. Do you believe in soulmates, Johnathon Boggs?"

"Now, I do." I nod firmly. "And I'm up for total submersion if you are." I nod to the sign.

She shifts nervously on her feet, pulling the robe tight around her. "Should we go all the way? All the way under, I mean?" she quickly clarifies.

"I'm game," I say, depositing the basket and towels I carried next to the edge.

Decision made, she unceremoniously shrugs out of her robe. The way she looks in my shirt, the way the neckline exposes her collarbone, is paralyzing.

"Me too." she smiles. "You're sure you don't mind?" She gestures at herself, my shirt.

"Go ahead." I wave her off. *Make my fucking day.*

I can tell she's only got panties on underneath. Her breasts sway under the shirt, and I have to bite down hard on my lip to keep from staring.

I clear my throat while I watch her hesitate, assessing how she's going to get in. "Having second thoughts?"

Before I can go to help her, she laughs good-naturedly. "Nope." She makes quick work of slipping into the spring, sitting on her butt first and pushing in with zero hesitation.

I think I know her well enough to see her dropping her guard. I was raised right. I know that no means *no*. Hell, I've schooled Meg in self-defense myself. Still, I can see her softening toward me, and it gives me serious hope that she's changed her mind about us.

She's waist-deep now, waiting for me to take off my jeans. "Coming in?"

"You sure?"

"We're officially off the clock, John. I wouldn't practically skinny dip with a client if... Let's just say half my job is done with the collectibles. The sale at the house will be done soon, too. And right now, I want it to be me and you."

When I don't move, utterly shocked by her words, she prompts, "You okay with that?"

"Yup." Shit, I'm a one-word wonder. Get ahold of yourself, Boggs. You've been around beautiful women. You've been around beautiful women more naked than this. Younger than this and older. What makes her any different?

I'm getting to know her. That's what. And I want her...for much more than a night.

"It's warm. Perfect." She sinks in, the water moving around her chest as I step out of my jeans.

She turns away, then peeks over her shoulder. "Boxers?"

I shrug. "Yeah?"

"I thought you'd be the kind to wear boxer briefs. I mean, I wasn't thinking about the kind of underwear you'd wear, but in this moment..."

I run my hands down my boxers covered in embroidered base-balls, admittedly a cliché that I can't deny I loved when I opened them on Christmas morning with Meg last year. Yes, it's odd that my sister gave me underwear and that they're my absolute favorite. I don't care.

A groan escapes me as I step down rough-cut stone stairs into the hot spring. I've always responded to heat treatment. I used to sit in tubs after games before the masseuse would work on my shoulder. When it was my turn to ice, I bitched the whole time, but my body was grateful.

The evening temperature is dropping. Trees sway in a slight breeze. The forest around us seems to exhale in the moonlight. One of those moments washes over me unbidden, those moments where everything feels suddenly perfect, and you're afraid to even question it because you know it won't last long anyway.

"I need to do this more often." I rub at my right shoulder. Both of them are blown, but I've always got tension in the right. "Tell me what's going on in that head of yours," I ask because I'm curious, and I need to do something with my mouth besides tossing all the rules and kissing the shit out of her.

"I'm having so much fun with you on this random little road trip, and I never want it to end."

Stupidly, my heart soars from knowing I'm not alone in this attraction. "Well, that calls for a classic road trip vacation game. Tell me the rose and the thorn from your day?"

This is a game I often play with Meg. What is the high and the low of your day? The guys even play every once in a while when we're all feeling melancholy around a fire or while holding fishing poles.

"Like the good and the bad," she confirms, surprising me by sliding around me and coming to stand between my legs. I sit on my hands to keep from grabbing her behind the knees and running my fingers up her thighs.

This is new...

"You already know," she says, swishing water between us with her hands. This way and that. It's mesmerizing. "Everything you saw me lust over today is my rose." She quirks her brow as if trying to communicate more, and I'm getting her meaning loud and clear. Coffee cups weren't the only thing on her mind today.

Same, baby.

"I talked you out of a lot of stuff. Kinda wish I wouldn't have." I cave and allow my fingertips to pull at the hem of my shirt, grazing her thighs.

"No, I'm grateful you did!" she says with enthusiasm. "And driving your truck, minus the literal fender bender that I swear I'll pay for." I wave her off as she continues. She can have my truck for all I care. "That was a win."

My wet T-shirt is hugging her like a second skin, and I have to pull at my boxers, praying they don't reveal exactly how turned on I am right now. I'm going to have a hard time concealing it when I get out of here as it is.

"Willow and Cat are always holding me back. If it were up to me, our apartment would be full of teacups and side tables. Curio cabinets and secretaries—"

"Secretaries?"

She takes a deep breath and one step closer through the water. I widen my knees, creating space for her between my legs. I don't know what game we're playing, but I'm pretty sure, at this point, I'm the only one who stands to get hurt.

"Old-fashioned desks that need a sand and polish and a cheery corner in a room for someone to write letters. Don't get me started on the artwork, bed frames, and woven baskets made from real fibers that you can't find anymore. Oh! Turkish rugs! Do you know what those cost new?"

"Next time we go to a Flea, you can fill my truck bed with whatever you want. I'll be your personal mule."

"But where would I put it all?" She laughs, looking up at the sky. The snow-capped mountain tops sparkle in the moonlight behind her as if sprinkled with glitter. "It would never fit in our pink row house..." She chews her lip, seriously contemplating where she's going to stash her next haul.

Bouncing on her toes, damn near in my lap, she waits for an answer to her very real question. She might actually take me up on this offer. I wonder if she realizes how much that delights me.

"You can store whatever you want in the basement of Boggs. Hell, you can fill up Ricky's house if you want. I've been cleaning out the hunting cabin on the property, thinking I might try sleeping there for a while when we get back. It could use a makeover."

"Really?" She's delighted. "That's the second phase of my business plan. I want to offer a renovation service along with the estate sale. Lots of times, the old homes need updating after they're cleared out before they can be sold. Oh my gosh. I'd get to play with pretty glass tile and marble samples all day. Can you imagine?"

I laugh at her. "It's easy to make you happy. I wish you'd been around when I started renovating Boggs. But I kinda enjoyed it, too. Might even do a flip myself if I find the right project."

We eye each other. The words, *we could do a flip together*, are on the tip of my tongue, and she knows it.

"You've done a great job with Boggs. I love the choices you made. You'd be good at flipping." She can't stop herself. She's amped up over a reno project.

"A couple of chipped coffee mugs, an old table or two, a dusty basement to store them in, and look at you, happy as a clam. I know what you like now," I say, trying for serious. "Tell me something you absolutely hate. Give me a thorn."

"My parents bickering."

"You've mentioned that." I nod, looking into her eyes. "You think the vow renewal will change things?"

She shrugs, then lets herself sink deep into the water. She's almost kneeling in front of me, and I can't help myself, I grasp the backs of her thighs and pull her slowly to straddle over me.

It's a surprise that she lets me. We're moving toward something tonight, and I desperately need her to tell me what.

I look up at her through water-tipped lashes, but I don't dare drag a hand over my face to clear them. I don't want to miss this for a second. She gives me all her weight, sinking down on top of me, causing my entire body to overheat despite the dropping temperature around us.

"I can't help but wonder if they have to renew it, was it solid to start with?" she asks. "I don't think they'd ever really leave each other, but..." She shrugs her shoulders. "The truth is, I don't know if I believe in forever anymore."

Fuck. What am I supposed to say to that? My heart is pounding so hard right now it could very well explode in my chest.

The number that asshole did on her makes me want to break bats as if I was back in the dugout and warring with a ref. There are different kinds of abusive relationships. Your fists aren't the only way to hurt someone. Words can do catastrophic damage. I know that from my relationship with Ricky.

"I don't know about forever." I let my hands wrap around her strong shoulders, dragging my thumbs across her collarbones. "But I do know about right here, right now," I say, offering her the only thing I have—my honesty. "I know there's no place I'd rather be. I know that I've never felt this way about anyone, *the pull I feel toward you*, and if I'd never met you, if our destinies hadn't been on a collision course one way or another... I might have gone forever without this feeling. I ache to be near you. It's the damn-dest thing." I laugh a little while forcing myself to be strong and meet her eyes as I pour my heart out, hoping it'll ease her mind a little.

The water between us is hot, the air around us cold, and in this obscure clearing marked as spellbound, I know for a fact that I'm on the tip of a knife. That I'm about to slide down the sharp edge, come what may, because I've got to get to the heart of it. Whatever this pull, this magnetic attraction I have to this woman is on the outside, it's growing tenfold on the inside.

And while I can control lust, I cannot control the burning need to soothe her—to erase her fears, to make her feel safe. To make her happy.

CHAPTER 19

John

I grasp her face between my hands and pull her close, close enough to kiss.

"John—" Her breath hits my cheeks, and my body responds instantly. With her knees on either side of me, I know she feels every inch of how much I want her, and I'll be damned if I try to hide it any longer.

I stay frozen, warring with myself over how much I'm willing to risk and search her eyes with mine. "Francesca, what's happening between us?"

There's a long sigh before she pulls from my grasp and puts a small amount of space between us. Not a lot, but enough. "I don't know."

My eyes are drawn to the uneven waterline in her T-shirt, lighter on the top, dark and wet on the bottom. "I get that you need to take things slow, but I'm starting to feel like I'll be the one getting my heart stomped on if you walk away—without even giving this a chance."

She presses her lips together while chews on my words. "If this becomes something...or if it doesn't, and then I'm left gluing myself back together—that was the point of the list, not to get attached Not to get hurt."

"I'll make you another deal—"

"Okay."

"No more friendship only—"

"But—" She bites her bottom lip, it's only the second time I've seen her do that and it guts me. If she thinks I'm pulling away, she's got another thing coming.

"Let me finish, sunshine," I gently press my thumb to her soft mouth, pulling her lip free, "I won't kiss you until you tell me you're done with your list. Until you believe me when I say, I'm interested in you. I want you, Francesca." To get her to the next step and to protect myself, it has to be that way. I want her to know how serious I am about her.

"But, it almost hurts how much I want you," she whispers through my fingers.

"Trust me, I got you." She's testing my ability to keep myself together when she says things like that, but I press my forehead against hers, willing her to believe me because I mean what I say. "When I do kiss you, baby," I drag a fingertip down the bridge of her nose and cup her cheeks in my hands, "it'll be because I plan on kissing you for a good long while. And you'll know, you'll believe, I only want you."

She holds my gaze, gulps, but doesn't offer a reply. So, I keep going, making this up as I go but following my heart nonetheless. "I'm afraid of getting hurt too."

"My heart is ready. It's my head that's not." Her eyes well with tears.

"I understand. I hate it, but I understand."

"But I can't seem to keep away from you," she says, mustering a small laugh.

"I want to touch you more than I've ever wanted anything in my entire life. You have to know that." I look into her eyes and push wisps of hair behind her ears with wet fingers. "Is that what you want?"

Maybe she's not ready for kissing because that means something more for both of us. But I need to please her, to take care of her.

She closes the tiny gap between us, exhaling as she presses her cheek to mine. Her lips graze the shell of my ear with another sigh as she wraps her arms around my neck. "You feel so good, I know I want to feel more of you. More of this." To my shock, she rocks against my hardening dick.

She is going to kill me with wanting but in the best way.

"We can do this," I whisper in her ear. "Baby steps, that's all this is. I want you to get comfortable with me, keep doing that." I flex just a little beneath her to give her encouragement. "I want to put my hands on you. Is that okay?"

She squeezes her thighs, but I flex into her again to keep us as closely linked as possible. "I think so," she answers.

"Francesca, you are everything I've ever wanted. You should know that. And that's why I'm going to take what I can get, okay? Please, don't break me." I flex my hips again and she meets my thrust with a gasp against my forehead, riding my length through my trunks. She wraps her hands around my neck, her thumbs press into me possessively.

"I won't. If you don't break me."

"I won't, I swear it." My hands trail the slope of her waist until I reach her ass and take her in both hands. "Fuck, *you* feel so good." It's embarrassing that merely having her on my lap is affecting me like this, but it's been a while. She continues to rock against me with light mewls and more pressure, seeking a release. "If you keep doing that, you're gonna make me—"

"Me too," she rasps. "It's been a while."

I chuckle, we are two pent-up peas in a pod. "Same, but I want this to be about you." I roll my hips again, relishing the feeling of the water moving between us and her weight pressing right where I need it.

"Why does this feel so right?" she asks. "Like your body and mine fit each other. Every little touch, your skin on mine, makes my heart race. It's not normal." She looks up at me, a flash of hesitation. "That was too much—"

"Nothing, no one, has ever felt so right to me. It sounds insane, but I knew the moment I saw you. I knew you fit me like a lost puzzle piece."

She grins at my confession and drops her mouth to my neck, kissing, sucking, and rolling her tongue against my skin like she wants to leave a mark.

I'm fine with that.

"I'm getting so confused," she whispers. "We don't want the same things. Why is this so hard to stop?" she asks as if reading from some rule book she's written to go along with her list.

"Sure, we do."

She quirks her head at me. I punch my hips into her, harder this time while dragging my hands down her front, the tight buds of her nipples pebbles under my hands reminding us both how close we are to the edge for each other, yet we still have most of our clothes on. And still, I haven't had my mouth on her—not in the places I'm dying for.

"And what's that?" she challenges, her body responding achingly slow now, moving up and down against the stiff tent in my trunks.

"Not to hurt anymore." I run my fingers up her thighs, squeezing at the top and letting my thumbs dip down toward her center.

It's as if I've been waiting for something solid to ground me since I left baseball, since Ricky left me, and here she is, in my arms. A girl I can talk to, who's driven, thoughtful, bright and sunny and wants me for more than the jersey on my back and a night to brag about after. Fucking finally.

I pull the hem of my shirt to the side while my other hand slides lower, slowly searching for that one singular spot between her thighs. She widens her knees, welcoming me, and my breath hitches in my throat.

I rub the flat part of my knuckle over thin cotton when I find it, and she gasps, looking up to the stars above us.

"Shhh," I tell her. She fidgets, chewing her lip. "Look at me, Francesca."

Her eyes squeeze tight as if I've stung her, the opposite of what I'm trying to do. "Can't," she squeaks.

I decide not to push her but ask firmly, "What do you want?"

"To forget," she answers immediately, and whether she's responding to my tone or my touch, it doesn't matter. She's all breathy and fighting something I can't see. But she's more than willing to keep going. She wants this. I think she needs this.

I switch to my thumb to press more directly through the thin cotton covering her, getting a better feel of her while desperately trying to keep myself in check. "What do you need to forget, baby? Whatever it is, let me take it for you. All of it."

"I want to forget him."

Him. That's not what I was hoping for, but I guess it works just as well. I can do that for her, be that for her. Yes, it scares the shit out of me. That she'll only need me for a short time—to play a specific part in her life, and then she'll easily be done with me.

Am I willing to trade her happiness for mine?

"I'll fucking erase him, Francesca. Say the words." *You want me. Say it.*

"Yes—John." The pressure I'm applying with my thumb is hitting the right spot, and she grinds harder against me, riding my hand like she was made for me. She moans and I return the sentiment with a gasp of my own and then a possessive grunt.

I've been so good, and I've waited as long as I can. I need my mouth on her. It feels luxurious to drag my lips across the wet fabric clinging to her chest and sink my teeth as gently as I can into the round of her breast. *Finally.*

She whimpers, and it fucking unravels me. "Please—John."

That's it. I tug the thin cotton to the side and push two fingers into her, my thumb finding that tight bud again, but now we're skin to skin. Nothing between my hands and her heat. Water moves around us, lapping at the edges of the spring as she meets my hand in perfect sync, as if it was me inside her and not just my fingers.

"Oh god—" her core clenches tight, her body throbbing, and it feels unbelievable.

"Say my name, baby." I drop my lips again to her chest, covered in my T-shirt but wet like second skin, and take her nipple in my mouth, sucking hard through the fabric.

"J-John, yes, please," she rasps. Her head falls back while her body constricts around my fingers, slick with her desire even in the water, her breath coming high and light.

"Is this what you want? I want to give you everything you need, baby." My only goal is to please her. She's got me tied up in knots.

She takes a shuddering breath, and then another. "Don't stop." Her forehead drops to my shoulder, lightly biting me back at the nape of my neck and moaning through her teeth.

I'll take that as a yes. She's close, I can feel it, sense it.

She rides my hand a little longer, throbbing around my fingers until I hear her breath hitch. She arches her back, head pressed up to the stars and comes with gasping breaths one after another.

She looks down at me and it's everything I can do to hold back and not let my mouth crash into hers. Her full lips are pink in the moonlight, open and panting, but I'm not a total masochist. I need so much more before I let that happen. I want her to be mine, no lists, no one else.

This is enough, making her feel good and claiming her pleasure as my own is enough, for now.

Shivers roll through her body as I wrap her up in my arms. "That was a good first run, but I promise next time..." I don't finish my thought because she freezes.

I watch it happen in real-time, her mind and all her worries and fears coming back to her as the hazy, happy after glow melts away.

"Wait." She pulls from me, and I let her go, all the way to the other side of the hot spring.

Her gaze drills into me, the weight of her stare like the weight of an anchor tied around my heart, dragging me deeper and deeper until I hit rock bottom. If I could move mountains for her, I would. And I think she wants that. She's warming to me. She does want more, but she's fucking terrified.

To my surprise, so am I.

"I'm afraid we're going to hurt each other," she says.

"That's the opposite of what I want," I rasp, my voice low and full of gravel.

She shakes her head as if confused and pushes all the pretty hair that's fallen from her bun away from her face. "This is all happening so fast. It's hard for me to trust it, trust you."

"What can I do?" I'm at a loss. I can't help the way we met, that we're both emotionally raw, that for better or worse, our story is unfolding the way it is.

Her eyes light up. She's working through her demons, and right now, I think she's winning. "Let's do what the sign says."

"I was thinking of doing about ten other things, but the sign?" I reach for my hat, but it's not there. I left it back in the room. Instead, I run my hand through my hair, using the water to keep it back so I can see her clearly. It's gotten to the deep, dark part of the night out here in the woods—my favorite. We're out a good distance from town, and the stars shine as if I'd turned on twinkle lights to glow above her.

"Total submersion—if we want to change our destiny, let's

217

sink deep into this water and wish for what we really want. You and me. Together."

"I want you, Francesca. I know you're scared. I am, too." There, I said it plainly.

"Maybe I need a little magic on my side. Maybe I need..." She looks around as if she'll find the words she wants in the trees. "I made a promise to myself. I swore I wouldn't put another man in a position to hurt me ever again. Or at least until I was fifty."

That makes me laugh but I hold her gaze, working out in my mind how I want to respond. She takes a deep, shaky breath and adds, "Thank you, by the way. For not telling me I'm taking it too hard, too seriously, too personally. I came here to start fresh, and I have, and you've been there the whole time."

"You're welcome," I say, still holding her gaze as she blinks but doesn't look away. "I see you, Francesca Bloomfield, and I want you for everything you are. I want the smiles as much as the tears. The way you bounce on your toes when you're happy but also for the way your face falls, lips turned down when you're sad and trying not to show it."

"Okay, then." She swims back toward me, and I meet her half-way, grasping her hips because my hands already miss her body. The cicadas and crickets cheer us on in whatever hair-brained scheme this is. I already decided I'll do anything to make her happy. "Ready?"

She's breathing harder now, the recent memory of what we just did crashing over both of us, I think. Is this what it's going to feel like every time I touch her from now on? An aching reminder? A devastating need?

"Yup." I nod.

We hold eye contact, and then I add, "How do we do this?"

"We count to three at the same time, and then we go under."

"Was that on the sign?"

"I'm improvising. We stay under for a count of ten." Both our chests are heaving with anticipation. "One, two, three."

I watch her until the very last second. Her eyes close, mine do too, and we sink.

My heart is in my ears as I reach out to her through the murky water. Beat by beat, I get close enough to grasp her shoulders. Bubbles ascend around us as we hold our breath, counting to ten. If we're in sync, we've just reached seven.

Eight.

Nine.

On ten, I pull her to me and kiss her.

CHAPTER 20
Fran

I t didn't count. His lips barely brushed mine, still, it was perfect. I keep telling myself that as we hike back to Dave's under the stars. It's good I've got the robe; it's freezing out here.

A plethora of goosebumps span John's broad chest, with two flimsy towels draped over his shoulders.

"You want the robe?" It wouldn't be a bad thing to put my senses on ice after everything that happened in the hot spring.

"I'm fine." He smiles at me.

We're pretty quiet as we make our way back to the house in the dark. He grasps my elbow as I stumble. My balance and eyesight are not helped by the darkened sky and the loss of starlight as we wind down a trail with a canopy of tall pine trees.

Dave's is locked up tight, but he's left a sign on the door telling us he hid a key. Why he didn't leave the door open is beyond me, but John fishes the key off the top of the molding, his chest brushing up against my shoulder. He leans in, pinning me in the entrance, but I slip under his arm the second the lock clicks, and the door falls open.

We creep up the stairs, and once in the room, I run for the bathroom so I can freak out in peace. The door closes with a snick.

Francesca, what are you doing?

Maybe I need a list to calm my nerves, *ten things Francesca should be focusing on right now instead of*—no. Maybe, maybe, no more lists. Maybe now it's time to live in the moment, to listen to what the man outside this door is saying to me. To take a chance...with him.

"Everything okay?" he asks.

Is everything okay? I don't think it is.

The school room has creaky floorboards, and the bathroom door cuts at an angle ending halfway down the wall. This room probably used to be attic space, and it's got shoddy insulation to prove it. The room itself is frigid. When I finally come out of the bathroom after a speedy rinse, he's still shivering.

"I tried not to use all the hot water. Your shirt's in there, I washed it out and hung it up to dry for tomorrow."

"I'll, uh, just be a minute," he says, moving around me and into the bathroom.

Wrapped up in my fuzzy Dave's robe and nothing else, I jump into bed, pulling the soft quilt up to my nose.

By the time he comes out in a pair of gym shorts he found stashed in the back of his truck, the room has gone dark except for a small unicorn night light plugged into an outlet near the door.

"How's it freezing in the middle of summer here?" I ask, not looking away and taking in every inch of him. After what he did in the hot spring, my body feels branded by him. My mind is whispering, *Mine, mine, mine.*

"We're up higher in the mountains. Want me to turn that out?" He nods toward the blue glow.

"No, I need to be able to see if I have to get up and p—I mean, use the bathroom." *How am I going to sleep the whole night next to him?* I'm so nervous I suddenly can't utter the word *pee* in his presence.

He stalks toward the bed, and I sink down deeper. "Scoot," he says, looming over the edge like a giant made of shoulders and muscle.

I do, and he tucks in next to me, his trim waist and all his abs disappearing under the blanket. It's for the best, but I inwardly mourn the loss.

After our mystical plunge, the not-kisses underwater, and all the destiny talk, I'm supremely aware my heart has knit itself dangerously close to his. Now, as we face each other with both our heads resting on fluffy down pillows, holding each other's gaze, having a conversation with our eyes in the silence, I wonder if this could be real.

What a pair we'd make. Both a little broken. Both a little brave.

"It's been a long day," I finally murmur as my eyes roam his face, taking in every detail cut in the moonlight from a large picture window mixed with blue unicorn glow.

"It has," he agrees, eyes searching mine. "How'd we get here? I'll be honest. I wasn't prepared for the situation we're in."

I've gotten used to the clarity he speaks with, and I push my hand out from beneath the heavy quilt to trace the cleft in his strong chin. "There's no place I'd rather be. Maybe it's fate we ended up here?"

"You believe in fate, now?"

"Maybe," I say, releasing a slow breath. It settles me, I feel good, I feel calm and happy next to him.

"I think fate is only fate if you want it to be, sunshine." His arm wraps around me under the blankets and pulls me close. "Happily ever after is a choice," he smirks, quoting the mug I bought him today.

"I couldn't agree more, JB."

"Sleep tight," he drops a kiss on my forehead, and I sigh, exhaustion taking over. I nuzzle into his chest, breathing deep and letting my eyes flutter closed. Happy, content, and safe in his arms. We drift off.

Something wakes me. Thoughts of water, but this time not cold. Everything is so, so hot. When I open my eyes, his face is so close to mine. Long lashes dust his cheeks. His arm is dropped over me, the source of all the warmth.

It takes me a moment to orient my thoughts, both wanting and not wanting to pull myself back to consciousness. Somehow, I manage to hover in that in-between, gray area of awake and not.

I burrow in closer, dropping my lips to his neck. He's so comfy. I wrap my arms around him, and he murmurs something I don't quite hear, pushing a strong thigh between my legs.

I gasp as my traitorous hips react and slot into his.

His eyes crack open and flutter closed again. "You okay?"

"Don't wake up," I say, hoping he won't remember this in the morning.

"Too late." His arms wrap around me, grasping my ass in both hands. "Mmmm," he murmurs, low and gruff.

This is only a snuggle. Sharing body heat in this fucking freezing room. Subconsciously, I knew this was where we'd end up, wrapped around each other. Harmless cuddling.

Fate is only fate if you want it to be. *After all, you can't win if you don't play the game, right?*

His arms tighten around me. "Go back to sleep, baby."

"Don't want to." The words are out of my mouth before I can

even lie to myself and act as if I want to hold them back. I'm done holding back.

His eyes open, and he nudges my nose with his, slowly inhaling as he presses his lips into my hair, my neck. He's asking me so much in this quiet moment. We both know it.

"John..." It's a sigh, tinged with surprise, as he begins dropping kisses as he goes.

"I'm here." I pull his mouth to mine, but he stops me. "I can't. Call it stubborn." His fingers trail reverently down the curve of my cheek. "That's not a word that offends me."

"John," I whine at him. Sure, I probably deserve this because I'm the one with the list and all the rules, but—I am desperate for his mouth on mine. Kissing is so intimate, at least, it is when you want it to be. I want that with him.

I want him to be mine.

"You know how to get what you want from me. Say the word."

"I was dreaming you were kissing me, and I was kissing you back—" I whisper, doing my best to coax him into giving me what I need.

"That's a good dream."

"Then do it."

He shakes his head, ruffling the pillow we share, pressed forehead to forehead. "You're not the only one who feels as if they've been thrown away, Francesca."

What? Is that how he feels? "I would never throw you away."

"What do you need? From me?" He's been so giving, so understanding, and now it's my turn. I want to make him happy.

"I just want you." I shrug in the dark.

"Then delete it," he whispers in my ear, his lips lightly biting my lobe. "And I'm yours."

"What?"

"Delete the list off your phone. I want to know this means something to you."

"Are you serious?" Fine. He wants proof that I'm done with

the list? That he's not another number? *Sweet, sensitive, stubborn man.*

I can do that for him, and what's more, I want to do it. I'm ready to be rid of the list. It's the last piece of my ex that I didn't realize I'd been holding on to.

"Okay, I will," I promise. "First thing tomorrow." My phone is on the floor and turned off, and I want him now.

I brush my lips against his, but he pulls away from me. A whine of exasperation falls from my mouth.

"Frustrated, baby?"

"This is a side of you I haven't seen yet," I huff in mock annoyance. "My phone is on the floor. It's off!"

"I'm only being demanding because it's you. This is new for me, too," he says reverently.

Leaning off the bed and fumbling on the floor, I pop my head back up and look at him. "Hold on." I raise a finger in the dark.

"Holding." He puts both his hands behind his head.

"You're enjoying this way too much," I say, tapping at my phone. I blow a piece of hair from my cheek, and it falls right back into place.

My phone illuminates in my hand. "Finally!" I exclaim, pecking at the keys with my thumbs to unlock it and pull up Notes. "Here, see?" I show him what I'm doing. "Aaaand, gone." A note numbered one through four with a gaping hole after number five disappears from the screen. "There, you happy?"

"Very."

"Now..." I look down at him, propped up a bit on the pillow and headboard, waiting for me.

"Now..." he repeats, eyes on fire but not making a move. He's not fooling me, though. His chest is pumping as if he's hiking uphill. He's just as nervous, excited, and frustrated as I am.

I crawl slowly up his front. With both hands on his chest, I brace myself against him as I drag one knee over his hips, sinking down and drinking in the most delicious look on his face.

He raises a hand and pulls my hair from its bun, securing my *happy face* scrunchie on his wrist. "Mine."

Yeah, back at you, JB.

Both of us work to draw breath, heavy and fast.

As I lean in, my robe gaping at my hips and even more at my chest, my hair falling around us, his hands remain pinned at his side.

"Thank you," I say, dropping light kisses across his face: cheeks, eyelids, and chin.

"For what?"

I pull back to smile at him, blue light shimmering over his features. "For waiting for me."

He grips my hips. "I've never wanted something so bad. You're worth the wait, Francesca."

While I lean over him, bracketing his head with my hands, our mouths meet light and tentative. I pull back, both of us panting while he hardens beneath me, and then I drop my lips to his again. His hands stay still but he kisses my top lip, then tugs at my bottom with his teeth before his lips part, and I lick lightly into his mouth. It's everything. Our mouths seal together, slow, sweet, until I gasp for air.

The kiss turns demanding in a flash like a firecracker that's used up all its wick. I couldn't control it if I tried. The reaction to us finally connecting is visceral, and I feel it glide down my body with heat and want. His hands are everywhere now, no longer holding back, dragging his fingers through my hair and his palms down my back. I'm very, very greedy with him, moaning into his mouth as our breath mingles and our lips take.

He breaks the kiss, biting at my neck and licking and sucking at the spot in apology.

But I grab his chin and take his mouth back, so much more demanding than I've ever been. But I feel comfortable with him. He knows me, and I know him.

How much of him can I have?

He meets the question in my eyes with his own demand, biting my bottom lip and tugging. "I could do this forever," he breathes, and then devours me again, our tongues moving against each other as if we were made to do this. Every lick, every hot press feels meant to be.

"Me too," I breathe, laughing at how raspy my voice is as I move against him where my knees are spread, and we're trying to connect. I desperately want him closer.

He releases a growl, and I stop for a moment, pushing up on his strong chest to give him an appreciative look.

He grins back. "I think I've been holding that in since I smelled your strawberry lips and sunscreen skin on the dance floor the night we met," he admits.

"Baby," I whisper, cocking my head in total wonder. "You growl." I didn't think that was a thing real men did. And it's fucking delightful. I had no idea *kissing* could be this exciting and effortless.

Done for. I'm done for. There will never be a day in my life when I don't remember this exact moment in time.

"Only for you," he responds.

"I want you," I gush because I need him to hear me say it.

"I'm yours."

Those words undo me, my chest aches with a feeling of safety. Trust. Because I believe him.

My hands find his, and I bring them up to cup my face. He rolls his hips in response, pressing his hard length between my legs, doing his best to please me through shorts while we both know it's not enough.

"Baby," he pants, hoarse and gulping. "Do you want me to make you come?"

Oh my god. No one has ever asked me that question. *Ever.* "*Please.*"

"God, that word on your lips. What do you want, Francesca?"

"I want all of you. I want you inside me." I can tell that shocks him.

"I don't have a condom. I'm sorry, I—"

Greedy, I'm so greedy. I guide his fingers between my robe. "Will you touch me again? I want you so bad it hurts, John. I didn't know it could be like this. It's never been like this for me."

"Look at you," he whispers. "So beautiful."

I'm slick and wet, and he groans, thrusting up when he feels how much I want him. My hands move over his—not that he needs my help, I already know that from the hot spring—but it feels good directing him. I hum in reply as he pushes two fingers inside me, and I press the heel of his palm against the tight bud of nerves at my center.

"You make me feel so good." It's never been this good with anyone, this natural, this easy.

"You ride my hand like you were made to do this," he replies with a sweet twist to his words. "You were meant for me. I'm sure of it," he finishes, and my heart swells.

"Yes," I groan, moving on top of him to find the depth and friction I desperately need. "More of that. So close..."

"Baby, if you keep bouncing with your ass like that, I'm gonna finish before you do."

"Don't stop, don't stop," I pant.

Desperately, I pull the robe away and run his free hand up my naked body. "I want to feel you come with me," I say, reaching back and pushing his shorts down to grip his length behind me, the waistband pushed down on his hips from me riding him. He's everything, more than stretching the circumference of my fingers, and I work my hand up and down while he groans.

"Fuck, Francesca." He squeezes my breast, then drags the palm of his hand flat down the center of my chest, across my belly, my hips. It's as if he's claiming me, all of me. "You are more... I'm more turned on than I think I've ever been. With anyone. Ever." He thrusts into my hand, his hard length pressed against the back of my ass, and I feel how excited he is when he glides even easier using the moisture from his tip. "I feel like a teenager."

His hands are insatiable as he palms my breast again, gripping and rolling my nipple, going back and forth, showing equal attention to both. His other still working my core as if he were made to do it.

"Your hands feel so good, baby," I moan.

"You're a fucking dream," he responds, all breathy and needy.

We're close, each of us bringing the other to the breaking point. Me with my hands on him, and him with his hands on me.

And why shouldn't we fly together? Why shouldn't he be mine? Why can't I be his?

"John, *yes*," I yell, coming hard on his hand, my core throbbing.

He breaks, too, spilling all over my hand and between my thighs.

Both our bodies shake as I lean down over him, dropping my bare chest to his and soaking in his warmth. I gasp when he adds more pressure to my center, wringing the last bits of my orgasm from my body.

I can't believe we just did that.

Now I kinda want him to be number five... Forever.

CHAPTER 21

Fran

The ride home is mostly silent, both of us stuck in our heads, and I'm pretty sure we're thinking about the same thing....

It was easy to delete the list of mediocre kisses. It was not easy to tell my heart it was safe to take a chance—but it was worth it. I'll always think of him as number five, though, that gap on my list remaining open, and I think maybe always destined for him.

You're not the only one who's been used and then thrown away.

I'll never un-hear his words. It's hard to believe a beautiful man like him has felt unwanted. It's absolutely terrifying that someone like him, who has it all compared to many, can feel so small. Just like me. It makes my heart ache and also makes me desperately want to be the one to cherish him.

Could I possibly keep him?

Our friendship pact was the thinnest rouse in the history of men and women trying to pretend they didn't want to tear each other's clothes off. The pull was there from the second we locked eyes at Throwbacks, but now, it's considerably worse. John is sweet, quiet, and thoughtfully damaged in ways I want to explore with healing balm and bandages made of kisses.

Who could blame me for asking him to touch me in the dark last night? That was unavoidable. The dream had been so vivid, John coming toward me in the water and wrapping his arms around me. He kissed me so deeply I was suddenly drowning, desperate for air, and then I woke up. Hot and needy. There was no way I could wake in that state, with him next to me, and not demand he make it real.

I blame a long day filled with shopping, role play, a ton of sugar, even by my standards, and that uncanny hot spring.

The truck jostles over a crumbling curb as we pull up at Thistle and Burr. The parking lot is empty. That's odd. Only Heidi's blue hatchback is parked front and center. The place isn't big, but over the last two weeks, the parking lot has been full of family vans and Jeeps filled with college kids looking for a place to crash, that sort of thing. It's eerily quiet while the rest of the town bustles with summertime tourism.

My plan is to hop out, say a quick goodbye, and sneak in a much-needed nap. Then I'll plan for the sale next week and, let's be honest, work through my feelings for Jonathan Boggs. I'm not sure how much longer I can hold them off or if I have at all.

Heidi comes barreling out the door, a pair of cowboy boots on her feet, kicking up dirt on the sidewalk. She leaps into the air and slaps a high-five on the Thistle and Burr sign. It swings on rusty hinges while a grin splits her face. John's out first, and she's talking a mile a minute by the time I round the front of the truck to greet her.

"And I'm so glad you're finally back because—"

"Slow down, slow down," John says.

"Everything okay, Heidi?" I ask.

"Everything is *amazing*!" she screams so loudly that a flock of birds abruptly flees a nearby tree, making me jump. "I won the *lottery!*" She dances a jig in a neon bikini top and what look like old Clover High School track shorts.

"You're kidding," I stammer. This can't be right. "I thought you scratched the tickets I gave you?"

"I did, but it was a real bummer to lose, ya know?"

Well, yeah, I do know.

"How the hell?" John stammers, pulling at the brim of his hat.

"I bought another one, with a million-dollar jackpot," she gushes, eyes bright.

I struggle to find my words, trying to understand what she's telling us. "One? You bought another *one?*"

"First one I've ever bought in my whole life. But I needed a win, Frannie. It was a total whim, but it felt like the universe sent me to the gas station—"

"Which one?" John and I blurt at the same time.

"Right there." She points. "Dickies, on the corner."

"A one-pump gas station. Probably the last of its kind. Figures." John laughs, rubbing at his chin.

"And it's all because of you, Frannie! If it hadn't been for you, I never would have bought a ticket. *It wouldn't have crossed my mind* because what are the odds? Right?"

"Right." I shake my head and look at John. He only raises his shoulders as if to say *go figure.*

"If my sister didn't need the cash, I'd cut you in, I swear."

I hold my hands up. "Absolutely not. You don't owe me a thing, Heidi. You deserve it, and if your sister needs it, that's great."

"Will Lucy take it from you?" John asks.

"She's a prickly pear these days, but I'm hopeful and she's desperate."

"What are you going to do with the rest of the money?" John asks.

"Oh, I've been up all night thinking..."

"You've got plenty of time to figure it out, right? Has the gazette gotten wind of this yet?" He pulls his hat off his head, flips it around. A tic I've realized he has when he gets nervous or excited.

"I've been avoiding them at every turn. A few reporters skulked around already."

"I've got a finance guy who helped me when I got my first big checks. Want me to connect you two?" His eyes begin surveying the property around us, immediately going into business mode. "You'll want to have savings, of course. But think of everything you could do to this place... New roof, new rooms—"

"You were saying you wanted to buy energy-efficient washing machines," I offer, happy to contribute to the conversation and surprised I'm more on the inside than I thought.

I pull John's cap off his head and pop it on mine. He gives me a funny, lopsided smile but doesn't seem to care that I've commandeered his emotional support hat to keep the sun out of my eyes.

I also want to be close to him, to smell him and touch him, and it's making me act like a love-drunk teenager.

"Maybe you put in a pool in the back? Bet your guests would like that, an infinity one that blends right into the lake," I suggest, hands on my hips and getting big ideas.

"That would be perfect," John says, turning to me. "Yellow chairs and towels, play up the summertime vibes—"

"Are you guys kidding?" She looks at the pair of us as if we've grown horns. "I've already called the realtor. He's going to list it, and I was wondering if I could leave the keys with you, John? Would you mind? I can't leave them with Lucy. She still won't leave the cottage..."

He scratches his neck and contemplates his options, but I know he wants to help her. "Yeah, Heidi, sure. I can hold the keys for you."

"You're a saint. My cars loaded for a drive to see my old college roommate that I've been crushing on via socials. Gonna show up on her doorstep and tell her exactly how I feel. I've got a ticket to Amsterdam in case she pulverizes my heart with the heel of her Doc Marten."

"Amsterdam? Of all the places?" I ask.

"There's an annual glass bead festival I've always wanted to go to. And then I'm headed to Munich for Octoberfest. I'll bum around in between—"

"You're leaving for that long?" John looks truly stricken. "What's the town going to do without a Motel? I mean, I guess that's not your problem. I'm not saying let it stop you. But you know the lake committee is going to lose their minds over this."

"What is up with the lake committee?" I ask.

"There are rules on the lake, rules both Clover and Novel have to adhere to. The lake committee is kinda like our town elders," John says, stealing his hat back and putting it on backward.

"I take it people don't come and go around here very often? Other than the tourists?" I ask, rubbing his arm to console him. He loves these towns so much. He's so serious about it.

"Everyone's gone. The guests I had were all about to turn over, and when I offered to comp the stay to the ones who still had a day or two they happily took me up on the offer. Yesterday, my numbers were verified and accepted by the state lotto. You're my last key, Frannie. Leave it on the counter, would you?"

"What do you mean? Today?" I'm paid up another month, and even if she planned to comp my stay, I've got nowhere else to go.

"Stay as long as you want. I just won't be here, and John will have the key, if that's okay. Please?" She adds the *please* with the sweetest smile. This girl has clearly needed to get out of town for quite some time, and she's not taking no for an answer.

"I got you covered," John says easily, light dancing in his eyes. "Come on," he takes me by the hand, "let's get your stuff in my truck. You can stay—"

"I can't stay with you," I object. A night filled with multiple orgasms does not equal magically living together. Though the thought does make my heart flutter. I clearly can't be trusted around him. "You don't even live anywhere. You live in a tent!"

"That's a great idea," Heidi says, clasping her hands and blinking at me. "And that way, I don't have to teach you how to use the laundry. Or the industrial cleaning supplies." She shoves her hands in my face. "Does awful things to your nails even with gloves."

Cleaning doesn't bother me at all, but I get the feeling I'm the last detail she needs to sort out before she can officially hit the road with a free conscience.

"She'll be fine with me." John gives Heidi a one-armed hug. "You be safe out there."

"Thanks guys." She pops up on her toes and kisses John, then me, on our cheeks.

"I can't believe this," I say, stunned by it all, as he continues to pull me along.

Heidi's hatchback fires up. She's tapping on her steering wheel, then rolls down the passenger window to shout as she passes us, "You really changed my life, Frannie. I never would have bought a ticket, not if you'd hadn't given me a loser that made me think, maybe I could be a winner?" She laughs at herself, giddy, and why shouldn't she be? She won the freaking lottery after playing once! I've been playing my whole life. "Wherever I go from here has been completely altered because of you!"

We wave goodbye.

"I can't sleep in your tent," I say again as John drags me to my door, and I fish out my key. "It's not that I'm not up for camping, but I'm more of a one-night-only in the wilderness girl... Then I like hot water and a cozy bed."

"You're not staying in my tent. Well, maybe someday I'll get you in there. But one night only works just fine. I'll find you a cozy bed."

"I can stay here."

"By yourself? In a motel? That's a B-list horror movie in the making. No." He shakes his head, moving past me into the room. I follow and shut the door. "There's the hunting cabin on Ricky's land, but it's rough. You should stay in the big house. It'll be convenient. I'll move into the cabin and be around if you need anything. I've been chewing on moving in there anyway."

There's going to be no arguing with him, and surprisingly, I don't really want to. I've got a ton of work to do on the house to get it ready for the sale, anyway.

"Meant to be." I laugh more to myself because this turn of events is all the things I fear. I plop onto the bed and let my gaze roam around the room, a visual goodbye to a space I started over in. The room I booked on a whim, the room I needed when I couldn't stand one more moment in San Francisco. The room where John made me my first pot roast. My sister was right, I did exile myself, but I don't regret it.

"Kismet, really." I shrug, on board faster than a starving woman snagging the last cookie off a plate. "Let's pack."

In no time flat, I'm shifting nervously in my sneakers on the sidewalk of Thistle and Burr, or what used to be Thistle and Burr. Who knows what it will become when someone buys it. Kinda sad, the place has loads of potential.

John hauls my bags to the sidewalk, and I lock the door behind him.

"I don't know if this is a good idea. Meg might not like it." Meg will hate it, and that thought alone causes my heart to double in speed.

"Meg? What's she got to do with this?" he asks, honestly stunned. "She won't care, I promise. She's been encouraging me to find someone and make an effort. This is the epitome of that. I'm definitely making an effort here, Francesca."

"John—"

"I want to do this for you. I want you there."

"This is not a good idea."

"Sure, it is. Come on." He tosses me his keys, and I catch them on reflex like we've been through this charade a thousand times. "You drive. I'll throw this in back."

"John, stop. Listen to me."

He freezes mid-step. "Okay, I'm sorry. What is it?"

"Your sister made me promise not to get involved with you." His face is blank for the longest time, so I add, "The day you had your party on the beach."

"Why would she do that?" he finally asks.

"She knows I'm only here for the summer. She knows I'm not looking for anything serious. And I promised her."

He nods, holding my gaze and leaning against his truck. "She was acting slightly off around us, now that you mention it. I'll talk to her, okay? I'll explain. She'll understand."

Blowing out a breath, I try to dislodge a chunk of hair that's become plastered to my forehead from standing too long in the sun now combined with nervous sweating.

"I don't want to be a problem or to come between you and your sister. After all you've been through, I won't do that. She was pretty serious when we spoke. I get it. She cares about you, and she's worried."

"You won't. It won't. I promise. I'll tell her we've become close friends, which is true, and that I care about you, *which is true*. After some time passes, we'll tell her that we're more." He hesitates, adjusts his hat, "We are more, right?"

"Yes, we're more," I admit.

"Okay." He smiles, pulling me to him 'til we're toe to toe, chest to chest, and cheek to cheek, propped up by his truck and drinking in the moment. "Until we know what this is," he drops his palm to the top of my head, slowly working down and wrapping around my chin to tilt my head up, "that's all she needs to know."

I kiss his lips softly at first, but it deepens quickly. He pulls me up by the back of my thighs until I'm wrapped around him. Then turns slowly, plants my butt on the hood of his truck, but pauses to look me in the eye. "Agreed?"

"Agreed." He squeezes my thighs right above my knees in a super ticklish spot, and I fly off, squealing while he laughs.

Watching him toss my bags into the bed of his truck as if they're nothing is deeply comforting. I've always felt I was somehow asking too much, needing too much in relationships and even sometimes with my family, but with John, he asks me what I need before I even think of it. My body hums when he's near. He's always turned toward me, and when our skin brushes together, we're like the bug zapper hanging in Heidi's entry—one touch between us and *zap!*

I've felt attraction before, but this is nothing like any of those feelings. This feels safer and more secure as if I've found someone I can count on. I doubt there's a problem that could be thrust at John that he wouldn't respond to with some sort of smile and a can-do attitude.

I pull out of the parking lot and begin to wind through the streets of Clover, through Novel, and toward the outskirts of town, where things are a little wider, a little more open.

"You look like you belong in this car," he says. "You really picked it up quick for a beginner."

"Minus the boo-boo."

"I've already messaged Logan. He thinks he can bend it back into shape no problem."

"Some things come naturally, I guess." I laugh because after I ran his truck into a tree, shifting did come pretty easily. I give him a sideways glance. "Why are you so focused on me driving stick?"

"It's good for you to take care of yourself. To have some basic survival skills and know how to handle yourself. I'll teach you how to change a tire next. Oh, and build a fire. Do you already know how to do those?"

"Not even close, but why do you care?"

We meet eyes while I idle at a stop. "I care because I care about my sister being safe when I'm not around. I care about the dudes, jackasses as they can be, because I don't want anyone to get hurt in some freak boating accident or break a leg hiking up a mountain. And I care about you..."

His words hang in the air.

"You're good at taking care of people."

"Thank you."

"Are you good at letting people take care of you?"

"Do you want to take care of me, sunshine? Cause I intend on letting you."

"Yeah," I smile and give him one of my absolute best, "I do." He reaches around the seat and plays with a piece of my hair, failing miserably to stuff it back into my bun.

My foot presses slowly on the break, we come to a crossroads.

"Do I turn right here?" I already know the answer, but I have to fill the silence before I say something I'm not ready to say...

I downshift, making a right turn behind a Wrangler with paddle boards strapped to its roof.

"Yes, Francesca. You turn right here."

John gives me a brief tour through his dad's house, similar to the one Meg gave me. Though when he does it, he points out towels and linens and everything I might possibly need. Butterflies explode in my stomach as if I've stumbled across a diamond ring in a junk drawer. This man wants to take care of me. He wants me to live in his house, so I'm not alone... I can't believe my luck.

"If you need anything, shoot me a text. I'm usually around camping. The hunting cabin is a few yards out back near the water. I've been thinking of using it more now that Meg's working full-time in the office. You can always holler off the deck. I'll hear you." His face turns red, and his chest heaves with rapid breaths.

Is he nervous?

"Remind me why you don't stay in the house?"

"Nope." We're both hesitating in the entry way, I'm all moved in. Now what?

"Well, if I'm here and you're in the cabin, why don't I at least cook you dinner? To say thank you?"

"Francesca, we both know you can't cook. I had to help you plug in a crockpot."

"Oh. That."

"And your motel fridge was filled with sugar cereal, cinnamon bears, and chocolate milk."

"That's what gave me away?" I laugh, but I bounce on my toes because I'm excited to play house with him.

"That and the last few weeks I've spent around you. Yeah."

"Then why don't you cook for me? Come out of the woods and force me to eat vegetables like you seem to enjoy so much." I'm not ready to let go of him.

We're both dancing around the fact that we could sleep together tonight. And for the rest of the summer, really, if that's what we wanted.

"You're up for that?"

"It shocked me, too. I really liked the roast. The onions were my favorite. I didn't see that coming." He pumps a fist in the air, and I beam at him. "It's just an onion. I doubt you'll ever get me to eat Kale. Calm down. You'll break a hip."

"Onions increase heart health and bone density. My hip is fine. I'm so glad you liked it. I won't be around much during the day. We're wrapping up construction at Boggs, but dinners sound good—"

"Oh, no," I add quickly. "I meant dinn-*er*. As in singular. Just tonight. You don't have to cook for me every night." God, he must think I'm so ungrateful. *Let me stay in your house, and come cook for me every night while you're at it. Kiss me silly and make me orgasm with only your touch.* "I already feel like a burden, crashing at your place."

"No take backs, I heard dinn-*ers*. Plural. Plan on it every night this week. I'll google recipes with onions, but throw in some surprises, too. How do you feel about grilled zucchini?"

"Pretty good, I think?"

Some things never change, but some things do, I guess.

I should ask him to stay. We're both adults, right? We've slept in a bed together. We've done things to each other—unspeakably hot things, hotter than any other things I've done with anyone else —it's only natural that we'd want to do it again, but this time, all of it and—

"I promised Gus I'd help out tonight because one of his guys is out with a broken nose." A whoosh of disappointment blows through me. So, he won't be around tonight. "Beam slipped and got him good. I need to head up there." He checks his watch. "Let's start tomorrow. Something to look forward to?"

Good. Great. I've got until tomorrow night to sort my feelings out, which is a much better plan than doing things to each other in the dark. As I stand here, I'm willing myself to believe the bald-faced lie.

"I should unpack tonight, anyway."

"So, you're good here?" His tone is so intentional like he really cares to know if I feel comfortable.

I wave him off, not knowing what to do with all this attention. "Yeah. I want to take inventory of the supplies I've got so I can start fresh in the morning and get the house organized. Tomorrow is good."

"Maybe this weekend I can show you around Novel a little more?"

"Sorry." I shake my head when his mouth drops into a pout. "I'll be back in San Francisco for the weekend. Remember?"

"Right. And this week?"

"This week is prepping and pricing. Then the whole next week the sale will run Monday through Friday. It'll be pretty crazy and totally exhausting. I, uh," this is embarrassing, "I didn't exactly book movers. It kinda slipped my mind. So, I'll be improvising on my own. But people are generally prepared to carry what they buy."

"Hmm." He nods. "Comes with the territory of starting a new business. You don't know what you don't know. When I took over the bar, I didn't place the Ketchup order for weeks. I guess I thought it magically replenished or something." His grin goes wide as he laughs sheepishly at himself. "You do not want to see half-tipsy boaters at seven p.m. with no condiments. Hoity-toity tourists with gold watches and tiny trunks went absolutely feral."

"I can imagine, being a rings and fries fan myself, of course. Condiments are essential."

"Noted." He laughs, his eyes dancing and looking deep into mine. "Need a date for the wedding?"

He says it like a joke, easy and breezy. But then he pulls at his cap, flipping it backward, then immediately back to the front. Whether he realizes it or not, he's waiting for a real answer.

"I don't think so—"

Tentatively, he reaches out and grasps my shoulders. "Don't you think Heidi winning the fucking lottery is a sign?" His voice is rough with emotion. "Perhaps the exact sign you asked for in the hot spring last night?"

"I don't know." I shake my head. I wish I could give him the answer he wants. "This is all happening so fast, and that's the opposite of what I promised myself."

We both linger in the doorway under the soft cast of light from the chandelier overhead.

He shrugs. "But now you're stuck with me. And I get the honor of proving to you that I'm taking this very seriously and that you can trust me." He tries to hide a small smile as he pulls the brim of his cap low. "If she hadn't won, and you hadn't moved in here, we wouldn't have a dinner date scheduled for every night this week."

He lets one fingertip trail the edge of my jaw, then grips my chin, dragging his thumb across my lower lip. Pulling down ever so softly until my lips part.

"I won't kiss anyone. At the wedding, if that's what you're thinking." And I mean it, because I don't want anyone but him.

He presses his mouth to mine softly once, then twice. I trail my tongue along his bottom lip and tug gently with my teeth. He groans. "If I didn't have to go help Gus right now…"

But it's good that he does because there's no denying what we're doing. No putting on the brakes now. I'm demolishing my dating rule and blowing past any sort of relationship rule.

"I'll see you tomorrow night," I say, lifting to my toes and speaking lightly against the shell of his ear.

Truth is, I'd tumble into bed with him right this minute if he only tugged me in that direction. I glance at the stairs behind me, thick treads of polished wood just begging for us to run up them, laughing with anticipation.

He dips his head, turning his hat backward with one hand as he devours my neck with an open-mouth kiss and gentle teeth, excruciating in its simplicity. I think he's trying to dig deeper, to tunnel down low into my heart, and set up camp. Light a fire. Tend it.

He searches my eyes and is seemingly happy with what he finds. "Welcome home, baby."

"For a few weeks!" I add quickly. "Until my friends come at the end of summer, then we'll find someplace to stay."

A hot flash of determination moves across his face, and he grins as if silently making me promise. Shit, did we just have a conversation and make an agreement in one look?

Adrenaline courses through my body and shoots through my heart straight to my toes. I'm not ready for the fall I see coming, the iron skillet that is surely going to smack me on the head like a cartoon dummy with hearts in my eyes. But here we go, anyway.

CHAPTER 22

John

"Remind me why you're living here and not there?"

Winter stands in the scant living room of the cabin on Dad's property. It's got log walls, plaid throws, and enough counter space for a family of elves. He's pointing out a window that looks directly at the big house framed by checkered curtains.

"Because I'm selling Ricky's place."

"Not yet. And instead of living over there with that beautiful woman, you're out here in the woods twiddling your dick." There's a mirror above the fireplace that reminds me of my mom, it's cracked and held together by the best wood glue I could find, and he stops to check his hair.

"I've got plenty going on at Boggs to keep me busy," I say, kicking my sneakers off and lining them up along a wall.

"Works not going to keep you warm at night. You really should have a dog or something. A rabbit?" He makes eye contact with me via the mirror. "You could be a rabbit hutch kinda guy, right?"

Instead of snapping at Winter about the one-night stands that only keep him warm for a small part of his nights and his odd zoo keeper habits that are only referred to as "colorful" because he's technically royal and most women are so into his ridiculous hair they ignore his quirks, I pull off the fleece I wore this morning for a run and chuck it at a side chair.

I've been there, sought comfort in the moment. It didn't last for me, and it won't last for him either. He feels too much, but he'll figure that out in his own time, I guess. I've barely figured out for myself that I want more. Achieving that *more* has been unexpectedly challenging. I had to go and pick someone who was unavailable. But now Francesca and I are trying, and I plan to tell her very soon that I'm falling hard for her.

Do I have enough to give someone like Francesca? It's not like I had a role model growing up, and I don't want to fall short for her. That's going from Little League to the majors in a heartbeat. I never thought that part through until I got serious about her.

There's a very real possibility she's feeling the same despite her fear of getting hurt. And if that's true, can I be sure I won't be awful at a relationship like my dad? After all, that's all I've known. I've been so focused on winning her over that I never stopped to think, is that what's best for her? Am I what's best for her?

There's no time to shower up because my run went long—as it has for the last few days because no matter how long I push my legs to the point of burning, I cannot forget that woman's ass flexing in one hand, her core firing off and pulsing in my other. If Dave's B&B could talk, that weird attic room would have some stories to tell.

But living so close to Francesca, yards away in a copse of trees for the last week, hasn't been all torture. Every night, I've trucked across the lawn after a shower at the cabin, pushing through the back doors after a day at Boggs as if I'm walking through the front door to a home with a woman permanently living there with me. It's been every bit the *Honey, I'm home* vibe it almost looks like.

Comforting. Real.

The part of the evening where we work out recipes together is comical, but I've taught her to use the most basic kitchen appliances at this point. The woman can now peel a potato, and I'm proud to be the one who empowered her. The first night, she dressed up and ruined a blouse with olive oil. The second night was jean shorts and a tank top. The two nights after that, she wore her PJs and asked what her job was in the kitchen.

I'd turn to her at the sink with a towel on my shoulder for washing veggies and hand her an onion to chop as if we'd been doing it for years. She'd cry, and I'd lick the tears off her cheeks and kiss her in the kitchen 'til I saw stars. Then she'd set up a kabob station as if she was born to do it. The girl loves onions, zucchini, and roasted peppers, basically any vegetable I serve her after charring it on my grill. Hand her a platter of cold vegetables with a sauce for dipping, and she'll hurl four-letter expletives back and go running for the candy dish that now lives on the Carrara marble island next to my fruit bowl.

"Logan's here," Winter says, lazily leaning in my doorway, letting all the bugs in.

I huff at him in acknowledgment. Francesca has no idea we're coming up to the big house to surprise her, and I hope Logan was stealthy about it.

She's been working even longer hours than I have. After dinner, she sits at the table with tags and ribbons and stacks of spreadsheets she's made to catalog the contents of the house. The lights in the kitchen remain visible from my cabin in the woods until midnight most nights. Almost completely due to her focus and determination, I've quietly walked back to the cabin after kissing her up against a wall so long my lips go numb, both of us promising to sleep in separate beds and keep things PG until we've gotten through this work week.

Boggs is coming to the end of its transformation, and Francesca ran the first day of the sale almost completely on her own yesterday. When I got home a little before five, I watched the woman carry items double her weight to cars and trucks of customers who were unable to lift themselves. Of course, I ran to her and offered to help. Of course, she waved me off and said she found some movers, but they weren't available the first two days. Said she could make it on her own until then, and I know she can...

But not today. Today, she's going to get a lot of help in that department, and I'm dying waiting to surprise her.

"Don't you think he needs a dog?" Winter asks as Logan approaches.

He grunts, looking every bit the lumberjack he is. Only Logan can pull off suspenders with his Carharts and ominous tattoos that look mean from afar but, up close, are actually quite thoughtful. In the distance, the lake reflects the rising sun behind him as he scratches at a beard that I know is his secret pride and joy.

"You're never convincing him to get a dog. Me either." Logan sticks his head through the door but doesn't let his feet cross the threshold, impatient for us to get a move on. "I remember bunking in here as a kid," he grumbles.

"I'm not lonely," I say around a toothbrush, bathroom door ajar, and then I spit. "We need to get up to the house. And I don't need an animal. I'm fine," I add for Winter.

"But you and Ricky—" Winter starts.

I silence him with a look.

He changes tack. "Lola's pups are almost ready to be weaned. You guys know it's going to be hard for me to farm them out."

"There's the truth," Logan says.

"Doc says St. Bernard's will get up to two hundred pounds. Plus, I want to train them all to be old-fashioned rescue dogs for ski season, little barrels around their necks. We could be like single bro dads," Winter says. He's got an actual menagerie of animals in his castle at this point; it's getting worrisome, and I give him a raised eyebrow and thin-lipped grimace to tell him so.

"Please never say that again," Logan grumbles, shifting in old hiking boots, laces barely intact. "I might actually consider it, if you never say that again."

"You know you're gonna keep them anyway," I add, pulling on fresh jeans.

"No—"

"You're going to keep them and live with a pack of wolves down in Vikingstrong like your ancestors have predetermined," I press, laughing at him so he knows I'm not judging—not entirely.

I'm pushing him because I can. It's fun to get a rise out of the pretty, calculated showman every once in a while. I'm still pissed at him for what he said at lunch a few weeks ago. Pissed at him for pushing. But he wasn't entirely wrong, either.

We've done the manly, *not going to talk about it and just move on* thing. I know he means well, poking into my private life, but if he can dish the advice, he needs to learn to take it. One of these days, I'm going to give him a real piece of my mind—a, *wake up and smell the childhood trauma festering inside you*, and do something about it besides hoarding animals and their unconditional love.

"Let's get on with it, then," Winter huffs and walks out without a backward glance, trucking up the hill toward Dad's old house.

"Hold up!" I shout, pulling the door closed and tripping over my own work boots to get down the path. Logan has caught up with Winter, and they both make faces as if I'm the slowest man alive.

Here come the old man jokes, in three, two, one—

"Jeez, old man. Need us to get you a walker? How about one of those lifts like mine?"

"Boss has still got some steps in him," Logan replies. "But let's keep that on the birthday list for next year." He laughs. Which is rare, and I don't give a shit if it's at my expense. That kid deserves some light in his life, whether it's laughing at my ass or otherwise.

"I'm only five years older than you guys." I point at them.

I don't mind the ribbing because they've stuck it out with me this long, pulled me through some dark as fuck nights when I was losing the game and everything I'd worked toward my entire life. If they need to make old man jokes, I'll pretend I hate it, just for them.

"You two shut your immature, puppy-loving, ass-kissing—" If I'm slightly out of breath, it's only because I've already worked out today, and slinging these pot shots at them is exhausting.

Winter halts in suede loafers glaringly out of place in the brush of the shadowy lawn. "Wait, who's ass-kissing?"

Definitely not Winter; he's torn his family apart with his unwillingness to comply.

"You know Logan's got a sweet tooth for Patty's," I say, clapping Logan on the back while I'm at it. He's a true Paul Bunion at six five, so I have to reach a bit.

Logan's cheeks turn the color of summer tomatoes—what parts are visible under his scruff—as I grip him good-naturedly by his neck. "Always in there clomping around in your boots, batting your eyes. Don't think we haven't noticed you flexing. You're going to give her a heart attack if you keep leading her on like you're a muffin top away from going for an older woman."

"Patty is a damn saint, and her pastry shop should be a landmark in town. I've worked hard to solidify my spot as her favorite." He allows himself a moment of laughter, though it's tight and through his nose.

Both Winter and I chuckle as we continue through the spotty green grass of a shaded trail, around the side of the big house, over a side path of river rock, and up the slate-paved walkway. There's a line forming, about twenty people deep already.

We all lumber onto the wide porch of my dad's house. "Sorry," I say to a woman with a bird's nest haircut. "This is my house."

She gives me a curt nod but doesn't give us much room on the porch. The rest of the line seems to press in a bit, clearly eager for the doors to open.

"Hold on." I pull three name tags I made this morning from my back pocket. "Put these on."

"What's this?" Winter asks, pressing the sticky tag to his shirt. It says, *ask me to move heavy stuff to your car.*

"You're the muscle, pretty pants. All those weights you lift in that fancy gym you tricked out in the basement of a hundred-year-old Viking castle are going to pay off. Though your ancestors would be horrified."

"Like I'm supposed to go out and hunt an elk for exercise."

"And I'm the brains?" Logan scoffs, shifting his weight, but I can tell he takes it as a compliment. "*Ask me all the hard questions,* huh?" He presses the tag into his shirt. I hope he gets pestered by little old ladies all day.

"What are you?" they ask me in unison. The woman behind us snickers—we must be winning her over.

I press my name tag onto my Henley.

Frannie's Finds Personal Assistant.

"Dude, you are so gone for that girl," Winter says, jabbing Logan in the shoulder as if he's won a bet.

I shrug and grin. "Whatever she needs."

Before I can press the bell, the door opens in a flash, and Francesca comes barreling out. "We'll open the doors in five minutes, people—Oh!" She pulls air pods from her ears, Alanis audibly blaring and making us all cringe. "Hey, Winter, Logan. John." Her hair is up in what might pass as a bun, but most of it's tumbling out and tickling her shoulders. She's wearing tight black bike shorts and a crop top. I'm staring, and I don't care. "What are you guys doing here?"

"The dude crew is at your service today," Winter says, bowing so low his knuckles graze concrete. He can't fucking help himself. He's been bred to charm, an elegant prince.

"What are you talking about?" she asks, her smile widening.

Does she notice she's still pressing a shoulder into my chest while she talks to my friends? I love that she leans on me.

The line shifts with anticipation behind us. "We want to help." I motion between us. "I know you've got movers coming tomor-

251

row, and I know you could go it on your own another day if you had to, but I've watched you clean, tag, bag, load, and generally run yourself ragged the past week. You don't have to do this alone. You've got backup."

"You *guys*," she gushes, high and light and adorable. "Thank you." She pulls us all into a huddle hug. "But you know, it can be emotional," she says, looking up at me. "To see people buying things that may hold some feelings or significance. You know, memories..." She trails off, and I know she's mentally warring with herself not to ask me for the millionth time if I want to keep anything of my father's.

It's about time I sat her down and set her straight. Like it or not, this isn't a normal estate sale, and this isn't how I expected to interact with the person responsible for clearing out all his shit. But here we are. It is personal.

"I'll be fine, I promise."

"Where do you want us?" Logan asks, breaking the slight tension that was building. It's no use wondering if the guys can tell or if they can feel it. They know exactly why I don't want one thing of my father's, now or ever.

"I've got coffee inside. Got up early and walked to Patty's for—"

Logan pushes past her, mumbling, "'*Scuse me,*" in a gruff voice but with a smile kicking up at the corner of his mouth. That guy cannot say no to a pastry.

The line behind us grumbles again, not happy someone's gotten through.

"Might as well open early." Francesca winks. "Come on in everyone. Time to shop!"

The morning is a raging success, and the dude crew is indispensable. They lift, they cart, they tote, but Francesca is a whirlwind of execution, direction, sunshine, and organization. The house is a zoo for about three hours straight, but she never falters, keeping everyone happy and sales ringing.

By the afternoon, I'm lifting a TV the size of Texas and hefting it out the door as Francesca rings up an old-timer I recognize as a regular from Boggs. She's set up a cash register via her phone, complete with gift wrap, bright red tissue paper, and white handled bags she's stamped with a Frannie's Finds logo.

"Need help?" she asks as I struggle to keep the mammoth TV from taking me down.

She shoves her hands under before I can answer, making it tip precariously.

"Sure," I grit. "Thanks." We gently place the TV in a bunch of old blankets, and I walk from side to side, helping the grateful grandpa with his bungees.

Francesca shakes hands with him, and we watch as he pulls away from the house, winding down the long drive.

It's oddly silent for the first time today, and when I look around, I realize everyone is gone.

She checks her phone tucked in the waistband of her shorts. "Five o'clock. Sale's over. You guys really helped out today. I don't know if I would have made it without you."

"You would have, but I'm glad you didn't have to. Congrats on a big success. You did it."

"Thanks." She stubs the toe of her sneaker in the gravel drive. "I did, didn't I?"

"You really nailed it." I drop an arm around her neck, pull her close, and kiss her forehead. She gasps and giggles. "One more week." I sigh, long and deep. Hating how aware I am that she's going to be gone all weekend at her parents' wedding.

She wraps her arms around my neck and pulls me in, but I wince. My shoulder smarts from the abuse of playing mover all day. "Are you okay?"

"Pulled something is all."

"You're hurting. I can tell."

"Acts up when I lift."

"Come inside and let me get some ice. Some heat?"

"Nah, I'll head back to the cabin. Maybe shower up unless I can help you with anything else?"

"With what?" She shrugs. "Everything is gone. We might not even run another full week."

That hits me somewhere low in the gut. And it's unbidden, unwanted, the thickness I feel moving up my throat. The water that pools in my eyes.

"Hey," she says, soft and sweet. Her eyes go wide. I try to look away, but she snags my jaw with her hand. "Oh, honey."

And that's all it takes. The tears fall freely now. I couldn't hold them in if I tried, and I am trying, but also... *Fuck it.* I let go. I let them go. It still hurts, but not holding back makes it hurt a fraction less.

"Breathe," she says, pulling me in. I have to hunch over, but I let my head fall to her shoulder. "Breathe with me. In and out."

"Can't. Can't," I gulp, and an ugly, guttural sob slips out of me despite the fact I'm trying to hold it in with everything I've got. Embarrassment and hot tears coat my cheeks as I struggle for shaky breaths. I'd like to run, to hide under a boulder somewhere, to drown my sorry ass in the lake. "Gonna go," I manage as I feel myself start to hyperventilate.

She doesn't let me pull away. "Don't. John, tell me what's going on."

She's been begging me to hold onto something of Ricky's, so worried I'd regret cutting these sour memories out of my life. She's right. It's time she knows the truth.

"Walk with me?" I motion with my chin toward the cabin, still struggling for breath.

"Anywhere," she replies without hesitation, and that helps.

We make it to my door, and I let my forehead fall, hands gripping the sides of the frame for support. Heaving breaths wrack my chest as I will myself to calm down, but my body won't listen.

Her hands snake up and around my shoulders, and she rubs at the knots there with her thumbs. "Let's get you inside."

I push the door open with my boot, and she follows me in.

"Sit," she says. I pull a chair from a small bistro set in the kitchen and follow orders. "I think you're having an anxiety attack."

She hunts around in the cabinets, finding mostly cobwebs. "Nothing? Definitely no paper bags, but no snacks, no dishes? JB, we can do better than this. You do need me." I think she's trying to cheer me up or at least stop the almost panic attack. "Let's do this the old-fashioned way." She stands between my feet, pushing down gently on my shoulder blades so my head hangs between my legs. "Catch your breath."

"I need to tell you something," I say from between my knees as she rubs my back.

"Okay."

Slowly, after some deep breaths and a silent prayer, I sit up, taking my time because I'm not looking forward to this. She sits on my lap and puts her arms around my shoulders.

"What happened up there? Do you want to talk bout it?" She nods toward the big house.

I shrug. "Yes? No?" Apparently, I have no walls with this girl. I haven't from the very beginning. "Ricky's not dead. I-I let you believe he was because I was acting like an idiot, and I *wasn't* ready to talk about it."

She blinks

Blinks again.

"Oh my god."

"Yeah," I sniff, looking up into concerned gray eyes. "Are you mad?"

"Not mad." She shakes her head slowly. "But confused."

I stare at her, incredulous. She's not angry, and she's not running for the hills. "He took off about a year ago after I refused to bail him out and give him the money to save the bar. He gave a big speech about getting his act together for me, for us to finally have a relationship. Signed the papers and gave me everything he had. And when he called a few weeks later, saying he'd dried out in a cabin on the mountain, I told him to fuck off."

"Wow." She lets a long exhale escape her lips, takes a deep breath, and meets my eyes, waiting for more.

"You don't seem very surprised." I excepted a much bigger reaction to *"My father's not dead, and the estate sale you're running is because I refuse to ever see him again."*

She shrugs. "It certainly answers a question I've been chewing on. I could never find an obituary online. Didn't come across any death certificates. Once I realized what a big deal he is, it was odd there were no articles chronicling his death. They all just sort of stopped on a timeline. I figured the family wanted to keep the details private. I didn't want to press you about it..."

"I'm so sorry."

She rubs my back and shushes me. "I'm glad you told me," she says. "I understand emotionally complicated. I also know you probably didn't plan on having to explain all this to the person running your estate sale."

"Thank you for understanding."

She shrugs. "I know you're a good person, Jonathan Boggs. So, what are you going to do about it?"

"What do you mean?" I let out a deep breath and instantly feel better. A weight off my shoulders.

I was afraid to come clean to her, to tell her what a moron I can be, and she's being an angel about it. She cares about me, that's clear, and it soothes me from the inside out.

"If he left to sober up, get himself together to have a relationship with you... Should you hear him out?"

"I mean, probably, yeah. Easier said than done," I grumble, rubbing her knee with the palm of my hand.

Maybe I have made things bigger than they really were, a mountain out of an angry childhood molehill. If he has changed, done the work, maybe I need to forgive him, just a little—for the past, at least. Neither of us can get that time back. It's not the crap in the house that's making me sad. It's the feeling of a door slowly sliding closed. A lock about to click if I don't stop it.

The time we're wasting now... The time we will have lost when one day, he's gone. Just like my mom.

"I wanted him to play catch as a kid. I wanted him to show up to one of my games. I wouldn't have even cared if he was blitzed." She nods, watching me closely.

"What I hear you saying is you've always wanted a relationship with your dad."

I nod slowly.

"It sounds like you want to try, but you're scared. I get that," she pulls the hat off my head and tosses it on the kitchen table. Her hands brush my hair back from my face.

"I'm asking you to try with this thing between us, and you're scared," I say, leaning into her touch.

"You're drawing that parallel too, huh?" She laughs softly.

"Hmm," I grunt, wrapping my arms tight around her waist, not wanting that small statement to ring so true. "I'll reach out. I'm not exactly sure how to contact him, I don't think he has a phone, but I'll ask around town and reach out."

She rubs my shoulders, taking my hat off the table and plopping it on hers. "Can I make you dinner?" she says with a lopsided smile.

"I don't know, can you?" I huff a laugh at my own dad joke, and she gently pushes against my chest.

"You've been making me dinner every night—" She halfheartedly grabs me by the cheeks and brings my face closer to hers.

"You've helped."

"Yeah, but my plan was to make you dinner tonight and show off my new skills before I head out for the weekend. How much I've learned from you. I'll invite the guys too—"

"Gone all weekend, and they get to share my time with you?" I say, though, I love that she likes my friends. It would never work with someone who didn't embrace my friends and my sister.

257

"As a thank you for today," she goes on, laughing. "But tonight, it's me and you. Okay?"

"Right. Fine. They'll love that, thanks."

"Give me an hour and be back up at the house?" She drops her lips to mine and we both smile, a smile-kiss. "You okay?"

"Yeah. Francesca, you don't have to—"

"Shoot me their numbers so I can text them myself. I want to. And John—" She twists my hat back on me but pushes the brim around backward so our eyes meet.

"Yeah?"

"I got you."

CHAPTER 23

Fran

"Hey, Winter, can I borrow you for a second?"

The pots on the stove can simmer. I thought I'd be in over my head by myself in the kitchen, but it turns out cooking is following directions with nice, organized lists of to-dos'.

"Sure, what's up?" He pulls up beside me in a Burberry T-shirt.

"I did something..." I pull lightly on his elbow, ushering him down a short hall.

"Something naughty?" My eyes go wide, and I drop his arm like a hot potato.

"I meant something sneaky?" He smiles and works a hand through his magnificent wave of hair. It's particularly on point since everyone's gone home and showered up. "Sneaky would have been a better choice of word there, Frannie. I'm sorry."

It is sneaky if he must know. And he must because I need advice. After my chat with John, watching tears roll down his face, I realized how much I recognize his pain. And I told him he could talk about it or not. His choice. A choice I wish my family would extend to me sometimes instead of hounding me because it makes

259

them feel uncomfortable when I'm upset and not ready to articulate why.

But I did do something sneaky.

"I stashed a few things," I say, rolling my eyes at him. Winter Larsen may spell trouble—a walking Molotov cocktail of easy wealth, unassuming confidence, and animal magnetism—but I know he wants the best for John. "I need your opinion."

I pull him into the mudroom and push a toile curtain back from the soapstone countertops they line. The room is cozy, both understated and elevated. A large black window box frames a pretty picture of the cabin not far off outside, barely visible in the woods around it, and the lake off to the left reflecting the sparkle of twilight on the water.

"What's all this?" he asks, picking up on my stealth mode.

It's heavy, but I lift a rusted metal toolbox from under the sink and plop it on the counter, careful not to make too much noise. "I kept a few things for John. I didn't read anything; just tried to deduce what was important and stuffed it in here. Hid it." I wince and twist my hands, waiting for one of John's best friends to tell me if I've overstepped horrendously or if I've done something good for his buddy. It could go either way.

He sorts through the box gently. One by one, he lines items up along the counter. A well-loved brown bear filled with beans, a photo album with black and whites of the great Ricky Boggs, some signed tickets, and a few baseball cards that look important. There's another album, too. Winter's eyes snag on it, and I wonder if he's seen it before. Gently, he flips through a few pages with news articles and clippings that I hadn't allowed myself to read, feeling too much like an invasion of privacy. He lets the book fall shut.

"You did the right thing, but he can't know about this."

"Found it in a closet on a top shelf covered in dust. Most of the things were already in there. I added the bear. The signed cards. It doesn't feel right, keeping it from him—"

"No, it doesn't."

"He told me everything, well, not the details, but most of it." I hesitate, judging the look on Winter's face. "I'm worried about him. And I don't want him to hate me for this." I motion to my hidden treasures.

"That's not who John is. I can't tell you how he'll react, but the guy doesn't hold a grudge unless it's with Ricky Boggs. His dad may not be physically in the ground, Frannie," he drags a hand down a clean-shaven face with a defined jaw, looks out the window, then back at me, "but they're both acting like it, stubborn mules that they are."

My mind is working in overdrive, sifting through each detail of the last month like a beachcomber. "It all makes sense now. Dave said something about getting ahead, that his signature would skyrocket when he passed. I didn't know what that meant. I thought it was some sort of sports term. Like when he *passed* ten years or twenty after playing the game. Milestones, or something—"

I pull a scrunchy covered in butterflies off my wrist, my absolute favorite if I was forced to choose, and pile my still-damp hair high on my head, wrapping it aggressively into a messy bun.

"He doesn't talk about it—but if he's opened up to you, that means something."

He did, and it does. John is important to me, and if I'm important enough to him to lean on, we might not be destined to hurt each other after all. I trust him, and he clearly trusts me.

"Do you think the two of them can fix things? Is the relationship worth saving?"

"Ricky's not a bad man. He was an absentee father—he shouldn't get a pass for that—but I think the past few years have taken their toll. He's reached out to me, and I know he wants to mend fences... Keep this stuff here. We'll come up with a plan... Logan, Ben, and I have been tossing ideas around for a while, but we haven't come up with anything to get the big dummy to pull his head out of his ass and call his dad."

"John said he didn't have a phone?"

"He's got a phone now, I set it up and got it to him shortly after he went up into the mountains to dry out. Ricky's not perfect. He made some mistakes, but I think John wants to forgive him. He's just got to figure out how."

"What about Meg? Can't she talk to him?" Is she going to kill me when she finds out I've stashed this box of stuff for John? Or that I've gotten so close to him that I want to take care of him like he takes care of everyone else.

"She's tried. He won't budge. It's not in our nature to let him get away with being a stubborn mule. We usually check each other, but this is different. He's been impenetrable. And Ricky's not much better. They're two asshats at opposite ends of an argument."

I shove the toolbox back under the counter and fluff the curtain.

Winter eyes me and gets quite close before he whispers low between us so no one will hear, "Do you love him?"

"No!" I shout. Then laugh. Then shout again, "God, no! Come on."

His eyes narrow and we exchange a knowing glance, this guy is good at reading people.

Maybe I do, love John Boggs. I think, despite my best judgement, I've fallen in love with an ex-athlete turned boat-up bar owner who loves hard and takes care of everyone he knows. I want to tell him. I've just got to figure out how...

"Don't say anything about this," I whisper-threaten as Winter and I make our way back into the kitchen.

My vegetable chopping lessons from John have paid off, and I'm taking my new skills to the next level as I man a thick chopping block with a sharp knife. A quick search yesterday on my phone led me to an easy veggie soup recipe with beer bread for a side, and I've got strawberry shortcake makings from Patty's for dessert. She packed them all up in separate containers, and all I have to do is assemble them on some of the pretty mismatched plates I scored at Revival on an afternoon shopping break last week. Jack and Wagner got back from their honeymoon, and while Jack wrapped my purchase, Wagner complained about all the inventory backing up in their tiny warehouse behind the store.

The guys sit in folding chairs someone found since there's no furniture left, and they surround a small TV from the garage that hasn't sold yet. There's something funny about the whole scene: me, engrossed with a recipe in the kitchen, a group of guys surrounding a tiny black and white bunny ear antenna TV in a ten-million-dollar mansion on the lake, my mix match tablescape outside set for six.

I kinda love us. I wish I had an apron with ruffles.

It feels like hanging with Cat and Willow, and I realize how much I do miss them but... What if this could be more than a summer? What if I left San Francisco permanently for the lake life?

Maybe—

"Baby, you peeled." His chest presses into my back, and he stares over my shoulder into the pot simmering on the stove.

"I peeled and chopped and diced," I say proudly. "Cried a river over an onion."

"Smells so good. I'm starving." You'd think he was talking about the soup, the soup I picked for his healthy heart lifestyle. But his nose is in my hair, drawing deep breaths in and releasing slow breaths out through his mouth that warm the curve of my neck. "Thanks again for listening to me. Earlier. I can't believe I cried on your shoulder. That was a first."

"You've never cried in front of a woman?"

"Does my sister count?"

"Sure." I inwardly wince. "And anytime." Laying the soup

ladle on a spoon rest, I turn into him and wrap my arms around his waist. "Have you told her? About us?"

"Not until there's something to tell... What, exactly, would you like me to say?"

"Don't put me on the spot!" I yelp when he pinches my waist and then drops his hands around my cheeks to squeeze me into a pucker before he plants a kiss on my fish lips.

"Seriously, though, I'm sorry. For what you're going through," I say when he pulls back. "I hate seeing you hurt. I want to help, but..." I trail off because I don't know how to finish. I might have already overstepped by holding items back from the sale, and I'm not sure how or when I should admit that to him.

His arms circle around me, and he pulls me to him, rough and tight. I can hear his breathing hitch as he fights to get his words out. "You're going to make me do it again," he manages on a bit of a laugh. "If you continue to be so sweet to me."

"I care about you," I say softly, giving him one last squeeze before releasing him and turning back to my dinner. "Now, beat it, JB. I'm about to serve."

He laughs and gives me a grateful wink before pulling his hat from his back pocket and making his way over to his friends. Immediately, they widen their bro-circle around the TV, welcoming him with slaps on the back and bad jokes.

We eat outside on the deck, enjoying each other while enjoying good food. I feel full by the end of the meal, but not just my stomach. All over, I feel full of a simple calm that comes with being satisfied with what you've got, where you are in life...who you're with. Happy.

The guys clear the table, hauling dishes inside. We walk them to the door like a couple who host rustic, delicious, intimate dinner parties with the epic woods and stunning lake as the backdrop all the time. The night was perfect.

"You guys have a good night." I wave before closing the door and turning to watch John put the last of my mix-match dishes in the dishwasher.

"Don't go back to that cabin," I say before I can stop myself, "or sleep in a tent or go wherever you normally go. Stay here with me."

He looks up, surprised, and lets the dishwasher click shut. It starts to hum. "There's no furniture."

I chuckle at him because I can tell that's not exactly what he meant to say. I caught him off guard.

"We can have a campout." I motion to the living room rug that didn't sell. I think there are still a few blankets in the linen closet, too.

"That would technically be a camp-in. I'm sorry we didn't think that through, where you'll be sleeping now that there's no bed, no couch, no nothing."

"Ironic that I'd end up with no bed. *Again.*"

"I take it back. I'm not sorry. Fate seems to be pushing you into mine, and I'm thankful for it," he says, taking determined steps toward me.

"What is it with you and destiny, and fate, and kismet?" I ask, backing up against the front door. I asked for this. I invited him to a sleepover, but am I ready for that?

"I'm a ballplayer. We're superstitious. Everyone knows that."

"No one knew Heidi was going to hit the jackpot, and Thistle and Burr would close in a matter of days." I laugh, backing against the door. "And you're right, her offer to stay was a horror movie in the making. But I'm grateful I'm staying here since it's the busy season, and I'd be driving over two hours to the bay otherwise. I couldn't manage that kind of commute day in and day out."

My heart constricts, and his advance on me freezes as that comment hangs in the air like dust motes in a slash of indoor sun. Our breath stills as our eyes hold. My babbling about commuting to and from the lake has caused us both to think the same thing,

I'm sure of it. *What happens when summer is over, and the job is done?*

"No one knew Heidi would ditch town the second she had the chance. Didn't see that coming. Did you do it on purpose?" he asks, changing the track of an uncomfortable conversation.

"Hand her a losing lottery ticket in hopes of planting a lifelong obsession, and she'd trot down the street and buy a winner?"

"So, no, then?" He unfreezes and takes the final step to bring him inches from me.

My chest pumps rapidly, searching for air, for the composure I lose when he's this close. "No, that was not on purpose. I'm optimistic but not that optimistic."

"Seems destiny didn't want you to have a winner. Maybe this is the way things were supposed to go the whole time." He pins me to the wall, his hands bracing right above my shoulders. "Maybe," he dips his head low so he can whisper in my ear, "you running from me the night we met just brought you back to me in the end."

"You sure do have a lot of faith in fate," I breathe.

"I told you I used to live for that kinda stuff," he speaks into my hair, still not touching me but taking up all my space.

"Did you wear the same socks for every game?" I tease.

"Worse."

"Oh, God, not underwear?" I look to the ceiling, trying hard to compose my thoughts instead of doing what I want.

"Ugh. I'd never." He pulls back to give me a crooked smile as if to say, *I would've if I had, to.* "I called my sister before every game. She'd say good luck, and I'd crush it every time. The games I didn't call because my phone was dead or we got off schedule or whatever, I tanked every time."

Finally, I touch him, but only to push him back.

"You okay?"

My mind trails off. His sister is important to him. He basically raised her. It makes the fact that I promised her I wouldn't get involved with him sit even heavier on my heart. Everything is moving so fast.

"Hey, baby?" He startles me from my thoughts and gives me a reason to ignore it a little longer. "Where'd you go?"

"Nowhere," I breathe. "I'm here." And I want to be here. Everything inside me wants to stay here in our house-playing, road-tripping, hot-kissing summer bubble.

"Good, because I got an idea." He laces his fingers through mine, and I can't help but melt at the boyish excitement in his voice. "Let's go pitch a tent."

CHAPTER 24

John

B uilding a fire is quick work for me, so is tossing up a tent. I've got four stakes in the ground, and before I know it, there's a shiny dome of green, barely visible, popped up in the dark night. Francesca watches me work, a contemplative look on her face.

"Can I help?" she asks.

"Sure, grab some logs with me." We both pull pieces of split wood from the pile Logan keeps stocked for my fires and drop them near the tent for later.

"It's so pretty here on the water in the summer. What's it like in the wintertime?"

"You've never come for ski season?"

"My sister used to do the annual school ski trip, but I've never been on skis in my life, well, except water skis when I was a kid." She kicks off her flip-flops and lets the grass tickle her feet, totally comfortable in her surroundings, which makes my heart soar. Nothing about my imperfect side seems to phase her—the camping, the issues with my dad, not even an anxiety attack and uncontrollable tears from a six-foot-plus man—and for that, I'm grateful.

An evening breeze rolls off the lake, and stray pieces of her hair float around her face. I could definitely do this for a good long time with her, easily forever. The land I love so much around us glows with stars and a few faint lights in the empty house behind us. The fire is burning, and the lake is lapping at the shore.

"Dance with me?" I ask, completely smitten. Past smitten, I've fallen hard, I just don't know how to tell her.

She moves into me, wrapping her arms around my neck. I put my hands on her hips and revel at how well I know her now compared to the last time we danced together.

"No crowd, now," she murmurs. "No disco ball. No chanting friends. Just us."

"Just us. I could get used to this." I dip her low and pull her back to me quickly.

"I love it when you do that," she breathes.

"It's been a while since I've felt this calm, I think," I say, pulling the crisp night air deep into my lungs.

"You work hard."

I raise an eyebrow at her because, while renovating Boggs hasn't been easy, this lake life is far from a city's hustle and bustle. Far from hard, if you let it be. Most people here are happy, fulfilled. A small life full of big moments. I wonder if she's up for all that.

She reads the look I'm giving her easily. "What? You do. Don't think I haven't noticed you taking care of everyone around you."

"Just how I was raised. I want to make my mom proud of the legacy she left." As I turn into her instinctually, I get a load of her profile in the low light of the fire and push a strand of hair that's fallen from her bun behind her ear, then think better of it and pull her hair tie free in one light tug and put it on my wrist. A piece of her wrapped around me, *mine*.

"Where are we headed?" I ask. "Me and you?" My hand drops to her neck, my thumb making tiny circles below her ear.

"You're always asking me questions like that." She smiles real slow and doesn't look away. "Right now, we're headed here." She pulls me down with her on top of my sleeping bag, where I've spent too many nights alone in front of a fire just like this.

"I want you to know I'm serious about you, about us. I'm all in, Francesca. I don't want you to leave." I'm still worried if I'm enough, good enough for her, but shit I'll try to be.

She fidgets, as if I've cornered her, which I kinda have, but it's the only way I know how to tell her how serious I am.

"All I know is I'm happy with you here, and I don't want to worry about the rest of it. I thought about making a list—"

"Like, pros and cons?"

"Yeah, you know I like my lists," she gives me a small smile, "and while they do help me organize my thoughts and feel less out of control, with you, I want to take a chance and figure the rest out later."

"Deal." I let my arm snake around her thigh, soft skin against skin, and rest my head on her shoulder as I squeeze, letting the fire take all my thoughts, anxiety, and worries, too.

When my chest is tight with emotion and close to bursting as I stare into the crackling fire, I move over her. It's quick, the way I push her into the blankets while cradling the back of her head with my hand, making sure we fall softly.

"John!" she whisper-laughs as I kiss her neck, trying to taste all her sweetness.

"Tell me what you need, baby."

"I have to be up really early tomorrow to drive to my parents." Rolling me gently to my back, she moves more of her weight over me, looking deep into my eyes. "I can't show up dazed and strung out over...no sleep."

I smirk, strung out over all the things I want to do to her, she means.

"You had a hard day," she says, leaning down and kissing me gently on the mouth.

"You were right. Letting go of the stuff hurt more than I expected." My hips roll under her. I can't help it. It's a natural reaction to her sitting on top of me and looking down like a fucking angel sent just for me.

She gasps and falls to my chest.

"I want to take care of you," she murmurs into my neck, dropping kisses as punctuation. "From now on, you cry in front of me any time you like. And I'll do the same." She looks up, meeting my eyes with a look of soft determination. "You got me, JB?"

"I do." I nod.

Fingers trail down my throat, down my front, then vanish under the hem of my Henley, pushing the fabric up and over my head in a flash.

"I want to make you feel good. Like you've done for me. I've been thinking about it, over and over, how I'm going to return the favor." She scoots back, her ass dragging over my very obvious erection.

"You don't have to return anything," I grit, and bite down on a groan.

"I know. But I want to."

On her knees between my thighs, she leans over me and drops her hands on my chest, slowly dragging her nails down my front. They bite into my skin just enough. "You make me want to do very naughty things."

A low growl releases from deep inside. "Fuck, me. Yes. Anything. Whatever you want, baby. Take it."

"Thinking about it," she replies, cheeky and toying with the button on my jeans. "First, I think I want you in my mouth."

I suck in a breath. This assertive side of her has come as a total surprise, but I'm not mad about it. "Shit, Francesca. Where did you come from? How did I get so lucky?"

She hesitates, all the bravado she's been showing off slipping. "I'm sorry. I kinda got carried away and..."

Her whole demeanor changed in half a second.

"Wait." I push up on my elbows. "What just happened?

271

What's wrong?" I squeeze her thighs and keep still, gazing up at her with firelight dancing across her sweet face.

"I, never mind. I don't want to bring it up right now, but..."

"You can say anything to me."

"I-I've been told I'm not very good at this. In the past... And I don't want to disappoint you. You've got such a history. I mean, I've seen your pictures online with women and..."

"That was a while ago. I haven't been with anyone in any way for almost a year. You're perfect. And if we're talking about fucking bulldog tie right now, I'm going to drive to San Francisco and knock some sense into that moron."

"It's silly. I'm being silly."

"What exactly did he say to you?" I press.

She holds my gaze—doesn't look away. "He said I was boring in bed."

What utter horse-shit. I remember him mumbling something to that effect the night we met at Throwbacks, but the way she's kissed me, moved with me already, I know for a fact that's impossible.

I shoot up, grabbing her hips so she doesn't move an inch, and she drops the button she was about to pop on my jeans. "Baby, you are everything. You are as fucking hot as the fire right next to us. That night at Throwbacks, when you pulled me onto the dance floor, I nearly fell to my knees—you were so gorgeous. Don't believe anything less."

She licks her lips and grabs my neck, kissing me as her response, soft and slow. I think it's a thank you, as if she needed to give one. I could tell this girl how wonderful she is for the rest of her life, and it still wouldn't be enough.

Pushing me back down, she pops the button on my fly and drags the zipper down, tugging down my jeans and boxers until my extremely hard dick is out and on full display.

Feeling her hands on me is sublime. She grips me soft but firm. Dipping low—

"Tell me if it's not...good."

A crack in the fire *pops*, and we both still, turning our heads to look at the blaze and the dark water lapping lazily behind it.

"Baby, I swear to God it'll be good. Your pretty little mouth wrapped around me, lit by the fire and under the stars, is going to obliterate every fantasy I've ever had out here when it's just been me and my own hand."

She turns back and has the biggest smile on her face, one I eagerly return.

As if turning down the volume, her grin melts as she intently gets back to her task. She's serious now, moving achingly slow as she drops her mouth and rolls her tongue around my tip.

"Oh, shit," I gasp. Her mouth is hot and takes the length of me in one go. No messing around. No taking her time. "Wait," I manage to say, grasping for her hair and gently pulling up so she meets my eyes. "Give me a minute," I manage to get out.

The fact I need a minute seems to embolden her, and I give her a look that says, *It's been a while.*

Fuck me. "Okay." I nod once, then again. "Remember, you don't have to do this." I want her to know I'm nothing like her ex. I want her to know she's going to undo me, but also, I value her, need her, for so much more than moments like these, though moments like these are quickly turning into some of my favorites.

"I want this," she responds with a long, lazy lick.

"Thank fuck, because I want you to want this." I thrust just a little into her mouth.

In a flash, she's back to business. Her mouth is genius, sucking and pulling exactly how I need it. She fits around me, teeth gently scraping as she takes me in all the way to the base. I can feel the back of her throat through the delicious suction.

She looks up. "I've heard it's good if I hum. Is that a real thing?"

I laugh, dragging a hand down my face. "You're blowing my

mind, sunshine, but sure, hum away." *How did I get so lucky?* loops in my mind on repeat.

She hums *Happy Birthday*, and it's so fucking adorable. I never knew adorable could be this sexy. But it is. *She is.*

It's not long before I'm at my edge, and while selfishly I'd like to hold out, both for ego's sake and for straight-up guilty pleasure, I want her to know how good she is. She's sexy as fuck and has brought me to finish in mere minutes.

"Gonna come," I grit, my breaths short and quick as a strike of pleasure surges through me.

It's an ecstatic release, one I feel deeply and continue to feel as her tongue laps up the sides of my dick, licking me clean. Our eyes meet, the last waves of orgasm still rolling through me. So damn proud.

After taking the time I need to gather my composure, I grin at her. "Roll over," I growl, fully sated but hungry in an entirely different way. "It's your turn."

Her face splits into a mega-watt smile in return, and I know I love her.

CHAPTER 25

Fran

"**K**itty-Cat! I'm home!" I shout, using my flowerpot key to push through the front door. The house is silent, not at all what I imagined I'd walk into the day before Mom and Dad's wedding. When we were growing up, there was music and cooking and arguing while cleaning—usually, all at the same time on special occasions.

Pulling myself out of John's sleeping bag this morning was tough, even tougher, when he wrapped strong arms around me and wouldn't let go. If we'd had the time, I would have made love to him right there. All morning long. We did *everything but* over and over the night before until I'd passed out, claiming I had to get enough sleep to drive myself safely in the morning. He agreed immediately. I don't think either of us wanted to sleep together then separate the next morning. I think when we finally do, it will be a marathon weekend. I'm giddy just thinking about it.

The entryway of my old house is exactly the same—the living room too. Driving away from the John this morning, I wondered if things would look different when I came back. They don't. I think the niggling feeling inside me is my own difference.

I've changed.

It's odd feeling more like I left home today instead of coming home.

"Outside, honey!" Dad calls through the sliding door in the kitchen. The Beach Boys pour through the house from the deck, and I breathe a sigh of relief.

Everything is right in the world.

For a moment, I imagined it was all gone. All changed. Mom and Dad had fallen apart as we all expected them to, and I was getting a glimpse into what would be if they hadn't patched things up. If they were getting a divorce instead of having a vow renewal. It warms me now to spend this weekend celebrating them, sends a buzzing down my spine filled with little girl memories—not all perfect, but there and intact—and I'm grateful. So grateful that they're proving us all wrong.

Not everyone gets a whole family. I know that. Willow didn't. Something that changed her as a child and altered her life forever. John didn't either, and that makes me sick to my stomach because he so clearly longs for his dad's love.

I weave through our entry hall filled with familiar smells and skirt around a vintage *Baywatch* pinball machine in the den that I remember Mom grudgingly conceding to living on the main level. Give and take, and all that.

Outside, Dad's got an acoustic guitar in his hands, and when my bare feet hit weathered wood, I know everything is going to be okay.

"Welcome back, daughter o' mine," he says with a pick stuck in his teeth, his fingers plucking at the strings.

"Dad." I take both his cheeks in my hands and kiss him square on the forehead as he strums along to crooning men who called themselves boys.

Mom mans the grill, her hair pulled back into a ponytail that makes her look so youthful I almost gasp. "Welcome home, Frannie. How's small-town life treating you? That was always a dream of mine, to experience a Hallmark movie life." She flips a piece of meat with a splat, and the grease sizzles. "Or, to travel, live like a vagabond. Maybe both."

My eyes dart to Dad, and I see it, that twitch in his shoulders. They don't realize they do this, but it's plain to me. They poke. Both of them poke at wounds in each other from time to time, throwing darts about their past and making the other feel guilty. I wish they wouldn't.

"Now, listen, if you wanted to live in a small town, all you had to do was ask," my dad says, putting his guitar down to give her his full attention. "And, I'll travel. I'd like to travel."

This is new.

"Oh," Mom responds, all the passive aggressiveness going out of her voice. "What about your warehouse full of toys?"

"As long as you let me keep the important pieces, I'd go anywhere you want. And can I add, it hurts my feelings when you refer to my collectibles as toys, even though I realize that's exactly what they are?"

"Well, thank you. And I apologize; I had no idea I was hurting your feelings and am happy to use the word collectibles."

He nods and then adds, "Maybe that's part of our second act?" He wiggles his eyebrows, knowing he's pleased her and looking damn proud of himself, like pleasing her has, in turn, pleased him. "Traveling around the world together. *Romantic.*"

Shit. It appears they've found the secret to life.

"What's going on here?" I ask Cat as I plop into a chair.

"Ignore them. Their new counselor has made epic progress. Turns out they're normal now. They talk things out like civilized people." Cat looks up from a margarita she's staring into while sitting at a checkered table-clothed table. "I *Amazon-ed* a massive number of earplugs and got plenty to share. You'll thank me."

I grimace, not because I'm not thrilled they're in love, but because I'm human, and they're my parents, and that's *gross.*

"How'd your first sale go?"

"Great. I should have hired staff for moving—"

"You didn't have any help?" Dad stops strumming.

"No, I did. The owner and a few buddies helped out, and then I finally found a reliable company."

"Was he okay with all his stuff flying out the door? With strangers commenting on his grandmother's china? Haggling for his dad's grill?" Mom motions to her own grill while she flips barbecue chicken thighs.

John's tear-stained face flashes across my mind. I miss him already. "It wasn't a grandmother's china kind of sale."

"Sports stuff, right? Did Dave take good care of you?"

My cheeks burn as I pour myself a margarita from a floral pitcher and more unbidden memories, this time steamy memories, wash over me. I spill a little when I smash into a mental picture of riding him with no shame in a Dave's B&B robe. What my hands did with his, John's lips at my ear.

"Yup, sure did."

"Platter!" Mom yells.

"I got you, babe." Dad's on his feet and moving fast. Cat and I make eye contact over our wide margarita rims, *unbelievable.*

"Now I'm gonna have that kind of father that ruins me for other men. His attentiveness is downright adorable." Cat tips her glass and slurps her drink.

"How *you* doin'?" I ask, invoking my best Joey from our days binge-watching *Friends* together, watching her pour herself another drink until the pitcher is completely upside-down. Empty.

"I don't know. We need a miracle move to keep Brand Hub open. My job is on the line..." she trails off.

"Sorry, I wasn't here. You were there for me when my heart was splattered all over the floor."

"It's fine. I'm fine, I mean." She looks up at me with watery eyes that I've never seen. She opens her mouth but bails on whatever she was going to say, instead muttering at her glass as if it's offended her, "This is empty."

"We'll make more." I pat her arm from across the table.

"But I can't make more, you know?" Her bottom lip quivers, and I don't think we're talking about cocktails anymore.

Cat is so together, so in charge, a lioness in her women-owned PR firm, but right now, she's cracking. And while I'm happy she's letting it out, I don't quite know how to respond. This isn't the playing field our relationship is usually on.

"Can I get you a tissue?" I offer.

"*I am not going to cry.*" She shakes her head, and as if she's that powerful, the water in her eyes disappears.

"What can I do?" I ask. "Anything. Name it." She's not going to let those tears drop. She's going to focus on a goal. That's the sister I know so well.

"Be my wingman at the wedding." She laughs while her face twists into a hopeful smile.

"Of course I will. It's just Mom and Dad's friends. We can probably hang together with good drinks at the reception, leave early—"

"No, I mean my *wingman*. Like, for hunting."

I can't tell if this is a good plan or the opposite of what she needs. "You're hunting, huh? Is Willow on board, too?"

"Willow can't come, stomach bug."

"That girl has the worst luck."

My sister nods in agreement. "I need a good, meaningless kiss to get me over the hump. A hot make-out with a stranger, like you did." Her face works to smile, and she raises her glass. "To kissing lists and no commitments," she croaks.

"What, honey?" Dad asks, preoccupied with googling the chords for "California Girls" on his phone.

I wave him off. "It's not all it's cracked up to be. The first few kisses after my breakup were awful. Then John…"

Her face descends right back into her empty margarita glass.

This does not feel like the time to tell her I've fallen for my *not-kiss* and run. Fallen hard. I've only just admitted it to myself.

"But if that's what you need, I'm here for you." I clink her glass. "And you're not empty, Cat. Whatever it takes, we'll find what we need to fill you up just like we'll find the good tequila under the sink to fill this pitcher up again."

"You two stay out of my tequila," Dad says, plopping a silver platter, probably antique and from an old woman's estate sale, on our pretty vintage tablecloth, most likely hand-sewn.

"Slumber party tonight?" Cat asks, eyes hopeful. She's alone so often, married to her job really, and I love when she needs me. This, I can deliver on.

"Absolutely. Anything you want. You pick the movie. You pick the treats."

"There's a viral TikTok dance I've been wanting to—"

"*Gah,*" I groan.

"It's my job to find what's trending! It specifically takes two partners. There are these bunny costumes that everyone has gone crazy over. I ordered two last week—"

"A bunny costume? Are you kidding me?"

"It's an Elle Woods theme. Pretty please, Frannie. It's for feminism!"

"Come on, honey, dance with your sister on the *Toker.*" Dad has no idea what he's talking about as he stuffs a napkin into his collar. And thank God, too. He was so protective when we were growing up, being a young dad and remembering quite clearly what teenagers were thinking, he'd go ballistic if he knew dancing on the *Toker* meant shaking my ass for the tens of thousands of followers Cat maintains to keep her finger on the pulse of trends. Hazard of the job, she always says.

"Fine. And then sleep. You know Mom's going to put us to work tomorrow before the ceremony." And I stayed up all night savoring a delicious man. I need some rest!

Mom appears in a red fifties-style dress and drops the bottle of Dad's good tequila in the center of the table. "I heard that, it's sweet that my offspring know me so well."

"Where have you been? Why did you change?" I've always

thought my mom had a sort of fairy magic to her. She can transform herself at a moment's notice.

"Couldn't grill in vintage." She does a twirl before sitting down for dinner.

"You look stunning. Red's my favorite color, especially on you," Dad says.

"I know," Mom replies. "Pass the salad."

CHAPTER 26

Fran

Cat and I are standing in matching midnight blue dresses on Pier Fifteen in San Francisco on the deck of the Exploratorium, a museum we came to as kids that frequently functions as a wedding venue. A large deck stretches over choppy water with the Golden Gate as a backdrop. High-top tables are draped with navy chiffon and littered with glasses and tiny plates with assorted bites.

A band is cueing up, and to my shock, my mom breaks from our circle of family and friends mid-conversation. She's made her rounds to almost everyone on the intimate guest list and boldly takes the mic.

She pulls the long cord attached to the microphone through her fingers, confidently stepping from side to side and giving the crowd a moment to take notice. Such a badass mom.

Tonight, she's transformed herself into a modern princess in flowing cream pants and a pearl-encrusted bodice. Large, gold heart earrings that we bought years ago, covered in crusty toothpaste in a stranger's vanity, are now polished to perfection and dangle in her ears, catching the light from the setting sun.

"Thank you, everyone, for joining us tonight. If you're in this crowd, you are beloved." Murmurs of appreciation float on warm wind as waves lap below us. "Mike and I went to summer school together. How many of you knew that?"

Almost every hand raises. "She's telling the summer school story? Again?" I ask Cat.

She shrugs, pulling at the sides of her strapless dress. "It's her favorite."

Mom launches into a gush that we've heard nearly a million times. But this time, it strikes me a bit differently.

"He was the coolest. I mean, the *coolest!* Confident, devil may care, bucking authority at every chance he got. I was hooked. Addicted from the very start. He had this car." She steps further into the crowd, the long cord of the mic allowing her plenty of room. Who knew Mom was so comfortable in front of a crowd? "He called it the *Ferrari.*" She raises an eyebrow, an indication to all of us that my dad might have been a little off with the nickname. "And he had a very, very big sound system." She fans herself as if getting all hot and bothered, and everyone chuckles because here comes the punchline. "*It was a hunk of junk!* A red, rusted bucket of scraps. Was it a Fiat, Mike?"

Hovering in the crowd, watching her every move with admiration and awe on his face, my father answers with light in his eyes, "It was a Ford Probe!"

Dad puffs out his chest and stands tall as if he's affronted by her making fun of his car. He laughs along with everyone else who remembers what a wanna-be sports car it was.

"Right," Mom continues. "An ancient, ridiculous, minuscule thing that Mike, the rugby player, could barely squeeze into but was so damn proud of. So confident..." She lets her gaze settle on my father, and all the fire that I've seen them use against each other in the past turns to a fire that's burning for each other in an instant.

Dad peels away from the crowd and joins her, embracing my very surprised mother, then sweeps her low while she clutches his neck with her free hand and lets the hand holding the mic elegantly sweep toward the floor. He kisses her madly. The crowd erupts and cheers.

"May I?" he says, sliding his arm down the length of hers and pulling the mic to his lips.

She hands it to him. Her movements are calm, her face full of rosy-cheeked understanding because she knows as high as the highs are, there are lows with him, too. But her eyes are burning. With respect? I think that's it. And I wonder if this time they're really going to change. Maybe this time, they've learned what it is to live and love and grow together while accepting their faults as well. This time feels different.

Dad pulls her to standing and continues holding the mic with one hand, her hand with the other. "I have to set the record straight." Whistles light up the night, and he chuckles, looking much younger than his already young dad age of fifty-four.

"Tell us your side of the story," Cat stuns me as she calls out. Then, just for me, she says, "I've always wondered what his point of view was for this particular chapter of their life. The Varsity rugby player and the craft nerd. We always hear Mom's side, falling for him, love at first sight. But he's never said what he was feeling in that exact moment."

"You're right," I whisper.

"Girls, listen up!" Dad catches our eyes, and we give an awkward wave to the crowd that pins us with their gaze. We both mime zipping our lips, tossing our keys into the ocean below, in a perfect sister moment that elicits more laughter. We really are the idyllic family tonight. Sometimes you get the best of us, sometimes the worst, but always a family unit. That never changes, and I'm grateful to have it. Grateful my parents haven't hidden their faults so Cat and I can see for ourselves that it's not always perfect.

"Okay, here goes." He clears his voice. "I've never had the guts to say this," he speaks to the crowd now, his closest friends and family, a man on a mission. "She fucking gutted me."

"Michael Bloomfield!" my mom hisses, her composure dissolving. Mom's not afraid of a few curse words thrown around the family table, at a ballgame, or even hurled at a particularly unfriendly driver, but this is their wedding. Well, their second wedding.

"Let me finish," Dad says, pulling her hand to his lips and kissing softly. "It felt good, knowing, maybe not believing, but hearing that you, uh, were so enamored by me. *Then.*" That meaningful tone permeates the space, hangs heavy for a moment, but finally dissipates into the night. Everyone here knows that nothing is perfect. I've been told, and I've seen with my own eyes, that relationships are hard. Feelings get hurt. Words misconstrued. "But I've never had the guts to tell you that you undid me the first moment we met."

He's still speaking into the mic and turns out toward the crowd as if putting on a Ted Talk. "She went to one session of summer school." He holds one finger up as a visual aide for the class. "*One.* Fell behind in math, is all." He waves his hand as if it was nothing. "I was there every summer, summer before college, too. Barely made it out. Didn't finish college. And what everyone needs to know is that *she* was the Rockstar. She had everyone's eyes, not just mine. Everyone was captivated by her. I had to peacock and show off and act way more confident than I really was because I knew I'd be fighting them off with a stick. And look what she did." He gestures to her with tears in his eyes. "She made it." He wipes a stray tear as he speaks directly to her. "You made it, Marin. You were an eighteen-year-old mom, yet you supported me through three years of school while raising a baby and didn't kill me when I said I didn't want to finish, supported me as I opened my dream business, and you got your own degree at night and ran the books a helluva lot more efficiently than I did. To spite me, I sometimes think." The crowd chuckles, and I see more than a few of my parent's friends wiping at wet eyes. Husbands and wives standing closer.

285

"Don't you see? You were the unbelievable one. You took my breath away. I spent every moment after walking into that hot-as-hell school in June in loathing, mourning my summer, and feeling sorry for myself like a jackass—except the bits with you. Because I fell in love with you that day, before you ever did with me. I saw you first. The bass in my car came in real handy. I blared it for *you* —to turn your head in my direction. I loved you first and in a flash. It hasn't been easy, and God knows, we've come so close, so close to ruining everything and calling it quits."

Mom moves to him quickly, crossing a short distance and wrapping her arms around him, pulling at his cheeks, knocking his bowtie lopsided.

"Don't ever give up on me, okay?" he says, his lips brushing hers, the muffled static of the mic pressing between them.

He's holding her when she finally responds, ever so softly, "Never."

After waves of applause, the rest of the wedding goes off without a hitch. The speeches made by the bride and groom infuse every single guest with a feeling of wonder, of chances, choices, twists and turns made in life. What can come of a moment, a glance, a kept commitment? As I trail around the crowd, everyone is telling stories about how they met and how they've worked to stay together, or for some, why they made the tough but brave choice to call it quits.

Stars light the summer night sky, and guests begin to dance while others continue to mingle, looking over the railing of the deck and into the water.

The band kicks into a swing dance. At the suggestion of their therapist, my parents took a few classes and now think they can cut a rug. Cat pulls me into a jovial crowd, everyone laughing, living it up, and tipping their heads back, letting the music and the night, and I think, my parent's love, wash over them.

"I'm ready," she says while twisting and turning in time to the music.

"For what?"

"To find someone to make out with!" she says, her voice raised to carry over the music and the crowd. "To take my mind off my potential joblessness."

"Oh, right. Okay!"

"You pick one, and I'll pick one."

"Are there that many single guys here?" I honestly haven't noticed. My mind is back at the lake...with John.

"Look around, Frannie. There are a ton of single guys here. All of our parent's friends have hot sons." She bites her bottom lip. She's excited, and I'm happy to see her this way. And yes, there are a lot of guys bopping around us. Seems there's a shortage of ladies and a surplus of sons. "How about him?" She eye-points to a White guy in a sports coat who immediately reminds me of my ex.

"Ugh, no, thank you."

"Okay, what about him?" She head-nods toward a tall Black man with a boyish face who looks sheepish when caught in her gaze. "Maybe for me." She decides before I can respond.

"Yeah, for you. Go get 'em, Kitty-Cat."

"What about you?"

"I've met someone," I suddenly blurt, slapping a hand over my mouth because I've shocked myself. It just came out! But I'm desperate to tell her everything, to gush and swoon, and I can't hold it in or pretend I'm man-hunting. "I wanted to tell you yesterday, but you were so upset—"

"Of course, I want you to tell me! Who is it?" she demands while keeping her dance moves easy and light under a string of twinkle lights, a master multi-tasker.

I bite my lip and give her a, *you're not going to believe this* look.

"Superman? The guy from the club who was shockingly also your first estate sale job? Who you swore you wouldn't even kiss, let alone get involved with?"

I nod. "I think I love him."

"Oh my God, Frannie." Her face twists, and it's not the look I was hoping for. It's a worried expression my sister wears now. "Isn't that what we were trying to avoid? After everything you went through?"

"It's different," I murmur. "He's different. And, I'm different, I think."

She stops dancing. "Then I fully support you, Baby Sister. Tell him I'll murder him in his sleep if he hurts you."

"You can tell him yourself when you and Wills come down at the end of summer."

"I can't believe summer is almost over, and all I've done is add to my follower count. You've started your own business and found a man..." she trails off.

"Everything will work out in the end, I promise."

"Right." She shakes me off. "I know, you're right."

"So, do you mind if I bail on the hunt? If you're good, I think I'm going to go check on Wills. See you back at our place? Say bye to Mom and Dad for me?"

"Okay, I will. Drive safe, Frannie. Brunch tomorrow before you go back to lover land?"

"You're on, and I'll cook." I flip my hair over my shoulder and beam at her.

She makes a face. "Aren't you a kidder—"

"No, seriously, I'll cook. Veggie omelet, and I'll look up a recipe for bacon."

"There's no recipe." She laughs. "It's just bacon."

"Well, plan on it. He taught me to cook, Kitty-Cat."

"I love him already."

CHAPTER 27

Fran

I climb the stairs of our pink house and quietly tiptoe through the living room. Willow is asleep on the couch with a book on her chest and a trashcan at her feet, moonlight from the bay window casting her face in a pasty glow. Gently, I let the back of my hand graze her forehead. She's warm but not burning up.

My room is nearest to the back of the house, the most private, and I'm glad for it when a shockingly sexy thought pops into my mind. I blame Willow's wall of romance novels. They give a girl ideas just by looking at them.

It takes a few minutes to dig through my overnight bag and find my pink bunny costume. Cat did make me do a TikTok last night and made me promise to leave the bunny costume in her room in case she needs to do more with Wills as my stand-in. It was kinda fun and I think we got a lot of views, which is what's giving me the guts to not think twice about my idea.

Shimmying into the polyester fur and plopping tall pink ears on my head, I grin, and a laugh escapes me as I creep back to my room and turn the lights out. Then, I flick the bathroom light on and crack the door. Propping my phone on a windowsill and kneeling next to my twin bed, I check my lighting. The bathroom door behind me casts a glow. I'm visible, but everything is softened. The bunny costume looks more pinup and less Halloween as I adjust the moldable ears.

I slide the zipper that runs the length of the front halfway down, letting it stop above my naval.

What the hell am I doing?

I hit call.

"Francesca?" There's a rustling of bedsheets as a mass of sun-kissed brown hair appears on screen, then a flash of his jawline dusted with stubble I want to lick, and a brief rush of bare chest before he pulls his phone back up toward his face. He blinks. "What the— "

"Just a friendly call from your neighborhood bunny," I say, which makes no sense. I've got no idea where I'm going with this, but press on. "You like?"

"Uh. Yeah. Hi. I like."

"Hey!"

"What?" He looks behind him into a dark bedroom.

"You're in a bed."

"I'm in the house."

"The cabin?"

"No, the big house. My house," he corrects. "I paid for it, figure I might as well make use of it."

"Well, Jonathan Boggs. I am proud of you."

"Thanks, bunny-girl. Felt like making some changes. Making room, just in case..." He trails off, looking at me meaningfully through the camera. I have to squeeze my thighs together and look away. He cannot look at me like that when we're not in the same room. "Are those ears?"

"What these?" I bend them up, then down. They're posable, and I try to find the sexiest way to position them as I watch my own image on the screen. "Up or down?"

"One up, one down. You look—"

"What?" This is taking a bit of a chance, I realize. It's the sort of thing I never would have had the guts to do with my ex because of fear he'd shoot me down.

"Just fucking adorable, Francesca." He laughs and shakes his head. Lightning strikes my heart from the joy of pleasing him— from him getting my humor, from him getting me.

He shifts in the bed, and I realize I can only see sheets piled around his waist. They've dipped low, and I don't think....

"Are you wearing underwear?"

His face flushes. Even in the dark, with only his phone to give me light to see, I can tell he's embarrassed. "I don't think so?" He's still half asleep and adorably mystified by this conversation.

"Do you always sleep naked?" The way I want him right now, I'm nearly drooling.

"No, unless I'm with you." He smirks, reminding us both of sleeping naked together, sharing a sleeping bag under the stars. "Laundry day. Now that I'm all settled in the house, I had a lot of backed-up laundry to tend to."

"But I sold the washer and dryer—and the bed!" I say, my head finally catching up with everything he's saying."

"Yeah, about that." He drags a hand over his face but can't fully wipe away a smile. "I bought new ones. I'm thinking of staying here for a bit..." he trails off.

My cheeks heat in the dark. I've got an inkling of where he's going with all this, but I'm not ready to talk about it.

"Bet you enjoyed that. Folding. Clean clothes smells. Bet you even loved putting everything away. Have you stocked the fridge?"

"Of course, I stocked the fridge, and I'm not as much of a neat freak as you think I am."

"Is your laundry all put away in drawers, JB?"

"I don't have any drawers. Bought this bed yesterday after you left and hauled it up to the primary by myself. I did stack everything against the wall, though." He sheepishly scratches the back of his neck, looking for a hat to fiddle with, no doubt. "Wanna know a secret?"

My heart kicks up. "Always."

"I did your laundry, too."

My jaw drops. "You didn't. That's personal stuff! My... All my... All my..." I can't say it and hide my face.

"All your panties. Yes. And bras. All so pretty—"

"Cat is obsessed with lingerie. She always gives me a set for birthdays and Christmas."

"I washed them. Let them air dry after Googling if that sort of thing was dryer-friendly. *The answer is no.* I folded them into tiny triangles. Stacked them right next to mine."

"You did not," I breathe, totally embarrassed but loving him for the effort all the same.

"Your undies are next to my undies. Deal with it," he smiles and leans back against the wall behind him, one arm behind his head showing off the tone and muscle of his biceps.

Despite the fact we've slept together and shared loads of secrets, my heart swells with this small act of kindness. "If this is your idea of knocking down my walls—"

"It's working," he says playfully. "All of it," he finishes more seriously.

I hum in agreement, satisfied with how well I already know him. With how well he can read me. "What made you decide to move in?" I meant for this to be a sexy call, but it's turning into what our conversations always are. Just...real.

He rakes a hand through his hair and leans forward again. I think I'm making him antsy. "Thought it was time. The thought crossed my mind... I could grow with this place. You know what I mean?" I do know what he means, but that doesn't mean I'm ready to think about it yet.

When I don't answer, he adds quickly, "It's all cleaned out, ready to sell. I've got still got an agent booked, but I'm not sure..."

"Maybe you should wait a while. Think on it a bit. You're still hurting, and that's never a good time to make big decisions."

"Are you saying you want me to keep the house, Francesca? Is there a possibility... I mean, I know it's soon, but I want to know if it's a possibility you might end up here. With me."

I suck in a breath, taking in his vulnerability through the screen. It's so refreshing to hear direct communication from a man instead of childish alluding and game-playing.

"Maybe." But that's not all I can give him. I push myself to be honest even though I'm terrified. "Maybe, yes."

"I'll take a *maybe-yes*," he sighs, relieved. "You make me very happy."

"Me, too."

"Why aren't you here right now? It's killing me. You in that costume. I can't take it."

My heart skips a beat. "You need to sleep. I'm sorry I woke you."

"I'm more than glad you did. I'm not gonna forget this for a long time."

"Good. Bunnies don't grow on trees, you know." Am I trying to tell him something? Am I trying to tell myself something? Like, maybe chances like these, like us, only come around once in a life? And I'm terrified to take that final step to solidify it. "Guess I'll go then. I'm glad you're in a cozy bed. Makes me happy."

"Francesca?"

"Yeah?"

"I'm glad you're coming home tomorrow. That makes me happy."

We both know what he said. The word *home* rolls around in my head like the last few sweet tarts in a dish as he waits calmly for my reply.

"Night then." I've taken the chicken exit on a rollercoaster. Again. If he's trying to talk me into moving in with him, me moving to the lake *permanently*, I'm not ready. It wasn't that long ago that I couldn't even kiss him, afraid of what it would mean, afraid it would hurt too much in the end.

"Oh, and Francesca? One more thing—"

"Are you ever going to call me Fran? Or, Frannie?" I shake my head at him, though we both know I've come to love his pet names for me. All of them.

"Never."

Shivers run the length of my body. I know I can count on him to make good on that promise. "I wish I was there too. I can't wait to get back to you."

"One more thing," he growls, eyes turning dark.

"Yes?"

"I'm a belly button man, did you know that?"

"Really..." I draw the word out as I slowly pull the zipper of my bunny suit all the way down. His groan and the way he drags a hand over his face gives me the courage to keep going, so I push the fabric away from my body completely and let it pool around my hips.

"You are so beautiful." His hand reaches beneath the sheet and everything in my core ignites, at the mere sight of him getting turned on just by looking at me. "Send me some pics. Please."

"You got it, JB."

I've been home, or rather, sleeping in John's house surrounded by tall trees and clear water for over two weeks. We leave the sliding door that leads to a balcony off the bedroom open when we sleep. I can hear the lake slapping gently against rocks that litter the shoreline.

Jonathan Boggs has kept me warm every night. In the same bed together, cuddling, talking, whispering things to make each other boil, and doing things to make each other burn. I want to tell him I love him, but I've been holding out because once we pass that intimate point, there will be no going back for me.

We still haven't told Meg. She's such an important part of his life, and I want her to know I would not, will not, ever hurt him. It's a promise we're going to have to make each other, and Meg's going to have to accept that. I had come clean to Cat and Willow at brunch the morning after my parents' wedding. They said they support it based on my blush alone.

The doorbell rings, and I rush down the stairs, my feet freezing on the wood treads in the early morning. Pretending to live here the past few weeks with John for the end of summer has been a dream, and I plan to pretend it's not ending right up until the very last minute. I've thrown on a swimsuit and shorts, ready to take a dip in the pool out back when John gets home from running errands. Though temperatures are still high, fall is creeping into town as shopkeepers turn windows and merchandise from *summer lovin' fun* to *fall festival* ready.

The sale is done. It only ran three additional days when I got back before all the old furnishings were thoroughly wiped out. I cut John a check, and I think we're both trying to make the most of the time we have left. Today's pool party feels like a swan song to the season. Then the grand re-opening party for Boggs, which I think Willow and Cat are driving down for.

With each passing day, I feel more and more confident that this man is in my life for the long haul. I have no idea what that looks like. Neither of us has talked about it since the night I woke him up in a bunny costume, and he hinted at me moving in. I don't know if we're both terrified of rocking the boat, or if we're just happy here in our little bubble and don't want to pop it with realistic thoughts until the last possible moment. I guess time will tell.

I stop to check myself in the hall mirror.

I look like a moony, out of her mind, madly in love, live-in girl-friend. My hair is down and messy. My lips are still swollen from a morning make-out session.

"Hello," a nice man in a fitted suit says when I open the door. "Are you Francesca Bloomfield?"

"That's me," I answer more cheerily than I think the stranger is prepared for.

"I'm here to get the house listed for Mr. Boggs? He said you'd be here..."

Oh. "Right. I, ugh, I didn't realize you were coming."

Pull it together, Fran. He told you he was selling the house. You assumed he'd changed his mind, but you should have asked.

"Please, come in," I add, swinging the door wide.

I give him a tour of the house, knowing all the nooks and cran-nies and information that might come in handy, and I realize I've gotten the tour myself twice. How quickly things change. I also realize how devasted I'm going to be when I eventually leave. Clearly, John is still planning on selling, which probably means he's planning on me going back to San Francisco. I'm sure we'll work it out. Long-distance relationships can work, right?

So, why is my heart sinking by the second?

"Well, I guess that about does it. The universal realtor lock will be on the door for the next ninety days, though I think this will be a quick sale. I've got my work cut out for me with the motel, though. If you happen to hear of anyone interested, please send them my way."

"Oh, you're listing Thistle and Burr?"

"Sure am. It's a nice place and would be a sound investment for a seasoned business owner. Just, not many people in the market to buy motels, you know? Motels on the strip do great in the summer, but in off-season, when everyone is up the mountains, it can be tough."

"Well, I will absolutely let you know if I come across anyone."

He tips an invisible hat. "Thanks for your time. Let Mr. Boggs know I'll be in touch."

"Will do, and thanks."

He turns to walk down the drive, but before I can close the door, I notice another car pulling in. An enormous shit-kicker truck like John's, but quite a bit older and a slightly worse for the wear. The thing looks like it hasn't seen a car wash in a decade after living full-time in the mountains.

I stand in the doorway and watch an older gentleman with wide shoulders and an even wider gait stride toward me. He pulls the bill of his cap low, thinks better of it, and pushes it up with a nudge from his knuckle as he comes to stand before me.

Bright blue eyes. Tan, weathered skin.

It's Ricky Boggs. I'd know him anywhere. I've stared at his photo online for hours while researching his career and his signature.

"Uh, hello there." Understated brown cowboy boots shift side to side. "John in?"

"No, Mr. Boggs. I'm sorry. He's not."

"Ah, you know who I am, then. Wouldn't think my son had told a girlfriend anything about me."

I start to say I'm not John's girlfriend, but I know better. As much as I tried not to get into a relationship, I'm one hundred percent in one now. "He has told me about you," I say instead. "I'm glad you're here. Saves me the trouble of tracking you down myself."

I push all my warring thoughts about the house, about John, and about what it all means for us aside and let his father in.

CHAPTER 28

John

"Y ou finally having a pool party?" Cindy at the Bargain Barn sizes up my haul of inflatables as she chews on minty gum I can smell from across the register.

"Nah, just hanging around the house," I reply, though the pile of pink margarita glasses with dancing limes beg to differ.

"Not your style, I suspect." Each glass beeps as she slides it through checkout, her wide smile showing off a blue wad of gum as she chews. "Glad you showed up to take this stuff off my hands so I don't have to store it for next season."

"Wrapping summer up already." I nod. "We're squeaking out our reopening for the restaurant to try and pick up what's left of summer traffic. Winter is coming."

"So, what's with the celebration?" She pops a bubble and eyes me with a suspicious smile tugging the corners of her lips. The conveyor belt comes to a stop with a pile of candy yet to be wrung.

"No celebration." My haul begs to differ.

"This you too?" she asks.

"For a friend."

"You bought our entire old-timey candy selection for a friend?"

"Yup."

"Must be a good friend." She winks.

I shrug. She is not going to get any details out of me. The second the lake committee hears I'm trying to get Francesca to stick around, they'll be all over her to join the business association of Novel or the gardening club in Clover. And I know Wanda Crosby, our resident grandma who wears afghans around her shoulders year-round, has been trying to con someone into buying her bookstore, packed floor to ceiling as if a hoarder lived there.

After thanking Cindy and dodging more questions about my dating status, my plans with the pretty girl from San Francisco, and what Chef Alec's fall menu might look like at Boggs, I cruise back to the house to see my girl.

I'm not even going to think about the fact she's supposed to be leaving soon, that summer is almost over, and that my time is running out to find the words and convince her to stay.

When I walk through my front door with an armload of rain-bow-colored pool noodles springing from my grasp like confetti cannons, I freeze mid-step and drop everything. The bag of candy spills across the floor, a tin of tape bubble gum rolling all the way into the living room.

"Son," he grunts.

"What are you doing here?"

He tucks salty black hair behind his ears, pulls a baseball cap out of his back pocket, and places it on his head. Old habits and all that. "I heard you were selling."

Shit. "From who?"

"Oh, I still keep my ear to the ground 'round these parts. Patty keeps me updated on town gossip. And you know I'm still on the committee." The lake committee is sacred. Once you're in, you're in for life, like one of those creepy Ivy League fraternities.

"How does she get ahold of you? Not much cell service in the mountains."

"Smoke signals," he replies straight-faced. I wouldn't put it past either of them.

"But I haven't seen you around in months." My eyes dart around the room, looking for Francesca, and he must pick up on it. "She's in the kitchen. Let me in. Sweet girl you got there."

"What do you want, Dad?" I don't know what I want him to say, but I'm waiting on needles to hear it.

"It's a small town, Son. I know how to avoid you. I keep to off hours, and Patty opens up early for baking most mornings. She lets me in. We've had some good chats." He scratches his chin, his eyes as bright and clear as I've seen them in years. "I think she wants to get in my pants." He chuckles.

I ignore his ego. "You're here to tell me not to sell?"

"Nah." He mimes spitting but doesn't actually spit. He gave up chew a few years ago when his gums started to wear away, but the reflex is ingrained in the old ball player. "The place is yours. Just because you're better with money than your old man doesn't mean this place wasn't the one thing I did right. Held onto it, didn't I?"

"You signed it over on the brink of foreclosure, same for the bar."

He taps his temple and clicks his tongue as if it were all part of his master plan, me bailing him out. "Property value. But you know what you're doing, don't you? I saw the new sign at Boggs."

I wince. All the time I spent removing every lick of him out of that restaurant, I never thought about the day he'd see it. The day I'd be confronted with my decision to erase him from my life completely, in one fell swoop, like when you've almost worn a paper clear through with an eraser, and you blow the bits away.

"It was time for a fresh start."

"Sure, sure. You sold everything, I suspect."

"Yeah."

"Fine. Fine. But there's something in one of the closets. It was on a top shelf, so I'm hoping it might still be here. Might have gone overlooked. Can I check? It means an awful lot."

I shake my head. "You came back here for one of your prized game balls? A signed card, maybe? After everything we've been through?"

"I came back for you once, like I said I would. You told me to *fuck off.*"

"Yeah." It's hard to get the words out, but I push anyway, praying I'll feel better for it. "I'm sorry about that."

Why is it so hard to be vulnerable with him? I don't hold back with people in my life. I've accepted the fact I'm a sensitive man—who cries for shit's sake! The guys from my locker room days would roast me. But it's damn near impossible to be that honest with my father.

"Did I hear the door?" Francesca comes in from the kitchen with two glasses of ice water in her hands. "Oh—you're back."

"I am. You met my dad, I see." Still frozen in the doorway, I finally take a few steps in. Being closer to her eases things.

Her eyes jump from me to Ricky and back. Something in the way she pops a hip, the way her feet fidget a bit, makes me wonder if something else is going on in the room, not just the unexpected visit with my dad.

"You need to tell me something?" I ask quietly, meant for her ears, but I know Ricky is watching like a hawk. These two seem to be in cahoots about something, and it damn well better not be me.

"I could ask you the same," she responds, a look on her face I don't recognize. She's holding something back.

I told the realtor she'd be here to open the door, but I also told him I wasn't sure if I'd end up selling at all. The guy insisted on keeping the appointment just in case I decided to go through with the deal.

"I'll get what I came for and get out of your hair," Ricky says.

"He's looking for something he left here."

"What sort of things? I'm sorry. I ran the estate sale myself, and most everything is gone." Quickly, she changes tack and takes a few steps away from me, centering herself between us.

"Francesca runs Frannie's Finds," I supply.

"That how you two met?" He gets up. His movements are much slower and more strained than I remember. He's aged ten years in ten months.

"Ugh, well—" Francesca stammers

"Not exactly," I say, giving her a quick wink. That seems to settle her nerves. She's clearly worried about what's happening in this living room right now. Shoot, as if I can blame her. I've given her every reason to worry. I've only told her the worst bits about my dad and me.

"Just some worthless stuff, really. Some photos that mean a lot. I told you all the memorabilia was yours to do with what you like. It was a cancer to me. Would have sold it all myself, I'm sure, in the end."

He opens a hall closet off the living room. Francesca and I watch him with equally sad expressions. We both know every closet in this house is empty—attic, too. She begged me not to get rid of everything. Not to throw my father and his memories out like trash. But I couldn't see reason then. I was so full of straight-laced, hot as a grand slam, anger.

Now? Not so much, it's simmered. Maybe she did that. Maybe it was time. Probably, it was both.

Still, I didn't save anything of his, let my pride steal his memories. I knew what I was doing. He hurt me, so I hurt him back.

Ricky turns back to us, face wiped blank but clearly struggling to keep it that way. "There's nothing there."

"Was it a green metal box?" Francesca's wringing out her hands. "Sort of rusted around the edges?" she asks quietly. "There were a couple of other things I found, too..."

My eyes dart to her. What has she—

Dad's eyes light up slowly, tentatively hopeful. "That's the one, darlin'."

"Follow me," she says with a tight grin. She's excited about whatever it is she's got hidden, but she's also nervous.

Like dumb puppies, both of us follow her with our mouths hanging open.

She pulls a box from underneath the counter in the laundry room, and we follow her again back to the kitchen.

"I was going to tell you about it when the time was right." The box hits the marble countertop with a *thunk*, and she looks up to see what must be the faces of the two most ridiculous men she's ever met. "Are you mad?" she asks me.

I scrub at my neck, "No."

I'm eager to be rid of all this tension I've been carrying for good. All the stuff, all the work at the bar, all the anger I've been holding in. I don't know what I am in this moment, but mad at my girl for saving my ass is not one of them. If this stuff means enough to Ricky to show up here, tail between his legs even after I told him to fuck off, I want him to have it.

"Can I?" Ricky asks.

I'm ashamed of what I've reduced us to. My father is asking me permission for something that's his. "Yeah, Dad."

"This is... This is exactly what I was hoping to find." He pulls items from the box one by one. Some of them are mine, some of them his. All of it blurring together into an old life I've been trying hard to forget. "It's been a while since I've been through it, but it's all here. Plus, some."

He looks meaningfully at Francesca. I've never seen his eyes so clear. It's good to see him sober again, and the hope that fills me up is suffocating.

"This is John's mom." He points to a photo, his voice quiet and rough like mine was before. He pulls another paper from the box. "This is how we met."

The great Ricky Boggs sheds a tear. I look away, the final bits of my anger with him settling because I'm ready to move on.

He lays a newspaper clipping on the counter, and spreads the wrinkles out as best he can with worn, gnarled hands.

"I didn't go through it all, just tucked things that looked old, or important, or both inside. Hoping it was the right move. Scared to death, I was overstepping."

She wraps an arm around my waist. Does she know she's been propping me up this past month? Supporting me as I tore out every piece of my dad, only to maybe be raw and ready for him to come back?

My hand folds around her neck. I'm not sure if I'm hanging on or saying thank you. It feels like both.

"Is that you?" she asks Ricky, looking at the washed-out clipping. "She ran onto the field?"

Francesca's eyes go wide. I probably should have told her this story, but I chose not to. And she's about to learn why.

"Sure did, wild woman. They called her the Kissing Bandit." Francesca's eyes are dinner plates now, but before she can make a peep, he goes on. "I wasn't the only one, see? She made sort of a habit out of it. For over a year, she had a thing for pitchers. Rushed the field at every game she went to, kissed 'em silly, and then took off."

"You're kidding." She's taking it better than I thought she would. "Not a terrible idea though, if you ask me."

Her eyes cut to mine briefly, and I see what's there. Aside from obviously being enamored with the story, she's drawing conclusions. Putting all the pieces of the puzzle together, of history repeating itself, of my mother's son meeting the love of his life in a similar, unorthodox way. Running from kisses, or to kisses, wanting love and acceptance but terrified of both.

What are the odds? Slim to none, they'd say. I've known that from the first night we met that we were going against all odds, that we were special, and that we *had* to be meant for each other. Ricky and my mom didn't quite make it, but I'm determined Francesca and I will.

"No, ma'am." Ricky shakes his head and sucks his front teeth, the light in his eyes firing up now as he tells Francesca his love story. "But as I said, most importantly, I was the last. The last pitcher she ever rushed the field for. She kissed me and once was all it took. I knew in that moment..." He pokes at the twenty-something faces on the clipping, my mom on the pitcher's mound with her arms thrown around my dad, her foot popped. "I knew she was my soulmate, the woman was meant for me, and I went and poured it down the drain, and for what? The game? The power? The party?"

"Alright, well, you got what you wanted." There's a ball cap around here somewhere. I move around the kitchen, find it by the toaster I bought last week, and pull it low. I'm about done with this walk down memory lane. Hurts too damn much.

Despite it I hear myself say, "Stay if you want."

"We can make something for lunch," Francesca adds. "I've been wanting to try the spinach John got from Grover's this week with a new strawberry vinaigrette dressing recipe I found."

"Can't." He grabs the box and begins a lanky walk to the front door. It's awkward to usher my father out of his own house, but this was his doing.

"Now, wait, you two. Mr. Boggs, you need to know your son is the very best person I know. He's been there for me, he treats his employees and his neighbors right, he takes care of his sister, and he misses the hell out of his mom. Don't leave things like this between the two of you."

Ricky looks stunned, and my heart explodes as Francesca, my girl, fights my monsters right along with me.

"That's a real nice sentiment," Ricky says from the doorway. "You hang on tight to this one," he says directly to me. His blue eyes bore into mine while his thin lips press into an emotional grimace, a hard line.

I'm torn between letting him walk out and fighting him to stay. Because I've missed him. I've missed my dad my whole life, and after all he's done in the end, wouldn't I be the idiot if I didn't give us a second chance? I'm hurt—down into my bones hurt. And I don't think that boy in me will ever fully heal, but I love him, too. It's a damn painful place to be. But his eyes are brighter and clearer than I can ever remember them. It's possible he's changed... Have I?

"Oh," he adds, shifting in his boots on the threshold. "The MLB has asked me to toss a charity pitch with you. At Oracle Park next month."

"They called me. Said they like the father-son angle, so if you're up for it, I guess I am..." That's a solid step in the right direction. And it's for the kids, so it's the least I can do.

"Well, I can't do lunch today, Son. I've got a meeting with my sponsor. But, you meet me on that mound, and I'll know you're ready to start over. I sure as hell am."

"I'll do you one better, old man. Come to the re-opening of Boggs." It's almost a dare, and he knows it. Meet me on my terms, Dad. Come through for me, just once.

"I'll try to remember that." With that, my dad walks out the door. Again.

CHAPTER 29

John

"What's the ETA on the cake?"

"They're delivering at five!" Meg shouts from her office overhead.

"What about the balloon arch?" I yell from the bar below, which I've thoroughly polished. I know I've polished it, but I keep rubbing at the lacquered wood as if people are going to be checking their reflections.

"The what?"

Tossing the rag, I truck up the stairs two at a time. Sure enough, she's frantically pounding away at her keyboard. I can't take the shouting today, I've got too much pent-up, nervous energy. "The balloon arch—didn't you say you were getting a balloon arch?"

"Easy, boss. You said it'd probably blow away," she retorts without looking up from her laptop.

"But you said it would be festive, and we needed to do this up right to draw a crowd. I think your exact words were, *'Don't be a tight-ass. Get the balloon arch.'*"

She turns, struggling to take her eyes off her screen. "But you said the renovation would be enough, that guests would have so much to look at inside that a balloon arch would be wasted. I also believe you said something about a child's birthday party?"

"Balloons remind me of kids' birthday parties...."

"So, I nixed the arch."

"But what if—"

"Everything's going to be great. Ben's doing free boat rides in the Gar Wood off the dock, right?"

"Yeah, he's bringing the vintage nineteen-footer. He'll be here in an hour."

"God, I do love a man driving a wooden boat. *Thank you, Ben.* And Winter is inviting all his stuffy, fluffy family, right?"

"Yeah, supposedly, his parents are coming to town. He's gotten marching orders to settle down—"

"Really?"

I nod, and my sister makes an uh-oh face but rushes on, "And Logan? He coming or hibernating?"

"He's bringing firewood for later tonight. Said he'll man the chimeneas we've got scattered around, keep them stoked and burning, and do a big bonfire at ten on the beach. There was something about fireworks, too, I think, even though we missed the Fourth of July by a week."

"He's such a pyro."

"You know he can't sit still. So, you think we're good?"

"We're good." She nods, pushing away from her computer to address me head-on. "You've done everything in your power to make this perfect, John. You've nailed it. Boggs looks beautiful, and even though you're still not talking to Ricky—"

Guilt crashes over me. I've been so busy with the bar and spending every second with Francesca that I haven't caught up with Meg in a while. "Talked to him recently, actually. Hey, there's also something I need to—" I need to tell her how serious things are with Francesca, that I'm going to officially ask her to move in with me after the party tonight.

But she plows on, understandably shocked that I've spoken to Ricky. "Seriously, when did that happen?"

"He stopped by the house looking for some of his things. Things he saved from his relationship with Mom."

"Oh shit, but everything's gone. Fran did a great job clearing that place out. Her check was posted yesterday."

"Yeah, uh, she actually saved some stuff."

Meg's eyes narrow. "Really? That's kind of forward of her."

Not if she knew how much I'd shared with her, how much she knows, and how much I trust her. I'm grateful she did it.

"She was trying to help, and she did. It was stuff I'd like to keep around, and Ricky was thrilled to find it, too."

"Hm." She nods, looking back at her computer and resuming typing. "Where is Frannie?"

"On her way, I told her not to come early because I'd be a basket case."

"Interesting that you care if your estate sale company sees you sweat at your own restaurant opening. When's she headed back to San Francisco? Soon, right?"

"Yeah, soon."

Her friends are driving to town as we speak for a final weekend. I will tell Meg about us once I know if or when Francesca is actually leaving. If I have it my way, she's not leaving at all, and I'll explain everything to friends, family, and the busybodies in town once I know for sure.

I leave her in the office to finish her work and head back down to the bar.

The day ticks on, and as the clock approaches five, I feel a sort of calm wash over me. My sister has planned a damn nice party, and the renovations look great. Though if I can admit it, there's a small spot in me that misses Ricky's crap.

Dammit, that'd be Francesca getting into my head. The beautiful, well-meaning, annoyingly observant, sensitive sweetheart that she is. Who just so happens to be blowing through the doors with sunshine in her hair right now.

She makes her way around the bar and hugs me around the middle. "Hi, how's it going?" She looks at me all concerned, knowing full well the kind of pressure hosting an event like this is. It's not that different than running the sale she did at Ricky's. I can't wait 'til it's done.

I glance up at the loft overhead and wonder if I should just holler up to Meg and tell her everything now. She'll be happy for us. I know she will when she sees how happy Francesca makes me.

"You," I point at her, "have some explaining to do."

"Am I late?" She looks around.

She's definitely not late. She's the only one here.

"I missed you." I take her chin in hand, kiss that tiny freckle under her eye that drives me crazy, and then pull her lips to mine.

"Are you worried about Ricky showing up?"

I kiss her. I kiss her hard and soft, and everything in between because I've missed her since I left her in my bed this morning and I can't believe I've found someone who cares about me enough to worry about me.

"We're here, as requested!" Winter's commanding voice rings through the restaurant.

Francesca rips her mouth from mine as Winter and Logan come sauntering around the bar. Her cheeks turn strawberry pink as she tries to hide a telling smile.

"The king and queen give their regrets," Winter says, sidling up to my bar, completely ignoring that he's broken up a good thing I had going. "I'll have a scotch, neat."

"They're not coming?" I ask, knowing that this is par for the course with his family. They're always swapping passive aggressive jabs.

"Delayed 'til closer to the holidays. You know they hate seeing me live a normal life here."

"You aren't seriously a prince, are you? I mean, I know the

castle used to be owned by a royal family, and they joke—" Francesca starts, motioning to me and Logan as if we'd make up something that would inflate Winter's ego even more than it is naturally.

"Unfortunately, it's true. Every last drop of blue blood in my veins is from a teeny, tiny town in Skagen." He scrunches his fingers to an eighth of an inch and peers through the crack at Francesca.

"Please don't get him started," Logan grumbles. "I'll have a Guinness, Boss."

"Didn't your parents get remarried?" Winter asks.

Francesca nods as she sips a salted-rim margarita I just handed her. "Getting back from their honeymoon in a few days. From what I've heard, they've decided to have another mid-life crisis, but together this time. They sold their business, and now, who knows what they'll do next. My parents are nuts, but they're in love."

"I don't think it's a bad thing, love making people want to take chances." I can't help myself. The words tumble from my lips.

Winter gives me a smirk. "Wouldn't know, bro, but it sure seems like you do."

Francesca's cheeks turn from strawberries to the color of cinnamon bears she's loves so much. "Cat's sorry she couldn't make it, by the way. Willow, too. They wanted to come early for the party, but Cat had a meeting come up. Willow's going to wait for her so they can drive down for our girls' weekend," she says.

"Too bad my parents can't sell the family business," Winter says, downing the remainder of his drink in one gulp.

"Oh, boohoo. Mr. Silver Spoon," I say, but my eyes stay focused on Francesca. She's looking out the windows at the view of the lake and the mountains as if she doesn't want to leave them. There's a longing in her gaze. Am I making all that up? I sure as hell hope not.

"Heavy is the head that wears the crown, my friend. Heavy is the head." Winter stands more deflated than I've ever seen him and walks out the back doors, down the stairs, and onto the beach.

"What do you need from us tonight?" Logan asks, quietly keeping to himself near the end of the bar. I'd almost forgotten he was there.

"Francesca, you're on greeting duty at the door, if you don't mind."

"Don't mind at all."

"Winter will be an extra bartender," I go on, thinking out loud.

"You're kidding?" Logan barks a laugh.

"How far the mighty have fallen," I reply with a wink. "I need you outside doing the setup. You brought the firewood?"

"That's like asking if a squirrel brought a nut."

Everyone's eyes track to the beach and note a huge pile of cut wood that's already been unloaded, along with stacks of folding chairs with large tables lying in the sand. Winter's already set about sorting them.

"I'll give him a hand," Logan grumbles as he stomps out the back doors.

With the guys gone, I'm left gazing at my girl with a belly full of anticipation—for all that is to come. I slap my hands together and rub my palms. "Let's open a restaurant, sunshine."

For the next hour solid, I shake hands, laugh at bad jokes, and sneak into the kitchen to steal a few bites, careful not to sample my favorite coconut shrimp because that might send my girl to the hospital when I kiss her silly tonight. Giving up shellfish is a small price to pay. Her kisses taste better than anything, anyway. The good people of Clover and Novel show up, putting aside their grudges for the night to partake in the open bar and clap me on the back in congratulations.

It's a real success. The place shines like a new penny, and everyone tells me I'm going to clean up in the summers to come, that tourists are going to drop cash not only to eat here but to enjoy the view under the new, crisp white umbrellas we've scattered around the deck. Our house drink, the Polar Bear Plunge, named for Francesca, is a hit and will draw a winter crowd from all the ski lodges on the mountain when I light a fire and add cozy blankets to the back of everyone's chair.

I catch her eye all night, and my mind plays tricks on me. Sometimes, I imagine her in those bunny ears, with the zipper of her furry onesie pulled all the way down, the way she palmed her own breasts in the photos, squeezing and looking at the camera with such an intentional gaze. I tell my brain to squash those thoughts really quickly, so I don't have to duck into the office to adjust myself. Instead, my traitorous thoughts flip to a completely new fantasy. Francesca is here like she is right now, but she's wearing a Boggs apron and manning the bar because I've just taken our kid to Little League practice.

I shake my head. *Shit, I've got it bad.*

It's time for the toast, according to my watch. I argued against it and tried my best to avoid it, but Winter insisted it was necessary. He handed me a bottle of champagne and told me to smash it against the deck as if I was christening a boat, but I refused. Had to put my foot down somewhere.

"Without further ado," Winter announces, pitching his voice for a large crowd, "I give you Mr. Jonathan Boggs."

The crowd claps, and I take my spot next to him near the back of the bar. Behind me, the sun is setting blood-orange into a blue-green lake. The mountains glow like snow-capped candy corn, strangely enough, and it's breathtaking. I have to force myself not to imagine a trick-or-treating family of five. Ricky wasn't a great dad, but I'm about ready to forgive him for it. He showed up for me once when I wasn't ready. If he shows up today, I think I am. And I'll use that as fuel to be the best dad I can be.

FIVE? What the hell?

"Thanks for coming," I say, roughly and without a drop of the finesse Winter showed. I've been ripped from my active dream, and I'm pissed about it. Standing here like an idiot with an empty champagne glass, I feel all their eyes on me.

"I'll keep this short. This town means a lot to me—"

"Towns!" Virgil Troutwine shouts, the man owns Mr. Bear Toys in Novel, but is ironically the biggest Grinch in town.

"You know I mean all of you, Virgil. Anyway, you backed my dad when the place was his, and you're backing me now." Murmurs roll through the crowd, and I know what they're thinking. Where is the great Ricky Boggs? Not invited to the reopening of his own bar? Except he was. And while it was last minute, the kid inside me is still hoping he shows. "I'd like to thank a few people specifically, and then we can get on with the party."

I roll through my list, shouting people out and counting them off on my fingers. Gus, the crew, my liquor vendors who don't let the supply chain stop them, and, of course, Meg. The dudes. Then, as I'm about to wrap it up, quickly as I promised, my mouth goes rogue.

"One more, and then it's back to open bar, I promise. Francesca Bloomfield," I pause and take a deep breath. "I couldn't have done this without you." My throat tightens. She happens to be standing right underneath the vintage sails we bought together.

Then the unthinkable happens: the front door to Boggs swings wide open. I'm certain, somewhere in the universe, a record scratches. The entire crowd follows my gaze, turning to look behind them.

"Uh, sorry I'm late." My dad strides in, rounds the bar, and whisper orders a ginger ale from Winter, who's resumed his duties.

"Glad you're here," I say with a shaky voice.

"Place looks great, Son. You did good." He raises his glass and drinks to me.

The crowd erupts with applause. Someone must've told the DJ to hit it because music fills the room with Van Morrison lyrics.

Nice choice.

It's all I can do to hold the tears back, but tonight, they're happy tears.

It's dark outside now. Everyone has gone. Ricky and I shared a few quick words at the bar and an even quicker one-armed hug. Then he was gone, an empty glass with a sweaty napkin the only sign he'd been here.

He came through. He showed up. And I'll take it.

A sense of peace washes over me in my bar with my girl. With my sunshine, even though it's midnight, exactly where I'm supposed to be.

"You worked your ass off tonight," I say while tossing the last dirty rag into a bin for laundry later. Chef Alec will hate that pile in the morning. I'll owe him fancy produce for a month.

"I didn't do anything. This was all you." She's perched on the bar, drinking a cold bottle of beer she's just reached for herself.

Not true. She helped clear tables, charmed guests, and poured drinks when the bar got so busy Winter couldn't keep up. We got away for about ten minutes together on a boat ride with Ben and a couple of friends. The bonfires on the beach were stoked and roaring due to Logan's constant attention, but other than that, it was an exhausting night.

I cross the distance and push myself between her legs. She opens them easily for me, a little laughter in her mouth as she takes a sip.

"You done?" I ask, eyeing the bottle.

"Not sure yet." Her pulse is jumping rapidly in her neck, and she takes another gulp. She's nervous.

I'm not sure why. I know this woman better than anyone I've ever slept with. That's where this is going. At least, where I want it to go, and then I'll beg her to stay with me for good.

"You know," I whisper, gripping her hips to pull her closer. "I kinda regret what I said in my speech."

She stills. "Which part?"

"Not what I said, exactly, but how I said it. *You are so important to me*, Francesca. I don't want things to end. There. I said it straight to you." I let my forehead drop to her shoulder with a low groan. "I'll tell Meg everything. I can't wait to tell the dudes, though I'm pretty sure Winter knows. But what I want to know is, what am I telling them? Are you still planning to move back to the bay? Or—"

"John..."

"It's almost out of our control now, right? Francesca, you have to know the way I feel about you is very serious." I shake my head. "I'm sorry." I look up at her, allowing my gaze to roam her face. "What I'm trying to say is," I gulp, "I love you. More than I thought I was capable of."

She sucks in a breath, surprised at my directness, I guess. I'm taking a gamble by laying all my cards on the table so early, but to pretend any differently, or play any more games, would just be delaying the inevitable at this point.

The electric tug between us is there and stronger than ever. We're inching closer with every breath we take, and I'm about to kiss her on my bar. I know what she wants. I know what she needs. I've been acutely aware of her needs ever since that night at the B&B. But I want to hear her say it before I'll touch her again.

"Say it, Francesca. Say it now. Please, I'm begging you to let it be what it really is—what it's been from the start."

"It's not that simple. I need to figure out how I'm going to deal with things at home... If, maybe, I don't go back."

"You're considering staying?" No reason to hide the hope in my tone. I'm sure my face says it all. We've danced around the subject, but this is the first solid thing she's said about moving... here...for me.

"Of course, I've thought about it. I don't want to leave you, John. Haven't you figured that out yet?" I grasp her chin and make sure our eye contact doesn't break as she speaks to me. "I am falling for you, but it's hard to trust it."

"Nothing bad is going to happen, I promise." I let my fingers trail her cheekbones down the bridge of her nose. The love I feel is overwhelming, but I don't want to push her. I'll happily take, *falling for me.*

"Everything is moving so fast."

"Time has nothing to do with the way I feel about you." My palms grasp under her thighs, and I pull her gingerly so she's flush against my stomach, legs spread, perched on my bar.

Her thighs widen easily, her hips opening naturally to me. My face falls to her chest. "Stop fighting it, baby."

CHAPTER 30

Fran

His lips drop to my shoulder in a delicate, closed mouth kiss. The spaghetti strap on my yellow sundress falls, the dress I was wearing the first time I walked into this bar.

"What do you want, Francesca?" He pushes his forehead into my neck, drags his nose through my hair, inhaling while dropping kisses behind my ear. He holds tight to my knees, my feet propped up on barstools.

When I don't respond, he lets out a soft, low moan as if I'm torturing him.

"You," I say in a rush, tipping my head back and opening up to him, pushing my knees even wider to welcome him into my space. "I want you, and you know it. Since Throwbacks, I've wanted you and tried to pretend I didn't. I hardly knew you. And now that I do, I think I was still holding on to old fears. But not anymore." I tilt my head, putting my chest on display, and waiting for his kisses. Real kisses. Kisses like the ones I got after I drove him over the edge in his tent with just my mouth while snuggled in one sleeping bag like teenagers.

"You have no idea how happy that makes me," he breaths in my ear.

How'd he get under my skin? How does he know how badly I need him? Because I do. I need this man, and as terrifying as it is that I've broken my promise to myself, that I've let myself fall again, in this moment, I don't care. In this moment, I'm no longer scared we'll hurt each other. I'm much more concerned we'll destroy ourselves, day by day, and from the inside out, without each other. So, I'll tell him everything. If he wants to hear a rush of needy words from me, he'll get them every time from now on.

Desperately, I pull his face to mine and look directly into his eyes. "You surprised me, Jonathan Boggs. I didn't see you coming."

"Sure, you did. You came to me, remember? You made the first move, and it was so fucking sexy."

"Yeah, but I didn't know you were going to put me back together so thoroughly. I wanted some glue, some comfort, if only for the moment. Just a kiss, right?" I press my mouth to his ear. "You healed me with your kiss, with one look, the way you touch me. You've ruined me for anyone else."

"Ugh," he groans as if he's gutted by my words, and he didn't ask for it specifically. "It's so good. I want more, but right now, I need you to kiss me." His lips drop to my mouth, and he gives me exactly what I want.

The kiss is soft at first until our lips part, his tongue stroking mine, needy and sweet. He's saying so many things with this kiss, and I try to respond. I tug at his bottom lip as we break for much-needed air, both of us gasping into each other, and I lick it better.

"You make me feel special, cherished. I've never felt as wanted as I have with you," I breathe.

Swiftly, he pushes me back onto my elbows and throws one of my legs over the bar so that I'm leaning back with one foot dangling on either side of the shiny mahogany.

His muscles tense under the short sleeves of his T-shirt sporting the colorful Boggs fish logo as he pushes up onto the bar with both hands, his forearms straining as he hovers over me. It's a feat of balance as he lowers my head onto the bar. The hardness of the wood isn't so bad because he's taking his weight, except for his hips, which begin to grind in slow circles against my center. Above me, past his beautiful face and smiling lips, are the wooden beams of the bar I remember admiring the first day I got here when Boggs was merely a place to meet a client, full of construction and chaos.

Who could have predicted this outcome? Me laid out on this exact bar, about to be a meal by the looks of his hungry eyes.

I push up slightly to capture his mouth—I can't stand him this close without his mouth on me—and sticky remnants of drinks pull at my shoulder blades. A giggle slips out of me when I think how long I made him wait to kiss me. He'll forever be number five. There will never be another list, and certainly not another man, for me.

He manages to balance while continuing to kiss me, slowly pushing his hips into my center so I can feel everything he wants to give me even though we've still got our clothes on. I bet he'll never look at his bar the same again, we're branding it, and I fucking love that about us.

"John, I want to say it back. I want to say I *love*—" I start in a rush as his lips drag down my sternum.

"You don't have to," he says between kisses. "I didn't mean to pressure you by saying it. I couldn't hold it in any longer," he says as he bites into the full crest of my breast. "If you're not ready, I can wait." Then in one quick motion, he pulls the bodice of my dress down to my waist. "*Fuck, Francesca.*"

I moan in response. It's not that I'm not ready to tell him, but holding onto my secret for a while longer just to be safe doesn't seem like a bad idea, either. A part of me is still scared of getting hurt.

"I'll take what I can get when it comes to you. I'll take anything I'm so gone for you, baby. If there are only pieces, if you're still broken, I'll hold those pieces in my hands until you're ready. I swear I will."

And I love that he's willing to accept me the way I am—on my time.

All I can do is whimper in reply. *I trust you. I believe you.*

My breasts are on full display, the dress doesn't need a bra, and I push myself together as his face hungrily goes back and forth, sucking each nipple into his mouth, hot and greedy.

"I'm glad I didn't know you were bare under this dress during the party. I never would have made it." He devours me again, his lips taking one nipple deftly and sucking hard. His hand palms the other.

A gasp leaves me, then a high-pitched mewl that I can't hold in as a sweet pressure builds in my core. I was always self-conscious of the sounds I made with my ex. I don't think he liked them. But John grinds his hips hard into me the second he hears my response to his mouth.

"Francesca," he murmurs lovingly into my skin, "I can't take what you do to me. You've cracked me open. I thought I was ready, but I wasn't ready for you."

How he's holding himself up and doing the things he's doing with his body, balancing over mine on this bar, is downright magical. "Wanted this," I pant, "since the night we danced—please."

"Fuck, that *word* on your lips is going to be my undoing." He pulls back and hops unceremoniously off the bar.

"Don't stop!" I push up on both my hands, my lips turning down in a huge pout.

"God, that fucking freckle right under your eye and the way your lips are pouting at me right now, it's kryptonite."

"You stopped!" I protest.

"Baby, I'm not stopping, but I can't do you justice on a bar top. C'mon." He pulls at my thighs until my legs are wrapped and locked at the ankles around him, and he plucks me easily from the bar.

I reach for his shirt and quickly pull it over his head, tossing it toward the bin of rags to be washed. Before he can do anything else, I burrow into him, then sigh deeply as he wraps his arms around my back, giving us a moment to just *be*. His skin, warm and smooth, pressed right up against my breasts and the flat of my stomach is pure bliss, and I wrap my arms tightly around his neck, giving him nowhere to go. He burrows right back into me, his mouth sucking at my neck in a way I know will leave a mark.

"Wait, your hat—" I say as he begins to move. Where we're going, I've got no idea.

"Later," he breathes, smothering his face into my chest. "I need this dress off you—now."

"Hat first," I demand with a grin.

He leans toward the bar so I can arch my back and grab his hat, plopping it on his head. The tan skin, hard chest, and baseball hat do things to my insides that feel like I've been starved for weeks.

"Where are we going?" I pant. I am not picky.

He grunts. "I'm taking you to bed. Are you ready?"

I shake my head. "I don't want to go to bed. No way I'm driving all the way to the house with you now."

We've waited to sleep together, maybe because I was scared of what crossing that final line would mean between us, maybe because we both needed time to adjust to our emotions, or maybe because we were so busy doing everything else.

"No?" He quirks a brow, and a smile tugs at one corner of his mouth. "You can't wait?"

"Not one more minute, can you?"

"I was trying to be a gentleman to take you back to a warm bed, and I don't know," he moves like if he didn't have his hands full of me right now, he'd probably fiddle with his hat, "light a candle or something."

"I don't need candles, John. I just need you. That's all." I shrug because I mean it. We don't need anything fancy. That's not us. We just need each other.

"You want me to—"

I nod eagerly, waiting for him to say it—begging him with my eyes to say it.

But he hedges. "You want me to..." he trails off again, uncertain.

"I want you to fuck me in your bar, JB."

"Holy shit, from your mouth, that's the hottest thing I've ever heard. I didn't know my sunshine had a dark side," he grumbles into my ear.

"Only because I trust you enough to show it."

My words must truly light a fire in him. He pulls an over-turned chair from a table by the window, pushes it off to the side, and plops my ass on the tabletop, then gently pulls my dress over my head. I raise my arms and let him. My feet dangle while he takes me in, and I hope he likes what he sees.

"Naked in my bar, this thong high on your hips," he says as he tugs at the thin pink fabric. I lift, and he rolls the scrap of lace down my thighs frustratingly slowly. "Fuck me."

He drops to his knees and kisses my thighs, his hands firmly wrapped around the backs of my calves, never pushing me before I'm ready. With nothing to hide from him and no reservations, I spread my thighs wide and arch my back, letting my hair brush the tabletop, eagerly awaiting his next move.

Determined, he twists his hat around backward, then looks up at me adoringly and licks his lips.

My own mouth drops open in a gasp at the sight. He is going to make a meal of me. "*Please*," I moan.

The more he keeps me waiting, the more I think I'll die without his lips, without his hands, *without him*.

In a flash, his mouth is on me. Hot and steady, he strokes his tongue against my center. My head falls back again, and I brace myself with my hands on the table that's smooth and clean as tension coils in my core.

When I let out a whimper, he places one foot on his shoulder, widening me for access, spreading me with his fingers. His mouth seals over the tight bud of nerves, and I stutter while calling out his name, my voice bouncing off the walls of his bar loud and bright. Sweet and shocking waves of pleasure wind me up tighter and tighter.

"I can't believe you're mine," he replies, easily pushing two fingers inside me because I'm soaked with need.

"Oh shit," I moan as pleasure rises up inside me. He curves his fingers, hooking me in just the right spot as my core grips him.

"*You are so fucking beautiful. Pure sunshine.* Do you know that? You walk into a room, and I swear it lights up brighter and warmer because you're in it. Your smile is magic."

My thighs squeeze against the pleasant agony he's creating between them, his thumb finding that bud of nerves and applying pressure. He moves first in slow circles, but as my breathing accelerates and my hips begin pushing back, riding his hand, he increases speed and pressure.

That coil bursts inside me, stretching out until I'm strung so tight I fall back against the table, pushing into his shoulders with my feet to ride the intense and sudden release. A chair behind me goes crashing to the ground as I pant through the shattering orgasm. The waves of hot, slick pleasure don't stop, and John doesn't stop pulling them from me, standing but leaving his hand pressed into me, wringing out every last drop.

"That's it. You're such a good girl."

"That was—" I gasp.

"So hot," he finishes. "I will never walk through this room or pour a drink at the bar without fantasizing about this exact moment."

"*More,*" is all I can say in answer, grabbing for his hips and unbuttoning his pants with shaking fingers. "We are not done."

"Didn't think we were, baby." He lets me have my way with him, pushing his zipper down until everything I'm aching for is within my reach.

His length is warm and heavy in my hand, the tip already shining with his arousal. "Do you have a—"

He bends quickly and hands me a condom from his shorts pocket. "Here—" He gasps as I move my hand up and down his shaft, my fingertips barely able to meet. He's perfect.

"You came prepared."

"I came hopeful," he manages to say.

After rolling the condom down his length, I guide him toward my center, and he grabs my hips, tilting them toward him. But he's still too far away. Just when I think we need to find another position, he reaches behind me and pushes the remaining chairs off the table, sending them crashing to the ground.

Holy shit.

A growl vibrates low in his throat. He leans hungrily over me, pulling one knee up and pressing it between us as his chest almost meets mine, creating more room for him to access me. I lean back on both my elbows as his tip presses against my entrance.

I can't go one more minute without him. "John, *please.*"

I'm begging.

That's all it takes for him to thrust into me fully. No warning, no more hesitation, no taking it easy. No more taking it slow. We are all in.

He pumps slowly at first, his biceps flexing as he again supports his weight on the table while I drop unceremoniously onto my back. One leg is bent and trapped between us, but I manage to ground my other foot on the leg of a fallen chair to give myself some purchase as I push back into him.

Hungrily, our mouths find each other as we set our pace, both of us moving harder and faster as our mouths take more and more.

"Francesca, it almost hurts," he says between biting kisses.

"What hurts, baby?" But I know.

"How much I want you. I'm going to want you forever. You

are. It. For. Me." He grips my waist and punctuates each word with a slick, fast thrust, hitting me so deep I see stars.

"Fuck," he curses, moving faster. "It's too good—"

"I know," I say before he can finish.

The way he's hitting me is already winding me up again. Add that to the fact I've wanted him inside me all night, watching him work hard at something he loves with people he cares about. Knowing he was watching me through it all as if I'm the only thing he wants in this world.

I grasp his cheeks with both my hands, tossing his hat to the floor because I need to run my finger through his hair and tug so he knows he's mine.

He continues plunging into me as we hold each other's gaze. I meet him halfway on every thrust, every whimper, every moan. He growls again, rough and right against the shell of my ear until there's no more holding on. We both spiral out together, trying to kiss in the moment, but it's more like gasping into each other's mouths as the pleasure overwhelms us.

There's no more movement as he collapses over me, my legs wrapping around his waist to keep him buried deep inside.

Three days later, the doorbell rings, and I drag my sleep mask off my face.

Cat and Willow are finally in town, staying in two rooms John and I cleaned up at Thistle and Burr under the guise that I was staying there too. Later today, we're headed out on our own road trip made for three, a much-needed reunion. I miss my buddies.

John and I are snuggled in bed, mid-day sun creeping through curtains I'm glad I forgot to price for the sale. We deserved a day to sleep late. We've both earned it turning over motel rooms on our own, and we stayed up all night last night earning it even more, making love in almost every room of the house.

"Who could that be?"

My mind wanders to the realtor who knocked on the door a few days ago. The one John didn't cancel. "I got it. Probably the realtor stopping by to drop off flyers."

He grunts and rolls over. Poor boy, I think I've worn him out. "Are you going to break the bad news, then?"

I still halfway across the room with newfound, happy energy. "Which is?"

We started the conversation of what our relationship was going to look like after the summer last night, but we never finished it.

John sits up, sheets pooling around his waist. "I'm staying, and I want to take it off the market..." he trails off.

My eyes water, and I nod, my lips quivering, but instead, I push them into a smile. "Sure, JB. If it is him, that's what I'll say."

"Good girl," he says, smiling softly and dropping back down into bed with a happy, sleepy moan.

Trotting down the stairs in bright yellow slippers that John surprised me with a few days ago and a Boggs bar and grill T-shirt, I throw the door open without thinking. Everything is exactly as it should be, and I'm ready to scream it from the mountaintops.

Meg Martinez stands on the doorstep with a box of Patty's pastries in hand.

"Morning, I thought...." Her smile falters as her words trail off. "I thought you were at the motel with your friends? I left a box on the doorstep of *your room*." She holds up the pink pastry box. She must have stopped at the motel before she came here.

I look down at myself and my slumber party attire. We haven't told Meg what's happening between us. We both wanted to take our time. We *needed time* to discuss exactly how we planned to make our relationship work. And then disinfecting a stale motel and my friends arriving in town sort of took over.

"Meg. Hi. I—"

"Laundry day, Fran?"

"Hey, baby?" John's rumbly morning voice booms from upstairs. My head snaps toward the landing, but there's no sign of him. "Tell him to beat it and get back up here, Francesca!"

My gaze drags back to Meg's, a knowing look on her face.

"So, when I told you not to get involved with my brother, break his heart, and bounce at the end of summer, you what? Thought it was a suggestion?"

Oh, shit. She is pissed. I've got a mouth full of sand and can't respond.

Padding feet sound above me, and I hear him stomp slowly down the stairs. "Meg, hey. Come in."

"No. I don't think I will," she says, shoving the box in John's hands when he comes to stand beside me at the door. "So, you're staying?" she asks me, point blank.

"No. I, we haven't... I'm leaving today, actually...."

A brisk fall wind blows through the entry as if a warning. Summer is over, and so is our secret. "I never thought my brother would lie to me like this."

"Come on, Meg!" John shouts when she turns on her heel. "Wait!"

But she's gone, stomping down the gravel drive toward her bike. And so are all the cozy feelings I woke up with.

"Ironic that today's the day I pack and head out, isn't it? Destiny's not on our side this morning, is she?"

John stands stoic next to me, shirtless and in a pair of gray sweatpants.

"Don't say that. It's my fault. I should have told her sooner. She'll come around," he says, rubbing at the back of his neck.

"It's my fault. I promised her in the first place. I told you she'd be pissed. You should go after her."

"I'm not leaving now, not when you've got, what? An hour before you meet the girls?" But his eyes are tracking her as she pops up her kickstand and mounts her bike.

"Honestly, I'm all packed up. I'll eat a doughnut and hit the road. Go." I motion toward Meg as she begins to peddle. "I know you need to fix things with her. I never feel right when things are bad between Cat and I."

"But, we need a plan."

Last night, we were supposed to talk about how we would move forward, what we wanted from each other, and how the distance between our lives was going to factor in. We barely made it past taking the house off the market before all our plans got eaten up by hot kisses.

"We have time for that. I have to go home and sort things out regardless, decide if, how, and when I can uproot my entire life. Check in with my parents. I rent with Cat and Willow—it'll affect them if I move out. I've been gone for so long. I've loved living in this bubble with you, but we both knew it wasn't forever."

"Why does it feel like this could be the end? Francesca, some of the people I've loved most have left. My mom, my dad—"

"This is not me leaving you. It's just the reality of the situation. Okay? Go talk to your sister. For now, I have to go home and figure things out, that's all."

Can he tell that I'm scared about leaving everything I know in San Francisco to move to the lake to be with him? And what if Meg doesn't forgive us? Forgive me? What then?

"Fine. I'll go because it kills me to know she's hurt. When she understands how I feel about you, all of this will blow over. I promise. Don't let this be something that stops you from coming back to me."

I pat him on the shoulder and try to muster an untroubled smile, but it wavers. And he sees it. "I promised the girls I'd pick them up. We're headed to Genoa first thing. I talked up Dave's B&B and Spellbound Springs a little too much."

"Staying in the kids' room?"

He takes a step back, the opposite direction I ever want him moving in regard to me, and scratches the back of his neck. His hand is looking for his hat and coming up empty.

"God, no," I say, a small laugh escaping my lips. I have very fond memories of that room. "We're sharing a king bed in the Camelot room. My sister bought crowns. Then, I'll drag them to a few sales on the way home."

"Come back to me, Francesca. Please. Don't let this be the end of us. We're more than just a summer..."

"This isn't the end, John," I say fervently, taking the steps needed to close the space between us and hugging him around the middle.

"Then why does it feel that way?" he murmurs over the top of my head.

My cheek falls to his chest. We share a moment together, the last moment of the summer and what we made of it. The truth is, neither of us can be sure what our futures hold.

"I'll call you when I get home, okay?"

"Okay." He gently drags a hand over my hair, petting me sweetly as if I'm his absolute favorite thing. "And baby, this is home. If you want it to be."

"Can't say I thought I'd see this day come," Ricky says as we jostle around on a bench seat on a bus. "Two pitchers, one ball, and one mound. Who can make it to catcher, ya think? You gonna punish me forever if it's me?"

The Oracle Park shuttle takes us around the back of the stadium, where players enter to warm up, suit up, and act a fool in the locker rooms well before game time.

It's been two weeks since I've seen Francesca. She and her friends were out on a road trip, and then she went straight back to San Francisco—and stayed because someone booked her for an estate sale. It wasn't ideal, not getting to say a real goodbye and not having her come straight back to me. But we've talked. We've skirted around issues like moving because she's been busy with the sale, and now I'm busy with all the media and organizing that's gone into today's charity pitch.

Still hurts that I haven't had my eyes or my hands on her in so long. Long distance is not going to work.

I brace myself on the seat in front of me as the bus comes to an abrupt stop, but neither of us moves. Players, agents, and press people make their way down the aisle and head out into the sun toward the stadium.

"You know," I answer him, "I wasn't trying to punish you. Is that how you felt?"

He turns to me. The bus driver kills the engine and gets off without a look at us. "It shouldn't have been about how I felt, Son."

"I was a hurt kid, which turned into an angry kid. I get *now* why you weren't around. You were working. Logistics, bills, all that comes with being an adult. But all you ever talked about was me playing ball or you slipping down the neck of a bottle. Never choosing me unless I was hitting homers, and sometimes that wasn't even enough."

"I put a lot of pressure on you."

"You did."

"And when my pie in the sky dreams went to shit—"

"You mean when I didn't automatically forgive you and go into business, bail you out, and rebrand as the happy father-son bar buddies you wanted us to be?"

He snatches his hat off his head and pulls it right back into place. "Think you got that deep into my head, huh? Got it all figured out?"

"I think kids pick up on everything when it comes to their parents."

"Maybe. But I loved you more than all that in the end."

"If things had gone differently, then wouldn't have minded if I'd eclipsed you? The great Ricky Boggs." Part of me wonders if even though he was hard on me all those years, if I had been better than him in the end, he would have resented me for it.

"Nah." He scratches at his chin with a knobby knuckle and gazes out the square bus window. "I wanted you to win, and I didn't care as much as I thought I did about the trophies in the end. I cleaned up for you. I didn't know my limits—the limits on my body and the bottle I tortured it with. I didn't know the consequences of all that wanting. But I do now."

"Yeah?"

"Yeah." He meets my eyes. "You can't live your life worried about what others think or what others want. You gotta live it for you."

"That what you're doing now?"

"Shoot, I guess." He smiles. "I lost the ability to play the game, lost my money, lost my bar, and lost my son." His eyes begin to water, and I have to look away. "Lost my wife, the love of my goddamn life. You know I wanted her back? But I was too damn scared of how much it'd hurt if she turned me down. I wasn't brave, not like you." He shakes his head. He sees in my eyes that I don't follow. I don't know when I've been brave. "Raising your baby sister the way you did."

I grunt. Mom would love to know that in the end, he loved her this damn much, and he was proud of me. Shit, I can't help loving the feeling myself.

"Speaking of," he pulls himself together, correcting his tone with a cough, "how's your girl?"

"You caught on to that, huh?"

"Told ya not to let her go. I could read the twinkle in your eye plain as day. So, where is she? She coming today?"

"No, she uh, couldn't make it work," I hedge, suddenly uncomfortable in my seat.

"Moved out as far as I can see. But you took the house off the market, I hear."

"Patty still sneaking you gossip and croissants?"

"Maybe. Maybe a little more sugar than that, even." I chuckle at that.

"Meg doesn't like it."

"Doesn't like Frannie?"

"Doesn't like that we hid our relationship from her, only for a while, when we didn't know what it was ourselves."

"Your sister is tough, strong and passionate like her momma. She'll come around."

"She has to. I'm not picking between them. I can't live without either one."

"How's Frannie taking all this?"

"I think it scared her off a bit, to be honest. She doesn't think she's made the best impression, starting out on the wrong foot with family. I need a chance to make it right. But she's been working here in the city, and I've been making sure Boggs is running smoothly and planning for today. After this is done, though, I can't be apart from her another minute. I do know that."

"And if she doesn't want to uproot her entire life for you?"

I shrug and answer without hesitation. "I'll move here." It's what I should have told her from the start. Whatever it takes, end of story.

The parking lot is bare, not a soul in sight as we sit a beat longer on the bus that feels like a little cocoon of overdue therapy. The sun shines down on the pavement like it does every day, whether we want it to or not. The stadium stands defiant against the blue sky, with no idea what it does to men and their dreams, for better or worse.

Chews 'em up, spits 'em out, one way or another.

And then what? What's left?

"You loved Mom," I say because I know he did, and I think he lives with the regret of not being there at the end. And I think that must hurt more than I hope to ever know.

"I did, and I lost that, too. Can't make it right now, but I can do right by you. That's what I was trying to do when I signed over the deed to the bar. I realized real quick I shouldn't have asked you for the money. You didn't owe me shit. A father who was never around, a guy who only turned up to critique your swing and compliment myself on your talents."

"I didn't want your bar, just wanted you. But thanks, all the same. You gave me something to cling to, to work for when I needed it."

I stand, uncomfortable with all the sharing, knowing my own eyes are welling up. "We'd better get inside."

Ricky's are watery, too, bright blue pools staring back at me. Like father, like son, I guess.

He follows me down the steps of the bus, both of us with bags over our shoulders. The team sent us uniforms so we could suit up and relive the glory days and also so they can take advantage via photo ops. After all, it's for the kids.

In a way, I'm glad the old man is getting what he wanted—at least in this small way. He's lived to play the game.

"What I don't get is," I say, "why'd you take off? Why'd you take to the woods and cut me out entirely?"

"Son, sometimes people don't know how to accept love when it's right in front of them. Don't know how to separate old pain from new beginnings...you understand?"

Francesca. "I think I do."

He pops a wad of gum in his mouth. Once a ballplayer, always a ballplayer. "And drying out just in time to smell your own funk and come to terms with all your mistakes... Man, if that don't set ya straight, I don't know what will. You gotta get that girl back."

I slap him on the shoulder as he swings the door of the locker room wide, and we're greeted by bare butts, good-natured jeering, and a smell I'll always recognize.

Some things never change. And some things do.

"I'm trying, Dad, and I don't plan to stop. The second this game is over, I'm headed straight to her and not taking no for an answer."

CHAPTER 32

Fran

The clock ticks like it's got something against me, agonizingly slow.

I woke up at five, unable to roll over and drift back off, my sleep mask still at the lake and probably tangled up somewhere in John's bed because I forgot to pack it. The second my eyes opened, I could only think about him. It's been the same way falling asleep. For the past two weeks, I've been running through our conversation over and over.

Why does it feel like this is the end? So many of the people I've loved have left.

"Morning, everyone."

There's a line already formed down the sidewalk of my current sale. It was a last-minute booking, and I left all my signage tucked away in the cabin in the woods at John's place. I'd planned on going right back for it. But a friend of my parents needed a favor when their mother died, and I got out my Sharpie and wrote Frannie's Finds on some cardboard. Sometimes, you don't need all the frills. Sometimes, you just need a Sharpie to get the job done.

It's in an old neighborhood with neat yards and colorful homes with tended gardens holding on tight to summer. The things inside are lovely—from a woman who died alone with no family nearby. Treasures for someone else to find now.

Stepping over the talisman left in line as a placeholder while they no doubt ran to a McDonald's for a bathroom and a mid-morning snack, I open the door and shimmy inside.

After readying the house, I check my phone before tucking it back into the waistband of my shorts. John's throwing his pitch today. It's silly, but I'd hoped I'd become his new lucky call. We spoke briefly last night, but both of us are hesitating. Him thinking perhaps I've left for good; me wondering if I've got the guts to risk it all and go back.

Focus, Frannie. It's time to open.

The onslaught of people is fast and hard at first but simmers by the time I've eaten all my Doritos and drained my Dr. Pepper, left wondering what I'll order for lunch.

I glance up from a particularly salty daydream about jumping in the lake and dying of hypothermia. This time, there's no rescue, and I sink to a very murky death that reminds me of a scary novel I read once that I was expecting to be a romance but found a much grimmer ending instead of a happily ever after—there's a life lesson in there somewhere, but I can't find it.

Meg still hasn't forgiven me. I've tried to call and get voice mail every time. Even if she answered, I have no idea how to explain what happened between John and me over the summer. How do you describe magic? A bolt of lightning striking twice?

I miss him down into my bones like a childhood happy place you're desperate to return to or a favorite hair tie that a boyfriend puts on his wrist and keeps so he has a piece of you, or the moments in life when you experience a rushing, flash of bravery—but times that by a billion. That's how much I want to kiss him again and call him mine.

A handsome young man is standing in front of my desk with all my ringing and wrapping supplies, quietly waiting.

"I'm sorry." I shake my head and look up when I finally register his presence. "Ready to check out?"

He's got nothing in his hands, music notes running up and down both arms, which are on display in a neon tank-top. Then he snaps his fingers like a magician, and a baseball appears in front of my nose with a flourish.

He chuckles, pleased with stunning me. "Found this in a bathroom drawer, isn't that odd?" His lips quirk, and his eyes narrow. "My buddy's kid started Little League, figured they're gonna lose a lot of balls. And this one's signed."

"The good stuff is always in the bathrooms." I take the ball and wrap it in tissue, noting there's no price. "I don't recognize the signature, but I don't really follow sports," I say, and my throat gets tight, thick with emotion for the one player I know intimately.

"There wasn't a price on it."

"I saw that. On the house today."

"Really?" he asks, incredulous. "It could be worth a lot."

"The family said to clear things out quickly. It's your lucky day."

"Wow. Thanks."

I shrug. "Sure. Reminds me of someone I know, and he'd probably love that this is happening to me. Right now. Today. Kismet."

"Ah." His eyes get dodgy as he takes the ball and starts to back away. "So, you believe in all that stuff?"

"Me?"

"I don't believe in destiny," he states with a confident nod.

"Destiny is a choice, I think." My eyes meet his, and I'm hopeful that he'll agree. "My friend has a coffee mug that says *happily ever after is a choice*. That's what it's all about, isn't it?"

I push up from my chair abruptly, rounding the table.

"Err...," he mutters, completely confused.

"It's about the choices we make," I explain. "*Oh my god.*" Adrenaline spikes, running the length of my body. I look up at the stranger who somehow sparked this realization. "Right?" I ask again, a smile splitting my face for the first time in two weeks. "We chose to stay in bad relationships. Or we don't. It's all up to us!"

I jump up and down on my toes, my reflection in an ornate gold mirror in the hall making it hard to ignore I'm having a very real, possibly unhinged epiphany.

He backs away slowly, forcing a smile, and quickly ducks out the front door hollering, "Good luck with that," as if he's dodged a bullet.

Well, shit. I guess not everyone's had a dunk in Spellbound Springs. Laughter bubbles out of me, and I do a twirl in the foyer. All alone. Just me and my choices.

Maybe I didn't believe in soulmates in the past, but maybe I believe in a touch of it now. But here's the kicker: none of it matters if I don't go after it and snatch it up in my hands like a mismarked antique at an estate sale.

I check my watch.

John is throwing out the first pitch at Oracle Stadium in an hour. And I should be there. I should tell him I want him forever, that I love him. And then, if he's still up for it, we should try. We should pick each other every day, fight for each other, and see where our love takes us.

I pick up my phone and call my mom and dad because I know they prefer it over texts. I also know they're home planning a trip to the Maldives this fall.

They answer on the first ring.

"Can you come run my sale for the rest of the day? There's something I need to do. And I need Cat and Willow's help, so I can't ask them." I'm cutting it close to game time. I mentally factor in the drive and traffic. I'm going to need a distraction if I want to catch him on the pitcher's mound.

"Text us the address, honey," Dad says. "We'll be right there."

I do, and when they burst into the door sixteen minutes later, I *run.*

"Bloomfield," Meg answers my video call on the first ring. *It's my lucky day.* I slam my car door and prop the screen on the dash.

"Martinez," I respond. *Stay cool, Frannie.* "I'll make this quick. I'm madly in love with your brother. I've been home for weeks, and I'm desperate for him." I turn my key in the ignition.

There's blue sky behind her on the screen and voices, but other than that, this is just between us. "You promised me you wouldn't hurt him. You said, and I quote, the last thing on earth you're looking for is a serious relationship—" I open my mouth to respond, but she barrels on. "You said—"

"I realize how bad it looks, Meg, but I swear, I fell for him. Instantly, I think, but that's something I'll chew on for the rest of my life. And I'm going to prove it to you."

I pull my seatbelt across my body and think of all the times John has done it for me. My cheeks heat as my belt *clicks* into place.

"Francesca, he's a grown man. If you want to be with him, then do it. I told John the same. Just don't expect me to support it. Not when I know your intentions."

"But all that's changed. That's why I'm calling. He said he calls you before he steps on the field for every game. That you're always in the stands watching him when you can be. It's part of his superstition. Right?"

"True."

"So, are you going to watch the pitch today?"

"I'm walking into the stadium now." To punctuate, she flashes the camera at Oracle stadium, a few puffy white clouds in the sky, fans in lines waiting to get in.

I slide my favorite aviators on. "Okay, good. Keep your eyes on that field Meg, and tell John to do the same. Before he throws the pitch, I'm going to do my best to prove to *you* and your brother how much I love him."

"I'm Francesca Bloomfield, and I have a ticket on hold here!" I shout at a man behind plexiglass.

"Hmmm." He twists a gray handlebar mustache and takes his sweet time rifling through a box in front of him.

"It was called in for me about an hour ago," I rush on, "by Winter Larsen. My friends should have already picked theirs up."

After calling in a favor from Winter and the dudes, I called Cat and Willow to beg them to cause a distraction on the field and hold off the pitch until I could get there. They've been texting me play-by-plays and made it here before the game, got their tickets with no issues, and are already inside.

A text pings, and I check my phone while the old man moves at a glacial pace.

It's a photo of them suited up in matching pink bunny suits, and a laugh that sounds more like a happy bark tumbles out of me. I owe them big time for the rest of my life. Cat says she's sweet-talking one of the players in the dugout from behind the safety netting, and Willow's trying to bribe someone for their press pass.

I push my phone back into the waistband of my shorts and franticly ask for an update. "Has the game started?"

"Did you know today's game is special?" the man asks, thumbing through a manila envelope that looks like it holds about thirty tickets, all paper clipped with sticky notes.

"You have no idea," I say, dancing in my sneakers, beads of sweat rolling down my back.

He eyes me as only the older generation, completely dumb-founded by youth, can. "Ah, here it is."

He slowly slides the ticket through the barrier. An announcer's voice bellows faintly from the stadium.

"Come on, come on," I whisper as the ticket crosses the barrier of plexiglass and my fingertips graze the edge.

"Game time," he says, smug in his striped shirt and still pulling at his long gray, gravity-defying facial hair.

"Thanks!" I shout, ticket in hand, and take off.

"Have a great day at the ballgame." His voice fades behind me as I approach the ticket taker and let her wave her security wand over me.

"You got a bag?" she asks.

"Nope!" I run through the front doors.

"Well, hello, welcome to Oracle Park," a young man with a stadium shirt proclaiming the same in classic baseball script says.

"Thanks." I shove my ticket in his face. "Where does this get me?"

"On the field! To the right and the first left into the tunnel will take you out to your seat. Behind the dugout. *Nice*." He grins with a mouth full of braces. "You'll probably want concessions first on a hot day like this—"

"No time!" I scream, probably scaring the peanuts out of him.

I pump my legs hard as I inhale popcorn and snack food smells, twisting and turning through the throngs of people until I get to the tunnel that will lead out into seats, the sunshine, and the open field.

A blast of sunlight assaults my eyes, and I make a visor out of my hand. Sure enough, the dugout is right in front of me.

Taking the stairs by two, I move fast until I'm behind home plate and in the last rows of seats. The stadium is packed. I'm an ant in an ocean, but I catch sight of two pink bunnies just as a fog horn blows.

Smack in the middle of the field, waving to the crowd on the pitcher's mound, are my two best friends.

John is there in a crisp white drool-worthy uniform, too, looking frantically around. Wondering what my sister and Willow are doing there in Halloween costumes, I'm sure. Who knows how much Cat and Willow have told him, but they're there in their bunny suits, doing a dance now to a rap song that's blasting overhead.

My sister dances with casually aloof model-type moves while Willow, to my shock and amazement, rocks her curves in such a sexy way the crowd explodes. The camera for the jumbotron zooms in on her ass as she swivels her hips. She's mesmerizing. The crowd gets to their feet, most of them joining in right along with her as she whoops and hollers, her bright blue eyes popping, red glossy lips shining, and strawberry hair glowing.

Where did these moves come from? It's like a fires been lit under her and she's exploding.

"We couldn't have asked for a better kickoff today. Thanks for coming ladies and for the generous donation." A man standing on the mound with a microphone tries to reel in the crowd when the song dies down. "Would you like to give another plug?"

"My pleasure," Cat pulls the microphone from the man and faces the crowd. "Thank you to Mr. Winter Larsen for allowing us to surprise Oracle Stadium with an additional donation today!"

Manager? Donation? What the hell has Cat done?

She smirks mischievously toward the crowd. "Let's give it up for Mr. Winter Larsen and his hundred-thousand-dollar donation to Children's Mercy Hospital."

I search the seats around me as Cat takes a bow, and I finally snag Winter's eyes. He's a few rows down, with all the guys, and the look on his face is one of pure hatred. That's when I realize an epic battle is about to begin between John's best friend and my sister because, judging by his reaction to what my sister just said, there is no way he authorized that donation.

The camera for the jumbotron pans to John as he bursts into a fit of laughter, pausing to brace his hands on his knees. Ricky waves to the crowd with a gloved hand good-naturedly.

So that's how they got out there. Cat must have offered up a donation, one big enough to get her invited onto the field for a personal thank you. The sexy bunny costumes probably helped, too.

"Our usher will see you back to your seats now." The man takes his microphone back a bit aggressively and shows the bunnies the way out. He turns to John and Ricky. "This is a moment for the books, a father-son pitch by the great Ricky Boggs and John Boggs, who holds the record in stats for his rookie year. Take it away, fellas."

The Boggs men nod, looking handsome in their matching white uniforms with red stripes.

Both of them take a pitcher's stance on the mound. John has a smile on his face. I think he means it as he watches his dad, but it's tight. There's pain in his eyes, too. He's happy for Ricky, but it must still hurt to be up there without being physically able to do something he loves.

It's Ricky who ultimately winds up and throws the pitch across home plate.

The crowd erupts.

"Take Me Out To The Ballgame" plays overhead.

And I jump the fence.

CHAPTER 33

John

"Hold this." I toss my glove to Ricky, which was really just for show anyway, and take two tentative steps off the pitcher's mound. Then I freeze as I watch her jump the fence.

The stands are dense with the crowd, and I'd been searching for her since Meg called to tell me Francesca was up to something, unable to find a needle in a haystack until now.

I pull the bill of my cap down but think better of it, ripping it off and stuffing it in the back pocket of my embarrassingly pristine uniform. My sister apologized for causing any trouble between us when I called her less than an hour ago. She said whatever Francesca had planned was going to happen before the pitch today.

My heart pounds so hard I think I need to sit down, but what kind of message would that send? A deep breath in and a slow breath out helps me to keep from collapsing as everything happens in slow motion.

Watching my girl run toward me is going to do me in.

The announcer shouts into the microphone, "Secur—"

A glance over my shoulder is all I've got time for. My voice is stuck in my throat, and I can't get the words out to tell the announcer to stuff it—she's with me.

But Ricky grabs the guy by the collar, pulling him close and speaking rapidly while he covers the microphone with his other hand.

Who knows what he said, but the announcer perks up and rearranges the look on his face. "Congratulations John Boggs!"

The crowd thunders, stomping in the stands with their feet, keeping time to a song that's playing overhead, but my mind can't register.

The jumbotron picks her up via video, following her as she runs right for me, her long blonde hair flowing behind her.

John! Her lips move, but I can't hear her, still pumping her legs, now halfway across the field.

I never realized quite how big a ball field is. It never felt like an ocean's worth of space until this moment until all I want is to hold her in my arms.

Shit, I should run to her. Why am I standing here tending daisies when I should be meeting her halfway? *Idiot.*

It's an effort to run while my whole body is thrumming with the beat of my heart, this damn uniform starched and heavy, not worn in, loose and soft.

"Before any of you get ideas, this stunt has been approved by Oracle Stadium." The announcer tips his hat to Ricky. "Not too long ago, a young woman named Rebecca Lee coined the term Kissing Bandit. She also led the MLB to instill a penalty for rushing the field. But this stunt is in memory of the first Kissing Bandit, whom many of you will remember rushing this exact field years ago."

Hearing my mom's name causes an out-of-body experience. My whole life has wrapped fully into a circle as if it was an open-ended thing, and now it's complete.

She's watching me now from heaven. Smiling. Laughing. Maybe she's the one who sent Francesca to me.

My feet pound into the turf, bringing me closer and closer, the crowd jumping to their feet, applauding while holding their breath. Will they see an epic kiss on a baseball field today? Will they witness history repeating itself? Can Francesca and I do better than my own mom and dad?

The questions loop in my mind while the crowd fades away until finally, she's in my arms.

I'm breathing heavily, grasping her cheeks and pressing my thumbs into her temples, letting my eyes rove her features as if she's not real. Her gray eyes are wide and bright.

"Hi," she says, squeezing my shoulders, chest heaving, looking into my eyes and nowhere else.

"Hi, sunshine."

She gulps. "I want to move to the lake," she says, all in a rush, "permanently, forever, 'til death do us part. Does that freak you out?"

Laughter falls freely from me, but I don't look away, not for one second, just in case this is a dream. "*I'm an idiot,*" I say, pushing my face into her neck, her hair, and inhaling deep and long. "I'll move to San Francisco. I'm so sorry, baby. I should have said this to you a long time ago."

"You said how you felt and what you wanted. I had every chance to accept it, but I didn't trust it. I was so scared I'd end up on my ass again, but this time instead of a bruised ego, my heart would be shattered into pieces."

"Baby, I will not let that happen."

"I know you won't. I want to be on the lake with you, at Boggs, in the mountains. I want to see if Winter's horses have more babies. I want to help Meg study. I want to hang out at the house with you and Ricky—and redecorate the cabin!" she screams as if in afterthought. "I want a life with you so much, Jonathan Boggs."

The Jumbotron has a heart-shaped frame around our faces, and flying cartoon cherubs shoot arrows that hit our heads and pop like bubbles. They zoom in, and the crowd begins to chant:

Kiss her, kiss her, kiss her, kiss her!

This time, I don't hesitate, and its sugar-sweet.

"Are you going to taste like candy bars and bubble gum every time I kiss you for the rest of your life?" I ask when our lips break into wide smiles.

She pulls back and crosses her arms. "There was traffic, I was hungry, and there were snacks in my car just looking at me—"

"Francesca?"

"Hmm?"

"You're delicious, and you're moving to the lake."

She nuzzles into my neck. "I love you. So, so much."

"Same, baby."

With that, I grip her waist and toss her easily over my shoulder, not caring that I'll have to ice it tomorrow, smack her on the ass, and start toward the locker room.

We're engulfed by a roar from the crowd. Fireworks go off behind the scoreboard, and I chuckle, knowing someone's going to get chewed for not saving them for the end of the game.

"They're cheering you on," she says.

She braces her hands on my shoulders, pushes up, and waves madly to the crowd. I know they're getting an eyeful of my girl and my jersey. It's the last time they'll see my name and number on the field: *Boggs, number five.*

Because I've officially left the game in the dust, it's time to teach someone else to play catch, and I plan on having at least three of them. A family of five just has a certain ring to it, the thought makes me smile up at the stands.

"I'm in love," she screams to the crowd, whipping them into an even bigger frenzy. I can imagine why. Those bright hazel eyes, long corn-colored hair, a mega-watt smile that's just got that *it-factor*—there's no other way to describe it.

I'll cheer her on for the rest of my life, too, and I've got a feeling she'll return the favor. When it comes to Francesca, I've trusted my gut from the start. I let her pull me into a dance I hadn't realized my heart was yearning for, and now she's gonna let me create the life for her she's been dreaming of—I'm at least going to try.

"The universe has been cheering us on the whole damn time, baby."

THE END

Epilogue

FRAN

It's a champagne cork exploding, the feeling I get before I kiss Jonathan Boggs. All that want building until—*pop!*

He takes the flute from my hands and exchanges it for a salty margarita. "I know this is what you really want."

"Thanks." I push the brim of his hat up and steal a kiss.

"To the happy couple and their insane choice to do manual labor for a living." Winter salutes us with his plastic champagne flute—Logan was in charge of bringing special glasses, Winter for bringing the Dom Perignon—the bottom falls off and he scoffs at it before draining it dry.

"And to Ben, for opening the Tipsy Taco," John adds. "Proud of you, brother. What is this, three business for you now?"

"Shucks. Thanks, Dad." Ben grins. "Enjoy, everyone, but I've gotta go check the schedule for tomorrow. Somebody already called in sick for the lunch shift."

"It's one thing to manage employees, but you two have signed up to run a motel? People are slovenly, you know." Winter is incredulous, but John and I are ecstatic with our choice to renovate and run Thistle and Burr together.

Logan looks mad at his glass but gestures in a toast and puts it back down.

"Now Novel has something they can lord over Clover, tacos and tequila," I add. Patty has been telling everyone Novel bribed Ben with low rent because Clover had all the best eateries.

My phone buzzes on the table. I've got a dress on tonight, so there was no stuffing it in the back pocket of my cutoffs or the waistband of my bikers. I'm expecting a call from Cat.

"You bought a motel—with a man," she says before I can say *hello.*

"We signed the papers today, yes!" I'm giddy.

I wrap an arm around John and bring him into the frame. "Hi, Cat," he says, a goofy smile on his handsome face. "Wait 'til you see what your sister has planned."

"You're gonna need to post so all your followers will come and stay. Chic as hell, I promise, but we'll need a little kickstart like any new business. Don't forget," I point at the screen, "you owe me for all the dancing videos."

"Um, did *you* forget I stopped a major league baseball game dressed as Elle Woods for you? We're even," she confirms. "But of course, I'll do anything I can to help my baby sister." She waves off my request. "I'm happy for you guys."

"How are things—" but before I can finish, Winter snatches the phone from my hand.

"Hey! Winter, give that back," I yelp, but he holds it over my head and moves closer to a bar with chili peppers wearing sombreros dangling from the ceiling.

"Speaking of that fateful game and how you managed to get on that field," he growls into the phone.

"Be nice," John insists, then says in my ear, "Probably best we let the kids work their own problems out, right?"

"What do you want, Winter?" I hear Cat groan.

John and I stay close, both of us wanting to find out if this is going to be an actual fight between my sister and his best friend.

"You cost me a hundred K, Bloom."

"It was for a good cause, and I enjoyed every minute of it," she retorts.

When I answered the phone, she was drawing a cat eye in a black silk robe split clear to her naval. I wonder if she's covered up or if she's boldly holding this meeting in French silk. That sounds like her, honestly.

"You know what they say about payback, don't you?" He taps the bar, and two shots appear in front of him.

"Bring it, Larsen," Cat replies. "My business is already in trouble, my sister just moved away, and my parents are enjoying a better sex life than me right now. Believe me when I say, you're the least of my worries."

He hesitates for a second, something washing over his face, before he slaps his smirk back in place and takes both shots in succession.

"Oh, I will," he says, licking his lips. He hands the phone back to me.

"Wait, where'd he go?" Cat asks, incredulous. I don't think she likes being threatened and then dropped like a hot potato.

"I don't know." I laugh. "He left."

"What an ass."

"Mommy and Daddy support you both," John says, taking up half my screen again.

"Work it out," I add. "Family is forever."

"I forgot you two are destined for matrimony and I'm going to have to deal with that guy forever," she groans as she perfects her liquid liner.

John and I fall into a fit of giggles.

"We need two ice waters, please," I say to the bartender.

352

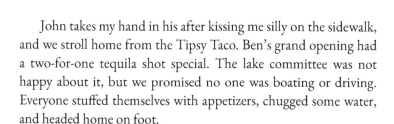

John takes my hand in his after kissing me silly on the sidewalk, and we stroll home from the Tipsy Taco. Ben's grand opening had a two-for-one tequila shot special. The lake committee was not happy about it, but we promised no one was boating or driving. Everyone stuffed themselves with appetizers, chugged some water, and headed home on foot.

Fall wind skirts around my heels, and I'm glad I'm wearing the new boots John gave me, complete with *serious-lake-girl* red laces. He wants me to have safe shoes to wear when we start our renovation on Thistle and Burr. I can't wait to smash walls and rebuild them with tiles that shine, fill up every room with second-hand treasures polished til they sparkle.

"Still feeling buzzed?" he asks, wrapping a strong arm around me and settling his chin on the crown of my head while we walk.

Stars press down on us overhead.

"I think the serving bowl of queso and basket of cantina chips I ate for my tenth course soaked up most of the alcohol, but I feel good if that's what you're asking, JB."

"Good. I'm feeling good, too... You know there's spinach in that queso, right?"

"I do, and I'm cool with it. I'm all for hiding vegetables in my food like a toddler when they're not charred to perfection by your grill."

"I'll remember that next time I try to get you to eat broccoli—"

"Bleh. Broccoli."

A full-on burst of laughter escapes him, and he pets my hair lovingly, letting his hand drop down my face and pinch my cheeks before his arm wraps around me possessively again. I clumsily trip over my new boots but let him manhandle me as we continue down the street, just the two of us.

When John officially asked me to move in, we begged Ricky to consider living in the cabin by the lake, to let us build onto it for him, but he moved back to town and got himself a cute apartment on Main Street near the state line. More importantly, an apartment right above Patty's pastry shop.

"Have I mentioned that you, in those boots and that dress, are absolutely killing me?"

The slow burn in my belly and the contented warmth in my heart give me the courage to slide my hand under his old Boggs Bar and Grill T-shirt to feel the ridges of his abs as we walk.

He's mine.

One street light clicks slowly through colors with no cars to mind it. He comes to a stop as I step over the state line, our hands still linked.

"I love being in two places with you at once." He gazes at me on one side while I stand on the other swaying in a breeze that slightly lifts my hem. "Have I mentioned that I want to always be with you? No matter where we are... You know that, right?"

He does. But I want to hear him say it because he's fought fears of that nature, and so have I.

"That day in my office, when you first came to the lake, you said being in two places at once was magical. I knew right then I wanted you to stay here with me forever."

Keeping me on the toes of my boots, he pulls me up stone steps. We both laugh at his hasty tugging, his own slightly clumsy man feet, even though he's got plenty of athletic grace. The sign for Clover, California and Novel, Nevada shines in pretty, scrolling gold script on the mint-green doors of town hall.

"What are we doing?"

"Sometimes Harry forgets to lock up, and with your hands all over me like they are right now, I was thinking we could slip inside real quick...."

"JB! You want to get sticky in a courthouse? What would the lake committee think if they knew? Their golden boy would be banned for life, and then where would we live?"

He jiggles the handle, his big puppy eyes filling with disappointment. "It's locked, anyways."

I push him against the door....

There's an extra perk to wearing a dress with a man you're stupid in love with.

Easy access.

"Do you have a condom?" I ask, slowly dragging the zipper of his washed-out khaki shorts down and reaching inside for my prize.

He sputters, "*Francesca Morgan Bloomfield*, are you serious? We're outside! You're suggesting we deflower the steps of town hall?"

"Absolutely." I snatch his hat and plop it on my head while my other hand grips him.

He groans. "Then I'm an idiot because I don't have one. But I will break into Dickies gas station right fucking now to get one. I'll leave a note, pay him for the window tomorrow, I swear."

He spins us so we've got the privacy of his wide shoulders, and braces one hand over my head, then drags my knee up with the other—all the way to his waist. His hand snakes under my dress, gripping my hip over a barely there thong.

"How much does a window cost?" I rasp. I already need him and my throats gone dry in anticipation.

"It'll be worth it," he growls in my ear, his hot breath fanning across my cheek, and I shiver. "You always surprise me."

That gives me the courage to say what I'm thinking next.

"Would it freak you out... I mean, what do you think if..."

Strong hands wrap around my ribcage, but I leave my leg hitched around him, pulling him closer. "If we skipped it?"

"Yeah." How did he know? Does he know it's been on my mind? This whole conversation, for some time?

He takes his hat off my head and chucks it onto a wicker settee with floral cushions. "I think I'm buying a ring next week on a secret shopping trip with your sister and Willow—"

"Wait—you're not driving to San Francisco on Thursday for a photo-op at Oracle Stadium?"

"Nope. That was our cover." He grips my cheeks in both hands, his eyes shining.

"What were you guys going to say when photos never materialized?" I ask, laughing through every word while the full weight of his plan settles deep inside, warming me from head to toe.

"I was hoping you'd be too busy researching wedding venues, or dress shopping, or convincing my sister to get ordained, to care." His hands slide down my front, gripping me again around my ribs, his thumbs brushing the underside of my breasts through my dress.

"Baby." I cup his face in my hands and kiss him softly on his full lips.

"Are you sure? About tonight? About everything?" he asks as I drop kisses all over his face: eyelids, nose, cheeks, chin. "I mean," he chuckles, "I figured we'd talk about it. I want a family, Francesca, and I'd like to be a dad who can play all the sports... Do all the things... I want all of it, but I'm scared."

I stop being silly and playful and look him in the eyes. "We can go home right now. We do have time to talk about this, John. I don't want to pressure you."

"That's not what I want." His gaze holds mine, and his face softens. "Just know that being a good dad will be my goal. I can't fail at that. Don't let me. Okay? We're partners now."

"You're the most thoughtful, caring, selfless man I know. You'll be perfect."

He releases his grip on me, and I'm momentarily confused. I thought we just settled things. But then he drags one strap of my dress down my shoulder, letting his hand fall to my chest to tug the bodice down with it.

"I knew it," he says hungrily. "You never have a bra on. Do you know how insane that makes me? How am I ever supposed to go in public with you?"

The warmth of his hand palming my breast in the moonlight, in the doorway of town hall, *or towns hall*, is in stark contrast to the night air raising goosebumps across my body. I'm bare to him and gasp when he takes my nipple in his mouth and sucks *hard*.

"Please," I whisper, pressing my hips into his.

"One of my favorite words from your mouth.'

So, I say it again. To make him happy. "Please, John."

He groans. "So needy, so fast?"

"Not so fast. You're not the only one who struggles in public. Watching you take down a taco in two bites was a carnal experience for me."

"Really?" He laughs, breathy and barely hanging on to his composure.

He buries his face in my neck and pulls the other side of my dress down, giving that nipple the same treatment as the other.

"Please, John," I beg again, barely holding on *myself.*

"God, I love it when you say my name. And out here, under the stars? This is my favorite way to be with you. Although, you know I'll take you any way I can get you. Always and forever, Francesca. Deal?"

Our eyes pin together, my hands around his length, my leg still wrapped around him so I can guide him to my center.

He pulls my thong quickly to the side before hoisting me up easily.

And slams into me.

Stars. I see stars literally above me as I try really hard not to scream into the night and wake everyone on Main Street. But also, my heart is exploding. Stars. Pixie dust. Something in the water in the lake? Full-blown forest magic in the majestic Jeffrey Pine trees? Who knows what it is? All I know is that I've never felt this alive.

"You good, baby?" Having him bare inside me is euphoric.

"More," I rasp, burying my face in his chest and inhaling him greedily.

"I got you," he breathes over the shell of my ear as he thrusts deep and slow.

"Always?"

"Forever," he promises.

It's not long until I unravel and go to pieces against the mint-green door, John following close behind.

I'll never look at town hall the same again. This little lake, and this man, are where I belong. I'm exactly where I'm supposed to be.

Acknowledgments

Big, huge, enormous thank you to the first readers of Kissing Bandit, my goodness, was this book a mess at the start. I had so many ideas and a title I was married to, and you all helped me bring it together when there were moments I seriously considered giving up. Hannah Bird was an Alpha reader extraordinaire, I'll forever be grateful for your comments on a a very messy first draft. Ray Riley, you helped the relationship arcs shine on the page the way they do in my head. Erin Thompson is single-handily responsible for John and Frannie's epilogue, how did I write the happily ever after and then *not write the happily ever after?* Erin! I couldn't have done it without you.

To my editor Jen Boles, thank you for a lovely edit, chat, and friendship.

To all my author buddies, book bloggers, and friends who make aesthetics and content with your marvelous creativity, I am so darn lucky to have you on my team. Also, to those who review, repost, and pre-order so I can keep writing books— THANK YOU.

My family has always been front of mind while I write, especially Le Husband, Jeff, thank you for being a man I can honestly call my hero.

Also by Margaret Rose

Sink Or Sell

Royal Hearts

On Holiday, (Spring '25)

Love Bug, (Fall '25)

About the Author

Margaret Rose is a true Gemini and the most extroverted introvert you'll ever meet. Before becoming an author, she worked as a personal stylist, secretly drafting novels and begging her friends to read them. Now, she enjoys wearing sweatpants just as much as sequins and watching her kids chase their dreams while she chases her own. You can find her online at Margaretrosebooks.Com.